Journey to Osm

The Blue Unicorn's Tale

Sybrina Durant

Edited by
Travis Erwin

Cover Art and all
other illustrations
by Dasguptarts

Journey to Osm
The Blue Unicorn's Tale

Story copyright 2018

Novel
Soft Cover Print ISBN-13: 978-1535455992, ISBN-10: 1535455993
Ebook ISBN-13: 978-1-942740-11-7, ISBN-10: 1-942740-11-5
Soft Cover ISBN: ISBN-13: 978-1-942740-12-4, ISBN-10: 1-942740-12-3

Illustrated Book In Color
Soft Cover Print ISBN-13: 978-1535127851 , ISBN-10: 1535127856
Soft Cover Print ISBN-13: 978-1-942740-07-0, ISBN-10: 1-942740-07-7
Ebook ISBN-13: 978-1-942740-08-7, ISBN-10: 1-942740-08-5
Hard Cover ISBN: ISBN-13: 978-1-942740-09-4, ISBN-10: 1-942740-09-3

Illustrated Read and Color Book
Soft Cover Print ISBN-13: 978-1-942740-16-2, ISBN-10: 1-942740-16-6

Coloring Book
Soft Cover Print ISBN-13: 978-1537021843, ISBN-10: 1537021842
Soft Cover Print ISBN-13: 978-1-942740-10-0, ISBN-10: 1-942740-10-7

BISAC Codes:
FIC009120 FICTION / Fantasy / Dragons & Mythical Creatures FIC010000
FICTION / Fairy Tales, Folk Tales, Legends & Mythology
FIC009000 FICTION / Fantasy / General

All rights reserved by Sybrina Publishing and Distribution Company
League City, Texas, United States of America

Contact Sybrina@sybrina.com.

~

TABLE OF CONTENTS

~

Prologue

No Metal. . .No Magic

*T*he entire tribe stood gathered in anticipation of his birth. Not so long ago, they would have been shoulder-to-shoulder, hoof-to-hoof at such a gathering, but their numbers had dwindled.

Bunched together in the Halstable courtyard, every member of the tribe squinted toward a closed door and waited. On the other side, Miral labored to deliver her baby.

The Oracle had foretold this day, but her vision lacked details, so the Metal Horn Tribe of Unicorns were filled with many unanswered questions.

What powerful magic would this foal's horn possess?

Which metal would define his essence?

When would this tiny new unicorn free them?

Would he enter the world with the power to rid them of the evil that hunted them?

Or—would they be forced to suffer for a while yet before the prophecy was fulfilled?

What was taking so long in the birthing room?

Finally, the door opened.

For a few seconds no one could see into the darkened entrance. Dust motes floated in the spectrum of light contrasting against the dim interior. Bits of straw tumbled out into the light.

Something stirred in the shadows.

Then, a tiny unicorn stepped forward on shaky legs. Behind him, his dam nuzzled the foal forward with her soft, velvety snout.

Blue. His body was dull blue, but no one focused on the color of his coat for long because something else was gravely wrong.

There, on his head. . .no metal. Only a small, ugly lump of what looked like. . .hide. It was not even a true horn as of yet.

Of course, all unicorns were born with dull, rounded horns to prevent damage to the mother, but this foal's horn appeared far more stumpy and much more odd than any the tribe had ever seen.

Disappointment rippled through the group as a dull hum of gasps and groans. Slowly, the tangle of mutters resolved into exclamations of disbelief.

"No metal. . .no magic." Only whispers at first. Then shouts: "No metal? No magic!"

The Oracle held up an aluminum hoof to silence the crowd. A hush fell upon them, until one lone, pitiful voice rang out, "We're doomed."

That set off the crowd in yet another round of frenzied outcries.

"No metal, no magic!"

"That thing doesn't even look like a real horn!"

"Look at his hooves. They have no metal either!"

The foal shrunk back, hiding beneath his mother's belly.

Never before, had a metal-less unicorn been born to the tribe. The foal's own mother, Miral, displayed a stunning horn of a shiny metal called indium, which gleamed as bright and pure as a looking glass. Any unicorn, who peered into its mirrored surface, saw their own image reflected in its soft, silvery veneer.

The magic of Miral's indium horn also allowed her to look straight into another's soul. Her heart ached for her child, for she knew the unforgiving world in which they lived. Without magic, life would be tough for any unicorn, although life had been plenty tough for them all since Magh rose to power and turned MarBryn into a frightening land.

Alumna, the unicorn Oracle, squinted at the tiny newborn. Her vision had foretold his birth and, yes, she had expected a stronger foal, but who was she to question the Moon-Star Spirit? Their savior looked very frail indeed, and in this moment, she had a hard time believing he would ever be anything but weak. However, as the Oracle, she must not let the tribe lose hope because hope was all the Metal Horns had left.

The wise Oracle felt sick at the injustice. This pitiful little thing would forever, be saddled with the disappointment of this day. So much hope had been placed on his small mundane shoulders, and now the entire tribe was ready to collapse under that heavy burden.

All around the Halstable courtyard she heard the mutters of condemnation … condemnation of … this little blue foal … of the prophecy borne of her own magic.

"He's too small, too weak!"

"The prophecy lied!"

"The Oracle was wrong!"

The Oracle wanted to calm down the herd. These ugly

comments were not dignified and in no way befitting a unicorn's good nature. She understood they were scared, and as a result, they were now both giving up hope and giving in to their fears. Nevertheless, this unnatural meanness had to stop.

Unicorns were never mean, but of course, the dark pall Magh had cast upon this land was changing the nature of all things in MarBryn. . .even unicorns.

Still, she would be compassionate, even if the others refused. The rose-colored Oracle called to the baby's mother loudly enough for the whole tribe to hear, "Miral, please forgive us on this most difficult day! If the Moon Star Spirit says he will grow to be a strong stallion, you must believe. We must all believe."

The sorrowful new mother raised her tearful eyes. "Do you really think so, Alumna?" The anguished unicorn's voice rose and fell as she wrestled with her despair in a battle that would not be won that day.

Alumna saw how much Miral wanted her words to be true. She desperately wanted to agree, but before she could find the words, another voice called out.

"No one believes this blue runt will save us! No one."

Tears fell from Miral's eyes as she bowed her head to nuzzle her foal.

"Enough!" Nix, a nickel-horned unicorn whom everyone in the tribe respected, stepped between the crowd and the mother and son. "No one here knows what the future holds," his eyes locked on Alumna's, "but, for better or worse, we must stick together. Savior or not, this foal is now one of us."

Alumna did not know if she should thank him or be offended, but at least the furor of disappointment had dimmed. She went to

Miral and leaned forward to gently touch the tip of her horn to her friend's in a gesture of solidarity. Then, she did the same with the tiny nub of the little blue foal. In that instant, she caught the vision of silvery blue moonlight cascading down through the clear dome of the Halstable. In that flickering image, she saw a magnificent blue stallion with a brilliant horn, aglow with powerful magic.

Hope rose within her once again, but the image faded and the sight of the disfigured little lump of the foal's plain hide horn reminded Alumna that, this was not the first vision she had gotten tragically wrong.

Chapter One
The Bravest Coward

*H*is dull blue coat blended with the dark shadows brought on by nightfall, giving him plenty of cover for his escape. Sneaking out of the Halstable was perhaps his single greatest skill, but then again no one save Ghel cared much about what he did. The tribe had long since given up on him as their savior.

In the two decades since his birth, Blue's horn had grown and was now as pronounced as any unicorn's, but the plainness of it marked him as an outcast. *No metal, no magic.*

That mantra echoed through Blue's mind every single day, although only one member of the tribe had spoken those words to him in recent years. Still, that truth permeated the air and thumped through Blue's body to the same rhythm as his heartbeat.

No metal, no magic.

These four words were why he snuck away from the tribe so often. He could not change the fact that his horn remained a tusk of hard, twisted hide. Not really bone, but certainly not metal, either. He had very little feeling or sensation in the appendage, and he certainly had no trace of magic. He knew because he had tried everything in the world to conjure something, anything, from his horn.

Tried and failed.

Blue failed at most endeavors, except for sneaking out. He was undoubtedly the best of the tribe at that. No one else dared stray far from the Halstable. The once proud herd now ranged only to the grove of trees near the watering hole and back. Even then, the unicorns were often forced to hurry back to the Halstable in order to escape the roving enemies Magh sent out in search of them. It was a sad state for a species that once roamed freely.

Save for a few protected spots, the entire land of MarBryn had become far too dangerous for unicorns, or any of the other free beings. Evil lurked behind every tree, bush, and rock, and the story of the last unicorn death haunted them all.

Even eight some odd years later, grass still did not grow at the ghastly battle site. Of course, only Blue knew this last fact since tribal decree forbade any unicorn to venture so far.

Half an hour into his journey, Blue again came to the very spot of the metal-horned tribe's last stand against Magh. Just over the ridge he would find another adversary and they, too, would wage battle on this moonless night. But first, the unicorn paused to pay his respects to the memory of all his fallen ancestors who had been killed and mutilated by the vile sorcerer, for no other reason than so the evil mage could claim their magic for himself.

Blue looked first to the barren earth that served as a testament to the unspeakable evil that had occurred there, and then he gazed upward at the stars.

His fate had been written, and while even he had a hard time believing the prophecy, he would forever be duty bound to try to fulfill the vision for himself, and for the remaining Metal Horns.

With a resigned breath he trudged onward to the waiting battle, even though he would surely fail, just like most of his endeavors.

He had no more than crested the hill when the charge came. A big, no. . .a giant—stag sideswiped Blue, sending him crashing to the ground. The air left his lungs in a rush and that was all the advantage the brute needed. Wheeling around, the stag jabbed the tine of a very sharp antler against Blue's jugular.

The battle was over before it even started.

"I thought you wanted to spar," Gaiso said. "That was an even worse start than last time!"

Once again, Blue had not delivered. He had no real excuse to offer his fighting mentor, but even if he had words, they would have been difficult to say aloud with that antler pressed so firmly against his throat.

The stag took a step back. "Get up. We shall go again, but this time I will not be so easy on you."

Hours later, Blue limped away from their secret meeting place out on the plains. Bruised, battered, and exhausted, he didn't even slow down at the barren patch of darkness as he trudged back toward home.

Stiff and sore after the grueling workout, he made such slow time that the sun rose before the Halstable came into view. He did not want to face the wrath of the tribe for sneaking out, so he angled off toward the stand of trees that circled the herd's watering hole. He knew of a nice shady spot where he could bed down and rest both his weary mind and his battle-ravaged body.

Gaiso never took it easy on him, but Blue knew the stag held back. In a real fight, those massive antlers would finish him off easily enough. However, little by little and week by week, Blue felt himself getting both stronger and more responsive during their sparring matches. He was learning to fight. But would it be enough when confronted with the worst of Magh's army?

That, was a question Blue could not answer. So, he laid down and closed his eyes, grateful for the whispering winds, which sailed through the trees. A cool breeze dried the sweat from his coat and ruffled his mane.

He slept for a time, until sounds broke through his dreamless slumber. Blue lay still on the cool ground beneath a densely leaved Jughead bush and listened. Voices carried on the flower-scented breeze.

Familiar voices.

I've got to get out of here before they see me! He cast his eyes from side to side without moving his head. Escaping undetected seemed unlikely, but maybe he would get lucky, and they would not linger at this spot for long.

Lying as still as he could, Blue next heard a different kind of noise.

"Ree-arrrl…"

The nerve-jangling sound whistled across his nose, leaving a scent in its wake. . .like honey and fear all blended into one.

"Aaarrrl…"

The sound whizzed past his left ear, cutting through both his fatigue and his desire to keep quiet.

Blue wrenched his head away, trying to escape the noise and, more importantly—the angry little creature responsible for the sound. He shuddered as his mind threw back in time to memories of tortured lungs and desperate gasps for breath. . .to painful welts and an almost out-of-body experience that felt like giant scabrous hands pushing his unresponsive body deeper and deeper into darkness.

When the sound circled around directly in front of him, Blue froze in place and went slightly cross-eyed as he stared into the face of the Buzzy-Biter, hovering just inches from his nose. Instinctively, he leaned his head back while avoiding making any sudden move that might startle the stinging little thing.

Years had passed since his last encounter, because Blue gave the mean little bugs a wide berth. One allergic reaction had been enough to make him wary. This particular bug seemed outraged beyond the norm. From the shaking of what appeared to be tiny, little fists—to the trembling of its antennae, Blue could tell the creature was yelling at him, but he could not understand a single word of the buzzy language.

Still, he whispered back, "Are you talking to me?"

The black and yellow bug vibrated with a low, angry drone and high-pitched buzz. Blue's spine tingled as the hairs up and down its length rose and trembled. The prick of the Buzzy-Biter's sharp stinger would burn like fire, and then the anaphylactic shock would take hold.

Blue was on the verge of bursting from his hiding spot when the bug surprisingly went silent. With a final shake of its fist, it buzzed off, leaving a curlicue trail of golden pollen specks shimmering in the sunlight.

Blue sneezed, then, froze again, realizing he still was not alone at the watering hole. A vibrant singsong of "Toodle-loodle-loo" drifted his way.

Next, a high-pitched squeal and exclamation of, "Ooh, that pond scum is thick today!"

There was no need to peek out through the leaves. He knew these voices, but he peeped through anyway. Using his right hoof, he pushed the sunshine-colored flowers away from his right eye. The branch immediately swung back into place, forcing him to move his head over a notch so that he could see out.

From his vantage point behind the bush, he could spy on the small clearing where a few unicorns from his tribe had gathered.

Silubhra, the silver-horned unicorn crooner, stood next to that lime-green buffoon Cornum. Sour in both appearance and attitude, Cornum looked particularly ridiculous today. Lemons and limes dangled from his mane, making him into a galloping fruit stand.

Blue struggled not to laugh out-loud, as Cornum pawed at the attached fruit. Style, the steel-horned unicorn, was always whipping up crazy mane-dos for the tribe. Being all but invisible to the herd, Blue had never been a beneficiary of her magic, and he fervently hoped he never would be, after seeing what she had done to Cornum.

A dark green filly stepped up closer to the water. Shaking her head like a judgmental schoolmarm, she gazed at the dirty pool of water before saying aloud, "Cleaning up this mess may take some extra work."

Beyond the pool, other members of his tribe ambled about. *Oh great,* Blue thought. *The gang's all here.*

That was an exaggeration. Not everyone was there, but Blue was cranky and sore after his night of sparring, not to mention his encounter with the Buzzy-Biter. Now, his nice quiet napping spot had been invaded and he did not feel very sociable.

Not that he ever socialized with most members of the tribe, anyway. He was an outcast, the only unicorn in the land without a metal horn. A fact Cornum loved to point out in subtle ways at every opportune moment, but Blue did not give him, or anyone else many such moments.

This little grove of trees and the watering hole provided the only outside escape for the Metal Horns. Being close to the Halstable, the trees offered a safe enough place to get some fresh air and enjoy nature's beauty. That, could not be said for the rest of MarBryn and even here, there were dangers, which was why the herd only ventured out a couple of times each month.

There was a big open area near the pond in the center of the grove. Thick hedges of heavily perfumed Jughead bushes in full flower bordered the dense outer ring of trees. The cool, sweet-scented shade underneath the bushes provided the perfect place for Blue to nap and hide, so he came here far more often than the others. Of course, he also ventured out on his own to places they would never risk. Still, he did not consider himself more brave than any of them—only more desperate.

If he truly were brave, Blue would come out of hiding now, but he did not want to face his tribe, and with only one way out, he couldn't escape without waltzing right out in front of those present.

Guess I'll be here awhile. Blue pouted, wishing he were anywhere else besides stuck there, hiding in the bushes.

He watched Nix, the nickel-horned unicorn. Everyone knew of his bravery. The unicorns loved to retell the stories of Nix's prowess, and even beyond the Halstable Blue had come across more than one creature who asked if the tales about Nix were true. He and his nickel horn were the stuff of legend all throughout MarBryn.

Nix watched over all of the Metal Horns with his sixth sense for danger. In these uncertain times, his magical ability, both to anticipate trouble and protect the others once it hit, made him indispensable. One blast from his horn could send a culprit with ill intent to an untimely end. As defender of the tribe, the brave thunder-gray unicorn had spent his entire life rushing headlong into danger to protect his fellow unicorns, but the safety of Nix's stable-mate, Silubhra, remained his primary concern. If she ventured outside the Halstable, the great unicorn defender could always be found at her side.

Blue longed to have a magical metal horn like the nickel-horned unicorn, but he was stuck with his ugly plain blue hide-covered horn.

The sun gleamed off Silubhra's silver horn as she warmed up her vocal cords, "La-la-la-la-la-la-lah!"

Blue leaned closer. He loved to listen to her sing. When he moved, one of the little pitcher-shaped flowers of the Jughead bush emptied its contents onto his backside. He tried to brush off the nectar with his tail, but the hairs that touched it stuck to the sweet, sticky stuff, so he left it alone.

Beyond the silver-horned singer, Blue saw Cuprum, the plump, moss green unicorn, dip her copper-horn into the slimy, stagnant pond. The murky water slowly churned and turned crystal clear before his eyes.

Blue smiled. He never tired of seeing that trick. Cuprum's horn allowed her to freshen their water supplies. No matter if it was too salty or too dirty, Cuprum had the ability to decontaminate and distill it into pure, clean water.

Watching the copper-horned unicorn perform her magic, he wished he could get some of the water to wash off the gooey juice. At the thought of water, he swallowed hard and realized just how dry his throat had become.

Thirsty from the vigorous sparring session, he badly wanted to walk right out and get a drink, but a nice refreshing slurp would have to wait, just like always.

He was an outsider. Even here, surrounded by his own tribe.

Chapter Two
It's All In The Horn

"*T*oodle-loodle-loo, toodle-loodle-loo."

The musical sounds floated merrily along to Blue, scrunched down on his belly under the dense hedgerow. Silubhra set the pitch so Cornum, the brass-horned unicorn, could tune his horn.

Unlike other unicorn spires, his ended in a flared bell shape, just like a trumpet. Cornum's magic allowed him to express a wide variety of musical sounds reminiscent of most any wind instrument. And windy he was. Cornum puffed out a lot of hot air whether he happened to be playing music or not.

Sometimes, his horn sounded like a sweet piccolo or an ethereal flute. Others, it emanated the sounds of a bright, metallic bugle or a velvety saxophone. When he felt mellow, his horn could easily produce the low, ponderous tones of a bass tuba, but when upset, Cornum's horn shrilled and screeched and whistled completely out of tune. Given how easily Cornum's fragile sensibilities were disturbed, the other unicorns were assaulted with those sounds quite often.

Be that as it may, Blue enjoyed listening to the duo as they rehearsed. Not that they needed practice. . .they'd performed these songs so many times; they were pitch perfect.

Silubhra, "Silver Tongue", as she was also known, sang along with Cornum's trumpeting accompaniment. In a persuasive lilting soprano, she serenaded the rest of the group,

"*In the Friendship Circle,*

we gather in peace.
Red, yellow, green or purple;
north, west, south or east . . ."

Her voice normally had the power to command anyone's attention, but this time the words of her song faded into the background of Blue's thoughts as he wished for the millionth time that he, too, had a metal-horn and a magical power. Being born without either made him feel like such a failure.

Any color is welcome in the friendship circle. . .except blue. No metal. . .no magic. Even Cornum has magic.

Blue cringed at the thought of spouting off the brash notes that sometimes erupted involuntarily from the brassy unicorn's horn, but ridiculous as he could be, Cornum at least belonged.

As he played, the lemons and limes attached to his mane swayed and bobbed in time to the music.

Okay, so maybe I don't envy Cornum quite as much as I do the others.

Cornum hit a note as sour as the adornments attached to his mane, and just like that, Silubhra stopped singing.

Cornum pranced around as if unaware he had ruined the song. As usual, he nodded his head in time to the beat. The movements caused his elaborately styled yellow-green shaded mane-do to bounce all about.

His mane could not hold all of the fruit in place, not even with Style, the steel-horned unicorn's magical assistance. Two lemons shook loose, falling to the ground.

Blue watched them roll in different directions and barely stifled a laugh. When he looked back up at Cornum, the two displaced lemons had been magically replaced by two more.

"Blat-t-t-t-t." trumpeted the distracted unicorn's brass horn. Cornum shook his head back and forth like he'd gone mad. That sent a couple more lemons and limes flying.

"Toodle-loodle-loot?" Silubhra tried to jump back in, but their timing was all off and the song abruptly ended on an odd note as a flying lime barely missed her nose.

Her silvery-white coat colored a bright shade of pink at the near miss. She again turned toward Cornum as if to speak, but this time he was engaged in a battle with the fruit. Biting at it, he twirled in circles like a dog chasing its tail.

Over by the pond, copper-horned Cuprum shook her head at the scene and said to her stable-mate Tinam, "If he weren't such a dandy, he wouldn't find himself in such predicaments."

"Too true." The tin-horned unicorn replied with a laugh before bending to help her fill another canteen with fresh water.

The blue unicorn squirmed around behind his bush, trying to keep himself from laughing out loud. Cornum looked so undignified, scrambling around trying to retrieve the fallen fruit, only to have it vanish from the ground and reappear in his mane-do.

Blue noticed Silubhra's ear swivel in his direction, and quickly choked back his laughter. He did not want to attract anyone's attention his way, but a whinnying laugh had slipped out.

A succession of rude sounds erupted from the brass-horned unicorn. . ."Bwamp, breeep, deedle-leeeet!"

Again, Blue snickered.

"Ahem," Silubhra said, peering at Blue through the bushes.

He jerked his head up in the direction of her voice, feeling a nip of embarrassment at being caught by the lovely creature. Where she stood, he could only see her head and silvery mane. Twigs of pure white baby's breath were woven through her long tresses, along with miniature posies of sunny daffodils and violet-colored beautyberries to add bright splashes of color.

The silver-horned unicorn regarded him with one arched brow. Her other eyelid was squinched shut, like the compressed bellows of an accordion. That curious expression seemed out of place on her otherwise flawless face.

She spoke in a whisper. "Blue, if you want to hear our music, you should come out to join us."

Blue's eyes widened. That idea made him feel particularly cranky. "I doubt Cornum feels the same way," he said.

Probably, many more than just Cornum felt that way. None of the others made any effort to include Blue in their activities, but he could not blame it all on them. Most of the unicorns had stopped asking after he had refused their offers so many times.

The dainty little mare angled her head around to catch a glimpse of Cornum from the corner of her eye. The brass-horned unicorn pounded the ground in frustration with both front hooves, causing another piece of fruit to jiggle loose and fall. No matter how many fell, they were immediately replaced.

"Yes," she admitted hesitantly." He can be brash and brassy, but he does love an audience. Besides," sunlight flashed on her diamond-encrusted horn and the hair of her coat bristled as she turned back to challenge Blue, "You don't make it easy for any of us, avoiding the tribe and singling yourself out the way you do."

The forlorn blue unicorn lowered his head, refusing to meet her eye. He had always known the tribe barely tolerated his presence among them, and here was Silubhra pointing out his failings as a member of the herd.

"No metal. . .no magic," was all he could think to say. He did not add his failure to be the savior the tribe had hoped for. He didn't have to.

Concern flickered in Silubhra's eyes as she admonished, "When you start thinking more highly of yourself, the other unicorns will too. No matter what you think, metal horn or not, no one holds your lack of magic against you . . . except for you."

Before Blue could respond, Cornum called out in a fussy tone, "Silubhra, are we going to finish this song or not?"

Blue's sad eyes met Silubhra's gaze. Her look of compassion made it hard to keep his voice level. "You should go before he comes nosing around here," he insisted with a touch of pleading.

She was about to reply, but instead sucked in her breath as Cornum approached.

"Just what are you up to over there, anyway? Is our savior hiding in the bushes again?" he asked, his voice going up a scale.

Blood flooded Blue's face, momentarily flushing it purple.

Rebuttals flew through his brain. *I won't take this from him! I'll fight back! I'll tell him I'd rather have no magic than something so stupid as a trumpet horn!* But instead, Blue shrank backward in an effort to be invisible.

Cornum tried to nudge in beside Silubhra to confirm his suspicions.

"There's no cause for that kind of talk," she admonished and in an act of kindness toward the despondent unicorn hiding in the bushes, she swung her derriere around to switch her tail right in the cheeky green stallion's nose. The action was enough to turn Cornum away from Blue's hiding spot.

"Have you finally given up trying to get rid of that fruit?" She swung her head around, nudging the flustered brass-horned unicorn back toward the clearing. "You know I can't concentrate when your fluting is off key."

Blue sighed, relieved that his secret location would remain safe a little longer.

As Silubhra guided the citrus decorated unicorn back to the center of the group, Cornum shook his head and another lemon fell to the ground. He stamped around it like a dancing donkey, finally skimming the side of it with his back hoof. It rolled in slow motion across the ground toward Blue's bush.

Blue prepared himself for the worst, in case Cornum came looking for his piece of fruit, but instead, the lime-green unicorn slipped into a full-blown temper tantrum, jumping and bucking and braying his horn until the entire group stopped their various activities to shout in unison, "Cornum, stop that!"

The brass-horned unicorn swung around so fast that two more lemons and at least three limes fell from his mane-do. Red rage turned his chartreuse hide an awful shade of puce.

Nix had had just about enough of Cornum's antics. "I'll nix that fruit," the dark grey unicorn declared.

He sent a magic lightning bolt toward the lemon heading across the ground for Blue's bush. With a satisfied snort, he blasted it to smithereens, but some sort of backlash ricocheted the charge straight back at the grey defender. Then, in the instant before the blast could harm him or any of the other unicorns, it imploded in a blaze of light, leaving behind a cloud of dark smoke.

"What the heck was that?" Nix demanded of no one in

particular. His attention was riveted to flakey bits of citrus peel drifting lazily back to the ground through the smoke.

Shaking his head from side to side, the unicorn defender said, "I've never had that happen!"

The forward blast from Nix's horn charred a few leaves, and blew a heated, acrid wind toward Blue's face. He had squeezed his eyes shut and tucked his chin into his chest, anticipating a horrific burn, but not one bit of heat reached him. Something had repelled Nix's lethal lightning and sent it careening back toward the tribe.

Blue was completely unharmed, although, the top of his face was somewhat blackened and the tip of his horn tingled. He was so shaken that he did not take the time to think about the fact that this was the very first time he had ever felt any sensation in his horn.

Chapter Three
The Outsider

*T*he group of unicorns lingered around the watering hole. They chatted excitedly about Nix's wayward blast but, were talking over each other so that Blue could not discern any of their actual words. All the voices meshed and blended into one cacophonous noise.

He eased to another vantage point, since a raggedy hole now exposed his previous hiding spot, and because he wondered if any of them had an explanation for the backlash and explosion. He did his best to be quiet, even though no one was listening for any sound from him. The attention of the tribe was split between the bewildered Nix, and Cornum, who was still fighting the fruit in his mane.

Style, the purple unicorn responsible for the wayward citrus attached to Cornum, watched his clownish activity with a smirk that Blue could not quite read. Was she angry, annoyed, or silently satisfied at her stable-mate's irritation?

She wore stylish striped leggings with alternating bands of fuchsia and carnation pink. Stepping forward, she declared, "Enough of that. I'll take care of that unruly 'do."

Looking Cornum up and down, she complained, "The way you're always prancing around, I knew it wouldn't stay put. I should've known to juice up this mane-do magic."

Truth be told, Style sometimes let her anger get the best of her. If she were less stubborn, she would have come up with a simpler mane-style at this point, but even from his distant vantage point, Blue could tell by the determined look on her face that Cornum would not be ridding himself of his fruity-do anytime soon.

She primped with the teased pouf of her mane for a moment. Then, she performed the tricky task of adjusting her leggings. She pulled the ones on her front legs taut with her teeth. Those on her back legs required a more acrobatic approach. Standing on three legs, she reached around with the cloven hoof of her right front leg to pull her right back legging up tight. She then performed the same maneuver on the other side. Being double jointed, all unicorns could move like that.

When she was finally done fidgeting and adjusting, she heaved a tortured sigh and tapped Cornum's head with her steel horn. The purple amethysts embedded in her horn sparkled as each citrus fruit fastened even tighter to Cornum's scalp.

"That fruit will not fall out again," she huffed and Blue thought he heard a stifled whimper escape Cornum but, given the distance, he could not be certain.

The one lemon that Nix had blown to pieces was not replaced. A barren patch where it had been was now in Cornum's mane, though no one dared to point out this fact, probably for fear that Style would twist something into their own locks.

Blue looked at the remnants of the fruit spread all over the ground. Plump little fluid sacs glistened in the sun. The essential oils released from the bruised, leathery rind lent a citrine freshness to the air, making Blue's stomach rumble at the memory of one of Tinam's Key Lime Pies. The unicorn chef could conjure up most any type of foodstuff, but he specialized in desserts.

Cornum bent his knee, raising a front hoof to pat a lemon secured tightly to the nape of his neck. He tried to loosen it by pushing at it with one of the tips of his split hoof without luck. This time, Style's magic assured they were all there to stay.

He offered a whiny, "Thanks, Style." That again left Blue

struggling not to laugh out loud.

Style shrugged off his sarcastic tone and turned to the bright yellow unicorn with the toque on his head to ask, "Tinam, what's for lunch?"

The chubby fellow's mane stuck straight out like uncooked spaghetti from under his chef's hat. "I plan to conjure up some sweet, steamy carrots drizzled with butter," Tinam said, licking his lips. The look on his face said he could almost taste it.

Now, when the tin-horned unicorn chef said 'conjure up', he meant it literally. He could pull together elements from far-flung places to make delicious concoctions nicely packed in tins to be enjoyed now, or later. All he had to do was use his imagination and with a little swirl of his tin horn—*poof!* Another gourmet delight from Chef Tinam magically appeared.

"And we'll have baked apples sprinkled with brown sugar and nutmeg for dessert," he coaxed.

Not as tasty as Key Lime Pie. . .nevertheless, the Chef's words made Blue's stomach grumble once again.

Tinam did not really have to try to convince anyone to eat the delicious meals he conjured. Everyone loved every dish he dreamed up.

"Sounds spectacular," said Cuprum. "Come on. Now that we've gathered some sweet fresh water to wash it down with, let's all go back to the Halstable to eat."

The jolly round unicorn eagerly lifted her copper horn, doing a little skip and a trot. The full wooden canteens strapped around her neck swung back and forth, thudding together like bells with wads of cotton around the clappers.

An old black stallion with a monocle over one eye chimed in,

"Lunch does sound good." He scratched his rough beard with a gnarled hoof, as if deep in thought, then touched his iron-horn to the charred leaves on the Jughead bush where Blue was hiding. The bush suddenly greened up and filled back in with new leaves and shoots.

Iown had a magical way with greenery. Whenever a plant showed signs of wilting or any other damage, he would sweep his iron horn tip across the affected areas of the plant, or through the dirt in which it grew. The soil would deepen to a rich dark brown color, and the plant would spring back to life. Leaves became greener and more pliable. The flower petals displayed more vivid colors and wafted increasingly fragrant perfumes, with just a little bit of attention from him.

The iron-horned unicorn smiled at his handiwork, gave a wink toward the bush, and then pointed homeward with his iron horn. "Let's go have lunch."

For a brief instant, Blue thought the venerable elder had winked at him, but surely, he was mistaken.

Iown happily led the Tribe of the Metal-Horned Unicorns toward the Halstable, but Nix stopped just on the edge of the grove and gave one last look back.

Blue worried that he had been spotted but Nix swept his gaze right past him and settled on something over on the far side. Blue squinted and made out the form of a yellow and brown Buzzy-Biter hovering above a bush. Could Nix really see the small bug all the way across the clearing? Was super sensitive eyesight how he spotted dangers?

That didn't strike Blue as so much of a magical ability as a freakish talent, but without any magic of his own, he didn't really know how any of it worked, so when Nix shook his head and trudged on toward the Halstable, Blue was again left alone in the grove.

Over across the way, the lethargic insectoid greedily sucked up Jughead nectar through the plump pistil of one of the many small pitcher-shaped flowers adorning the heavily leaved bush. His long, tubular tongue bulged in spots as the thick, sticky nectar rose up through it. His fluttering wings shimmered like stained glass glinting in the sun.

Blue watched the insect while feeling oddly disappointed that the herd had left him there alone, despite the fact he had been wishing for them to do exactly that.

Chapter Four
Feel The Burn

*B*lue sighed, lowering his head. "What is wrong with me? Why didn't I just crawl out from under these bushes and join them? Why do I feel like I don't belong?" he pitifully asked himself. Then, he answered his own questions with the pathetic mantra, which had been burned into his brain since he was a wee foal, "Oh yeah...*no metal, no magic.* That's why."

He twitched his tail slowly back and forth, unaware that the motion swatted away the same buzzing little hymenopter who had frightened him earlier.

"Rearlll!" The very angry critter buzzed past Blue's ear and around his nose, stopping right at eye level. The unicorn could tell that the insect was enraged and its anger seemed to be directed at him. He was pretty sure the fuming mad creature was giving him 'what-for' but all he could make out was, "Buzzzzybiter, buzzzzybiter!"

Then, he heard something that sounded like a war-cry and with that, the bug zipped past his ear again. Blue swiveled his head to see that it was making a beeline for his backside. Trying to defend himself, he frantically flung his tail back and forth across his vulnerable rump. More hairs clung to the sticky Jughead juice there with every swipe.

The Buzzy-Biter zigged and zagged, neatly avoiding each tail swish.

All Blue heard was, '"Buzzy-biter-buzzy-biter-buzzy-biter," as the hymenopter zeroed in on his backside.

Blue felt the needle penetrate his thick hide, and the painful pop forced him to stifle the, "Yeow!" that burst from his mouth. It was all he could do to choke back a more emphatic yelp, but despite the stabbing pain, the injured unicorn kept quiet.

The tribe was still within hearing range, and the thought of drawing their attention deterred him from crying out very loud. He did not want them to come back to witness his discomfort. Especially Cornum, who would never keep his snarky remarks to himself.

In the meantime, the stabbing pain of the sting exploded into a deep burning sensation that was quickly becoming unbearable. Blue twisted his head around again to see the Buzzy-Biter still attached to his rear end. Its barbed stinger had penetrated all the way through his hide.

The bug flapped about and droned in a way that made it clear he was stuck. Embedded there in Blue's flesh, the insect struggled mightily and the sight only made the unicorn feel worse.

Blue began to sweat. . .from the poison already entering his system, or just the fear of what was to come? He did not know, but he had to get rid of the nasty pest. He tried to dislodge it by twitching the hide of his rump.

When that did not work, Blue angrily angled his horn back toward the insect. With one eye trained squarely on the horrid bug, he motioned with his horn-tip to make it clear he intended to bludgeon the creature.

Imminent death made the Buzzy-Biter desperate. It launched into a frenzied struggle to free its sharp barbed end. Blue ground his teeth in pain each time the creature jerked outward; that barbed stinger was not coming out easily. The sickly-sweet stench of the jughead flowers filled the air, adding to the nauseous wave churning through Blue's gut.

The hymenopter's wings batted violently against the air as it tried to gain enough momentum to escape, but the bellows-like projection between the hook and its body acted like a powerful spring.

The bug's body snapped back viciously against Blue's rump, injecting even more venom into the unicorn.

Two. . . three. . .four more times, the insect's attempt at escape was aborted as even more poison pumped into Blue's system.

On the fifth try, the Buzzy-Biter finally attained enough thrust to break free from its victim, but its venomous weapon remained embedded in Blue's tough hide.

"Bzz-bzz-bzz." The insect zoomed past Blue's head. It bounced end over end across the bush, finally landing with a thud on the soft dirt below. The dizzy creature slowly pushed itself up to a standing position. Weaving back and forth a couple of times, it managed to brush the dirt off its wings before throwing itself into the air.

Blue swore he could hear the insufferable creature laugh as it flew away. Another stinger was already growing out to replace the one lost.

The pain in Blue's rump burned hot and raw. Try as he might, his horn could not reach the tender spot where the Buzzy-Biter's two-inch-long stinger remained buried in his skin. The hooked shape of the sharp object would never allow him to remove it himself.

He needed help.

"I don't feel so good," he groaned. The trees began to swim in circles before his eyes as he shuffled out of the bushes.

He could barely walk and his knees started to buckle. He understood well enough the dangers of a Buzzy-Biter sting. He had to get back to the Halstable.

Anyone stung by a Buzzy-Biter needed medical attention quickly, but someone with an allergy to the venom needed help even faster. An allergic reaction could be lethal.

Blue fell into that category, and he had just received five times more venom than normally delivered in a Buzzy-Biter attack.

The sun blazed high in the sky, he had no magic, and he was in serious danger. The distance to the Halstable was short, but he feared his grip on life might be even shorter.

Chapter Five

Two-Legged Danger

Blue emerged from the little grove of trees on shaky knees. Far ahead, he saw the majestic fortress of the Halstable planted on the grassy plain. The metal-horned tribe had lived there since before the Halstable had arrived on MarBryn and in that moment, Blue only hoped that he could make it back inside those walls.

The structure was, basically, a boxy rectangle with a hollowed-out center, which formed a big courtyard. Originally constructed to house hundreds of unicorns, the long rambling hallways of the massive five-story formation now led to the homes of only twelve. The dozen unicorns were the only survivors of Magh's ongoing pursuit and slaughter.

Far off in the distance, Blue thought he saw a group of creatures walking upright on two legs, approaching the Halstable. There were no discernible footpaths nearby, so he was immediately concerned that the venom in his body was making him hallucinate.

Unsure if the danger was real or not, his instincts told him to hide although time was not his friend. He dodged behind a bush to watch and see if the intruders were real or imaginary.

"Two-leggers . . ." he whispered, lifting a hind leg off the ground to ease the very real throbbing pain. He studied the approaching figures carefully. They too were real, he decided, and he immediately recognized them for what they were.

Many two-leggers populated MarBryn. There were Bugans from Bugansville and Letheans from the Silvan Forest. There were Ragamoffyns from the Red Band of Weita, and many others. Some two-leggers were gentle but, sadly, most two-leggers were no longer friends of the unicorns.

In the beginning, when the Halstable first came to MarBryn, nearly all two-leggers and other creatures had welcomed them. The manticore welcomed them, too but for very unsavory reasons. Many two-leggers now worked for Magh. Some did so willingly, while others had no choice, since they'd been ensnared under the sorcerer's binding spells. Now, far more two-leggers were dangerous than not.

Magh sent those under his control out to scour MarBryn, their mission always to find and gather all of the unicorn horns and hooves they could. Once, there had been hundreds of unicorns, but the two-leggers had been so successful in taking their horns and hooves that now there were only twelve. Dangerously close to extinction, the tribe now avoided all two-leggers, because it had become impossible to tell the good from the evil.

One on one, no two-legger could overpower a unicorn, especially not one who wielded magic. But unicorns were not prone to violence, nor did they do well with the guilt of taking another life. This left them susceptible to danger from not only the two-leggers, but also other creatures more intent on wreaking havoc. Unicorns could and would defend themselves when necessary, but to lay waste to beings trapped in an evil spell left the herd with a moral dilemma.

What are they up to? Blue watched as blood pounded through the veins in his neck. The poison racing through his system left him confused and unsure. *Why are they so close to the Halstable?*

The unicorn watched them move even closer. They argued and bonked each other on the head, as their voices grew loud and angry.

"Horsehocky!" one yelled at another.

"Blast it all, if you can talk that fudgeluffle smack to me!" the other yelled back.

Oh, it's only those Cussers from Egada, Blue realized. They were a group of short two-leggers, heads barely topping Blue's shoulders, but he did not want them to notice his presence. Their bark was traditionally worse than their bite, but he did not want to deal with them on this day so he took a step back, trying to become more enclosed by the bushes. Blue tried to stay as still as possible, which was not easy with the throbbing pain.

"Holy-Maroly! You two draggle-draggles cut it out!" their leader commanded, causing the curling mustache above his lips to shimmy. He was taller than the others and his ears were pointier, too. He bopped both of them on the head with his staff for emphasis.

"Snorksnot! That ferfernuggin' hurt!" ranted one of the short stocky Cussers. His beady little eyes and warty nose gave him a decidedly rat-like appearance.

He slapped the shortest Cusser on the back of the head. His leather glove made a loud *splat* sound where the material connected with the other's balding pate.

The little guy rounded on him, red-faced with anger. "Goldangit! If you hit me again, you'll be sorrier than sorry!" he promised, but being smaller and obviously, of lower rank than his larger compatriot, it was obvious he did not pose much of a threat.

"Ding-dong and double dang it! Just keep moving!" the Cusser leader shouted. The handlebars above his upper lip shook violently once again.

Just as the motley crew got within twenty feet of the Halstable's outer wall, its turn-about spell kicked in, causing the loud-mouthed ruffians to make an abrupt ninety-degree twist that pointed them away from the unicorns safeguarded home.

The Cussers were so confused by the change of direction; they began to argue even louder.

"What're we goin' this frazzlin' way fer? There's no reason fer changin' dadburn course," the shortest scruffy Cusser whined. He stamped his feet, like a child having a temper tantrum, but he did not stop walking. He knew better than that.

Their leader seemed just as bewildered as the others, but he kept right on going as if he did not want to them to know that he, too, was as disorientated as they were. He plunged ahead in their new direction and shouted, "Because it's the way I want to go, you groobstampers! Just keep moving, you buhdangled sluggards! We've been at it since dawn, and we won't be finding any flackity unicorns today!"

"But Magh said we gotta keep huntin' til we find—" the whiner began.

His leader puffed up his chest in pretense of a brave front, "I don't care what Magh told us to do! My gut is gnawing on my spine, so I aim to get back to Egada before suppertime."

He raised his staff again threatening another head bop. That was enough incentive for the other two Cussers to keep on moving. The town of Egada was still hours away and they did not want to miss supper, either.

Everything about the Halstable was constructed with magical properties, which rendered the entire structure invisible to the eyes of all other living beings. Therefore, the Cussers passed by without ever knowing how close their quarry had been. It was a relief to know the Halstable still had magical protection surrounding it.

In the past, most unicorns had thought it humorous to watch

creatures approach, and then unwittingly make sharply angled turns that led them away from the outer walls of their invisible home. It slightly amused the blue unicorn now, despite all the pain he was in, but it also frightened him to learn that even the Cussers were now doing Magh's foul bidding.

At this point, Blue's only comfort was the knowledge that it was still safe inside the Halstable. He was anxious to be inside, because the rest of MarBryn definitely was not safe.

Blue waited until the Cussers were completely out of the area before he moved.

The big voices of the little two-leggers rose and fell with each step they took. As the Cussers rounded a bend the sounds of their bickering all but disappeared from the landscape, but still Blue stayed hidden until their vocalizations faded away altogether. Allergic reaction or not, he would not be the one responsible for revealing the Halstable to these two-leggers, or any others.

His vision was becoming hazy, and so were his thoughts. He lurched away from the bush, the venom in his blood making his back leg so numb that he could not tell if it even touched the ground.

With the Cussers completely out of sight and hearing, he left the grove of trees. He felt weak, and the short distance seemed greater with every step. The smooth, dusty red ground seemed to move in undulating waves.

Blue found himself remembering recent incidents of failures in the magical system. Just a few weeks back, Gaiso had wandered in as if he owned the place. That had alarmed everyone, since he had never been there before.

Until then, none of the tribe knew the stag except Blue, but in true unicorn fashion, the sociable natures of the tribe members soon took over. Gaiso had proved to be such a pleasant fellow. . .what could they do but invite him to stay for dinner? Blue wished he had been there for that meal, even though he rarely dined with the others.

He wished Gaiso were here to help him now. His body shivered hard as the poison surged through his system. He shuddered again at the thought of what horrors might befall his tribe if any of the random malcontents had slipped through the Halstable's magical defenses the way Gaiso had done.

The Cussers were working for Magh. So were many others, so the Metal Horn tribe needed to be even more careful. Those little two-leggers talked and acted tough, but once upon a time, they had been somewhat kind to the unicorns. There was nothing kind about Magh, or anyone who did his dirty work.

I must remember to tell Alumna about the Cussers, he thought sluggishly.

As he trudged forward, his vision narrowed to a small spot of light at the end of a tunnel of darkness. The Halstable seemed like it was miles away, rather than yards.

His thoughts skittered from one danger to the next until he began to worry about manticores. He hoped one of them did not come swooping down upon him. He cringed as fear forced his eyes skyward, but nothing lurked in the cloudless expanse above.

Manticores were the most feared natural predators of the unicorns. The beasts had the head of a man, big bat-like wings, the powerful body of a lion, and a dragon's barbed tail tipped with a scorpion's stinger. Blue shivered again, when he realized that, if the magical security system ever failed, the manticores would have access to a virtual feast of their favorite meal. . .unicorns.

Thinking of the manticore's needle-like instrument of death reminded him of the much tinier Buzzy-Biter's much tinier barb. The poison made him tired and confused and incapable of a coherent stream of thought. His legs shook, and his rump throbbed with urgent reminders of the painful end awaiting him if the thing was not removed soon.

He needed a dose of Buzzy-Biter antidote before the poison worked its way completely through his system, but he felt so weak. Each step sent waves of pain shooting through his rump.

"I will make it. I have to make it," he told himself, "I have to warn the others that the Cussers are working for Magh."

Replaying this mantra in his mind helped him keep focused and gave him a new surge of energy. He closed his eyes, gritted his teeth, and trudged faster and faster until he was out of breath. Finally, Blue limped up to the large double doors of the Halstable. He inserted his blue hide-covered horn into an indentation where a doorknob would be—if the Halstable had been an ordinary abode.

He could see the indentation, as all unicorns could, but it was invisible to other creatures. As the doors swung inward, he staggered through. They closed immediately behind him.

"Ghel," he called in a whisper, limping through the maze of hallways to his living quarters. Spent as he was, Blue had to find his stable-mate quickly.

The golden-horned unicorn had saved him more than once, and she would know what to do.

Chapter Six

Only The Heart Knows For Sure

Blue and Ghel shared a stall comprised of several rooms.

They had been stable-mates since before the deaths of each of their parents, so it was natural for them to make their home together.

Blue's sire and dam had both become victims of the sorcerer. Blue had only been eight years old at the time of their death. The tragedy of the tribe was made all the worse with the common knowledge that all of the murdered unicorns' magic was exploited and used by Magh to further advance his evil. From Blue's parents, to Ghel's. . .to many, many others. . .all of them had suffered grave losses.

At that young age, he had heard a rumor claiming that Magh used the magic of his mother's indium-horn as a looking glass to keep an eye on events throughout MarBryn. He hated the thought that the despicable sorcerer used his mother's magic to advance his own evil, so the very moment he heard that news, he vowed aloud to Ghel that he would avenge his mother.

Privately, though, he had nightmares about Magh wielding control over his mother's spirit. He hoped the rumors were not true, but some inclination deep inside him confirmed that his mother was still watching over him somehow.

The golden unicorn tried hard to dissuade Blue from vowing to take on such a dangerous mission, but when she realized he was determined, she instead begged him for a promise that he would never do anything rash or venture out on his own trying to accomplish such a feat.

He had refused to deliver such a promise.

Blue never did hear what the sorcerer used his father's platinum horn for, but it was just as well he did not bear that burden, too. He had asked about his father, but few of the surviving unicorns knew much about him, and those who did seemed reluctant to tell him much about his sire, or the magic he had wielded with his platinum horn.

Blue's life would have been unbearably lonely, if not for his bond with the gold-horned unicorn. She had been born just days before him. Being nearly the same age, they had spent a lot of time playing together as ponies. When Blue lost his parents, Ghel's family took him in, even though he had been a despondent and withdrawn young unicorn.

By the time Blue and Ghel turned twelve, Magh had taken the horns and hooves from her parents too. They fell in a battle known as the Great Unicorn Massacre, and their premature deaths left both, Ghel and Blue, orphans with only each other to rely upon. So devastated were the few remaining adults, by the massive losses to the tribe, that there was no one left to pay them much mind. Over time, the bond between Blue and Ghel grew. They were two neglected souls seeking comfort in the only thing that made sense to them—their friendship.

Ghel's magic allowed her to look beyond what lay on the surface of another. When her golden horn rested on the heart girth of another unicorn; she sensed his or her emotional strengths, their hopes, and their dreams.

Her gift made her certain that underneath Blue's plain blue hide thumped the heart of a unicorn meant for greatness. . .even if no one else held that hope. While the rest of the metal-horned unicorns had all but given up on Blue saving them, Ghel had not.

Blue found the golden unicorn in their stall, relaxing on a long, low sofa. In one split hoof, she held a feather pen. Her flaxen mane hid her expression.

She gazed out a large, dark-glassed window into the central courtyard. She murmured words. . .words to a song, Blue guessed. Her singing voice did not possess the magical allure of Silubhra's, but despite, or maybe because of that, the raw genuineness of her singing spoke directly to Blue's heart.

*"You can't tell a book by its cover.
You must open it to read what's within."*

Looking up, her eyes locked with Blue's, but then his vision went blurry.

She quickly closed her songbook, before whispering, "Blue?"

A low moan escaped the blue unicorn as he stumbled through the doorway. He wanted to speak, to say a thousand things that sprang into his mind at the sight of her, but no words came as he gasped a pitiful sound and crumpled in a heap.

"A Buzzy-Biter. . .the stinger. . ." he managed to whisper before losing consciousness.

Ghel gasped. The stinger was still there jutting from Blue's backside. She remembered the allergic reaction he'd had after a similar attack years ago. This one seemed much worse.

I must act quickly, she thought urgently.

She went to remove the stinger with her teeth, but thought better of it. *What if that, squeezed more venom into the wound?* She gently probed the inflamed place with the point of her golden horn, wiggling the little hooked stinger until one end was more fully exposed. With careful precision she used the tips of her cloven hooves to grasp the sharp barb and extract it from Blue's swollen flesh.

With the stinger removed, the battle was half won, but he remained in danger. Most unicorns were not allergic to such stings, but Blue was not most unicorns. That was why the pair kept Buzzy-Biter anti-venom in their stall for just such an emergency. One quick dose could quell an allergic reaction, but without the shot, the consequences would be dire.

She pawed around in the drawer where they kept the antidote, but over the years, they had tossed all manner of odds and ends in there. She found the injection pen, but not the actual medicine. "Where's the ampoule?" Ghel panicked and jerked hard on another drawer. The big wooden box flew free and spilled its contents across the floor. She jumped back from the mess, only to hear a loud crack.

"No!" she cried, looking down at the splintered glass capsule lying in a pool of thick liquid. One drop of blood bubbled from her soft padded hoof. "That was the only one!" She bent to pull a sliver of thin glass from her hoof pad. It hurt but she could not worry about her own wound while Blue lay inert on the ground nearby.

Her pulse quickened as another low moan emanated from Blue's throat. She rushed to his side as he expelled what sounded frightfully like a sigh of defeat. Her heart hammered inside her chest. His normally blue muzzle was already tinged with white.

"He's stopped breathing!"

She nuzzled his muscular neck with her soft nose, trying to wake him.

He did not stir.

"Blue," she prodded, nudging him with a hoof. No effect.

She feared the worst, but then he jerked violently, kicking out his front leg as if defending himself from an attacker. He gasped then, and she saw that his breathing was labored, but still steady.

Tears pricked at her eyes, and she shook her horn impatiently. Her muzzle quivered as she listened to his harsh, forced breaths. The Buzzy-Biter poison was killing him.

She leaned her head against his heart so her ear rested just above his right lung. Ghel heard short, wheezing breaths and just beyond that, the faintest heartbeat.

She concentrated on that sound until it pulled her in and up through a dark space inside his unconscious mind. She tried to communicate to him that she was going for help and that he should hang on, but a pinprick of light flashed in the distance. Then, another. And another.

Within moments, colored flashes and arcs of light surrounded her and Blue.

Yes, there he was, lying on the ground—next to her—in the center of a ring of brilliantly colored lights. The entire tribe surrounded them. They stood horn-tip to horn-tip under a glowing golden pavilion of translucent cloth. Beyond the luminous canopy, she saw many unfamiliar faces anxiously watching from within a circling shelter of massive trees with colorful shimmering leaves. All of the creatures gathered there exuded a palpable anticipation of some long expected glorious event that pummeled Ghel's psyche like colossal rogue waves crashing upon a rocky shore.

Then, all went black again.

When next she could see, a multi-hued blue stallion stood before her, pawing at the air in triumph.

"Blue ..." the word fell, awestruck, from her lips before she was flung back into reality.

Lifting her head, she jumped up on all fours. "The prophecy! It's true!" Yes, he looked different, but there was no doubt in her mind that she had just seen a transformed Blue.

"You still have a destiny to fulfill."

She paced back and forth, weighing the odds for a moment. Blue was reluctant to associate with the rest of the tribe and he would be upset with her for involving the others, but his life was in danger and without the antidote, it was beyond her power to save him.

She told his unhearing ears, "You're not going to be happy, but I've got to bring Dr. Zinko here. I won't lose you. You are my world, but more than that, the tribe needs you!" She hurried off to find the unicorn with the magical medicinal horn.

Ghel galloped through the halls as if pursued by Magh's minions. "Dr. Zinko! Dr. Zinko, where are you?"

Rounding a corner at full speed, she nearly slammed into Lauda, the Lead-Horned unicorn.

"Whoa, there, young filly," Lauda exclaimed. "Are you okay?" The lead-horned mare's cropped mane curled loosely about her ears like a cap, giving her a grandmotherly appearance.

"I'm fine, I'm fine," Ghel gasped, "But Blue is not. A Buzzy-Biter stung him. He's unconscious!"

"Unconscious? From a Buzzy- Biter? I know he's allergic but that seems kind of drastic." Lauda pondered.

"I'm not sure what's going on," Ghel said, "The stinger was

stuck. I managed to remove it but I couldn't give him the anti-venom," she paused, looked down and lifted her hoof off the floor, revealing a small spot of blood. She sighed and continued, "I. . .I broke the only ampoule we had. Now Blue is in some kind of shock. I've got to find Dr. Zinko."

"Zinko was right behind me," Lauda said, looking back down the hall. No one was there. "He must have stopped to talk or look at something, but I imagine he will catch up to us soon."

"This is urgent, Lauda!" Ghel maneuvered around the old mare. "I can't wait for him to get to us. I've got to find him now!"

"Yes, quickly, go find him," Lauda urged as Ghel disappeared.

Chapter Seven
The Hard Way

*T*he lead-horned unicorn regained her composure and realized she stood but a few feet from her laboratory, where there was an entire cabinet stocked with anti-venom. She slid open a glass door and removed a small box marked *B-B Anti-Venom*. Inside were twelve tiny containers of the stuff.

"I'll rush this to Blue now," she said aloud. "Maybe I can stabilize him until Ghel gets back with Zinko."

When Lauda reached Blue, large white splotches covered his entire body. His breath was so shallow; she could not hear it until her ear was right next to his mouth.

The old mare immediately injected him with the antidote, but to no effect. The poisons had raced through his system, already ravaging his defenses. By the time Dr. Zinko and Ghel made their way to the stall, Lauda was frantically pounding the injection site with her front elbows, thinking that she could speed the anti-venom into Blue's blood stream.

But he just lay there, motionless.

"Lauda, stop. You're wearing yourself out," Dr. Zinko said to the frazzled old mare. "Let me have a look at him."

"The antidote didn't work, Zinko. He's too far gone," Lauda panted from her exertions.

A huge tear hung suspended from Ghel's eyelashes. "Please, save him! He's the best friend I've got in this world." Her voice cracked.

Lauda's heart squeezed hard. "Zinko will save him," she told Ghel gently while swallowing the extra thought, *if anyone can.*

The doctor gave his stable-mate a long, uncertain look, and then acknowledged, "My magic may be the only way to strengthen his system enough to reject the poison."

The zinc-horned unicorn rarely used his horn's magic that way, especially now that he had grown older and weaker, and the act left him exhausted.

Lauda's potions offered sufficient protection to prevent most ailments, and they could even cure some, but not all. Some maladies required his magical touch, and that came at a cost to Zinko's own health. But she knew the doctor would risk this, for Blue was worth the cost.

Lauda tut-tutted as she and Ghel watched the elderly white unicorn physician use his zinc-horn to administer a magical curative to Blue. This was not an injection from his horn to Blue's wound, although they were physically connected. It was a sharing of his own life-force with that of the dying unicorn.

The wound was the conduit for Zinko's horn magic to enter Blue's failing system. A thin bright white stream leapt from the unicorn doctor's magical horn into the wound. Static electricity crackled through the air and the faint scent of ozone hung in the room.

Blue's circulatory and nervous systems had both been severely damaged. His body instinctively latched on to the life-giving energy pouring from the elderly unicorn and rapaciously sucked it up.

Dr. Zinko's face froze; his eyes wide and protruding. His lips pulled back in a tortured grimace and his legs shook furiously as the tip of the wounded unicorn's horn began to take on the faint glow a cloudless blue sky. It was almost impossible to see against his hide, which was close to the same color as the soft light.

The pale glow began to revolve, until it became a small maelstrom of various shades of blue. The crackle of static grew louder and louder, building into a strong thrum of power.

"What in the world?" Lauda shouted.

Ghel exclaimed, "What's happening to Blue?"

Lauda had never before witnessed such a thing, and the sight scared the dickens out of her. Her stable-mate, the venerable doctor, looked to be on his last legs—as if every bit of his magic was being siphoned away.

The lead-horned unicorn ran to her mate and shoved his head hard, breaking contact between him and Blue. "Enough! No more, Zinko. I will not let you die!"

As soon as the contact was broken, the glow emanating from Blue's horn blinked out—as if it had never been there, leaving Lauda to wonder if it had actually happened. She would have tried to convince herself that it was just her eyes playing tricks, but then Ghel said, "That blue light. . .is that normal?"

Lauda ignored Ghel and instead took a long silent look at the blue unicorn. Then, she turned her attention back to her mate. The old stallion swayed slightly from side-to-side, but he managed to stay upright. In a gentler tone, she told him, "Blue is on his own now."

Lauda's lead-horn brushed against her mate's indigo-mane as she leaned in close to inspect the site of the Buzzy-Biter sting. The wounded area had already begun to resume its normal healthy shade of blue.

She straightened, stretching a stitch out of her neck, relieved that Zinko's horn magic was still so strong. Healing someone so close to death could take a disastrous toll on Zinko's own health, but still, she had never seen such a look come over his face before.

Had this time almost been too much for him? Or had the fact that Blue had no metal and no magic meant that the doctor had to work harder to save him? And what was that light that flickered briefly in Blue's horn?

Relief flooded through her when the magical physician drew a deep breath, shook his head, and rippled his shoulder muscles to shake off the remnants of using so much of his magic. When he turned to face her, she was pleased to see his own completely unblotched complexion, with no sign of undue stress or strain on his face.

"Don't know how much longer I would've lasted if you hadn't broken the connection between us," the unicorn doctor told her shakily. "Nothing has ever drained my life-force so quickly."

"I know," Lauda said, staring at Blue's horn tip. The dull, blue shade offered no evidence of the glowing light. "I could see you had lost all control. I'm glad I was here to help you break free."

"Me, too," he said with a shiver. "I fear to think how much worse it could have been. I had already delivered a full dose of my metal magic by the time you pushed my horn away, yet something kept pulling more and I could do nothing to stop it."

Lauda's fearful anger at nearly losing her life-long companion put her over the edge. Completely beside herself, she exploded, "If Blue had the sense to let me give him a dose of BB Repellant before he went sneaking off into bug-infested bushes, this would never have happened!" A brusque shake of her head sent her light-gray curls a-flutter.

She turned to regard Ghel over spectacles balanced

precariously across her dark gray nose. "There's always some young whippersnapper who refuses to be dosed because they think it makes their hide smell funny!" she said sternly. Her nostrils dilated as she *harrumphed* indignantly.

Lauda had yet to come up with a formula for the stuff that did not leave an unpleasant odor on the skin. She had mixed countless combinations, using many different ingredients. This latest batch contained birch tar and bog myrtle—both of which stunk to high heaven, but they were effective. Now, lemon eucalyptus and citronella smelled divine, but neither of them worked worth a hoot. Most of the unicorns preferred not to use her bug repelling concoctions because they were so repelled by the odious nature of them. But, then, most unicorns stayed close to home.

The unicorn doctor smiled fondly at his stable-mate saying, "Now calm down, Lauda my dear. I'm sure Blue will use your repellant from now on."

Lauda furiously ground a hoof into the floor, saying, "Yes, but did he have to learn such a hard lesson first?"

Her question was meant to intimidate, and it did. Ghel bowed her horn in deference but in truth, Lauda was not really trying to lay the blame for Blue's troubles on the golden-horned unicorn. He brought that on himself.

Dr. Zinko called their attention to Blue, who was starting to come around. "Ladies ... Blue is stirring," he observed, rescuing Ghel before the lead-horned unicorn could make another remark.

"Well, young stallion," Dr. Zinko said briskly, "You are one lucky unicorn to have someone like Ghel looking out for you."

Blue looked around the room at the others, as if confused. "Why are you all looking at me like that?"

Lauda pounced on the remark, asking, "Why?" After a fuming pause, she added, "You almost died, you nincompoop! That's why! You should have gone straight to Dr. Zinko. Or stayed here, where you belong, instead of gallivanting about the countryside. If not for Ghel's quick action, you wouldn't even be talking to us right now!"

The blue unicorn was so taken aback by the old mare's gruffness that his misery came flooding back in a rush. He felt like a wretched mess. Squirming under Lauda's stern scowl, he turned to face Ghel.

She looked so sad and lovely standing there as her golden blonde mane caressed her sweet-clover-honey-colored shoulders. Poor Ghel—she often took on trouble for his sake because, while he was off hiding from the tribe, she was left to answer their questions.

Embarrassed, he flopped over on the floor and closed his eyes to shut out their expressions of scorn and pity. A little voice inside his head niggled at him: *Nobody loves you! Everybody hates you! You may just as well have died!*

He knew, deep down, that it was not true—but like always he struggled with being so different from all the others.

Wallowing in shame, he heard Ghel's reassuring voice filter through his misery. "Don't listen to Lauda. She's just being a grump." She kissed him on the cheek. "You rest now, dearest. I'll bring you some dinner later." Her affectionate gesture comforted him, as a kiss from the golden unicorn always did.

Lauda's antidote, along with Dr. Zinko's healing magic, left him groggy and fighting sleep.

The other three unicorns talked softly, but on the way out Blue heard the doctor say, "I'm glad he made it home alive. He might not be our savior, but he's still a member of our tribe."

Chapter Eight

Not All That Glitters

*D*r. Zinko, Ghel, and Lauda proceeded down the long windowless hall toward the great room at the opposite end of the Halstable. The unicorn doctor said a good meal would help Blue heal faster, so Ghel looked forward to getting something tasty to bring back to him. Delicious aromas reached her nostrils before they were even halfway down the hall, making her stomach rumble.

Other unicorns smelled the tantalizing scents wafting through the air and headed to the kitchen, too. Two fillies were just leaving the Groomane Salon together as the trio passed by.

"I told you it would look great," Style, the steel-horned unicorn was saying to her friend as they strutted toward the trio.

"You were right, as usual," Cuprum agreed. The copper-horned unicorn seemed genuinely happy with her new 'do, but Ghel wondered if her encouraging tone was more to flatter Style than any other reason. The steel-horned stylist tended to get huffy when others did not show excitement over her work.

Style ran both the Groomane Salon and the fitness center next to it. The steel-horned unicorn liked to stay in shape, so she worked out a lot. Although she encouraged other unicorns to exercise as much as possible, too, there were a few who had no interest in her fitness programs even though outside opportunities to stay in shape were scant with the threat of Magh keeping the tribe mostly confined to the Halstable.

Some unicorns, like Blue, preferred running and jumping and climbing on his own, while others simply didn't like to break a sweat any place, or anytime.

Style had her faults, but she enjoyed helping the others look and feel good. She created magnificent mane and tail styles with just a touch of her horn. Her artwork, as she liked to call it, was something that got the fillies excited every time she came up with another fabulous painted hoof design. They went to see her often for an updated look, and Style always obliged with some fantastic new creation.

When Style conjured up elegantly styled mane-do's and hoof art, the recipient of her magical stylings was transformed in a matter of seconds. Style's motto was: *When you look good, you feel good, too!* Most of the time, it did work out that way.

Cuprum's latest makeover had her mane adorned with dragonfly-shaped barrettes. Rubies and emeralds hung loosely from her shiny, freshly brushed mane and tail. Her hooves were not left out, either. They were painted with crimson undercoats overlain with emerald outlines of dragonflies. The colors on her hoof-nails perfectly matched the red and green jewels.

Style, of course, had a new 'do, too. It was topped off with a butterfly-shaped tiara. The little princess crown glowed with a bright purple shine from the amethysts studded in it. Her front hoof-nails were painted purple with white butterflies.

The two fillies looked fantabulous. Style had worked her amazing magic again.

"Style, you've outdone yourself this time," Ghel complimented. "I love that tiara."

"Yes, it is very pretty," Lauda agreed. "Those dragonfly barrettes are exquisite, too."

Everyone agreed that the fillies looked sensational, but for the first time, their fashion-sense seemed frivolous to Ghel. Didn't they all realize how close Blue had come to dying? And from a simple bug sting, too!

In the grand scheme of things, the danger of the Buzzy-Biter paled next to the devastation Magh could unleash. And yet, they all had grown somewhat complacent, relying on the safety of the Halstable.

The unease wedged into Ghel's brain just as that stinger had been embedded in Blue's flesh. She could not shake the idea that the tribe had strayed far from their purpose. Surely, they were meant for more than hiding out behind the walls of the Halstable, only daring to venture out for short jaunts to a watering hole! A safe house that held them prisoner was not nearly as safe as any of them believed.

None of it sat right with Ghel. Truth be told, she had been having this growing sensation for a long while now, but Blue's near-death had brought it all home in a way her mind had never been able to puzzle out before.

To this point, every last member of the tribe had failed to live up to their true potential, and even after seeing within Blue, she feared none of them ever would.

She worried they were too vulnerable, too complacent, too fragile to fulfill their destiny. But if they did not, they would all die. Either long, slow, painful deaths trapped here in the Halstable or at the hands of Magh or his minions if they got careless.

Chapter Nine

A Pitiful Excuse

The group entered the Great Room, where the tribe always gathered to eat the delicious meals the tin-horned unicorn chef conjured up. Ghel watched Tinam's lemon-colored eyes light up like those of happy child when he saw Cuprum.

"Oh, you look delectable, my little dumpling!" the unicorn chef blurted with relish.

The dolled-up filly executed a perfect pirouette on the very hoof-tip of her left hind leg, sending her red and green mane flying out around her as she spun in place. "Don't I look a sight, though?" She laughed gaily; obviously loving the attention her new look brought. The other unicorns present looked fondly on the two lovebirds, while some fillies tittered at Cuprum's silly twirl.

Ghel swallowed a lump in her throat.

"You may be a sight, but look at this spread Tinam has created," Style observed. Her eyes widened as she admired the lavish array of luscious foods, which the unicorn chef had conjured. Everything she loved to eat was laid out on the table just waiting for a bite.

It was a well-known secret that Style badgered Tinam to come up with dishes just to suit her. The steel-horned unicorn was a foodie but love of food was no real cause for worry for her. After a big meal, she would just work out twice as hard and never gain a single unwanted pound. Ghel appraised the rest of the tribe with a narrowed focus that she never had before and realized that was not the case with everyone. She noted that more than one of the unicorns could do well to lay off of Tinam's creations.

A tough task, given the room swirled with delicious scents that captured the nose of every unicorn in the tribe.

Spread out on the table this day were tin bowls of spicy pink beans which had the sharp bite of onion and the pungency of nightshade peppers, served alongside tins of crunchy golden corn fritters sprinkled with refreshing sprigs of citrusy cilantro.

For those with a sweet tooth (and most unicorns had one), there were tin platters of sweet mace-laced potato haystack pancakes, dripping with maple syrup.

Tin containers of warm, fragrant banana raisin bread sat beside aromatic cinnamon-oatmeal cookies. Tinam never failed to please all of the unicorns—or himself, for that matter. His rotund body was the most noticeably out of shape.

The unicorn chef always outdid himself with each new recipe, so the unicorns eagerly anticipated each repast and for a short time, the Great Room vibrated with all the hullabaloo.

Rumps balanced on the tall square stools, spaced evenly around the long table. The unicorns *oohed* and *ahhed*, plucking up morsels of food with their cloven fore-hooves and dropping them into delighted mouths. Excited over the food, everyone was buoyantly happy to ignore the dangers outside the Halstable.

Everyone, that was, except for Ghel. She stared blankly at her food, pushing it around on the plate with the fork that she gripped daintily in the cleft of her split hoof. She had been ravenous, but she soon had to force every bite past the lump, which had taken up residence in her throat. Nothing would taste good or be right until Blue fully recovered from his life-threatening ordeal.

She wondered how he got stung in the first place. He often disappeared for hours, and sometimes days at a time. There was no telling what dangers he encountered when off by himself, but she worried every time he snuck away. Enemies lurked everywhere, even tiny ones, like Buzzy-Biters.

Life would be certainly be simpler if he didn't go off on his own all the time, and if he would spend more time with the rest of the tribe, she thought morosely, *but then, again maybe Blue was the only member of the tribe really living these days.*

Still, she wished Blue was not such a loner. She understood why he was better than most, but so much solitude only fed his self-pity. Besides, she missed him, and his departures often left her lonely.

The rickety old unicorn seated beside her must have sensed something weighed heavily on her mind. "Don't worry, Ghel," Iown, the iron-horned unicorn, offered in his wise, gentle voice. "Most problems can be ironed out, given enough time."

Not only did Iown have a way with coaxing the best from plants, he had a talent for doing the same with sentient beings, as well. In fact, the magic of his horn allowed him to 'iron out' most any problem. Whether called upon to intervene in a petty squabble between two unicorns, or to judge the best way to right a major wrong, the tribe depended on his wisdom as their Sage Counselor.

Ghel looked at her elder and, noting the dusky-gray bristles framing his muzzle, she managed a genuine smile. She had apprenticed with him for five years, and she knew very well that, if any of the tribe were having a hard time with their stable-mate or anyone else, they went to see Iown. Her mentor would give each party a soothing touch on their poll with that iron-horn of his, and then share a little of his sagacious advice. This never failed to resolve the problem. . .at least for a while.

She had seen this magic in action countless times, but somehow, she did not feel such a simple cure would help her problems with Blue. She had a sudden urge to confide both her earlier vision and the subsequent melancholy with Iown, but something held her back.

What if Iown did not believe she had seen Blue's future? Or that she was simply being a pessimist by pointing out the tribe's stagnancy? Ghel feared embarrassing herself so, instead, she said, "I wish I could believe that, Iown, but this isn't as simple as one of Style and Cornum's ego-centered spats."

The iron-horned unicorn's eyes went wide, and his lips drew back into a tight, grimacing smile. He flattened his ears straight back, looking very silly, and said, "Oh-ho! Nay, would I mention you in the same breath with those two? No, no, never, my dear," he assured her. White teeth flashed a smile tinged with mock-horror as he looked down the table toward the bickering couple.

Cornum and Style were whispering, or at least they seemed to be attempting to whisper, but their argument could clearly be heard: "Why lemons?" Cornum whined with a drawn face.

"Because—you—are a sour-puss through and through," Style snapped back.

Iown looked back at Ghel with raised eyebrows and round eyes. His clowning made her laugh, so she said warmly, "Alumna is so lucky to have you."

A ripple of laughter colored his voice as he bent closer to whisper back, "Well, I'd better go see what they are fighting about. It looks as if they need a little help ironing this one out."

Iown chomped down noisily on a stalk of celery and deliberately ambled down to the opposite end of the table, chewing as he went.

Ghel gazed sadly at Blue's empty stool, catty-cornered from hers. Empty, as always. Today, his absence cut a sharp pain in her heart, but if she shared any of her lonely thoughts with Blue, he would tell her, "You are wasting your life being the stable-mate of a pitiful excuse for a unicorn like me."

He had used those exact words before, and they stabbed her like a knife.

"Magic and a metal-horn would not make me love you more," she had responded angrily.

She had wanted, even hoped for him to say he loved her too, but like always, Blue simply turned inward and said nothing at all.

Chapter Ten
A Voice From The Orb

Alumna gazed into the big glass orb mounted on a three-legged stand in the room the others had all dubbed, The Oracle's Sanctuary.

The pewter stand holding the crystal ball was a peculiar piece of artwork. Each 'leg' was a full-grown unicorn rearing up on its hind legs. All six forelegs were up-raised, to securely nestle the clear glass orb in place on the tops of their hooves. Alumna loved the artisanship of the piece and wondered who had created it. *Some long gone ancestor, no doubt.*

On the desk, between her and the orb, lay a long piece of parchment with images splattered across it. The upper edges were held down by an ink bottle and a big chunk of rose-pink quartz crystal.

"Hmph." She stared down critically at the picture she had just drawn. "It should look more like this." She meticulously drew what looked like a mountain on the right side of the paper.

Many more maps and other fantastical renderings were stacked around the room. She had long ago given up trying to keep her piles of drawings and papers tidy and neat.

Alumna had stumbled upon this room with its great crystalline orb decades ago, while exploring the uppermost floor of the Halstable. It was one of the few places in the fortress, which did not have a window looking down upon the courtyard.

But it was not a dark place. Softly glowing tubes of light ran along the tops of all four walls, and a big skylight above her desk allowed diffused sunlight to flood the room.

When she first found the mysterious room, she immediately told the other members of the tribe, hoping they might all work together to ferret out its purpose. To Alumna's surprise, however, no one else saw anything in the orb when they gazed into it, so their interest in the place soon waned.

Colors swirling in the glass sphere had drawn every unicorn's eye into it, but she was the only one who saw distinct words and images. Alumna was also the only one who had read all the books lining the walls, because reading had become a neglected skill in the tribe. The others could read, but most unicorns chose not to, after they got past their mandatory studies. This generation simply did not believe in the magic of a good book. To most of them, books were just … boring.

Among the many books, she had found an unfinished work inside a thick leather-bound journal. Hand-lettered writing dubbed it *The MarBryn Compendium,* and inside were pages and pages of notes written in a wide variety of styles by what was obviously a number of different authors. Some of the pages were hard to read due to poor penmanship, so Alumna had spent hours trying to decipher the words. Others were written in clear and concise script.

They described things both new and familiar to Alumna, so she quickly understood that the journal was created as an encyclopedia of sorts, for all things MarBryn. From fauna and flora to geography and weather, *The MarBryn Compendium* was a source she turned to often, but even its cherished pages failed to spark much interest from the remainder of the tribe.

Though, neither the books, nor the orb captivated the others the way they did Alumna, she simply could not stay away. Gathering bits of information had become her sole compulsion, to the point that she spent every available moment she could in this room, and now everyone referred to it as The Oracle's Sanctuary.

They called it that because every time she emerged from the room, she had some new tidbit of information— information that, often as not, came from the big glass orb.

The first time Alumna looked into the crystal ball, her mind filled with images of events that could not possibly have occurred in this world so, mimicking the actions of those who wrote in *The MarBryn Compendium*, she began recording what she saw. She drew what she could and wrote out things too complex for her artistic abilities.

Even after years of practice, Alumna's artistic abilities were still primitive. Her drawings were often simple lines and curves, splashed with a little paint. She did her best to depict the foreign faces, buildings, and landscapes that came to her via the glass because it struck her as important to do so. Now, countless renderings filled the room.

Years into the task, she heard a voice emanate from the orb. She thought her mind might have finally gone over the edge, but the orb had hissed and crackled before, so that helped her understand the source of the voice.

In gentle tones, the voice said, "*Alumna, I am Numen, the spirit of the Moon-Star, and you are a descendent of a long line of aluminum-horned Navigators. The magic of your horn drew you to this room, and to this orb.*"

Alumna had stared deeper into the glass hoping to see the face of the speaker, but saw nothing within its enigmatic depths. "Numen? Why have you never spoken to me before?" she asked, thinking of all the hours she had spent staring at the silent globe.

"*Many generations have passed since my last communication with a Navigator. You were the first to enter this room in nearly a century. With no one to guide you, it took years before the connection between our psyches grew strong enough.*"

"Who are you?" Alumna had asked in wonder.

"I am an astral entity that contains the combined knowledge of all unicorns. Your ancestors created me eons ago with the ability to transmit and receive information across the universes. It is my divine duty to watch over and guide all unicorns beyond Unimaise."

"Unimaise? I have so many questions. . ." Words began to spill from Alumna's mouth. "These images and pictures . . . Who are they? What are they? Where are these places?"

Numen sighed and said, *"I have much to teach you."* Then, his voice faded away.

Thusly had gone all communication with the Numen. It would start out strong, then fade after a few minutes. Sometimes, weeks would pass with no contact at all.

Sometimes, the Numen shared very important details. . .like the prophecy about Blue. Other times, the Moon-Star Spirit revealed only the mundane.

Today, there were no voices coming through, only images and Alumna remained so intent on copying them all down that she did not hear Ghel's approach.

"What are you working on, Alumna?"

Startled by the interruption, the rose-colored unicorn hastily moved the items holding the paper flat on the desk. She rolled the parchment up tight so no images could be seen, but she worried terribly that doing so would smear the ink.

Ghel did not seem to notice Alumna's odd behavior as she stood near a bookshelf, swishing her tail and shifting from hoof to hoof. Her eyes betrayed the look of someone deeply troubled.

The expression changed Alumna's irritation at being interrupted to one of concern for the younger unicorn. "Nothing so important I can't help you. You look pained, my dear. What brings you here to the sanctuary?"

"I'm worried about Blue," Ghel started and then stopped, before plunging on. "Since the incident with the Buzzy-Biter, he seems even more withdrawn. I was wondering if you've had any recent contact with the Numen. Or if you've learned any more about the future of the tribe. I . . ."

Her voice trailed off without completing her last thought, but Alumna thought she knew what was on Ghel's mind and she felt for the poor dear.

The young filly had confided more than once that she hoped to one day bear a little blue foal. That seemed less likely all the time, given both the innate protections instilled within unicorns in times of peril, and Blue's lack of commitment to the tribe or anything else.

The red unicorn thought back to the Numen's prophecy about Blue's birth. The words of the Moon-Star Spirit, on the day Blue was born had come with a warning that clenched her heart: *"There are two potential futures for the metal-horned unicorn tribe. The first is a dark and gloomy possibility, with no new unicorn births after the blue unicorn's arrival. All unicorns will fade from MarBryn if Blue fails to fulfill his destiny."*

". . .and the other possibility?" Alumna had almost been afraid to ask.

"The other offers hope, but only if the blue unicorn gains the tools and knowledge required to save all others."

Alumna remembered the flood of relief that had washed over her when the Spirit of the Moon-Star went on to promise, *"Should the blue unicorn succeed, he will lead the tribe of metal-*

horned unicorns back to prominence where they will live safely and prosper in Unimaise, the land of their ancestors."

He had shown her so many images of that place by then that she felt like she had already been there. There were no two-leggers on Unimaise, only unicorns. In fact, there were many different breeds of unicorns on Unimaise: Metal-horns, Peacorns, Watercorns, Unicus, and several others.

Alumna had seen their true home in the orb, and it was a beautiful place, one like none of the unicorns of the Halstable had ever seen. Alumna wondered if any of them would ever see it for real.

The unicorn oracle had also learned that each breed of unicorn contained a variety of herds. She belonged to the Metal Horn unicorn breed as a descendant of the Navigator herd.

When he said, "You are the only Navigator in all of MarBryn," she had asked, "What is a Navigator?"

"Navigators chart the courses for the Jump Ships," Numen replied, though the information meant nothing to her.

"Chart the courses? Jump Ships?" Alumna repeated the Moon-Star spirit's words wonderingly.

She had feared they had lost their connection, because the Numen said nothing until she spoke again. "Do you mean to say that I will navigate us back to Unimaise in some kind of ship?"

"You will chart the way, but only a Pilot can bring the Metal Horns of MarBryn home."

"A Pilot?"

"There has not been a Pilot born on MarBryn in over a century," Numen told the devastated unicorn. "Soon, that will change."

"This new foal will be the first?" Alumna asked, but the Numen was gone again, so no answer came. At least, not before the birth they had all been anticipating.

Blue had been born with a plain hide horn and hooves a few months later.

Sadly, there had not been a single unicorn born into the tribe since, and twenty years later Blue still had no metal. . .and no magic.

Chapter Eleven
You Can't Find It On The Map

Ghel waited for Alumna to say something—anything—but the oracle seemed completely lost in her own head. She cleared her throat and said, "Alumna, has the Numen contacted you or revealed any more about Blue's prophecy? What aren't you telling me?"

"Whether our tribe expands or not isn't only an individual matter. It's not your fault or even Blue's."

Ghel was confused until Alumna said, "I remember you telling me you hoped to have a little blue foal one day."

Surprised, Ghel did not know what to say. They had discussed this topic long ago, but the gold-horned unicorn had pretty much given up on the subject, and it had been a long time since motherhood had even entered her mind.

"The aura of the entire tribe is tattered," Alumna went on. "We've been struck by tragedy, here in MarBryn. There's been so much loss of life that the fertility aura has faded away to the point that there can be no new births."

The golden-horned unicorn lowered her head for a moment in silent remembrance, then replied, "I know." Her voice cracked as she recounted what every unicorn wished they did not know. "I would not want to bring a baby into this world with the fear of Magh ever-present."

Alumna carried on, despite Ghel's words. "This is a natural protection put in place to protect against an evil being from harvesting an endless supply of our magic. Magh's Metal Horn Massacre tipped the balance, and until the power shifts, there will be no births possible. All of those thuggish manticores and spellbound soldiers mindlessly murdered our family and friends. Now we are so few in number. . ."   Her voice caught and she did not continue for nearly a minute.

"For eighty long and terrible years, they've ravaged our tribe, collecting horns and hooves for Magh." Alumna kept at the harsh history lesson even though Ghel knew every last one of these facts. "There have been no new deaths for over eight years. But as long as we stay close to the Halstable, it seems we are safe."

Ghel could listen no more. "For how long?" she demanded "We are prisoners! Yes, it is a good thing we are still alive, but how much longer can we last like this? The protections mean nothing if we all go extinct, and we aren't really living now!" The pain in her heart spilled into her veins and spread throughout her entire being. "I'm sorry, Alumna. I need to go," she choked out. She left the room, completely forgetting her original intent for the visit.

On her way out the door, the golden-horned unicorn brushed past Iown without even the courtesy of a how-do-you-do.

"My goodness, what just happened here, my dear?" he asked his stable-mate. "Ghel is usually so sweet and friendly."

Alumna slumped over the desk with her head cradled in her forelegs. Iown came over and nuzzled her cheek. His comforting touch chased away enough of her sorrow that she managed a smile.

"Iown, I fear for our future," she revealed. "What if Blue never comes into his own and our tribe fades to nothing?"

"There's still hope," Iown reminded her. "It's not as if he's a decrepit geriatric like me."

"Don't say that, Iown. I'd prefer to think of you as a venerated gray-beard, and you're certainly not decrepit."

Iown lifted his eyebrows in a playful manner. "Gray-beard! Ha! You've got me there," Iown laughed, "At least my mind is sharp."

To that, Alumna only nodded.

"You mustn't give in to despair," he urged. "There's still a chance Blue will find his purpose and lead us all to Unimaise."

Iown's iron hooves clanged dully on the floor's hard surface as he moved across the room to a sketch of a hilltop.

"Without metal? Or magic?"

He did not respond to Alumna, and instead stared down at the drawing. Scattered around the landscape were several buildings that looked like variations of their own home. Off in the distance ran a wide river where two unicorns swam. Alumna had also drawn two unicorns with giant wings beside one of the buildings.

Iown touched the picture with his horn. "This is Unimaise?"

She could only shrug.

He turned to face her. "The Numen said the tribe will be safe on Unimaise. It would be grand to live somewhere with no manticores to swoop down upon us. Every day, I imagine a world with no warring tribes, and no motive to kill magical creatures."

"The Numen did promise that, but only if the prophecy about Blue is fulfilled."

Alumna felt a rising irritation with the Numen and his promises. Over the years, the Spirit of the Moon-Star had revealed so much knowledge, but held back the most vital information. "Our ancestors were so smart. They had magic and technology. They created the Numen and the Moon-Star. They sent our tribe from Unimaise here to MarBryn, but we don't even know why. Or how? What went so wrong, that we have lost both the know-how, and the will?"

Iown wished he had an answer, but this was one problem he could not iron out. He had faith, however, that Alumna and, hopefully, Blue could solve the mystery. So he kissed her on the cheek, and said, "You will find a way to help Blue. . .and the rest of us."

"I have no idea why you are so certain," she replied, "but if that is indeed the case, then I'd better get back to it." Communicating with the spirit of the Moon-Star felt like the only chance to help Blue fulfill the prophecy.

Iown left her alone with her thoughts, but she did not mind. He had other things to attend, and, despite the dangers, the tribe somehow managed to go about their daily business.

Admittedly, most of that business was of little importance, but this did not rile Alumna. By their very nature, unicorns had a way of making their reality seem better than it actually was and inwardly, she applauded the others' ability to sing, dance, and play through such adversity.

The weight of her task sometimes made her feel nothing but gloom, yet Alumna knew that if push came to shove, each unicorn would do their part to shoulder the burden of saving their race. Though, sometimes, she wished they were more inclined to help now.

"Why must I, alone, be haunted by the Numen's words?" Frustrated, she threw her question at the unresponsive orb. "Why won't you show me how to help Blue?"

Though Alumna had asked this question of the Moon-Star Spirit countless times, there had never been a satisfactory answer. She could not help wishing they had a better way of communicating. The orb always seemed to be plagued with a bad connection to the

Numen. . .when there was a connection at all.

She unrolled the map to take another look at her latest effort. She felt a little guilty about hiding it from Ghel, but she did not want to get her hopes up about Blue's magic. Happy to see that the ink had not smeared after all, she thought the map looked all but finished.

On the left side, she had drawn a building that clearly looked like the Halstable. And there, just to the left, was the little grove of trees where the unicorns went from time to time. Tracing a path to the northeast with her hoof, she came to a larger grove. No—not a grove—a forest. In fact, it was the Guarded Forest, the only other safe haven for magical creatures in all of MarBryn.

The other places she had drawn were new territories unknown to her or the other unicorns. Some she had read about in the *MarBryn Compendium,* but some were altogether new. She could not even be certain they were real places, but they had shown themselves to her in the orb, along with names and coordinates.

Phlat Plains. . .Heptagonos Valley. . .Smaul Mountain. . . Lethean Silva. . .Jeribild. . . and others.

Finally, at the southeast corner of the parchment, the location that had shined brighter than anything ever had within the orb: Muzika Woods.

She leaned closer to peer more deeply into the glass ball, urging it to reveal a firm path forward. "Numen, please, tell me what's to be done."

To her great surprise, he immediately answered, "A plan has been devised."

Alumna's face lit up at that piece of great news, until the Numen added, "But it is fraught with danger, and no one will be safe should even one of you fail."

Chapter Twelve

Of Descendants and Ancestors

*B*lue woke to the sound of hoof-steps. Sunlight filtered into the room, but he had done little more than eat and sleep for days, so he had no idea if it was morning or afternoon.

"Ghel?"

"No, Blue, it's Alumna. I've just received a message from the Moon-Star Spirit. A message for you." She thrust her face close to his. The abrupt movement made the rubies in her aluminum-horn shimmer.

"A message from the Numen? For me?" He leapt to his hooves. His wound had healed, but not his spirit, so he swayed unsteadily after days of inactivity.

"Yes. The Numen claims you are to receive the powers of the Moon-Star Spirit," Alumna told him. "No unicorn has ever possessed such magic."

"What? How? When? Where?" Blue shook his head to clear the fatigue. The news sounded promising, but also unbelievable.

Alumna sat on the window seat and stared out at the courtyard before saying, "You will meet your destiny in the Muzika Woods. You must be there when the Moon-Star arrives."

"So, the prophecy is true? I'm going to receive magic without a metal horn? How is that possible?" He still could not believe the words coming from her mouth.

"Blue, this is what was foretold," she told him solemnly.

"Some thought it would never happen, but now it appears to be coming to pass. Your fate may indeed be to save us all."

His mind raced. *He would save them. And he would avenge his parents. Maybe doing one would bring about the other?*

The aluminum-horned oracle went on, "All I know is that when you get to Muzika Woods, you will receive the powers of the Moon-Star."

Blue was so excited he could not keep still.

"Now listen, Blue, this is important. The Moon-Star is coming."

With her split hoof, she withdrew a rolled piece of parchment from the leather quiver on her back. Shaking it at him, she said, "You must be at the appointed place when it appears from the other side of the moon. When it joins with you, the rest of the tribe may finally be safe from the threat of extinction."

Alumna's tone was so grave, Blue stopped shifting about. The tone of her words cut through his excitement. "Joins with me, how?" Fear weakened his knees. Touching a star suddenly sounded like a perilous task.

Alumna puffed out her breath in an annoyed whinny. "I'm not certain what the process entails, but I am certain we must travel a great distance in a short time to make the rendezvous."

Her words were not all that comforting, and they reminded Blue that he had not told anyone about his encounter with the Cussers. "Alumna, there is a lot of danger in MarBryn right now. Magh has spies and scouts everywhere."

The unicorn oracle stared hard at the young stallion. "I know."

Blue shook his head. "No, even the Cussers are with him now." He told her what he had heard and seen after being stung."

Alumna bit her lower lip and looked at the rolled-up map as if she could divine answers from it. "The Numen did not mention we had lost the Cussers as friends. Of course, he might not be fully aware of all of the happenings in MarBryn."

"If he doesn't know that, how does—"

"We have a lot of things to go over as a tribe," she said, cutting Blue's protest short. Shoving the map back into its holder she looked at him intently and said, "I will gather everyone in the courtyard. Be there in half an hour so we can go over this map and make our plans for the journey to the Muzika Woods together," she spoke very sternly.

"Yes, ma'am," Blue said, as she hurried away with the tassel on her cap swinging right, left, and 'round and 'round like the hands of a frenzied clock.

Blue felt the doubt drain out of him. . .the childish excitement, too. This was the very thing he'd been waiting for. It was why he had been sneaking away to train alone all of this time.

Alone.

He didn't need to wait for the tribe to gather. He knew what had to be done and where he needed to travel to make it happen. He was more than ready to meet his destiny, because he had been training hard for years now. He could and would face whatever was in store.

The day he learned about Magh's desecration of his mother's horn, he had begun preparing his body for an arduous challenge.

Avenging her death had always been his ultimate

motivation, but he could not hope to confront the sorcerer with the puny body he'd been born with. He had determined to make himself stronger, swifter, and more agile. Given that he had no magic, he would also need a keen wit.

Preparing himself took time. For years, he had run back and forth across the plains, imagining Magh's warriors in close pursuit. He had jousted hay targets with his hide-covered horn. And he had endured the grueling sparring sessions with his friend Gaiso.

Now, he remembered their first meeting. Blue had been on a practice run when he came upon the frightening scene.

A small manticore swooped silently down behind the stag. The manticore landed with a loud thud, and Blue was certain the deer would be instantly vanquished. Instead, the hart turned to challenge his stalker.

The big deer had turned with such an air of confidence that, for one brief second, Blue had been jealous, but then he had come to his senses. Grand in stature as he was, Blue felt the cocky stag had no chance to outlast a manticore in battle.

Though small for a manticore, the creature still loomed much larger than the big buck. The combatants smashed and clashed until the manticore found an opportune moment to reach out with a powerful paw, slamming the stag's antler to the ground.

When that happened, Blue could no longer stand idly by. Racing into the fray without a second thought, Blue plunged in with no idea what to do next. The move proved enough of a distraction to divert the manticore's attention away from the stag.

Unicorn meat was a tastier treat than that of a muscle-bound deer, so the carnivorous creature dropped the antlered beast to pursue Blue. That returned the advantage back to the buck and in the blink of an eye, Gaiso speared the monster with six prongs of one powerful antler. The manticore crumpled into an ugly heap and was down for good.

Turning to Blue, the stag gallantly bowed and professed, "You have saved me, Sir Unicorn."

Stunned, Blue objected, "Saved you? You dispatched him yourself!"

"Only upon your fortuitous arrival! How can I repay you?"

Blue instinctively began to shake his head, but then he blurted out, "Train me to fight like you!"

And on that very day, their training sessions began.

The buck had taught him to jab to the left, strike up high, and then, move back to the center for the kill. Thanks to Gaiso, Blue's horn strike grew swifter with each exercise and before long, his cloven hooves could cling to the steepest cliff ledge with ease.

Gaiso has prepared me well. He is the one who has believed in me. Not the tribe. Blue moved about the room collecting things for the journey.

He justified his decision by telling himself, *There's too much danger out there, and most of the tribe has no idea how to fight or even run. I need to do this alone! I don't want anyone else to get hurt.*

Determined that he was on the right course, he ignored the selfish motivations behind his actions. He wanted to prove himself to the tribe. He wanted to show them he could do things without metal or magic. He could not do that, if they joined in to help with their own magical abilities.

No matter his motivations, Blue felt a sudden and intense feeling of deep loss in his knees. It might be a long time before he saw any of his tribe again—including Ghel.

Especially Ghel.

Blue's head was spinning, but he smiled at the realization that if he succeeded, Ghel would finally have a reason to be proud of him.

Leaving her was the hardest of all. He wished he could take her along. She was his best friend and confidant, but even she did not know what he had been planning all these years.

Had he shared his training regiment and the depth of his commitment, she would have wanted to be a part of it. But Blue would never put her in harm's way to satisfy his own desire for revenge.

He also knew he'd hurt her by holding back from their relationship all these years. His track record was not good. If he failed at any point, he would die, and the closer he and Ghel were, the worse she would grieve.

She would be hurt to discover he had left without her. Blue felt bad about that and wanted to leave something behind to show his deep feelings for her. His eyes scanned the room before settling on the ornately carved wardrobe. Inside the door, on a hook, hung a gold heart charm on a ribbon.

The pendant had once belonged to his mother.

The hinges creaked with a harsh, high pitch as he opened the door and touched the golden charm. His mind flashed with fond memories of his dam's warm cinnamon-y breath. He could almost feel her embrace as she snuggled him back to sleep in the middle of the night.

Those warm thoughts cooled at the memory of the day Alumna told him his mother would never return. He had blamed the messenger, kicking his little legs out at her in anger.

"Leave me alone," he cried, when she tried to soothe him. "Just go away!"

She had done as he had demanded, and he supposed it was on that day that he realized it was easier to push others away than it was to allow them to get close.

*His dam...his mother...*his heart squeezed as he gazed at the charm's unusual center, where a faded silvery ring was soldered into place. He briefly wondered, as he had many times in the past, why the silver had been added there when it took away from the beauty of the gold heart. He also wondered, again, why his dam had left it behind when she left the Halstable for her last battle. *Had she known she wouldn't be coming back?* So many questions he might never get answers for.

He did know the heart-shaped necklace had been a gift to his mother from his sire. It was the only possession left to Blue from both of his parents. He had planned to gift it to the gold-horned unicorn someday, and he could not think of a better time to give it to her than now.

Especially since, like his mother the day she gave it to him, he might not be returning.

He hung the ribbon over Ghel's chair, where she would be certain to see the pendant, before moving over to the desk they shared. He took up a feathered quill and dipped the sharpened end into an ornate inkwell. He lost precious time studying a blank sheet of paper, wondering what he should say, but after a moment, he quickly wrote the golden-horned unicorn this note:

My Dearest Ghel,

My destiny has finally been revealed by the Numen. Alumna says I must meet with the Moon-Star to receive my magic. Joining

Filled with a newfound sense of purpose, he loaded a knapsack with ready-to-eat tins and other supplies, and then slung it across his back. He took the time for one final, longing look about the room, before galloping down the hall and through the Halstable gate.

The Guarded Forest would be his first destination. There, he would seek out Gaiso, with the hope of persuading the stag to join him on the quest, because Blue felt far more at home alongside the trusty stag than he did here, among his tribe.

Chapter Thirteen

A Trail Of Blood

*T*he tribe milled about the courtyard, each member guessing and speculating at what the sudden hullabaloo was all about.

Word had spread quickly that they were waiting for Blue to join them and then there would be a big announcement, but a quarter-hour had passed and Blue had not appeared. Soft murmurings could be heard from each little group.

"What are we here for?"

"What news could be so important?"

"What is Alumna waiting for?"

"When is she going to tell us what is going on?"

Alumna was waiting for Blue so he could be there when the news was revealed to the others. Quietly, she shared some of the information with Ghel, but only because she thought Blue would need his closest ally to rely on. "Blue is going to be tested very soon," she told Ghel. "If he passes, he will finally receive his magic."

"Tested?" Ghel's chest constricted with both concern and excitement.

"Yes, the Moon-Star is coming and Blue must be at the appointed place when it arrives," Alumna whispered, but not quietly enough.

"Did she say the Moon-Star is coming?" Style asked Cornum.

That was all it took for the news to fly across the courtyard.

"I've said too much," Alumna fretted. "I should have waited for Blue before saying anything."

But the damage was done. In mere seconds, she and Ghel were surrounded by the others, all of them talking at once. Alumna scrunched her eyes tight, rubbing her forehead with her pastern.

Where was Blue? He had seemed so excited. Then, it dawned on her that maybe he felt uncomfortable at being thrust into the focal point of the entire tribe.

The aluminum-horned oracle found a break in the barrage of questions and leaned close to whisper in Ghel's ear, "Please go check on Blue. I'm afraid he might not like the idea of being the center of attention in this meeting, but we really need him out here."

"Don't worry Alumna, I'll convince him to come," Ghel promised. She slipped away from the group of anxious unicorns and sprinted for the stall she shared with Blue.

*T*he golden-horned unicorn entered their stable-suite, only to find the note Blue had left behind. Tears leaked from her eyes as she absorbed the words he had written only minutes before.

She took up the necklace and held it against her chest, "His mother's pendant," she whispered. "Oh, he does love me!" She smiled at this new realization, even as fear took hold of her heart. He had gone off alone to face a dangerous and unknown mission. That part terrified her, but the underlying meaning of him leaving the pendant proved how he felt about her, even if he had never said the actual words.

Blue loved her.

Trembling, she struggled to secure the ribbon around her neck. She would not lose him now. "He can't have gotten very far. I'll go find him and bring him back."

Once the necklace was firmly in place, she surged after her wayward love, believing she could easily catch him and convince him to return before anyone even knew they were missing.

Outside the Halstable, she followed Blue's hoof tracks for several miles until they ended in hard rocky dirt. She had concentrated so heavily on the impressions in the dirt that she had barely looked up to take note of her surroundings, but now she stopped and did a wide sweep of the unfamiliar landscape. "Where am I?"

She had not meant to go so far or so fast but her adrenaline had propelled her headlong to this point. Now she was lost, with no idea what to do.

Go forward or turn back?

Frantically, she moved forward, stretching her neck to look for anything recognizable. She had hoped to help, but now she had gone and made the situation worse.

Where are you, Blue? I need you!

She wandered about, looking far ahead until she tripped and gashed her knee on a sharp rock jutting from the ground. Sticky, sweet-scented blood oozed from the deep cut.

Ghel looked down at her leg, then back up at the inhospitable countryside. She regretted her hastiness. Nothing was familiar, and her complete lack of an internal compass left her hopelessly untethered.

No unicorn had any business wandering around lost on the outskirts of the Kinubalu Desert. With no trees to be seen, that had to be where she now was. Endless hard, rocky earth stretched out for miles. She shivered and thought, *I'm way too close to manticore territory!*

Eight years had passed since the last time a manticore had tasted unicorn flesh, but the alluring scent of fresh blood would drift for miles on the wind.

Nothing but small scrub bushes and sharp angular rocks surrounded Ghel. The jagged stones were all about knee height and jutted dangerously from the hardscrabble soil. The sun beat down mercilessly and with no hint of any trees, finding shade was not an option. The sun hung low on the horizon, so it would be cooler soon, but manticores hunted at night.

First things first, Ghel thought: *find water.* Both to drink, and to wash away her blood. She didn't remember seeing any on the trail behind her, but she had been looking for Blue and nothing else so she turned back toward what she hoped was the direction home and plodded into the wind in search of water.

*S*everal miles away, the sweet scent of unicorn blood teased at the nostrils of a hungry manticore who had not eaten a full meal in four long days. His taste buds tingled in anticipation, and being downwind of his prey, he had little problem racing quietly along on his four padded paws so as not to alert the wounded unicorn.

The manticore stopped short upon seeing his prey much closer than he had anticipated. He again sniffed the wind, unsure why the blood scent seemed wrong in relation to the location of the unicorn now galloping across a natural rock bridge right at the northwestern tip of the Kinubalu Desert.

No matter what his nose told him, he had to get ahead of his prey, so the manticore dashed for the bridge, hoping to catch the unicorn unaware.

The formation was the only quick way across a deep slash in the land— a short cut across a deep, wide canyon that ended near the edge of the Guarded Forest. Without the bridge, it would have been very long detour to get to the other side, so the manticore held an advantage by knowing exactly where the unicorn had to go.

The manticore, of course, could have crossed by launching himself from one of the high plateaus and gliding over the gap. But he was not on a high point now and with his small wings, he could not gain enough thrust to launch himself into flight from the ground. So, he stealthily followed the blue unicorn on foot.

The closer he got, the more confused he became. *What happened to the blood scent?* He was certain he had smelled blood, but this unicorn did not appear to be bleeding, and the alluring scent had all but faded away.

The beast stood in the middle of the bridge trying to figure it out. Watching the blue unicorn approach the Guarded Forest, the manticore smiled, *"He's trapped."*

The Guarded Forest was surrounded by a tall, barbed-vine fence. The ancient vines bristled with huge thorns that would easily pierce the toughest hide. There was no getting through them, or over them.

I've got him now, the hungry beast thought, grinning wickedly.

He raced on toward the unsuspecting unicorn.

Chapter Fourteen
Nix That Needle

*T*oward the end of the bridge, Blue felt the hairs rise on the back of his neck. A lurking dread filled him, but the dark green wall of the forest lay just ahead so Blue hurried forward.

He had never been to the forest, though Gaiso had mentioned the place many times. Staring at the tall, gnarled wall of vines, Blue realized there was no path through the pre-historic vegetation. No matter where he looked, huge thorns more plentiful than leaves jutted out dangerously.

As Blue stared upward, his attention was caught by a dim path of light moving up the darkness of the wall. He angled his head down and to the right, and the soft, diffused beam furtively followed his every movement.

The light was made up of a strange glowing mélange of shimmering and shifting shades of blue. A slight tingle at the very tip of his horn made Blue feel weird, almost as if he were going to pass out, and that prickling sensation at the nape of his neck was becoming more intense.

Blue wondered briefly if these feelings had something to do with the Numen's prophecy, but as he leaned closer to inspect the colossal spiked wall, the vines began to untangle like a thousand strings slowly unraveling their own knots.

The sight bewildered Blue and wiped away whatever thoughts had begun to form in his brain, just as a space opened up directly in front of him.

As soon as the unicorn had cautiously stepped through the

hole, the undulating tendrils immediately reached out and intertwined, closing the portal behind him. In the time it took to blink, the wall was once again a solid mass of vines.

The hackles on his neck relaxed, and the tension in his muscles eased away.

The manticore raced to the wall and reached out to touch the spot where the unicorn had disappeared. He growled in pain and pulled back a bloody paw, which had been impaled by one of the thorns.

His empty belly rumbled. Disappointed at losing his dinner, the beast turned back across the bridge dumbfounded by what it had just witnessed.

There would be no further pursuit. The Guarded Forest would not let the manticore in.

Halfway across the land bridge an unexpected delight tickled his nose. He had picked up the scent of blood again, and when the defeated manticore lifted his head, there stood a golden unicorn on the path ahead.

Head down, stumbling in his direction, this unicorn was clearly wounded and paying no attention to its surroundings.

The manticore wetted his lips.

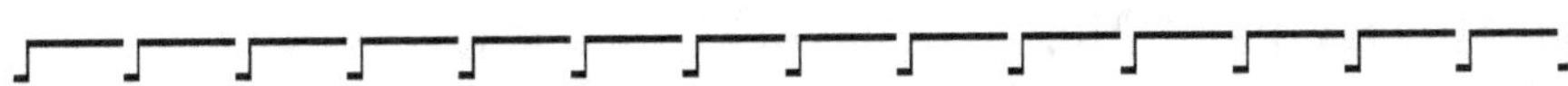

*B*ack at the Halstable, the tribe stood around the courtyard in, what, could best be described as—a frenzied standstill.

Blue had disappeared, which wasn't all that usual, but then Ghel had vanished as well, and now Alumna was left to field a million questions for which she had few answers, though she knew the entire tribe expected her to somehow fix whatever had gone wrong.

But she was an oracle, not a leader, and she, too, had unanswered questions.

A song rose up, and all eyes turned to Silubhra as she sang:

> *Brave Nix Nickel-Horn,*
> *Defender of the Unicorns.*
> *The only one with a magical knack*
> *to Nix a disaster, and that's a fact.*

She sang to Nix, who seemed to stand in a trance. His eyes were clouded over and he remained unnaturally rigid. Everyone knew what this meant.

Somewhere, a unicorn was in danger.

My brave Nix Nickel-Horn, the Great Unicorn Hero, Silubhra sang proudly, just as Nix came out of his trance. His head swung abruptly around, as if on point. With a shake of his dark gray mane, he spoke out: "Ghel is in danger, but never fear, I will rescue her in the nick of time!"

A solid blaze of light filled the air with silvery sparkles. "I'm off!" Nix shouted, disappearing into the brightness.

Nix's nickel-horn was much more powerful than most of the magic already stolen by Magh. Some nickel-horns had only been able to detect danger from a few feet away. Nix's magical detection range spanned for miles and miles, and the blasting potential of his horn had proven to be greater than a stick of dynamite.

Some of the other nickel-horns had barely been able to conjure enough firepower to ignite a dry candlewick. So it was no accident that Nix had survived for so long. The other nickel-horns were lost, years ago, during the Metal Horn Massacre.

With so few metal-horned unicorns left, if any of the survivors happened to get themselves into trouble, Nix's magical ability transported him directly to their location in plenty of time to nix whatever disaster was about to occur.

This is why there had been no deaths over the last eight years.

But Nix could not protect everyone. Without a metal-horn to anchor Nix's compass, Blue was stranded on his own.

A shiver ran along Ghel's spine. A fear unlike any she had ever known clenched her heart and made it beat faster.

Something was out there. She could hear it breathing.

Terrified, Ghel looked all around until her eyes locked on those of a slobbering manticore. Its dirty, lion-like body was crouched low to the ground, preparing to spring on her, its scaly black dragon's tail arched high into the air. The crimson scorpion stinger poised to deliver a death stroke.

She cowered from the leering expression on its ugly, ravenous face. Its hungry eyes gleamed as it licked its chops hungrily, and even from this distance, she could smell its fetid odor.

Ghel's fearful eyes darted first one way, then another, searching for an escape.

The sun had sunk so low that darkness had overtaken the horizon.

The manticore sprang forward just as a blinding light

exploded in its face. The brute was disoriented for only a couple of heartbeats. By the time it could clearly see again, the golden unicorn was half-way across the bridge—heading for the Guarded Forest. . .and a thunder-gray unicorn was between them on the rocky structure.

Slicing the air with his horn, Nix sent a powerful blast at the beast, who skittered away from the fiery detonation. The explosive charge missed the manticore, wreaking havoc on the rock formation. The bridge splintered into countless shards of debris. Boulders, rocks, and pebbles plunged down into the gaping hole in the land. Nix turned to Ghel and yelled, "Run!" as the short cut to the Guarded Forest crumbled to dust and slipped into oblivion.

The two unicorns dove and made it to safety just as the last of the remnants of the bridge that formerly spanned the gap tumbled into the chasm.

Over on the other side, the manticore stared at them through goggle-eyes.

Furious that he had missed and accidently destroyed the bridge, Nix lowered his horn and proclaimed, "NIX that needle!"

In a flash, the manticore's scorpion stinger disappeared in a single black puff of ash.

With a horrified expression on his face, the beast cried out, "Spare me, please, Brave Nix!" His pleading eyes were wide with terror, for the legendary prowess of Nix was well known throughout MarBryn. "Please," the manticore begged again.

Nix flicked a questioning look at Ghel. She nodded to approve the idea of mercy. Given her heart of gold, she could not sustain malice toward any living creature, even one who would have taken her life.

The smooth-gray unicorn snorted and flared his nostrils and bellowed in triumph. Standing at equine attention, he clicked his rear hooves together and, with a quiet, authoritative drawl, said, "If you know what's good for you, you'll beat it back to where you came from before I am forced to NIX your nose the way I NIXED your noxious needle!"

"No! Please, not that!" the manticore pleaded, grabbing at his snout as if he could protect it from being nixed.

"Beat it, before I change my mind," Nix warned.

The manticore answered meekly, "Thank you, kind sir! Thank you!" then scampered away on shaking knees.

Chapter Fifteen
Lucky Mr. Unicorn

*B*lue slipped into the Guarded Forest still a bit bewildered by the odd blue light he had seen and that crawling itch of impending doom he'd felt before the forest magically unraveled and let him walk in. Nevertheless, the important thing was to find his mentor and continue the journey.

Though Gaiso had told him plenty about this place, and he had seen the vine protected walls from a distance, Blue had never actually ventured inside until now. History told him no evil had ever penetrated this place, but between the strange blue light and the sensation that something bad was about to happen, Blue still felt very vulnerable as he moved deeper into the forest.

His unease might have come from the pressure of the trip, or simply from stepping into this new place, which smelled dank and earthy.

There had once been a time when the Metal Horns roamed freely here. They came and went as they wished, because, while the spirit of the forest moved its thorny undergrowth into the path of any creature with bad intentions, everyone knew the good nature of unicorns never led them to initiate aggression. But a lot had changed over the years, and the few remaining free creatures were extra cautious these days, so Blue had expected to be tested somehow before being allowed access.

The ever-present dangers in MarBryn kept the Metal Horns from traveling so far from the Halstable these days, so it had been a long time since any unicorn had stepped into these woods.

Blue entered hoping to convince Gaiso to travel with him to

Muzika Woods, because he could think of no better companion for such an important journey. Although he knew the stag well, he did not know where in the forest he called home. Blue took a few steps to his right, then stopped and thought better of that choice as a premonition came over him that left was the better way to go.

He went only a short way before two small, winged creatures zoomed up level with his head. Fairies. He only knew of the creatures from stories he had heard since ponyhood, but still he was glad to see a couple of friendly faces. At least, they looked friendly.

They flitted about with great precision as they checked him out. Exquisitely patterned butterfly wings fluttered in the air above his head, but he couldn't really focus on either as they looped and swirled and crossed over each other.

"I'm Fleoge. And this is Pido!" One said, but Blue could not tell which had spoken in the flurry of activity.

"Wanna play tag with us?" Before he could answer, the pair zoomed upward and through the tree branches only to circle back around his head in the time it took for Blue to blink twice.

"Of course, we never get caught," they said before doing another set of impressive aerial acrobats through the branches. "Fairies never lose at tag!"

"My name is Blue," the unicorn announced.

"Oh, we know who you are," the pair said in unison while flitting by his head yet again.

They seemed to be quite enjoying their antics, but already eager to find his mentor, Blue couldn't help feeling all the more anxious by their whirlwind flights. The fairies flitted to and fro before his eyes, then began to chase one another around his head.

"Fleoge! Pido! Would you two be still for a minute?" he said, dizzy from watching their antics. "I need some help."

The larger one was about as tall as a field mouse standing upright on its hind legs, and half as wide. The markings on the little guy's wings looked like ascending bubbles, decreasing in size as they rose. He skidded to a halt in mid-air, saying, "Fleoge and I are busy, Blue! Can't this wait until after our game of tag?"

"I don't have time to play," Blue said. "And you guys are too fast and nimble for me to catch anyway," he added, hoping flattery might make them stop for a few wing beats at least.

Fleoge continued to flutter her delicate orange butterfly wings, spinning about in a marvelous aerial ballet. "What is it you need?" she asked.

"I'm looking for Gaiso. He lives somewhere in the Guarded Forest, but I've never been to his home."

"Never heard of any Gaiso," Pido answered curtly, zipping back and forth through the air behind his sister.

"What does this Gaiso look like?" Fleoge asked.

How could anyone not know Gaiso? Surely, his massive antlers made him quite impressive in any surrounding. "Well, let's see. He is quite a large stag. . .larger than me. His antlers span at least seven feet across from tip to tip."

"Nope, don't know him," Pido butted in.

"Pido, don't interrupt. . ." his sister admonished. She raised her eyes and eyebrows skyward, then got back to Blue. "Any other identifying features?"

"Yes, his coat is a rusty red and he has a long beard jutting from his bottom lip," Blue finished.

Fleoge thought a moment, "Maybe I've seen him around, and maybe I haven't, but I don't know where he lives. Let's go see Waap and see what he has to say!" She flew up to an o'possum hanging upside down from a tree branch.

She brushed her beating wings against the snoozing critter's nose, causing him to swipe at her with a front paw. The resulting breeze rolled her end-over-end through the air. When she finally stabilized, she giggled and said, "Sorry, Waap. I deserved that."

She flew back to the sleeping o'possum. "Come on. Wake up, sleepy head!"

Waap yawned and stretched all four legs. His tail was curled around the branch, holding him in place so he could perform this sleeping trick. He looked at her all squinty-eyed, saying, "I don't wanna, and you can't make me."

Pido decided it would be fun to harass the sleepy critter, too. He flew up, joining Fleoge in her attempts to wake the lazy creature. The larger fairy mimicked his sister, tickling the grumpy animal's nose.

Waap backhanded the nuisance away, causing Pido to sail to the ground, where the fairy hit the dirt hard. A star with a tail ricocheted back and forth between his antennae and released a spattering of angry electrical charges. Sparks flew all around the fairy's head like tiny fireworks.

After the charge was spent, Blue used his hide-covered horn to lift the unfortunate little guy to his feet. "Maybe we should forget about asking him for help," he suggested as Fleoge arrived on the scene.

The delicate smaller fairy covered her mouth to stifle a giggle. "Ooh! You made Waap mad."

Undiscouraged, Pido launched himself back into the air without a care. "You started it, so it was really all your fault, but who needs his help anyway?" He retorted airily. "Come with me. I know who we can ask."

Fleoge clapped her hands and zoomed away, leaving Blue hurrying to catch up.

"Follow me," Pido called. His antennas trembled madly as he zigzagged away through the trees. The blue unicorn galloped fast to keep pace with the zooming fairies in their winding path through the woods. He ducked and dodged trees and bushes as best he could, but twice, branches slapped him in the face as he ran.

Finally, with Blue's eyes still watering from the sting, they came upon two cute little squirrels with huge furry tails.

"Ooh, look, Oura. It's Pido and Fleoge," one of them chattered to the other. "Have you come to play tag?" she called to the fairies.

"Oh boy, Olina, they brought a unicorn to play too!" the other squealed happily.

Blue gritted his teeth. Is that all the inhabitants of this forest did, play tag? He had important business to attend to and he did not have time to waste playing games.

"No, you sillies," Pido replied. "We are on a mission and we need some info."

Fleoge landed on top of a big daisy with lovely white petals and a bright yellow center. It tipped forward a bit from her slight weight, spilling a smattering of pollen that sparkled in a beam of sunlight.

"Alright, business it is, then. Maybe we can help. What is it you need? We keep our paws on the pulse of this entire forest," one of them—Blue had trouble telling them apart—bragged.

The blue unicorn asked if they knew the whereabouts of the big red buck. "I'm trying to track him down to discuss something of great importance. We've spent a lot of time together out on the plains, but I've never been to his home."

The gossipy little squirrels put their heads together to chitter-chatter privately for a moment. As they discussed, their fluffy tails whipped back and forth for emphasis, like conductors leading separate orchestras.

"Sure, we know exactly where Gaiso. . .and his sister, Springen live," Olina informed them.

She dusted off the acorn she held in her tiny fingers. When it was suitably clean, she popped it between her sharp teeth, cracking it expertly.

"Anyone, care for some?" she inquired, holding the nutmeat out in an open palm.

No one did.

"Okay, then. More for me." She shrugged and scarfed it down herself. "Yum," she said with a satisfied smile.

She seemed so tranquil that Blue wondered if she had forgotten his question. He fought to keep the urgency out of his voice as he asked, "Do you think you might point me in the right direction? I need to see Gaiso as soon as possible."

The two squirrels busted out in an annoying chatter like laughter that left Blue all the more impatient and irritated. He hadn't said anything funny. At least, he didn't think so.

The fuzzy duo paused, looked at each other and said in

unison," He *NEEDS* to see Gaiso." Then they burst into laughter yet again.

This time the Fairies joined in on the merriment, but not Blue.

He was just on the verge of shouting at all of them when one of the squirrels stopped and pointed with a flourish, "And here comes your good friend now." The squirrel pointed.

"Well, look at that! You are in luck Mr. Unicorn?" Oura quipped.

There, just emerging from some heavy growth was Gaiso and his sister, Springen. They happened to be foraging in the area for one of their favorite treats—acorns.

Finding Gaiso so quickly was indeed the stroke of luck Blue needed, but another one of his strange hunches hit Blue and he realized more than luck had been involved.

Chapter Sixteen
A Friend Joins The Fight

*T*he big buck strode toward them, as impressive as ever. His fifteen-point rack spanned at least seven feet from endpoint to endpoint, but even without the massive antlers, the stag stood taller than Blue.

Beside him strolled a small, spotted doe. Though no longer a fawn, the dainty little thing was less than half the size of the stag. She was a tiny, damsel deer, and as pretty as a doll.

As the deer approached the little group, the others were surprised to see the big buck brandish his rack at the blue unicorn. Raising his mighty head, he challenged Blue with a robust, "Hello, Sir Unicorn. Are you here seeking another jousting lesson?"

Blue laughed at his friend's antics. He knew Gaiso did not mean any harm. "Not today, my friend, but I am very happy to see you. Much has happened since our last lesson."

Gaiso nodded. "I am pleased to see you too, sir. Tell me, what brings you to the Guarded Forest?"

Blue told the stag of the message from the Numen, finishing with, "He told Alumna that it's my fate to join up with the Moon-Star."

"The Moon-Star?" the stag asked, surprised. "How do you join with a star? I have seen shooting stars and heard of one falling from the sky, but it is said to have left a crater and anything that can dent the ground will surely spell doom for any beast. Unicorns included."

Blue shrugged. "I must fulfill the prophecy, so somehow I must succeed in what seems impossible. I'll do whatever it takes to save my tribe, even if that means sacrificing myself."

Gaiso's eyes widened. His antlers made a soft clacking noise as he shook his head. "I know nothing of this Numen, or Moon-Stars, or legends of any kind regarding the unicorns, but the whole thing does sound grim. I fear no beast will stand a chance against a blazing star."

The stag seemed completely lost in thought until Blue said, "The joining isn't a fight. The star is. . .is meant to join with me. But getting there will be difficult, which is why I was hoping to convince you to accompany me to the Muzika Woods."

As crazy as the whole idea was, Gaiso answered with the speed of galloping hoof beats, "Of course I'll go. I owe you my life."

Blue was a little embarrassed at his words. The stag had done all the fighting against the manticore. "I only provided a distraction," he said, cheeks coloring with embarrassment that he had not done more. "I only happened to be in the right place at the right time."

"Your presence saved me just the same," Gaiso insisted. "You could have walked away and if you had, I would not be here now,"

Blue could not help protesting again, "But I did nothing—" he began until the stag cut him off.

"No more of that. Besides, this sounds like just the type of adventure I'm up for," Gaiso said heartily. "And you've yet to graduate my fighting academy, so I am duty bound as your teacher to continue the lessons along the way." The stag then added, "It seems I'm always stumbling into something interesting where you unicorns are concerned."

"Oh, about that ... forgot to ask you about the meal you shared with my tribe," Blue said. "I'm sorry I missed you, but I rarely eat in the dining hall." He lowered his head gazing at the ground in the hope no one would ask why.

They didn't.

Shaking off his melancholy, Blue continued, "You gave the rest of the tribe a fright, appearing so suddenly. We've never had an uninvited visitor get inside the Halstable."

"It was rather rude of me to intrude into your home as I did," Gaiso began.

"I'm not trying to saddle you with guilt," Blue interjected. "They just couldn't figure out how you managed to get in. No one else has ever crossed the magical boundary without an escort."

"It's kind of a strange story," Gaiso acknowledged. "I was just walking westward across an open plain, minding my own business, when one of my antler points jammed into something. Actually, into nothing. It seemed to be stuck in the mid air, but as I wriggled it around, I heard a swishing sound. My antler suddenly freed from whatever had grasped it and I was able to move. I stepped forward into the most astonishing sight. Gone was the open plain. Instead, I found myself in the entrance way of a grand abode. My curiosity got the best of me. I'm afraid I had to explore the place. . .your place, it turned out."

"Your antler point unlocked the door, just like a unicorn's," Blue said aloud. The revelation scared him. The Halstable was invisible to other creatures, but what if one of Magh's henchmen found it, and used a horn of some sort? Could he, too, get in?

"I suppose that's what happened. But it was quite by accident, I assure you," Gaiso said.

"Now, tell me about this quest. I must say, I hope we see some action. Nothing churns up the adrenaline like jousting with an actual foe in a life or death duel."

Springen, his sister, swiftly chimed in, "He does love combat. Why, not long ago, just south of the Guarded Forest, he fought a lynx! I was there. It came stalking us from behind. Gaiso heard a twig snap just in time, and turned to catch the beast on a rack point as it lunged for us. He speared its leg clean through as it attacked, but it still was a nasty fight for a few minutes. That cat won't be a threat to any of us again." She smiled a bright, pretty smile, despite the memory of what had to be a horrifying experience.

The blue unicorn could not help but smile back. She reminded him of his Ghel, who was also warm and friendly to everyone, even in the face of adversity. A pang of loneliness washed over him. He missed the golden unicorn already.

Blue turned to his friend, "It will be great to have you along, Gaiso. There's no telling what we will run up against along the way, so knowing you'll be there to have my back means the world."

Throughout their conversation, the squirrels kept popping nuts into their little jaws. The enjoyment they appeared to get from chomping brought on a hunger within Blue, but he did not care for acorns. He needed something more substantial than a few nuts.

When his stomach rumbled loudly enough for those closest to hear, Blue rummaged around in the bag slung over his withers. It was so stuffed with Chef Tinam's ready-to-eat meals, he had trouble grabbing two tins with his cloven hoof, but eventually he managed to pull them free of the bag.

One was clearly labeled "Vegetable Barley Soup" while the other had a squiggly print that was hard to read—"*Sweet Red Beets sprinkled with Blueberries.*"

Tinam's to-go containers were designed so that anyone could easily open them with a touch of a stick, an antler, a finger or anything solid so Blue tapped each lid with his horn, causing them to roll back and release delicious aromas.

The soup had a thick creamy base of shredded carrots and potatoes. Barley lent a nutty flavor to the mix. The beets smelled like freshly turned dirt after a light rain. They'd been roasted so they would taste slightly sweet. The blueberries were so fragrant that just their tart scent made his taste buds tingle in anticipation. This earthy chow smelled like home to the hungry unicorn.

Oura's eyes popped wide open. "I've never seen food preserved in such magical fashion. And it all smells wonderful! May I have a taste?"

Quick to reply, Blue said, "Yes, please, everyone have some. Tinam is a great chef."

The two little squirrels quickly brought out some large, sturdy bowl-shaped leaves for Blue to serve up Tinam's treats. There was enough for everyone to have a small, yet filling sample of unicorn cuisine.

Clearly impressed, Springen gushed, "Tinam certainly has a wonderful knack for preserving foods."

"Amazing," Gaiso said over a bite of warm chewy soup. "These spices are beyond my tongue's ability to identify, but they are delectable, whatever they are." The stag closed his eyes to fully savor each taste. "This is every bit as wonderful as the freshly conjured meal Tinam served the day I wandered into the Halstable."

"Oh, this is divine," said Fleoge. "Just, one little barley pearl fills me to bursting!" She fluttered to the ground and sat down to rest.

Pido agreed with a satisfied burp. He leaned back, rubbing his full belly.

Overcome by a sense of tribal pride, a shy smile crept across Blue's face as he took in all the compliments on behalf of Tinam, the tin-horned unicorn chef. Sharing his food made him very happy, and hearing their compliments made him especially proud of Tinam's magic.

Over the years, he had been so jealous of the magical abilities of his tribe that he'd never fully appreciated how special it was, to be a magical unicorn. But sitting there with new friends and old, it dawned on Blue that every last unicorn in the tribe possessed extraordinary talent. Perhaps his talent would be in saving them and preserving their magic for their world.

His destiny lay before him and if all that meant was that magic would live on, then he would fight to the end to give that to his tribe, and to the world.

Chapter Seventeen
A Nutty Goodbye

After the meal, Blue and Gaiso huddled together, laying out a plan for the journey ahead. They considered every possible route and spent a long time making plans until they reached the conclusion that they should head east across the Phlat Plains, following the tallest mountain on the eastern horizon until they reached it.

By the time they settled on this course, the sun had dipped low, so they decided to wait and get a fresh start come morning, to maximize their daylight.

"Muzika Woods lies to the south," Gaiso said, "but I think it would be better to head due east for a while before turning that direction. I don't want to get anywhere near Magh's castle.

Blue agreed. He did not want to get any closer to Magh than necessary—at least, not before the joining, when he was said to gain all of the power and knowledge of the Numen. Perhaps then, if he survived, he would seek out the evil sorcerer to exact the revenge he had vowed to deliver.

Having never ranged further from home than the edge of the Guarded Forest, Blue was curious about many things. "Do you know anything about the landscapes or the populations we might come across on our route?" he asked.

"Most of my travels have been to the west of the forest. The foraging is better over there," the stag admitted. "This journey will mostly be new to me as well, but I am excited for a grand adventure."

The moon had risen to its highest point. Gaiso yawned and said, "Time to sleep. The earlier we turn in, the sooner our quest can begin."

"Early to bed, early to rise," Blue said without enthusiasm since he doubted sleep would come easy on this night. Bright rays of moonlight filtered through the thickly leaved trees, making it harder for Blue to relax. He shifted, trying to find a comfortable spot to rest his head on the hard ground, but nothing led him to find sleep. He stared up at the moon and stars and thought about Ghel sleeping back in their shared stall. At least he hoped she was sleeping and not up worrying about him. He hoped she would understand why he had to leave and accomplish this without the tribe. Then, his thoughts ranged out further to unknown realms.

I wonder what's out there. Will there be monsters? What kind of creatures will we fight? I've never been so far from home before. Will we make it to Muzika Woods in time? Will we make it there at all? At least I'm not going alone.

He turned toward Gaiso and whispered, "Thank you."

"Are you talking to me?" Gaiso mumbled. His voice was heavy with sleep.

"Yes," Blue said, though he had not intended for Gaiso to hear his gratitude—because the stag was not one for sentimental words.

Gaiso's confusion came through in his voice as he asked, "Whatever for?"

"For being my friend," Blue said, humbly.

Gaiso snorted rather loudly and sputtered, "Why yes, of course. We all need friends sooner or later. Now, get some sleep. Morning will be here soon."

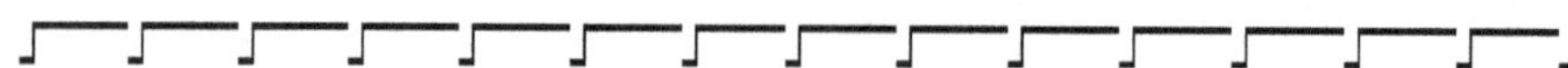

*M*orning came with the beginning of sunrise. An orange glow had spread across the entire sky by the time the young unicorn and brave stag made their farewells.

"I have a bad feeling, my brother," Springen said, looking at Gaiso with large soulful eyes. "I wish you wouldn't go."

The stag laughed off her worries. "Your female nature makes you worry too much, sister. I can take care of myself, and have no fear; you will be safe here in the Guarded Forest." Gaiso gave her a brotherly kiss on her forehead before trotting off to meet his fate without a backward glance.

An acorn whizzed by Blue's head and landed in the dirt several feet in front of the unicorn. Blue turned around to find two furry rodents scowling down from the branches of a tree.

"We can take care of ourselves, too," Fleoge yelled at Gaiso, who quickened his step in reaction.

"Yeah," Pido chimed in before raising her paw. "Go on, Mr. Fancy Antlers! And you. . .Mr. Unicorn. . .hurry and catch up to your chauvinist pal before my 'female nature' decides to peg you upside the noggin' with this nut!"

Springen laughed and said, "You get 'em, girls!"

Blue ducked two more acorns before deciding to leave well enough alone and skedaddle.

Gaiso could fight this battle when he returned. . .if he returned. Two angry squirrels and flying acorns were one thing; dodging Magh's army had the potential to be far more deadly.

Chapter Eighteen
To The Last Breath

Though Nix had saved many over the years, he had not saved them all. He simply could not be everywhere at once. That was one limitation of his magic.

Another was that he could not get himself and Ghel back home the same way he had arrived. Without the jolt of adrenaline imminent danger provided, he could not make such leaps across distance. And even if there were danger back at the Halstable, he could not have brought Ghel along when he made such a leap.

So, they would have to hoof it back and given Ghel's wound, the return journey would take a while. Nix was not a healer.

The trip back to the Halstable was mostly silent and it was much longer, since, with the land-bridge destroyed, they had to find a detour around the crevasse.

Before starting back, the gold-horned unicorn pleaded with Nix to help her find Blue, but he explained away that idea. "It's not that I don't want to find him, but you know I can't detect his whereabouts, Ghel."

No metal, no magic.

Neither said the words aloud, but they didn't have to.

"That's what frightens me so much," she insisted. "He could die out there all alone. We'd never even know he'd been in danger."

"Let's not think about that," replied Nix. "We can't go after him without the rest of the tribe. It's too dangerous, so let's not agonize over things we can't control. We don't even know what route he took. The best course of action is to go back and hear what Alumna has to say about her vision."

By the time Nix and Ghel neared the Halstable, the sun was throwing long shadows across the plains as morning broke over the horizon. The tribe had waited up all night.

The crowd of sleepy unicorns huddled in small groups anxiously awaiting Nix and Ghel's return.

Cornum saw them first and blew a victory blast from his brass-horn, "Too-to-ta-tooo! Look everyone! She's safe!"

Everyone perked up and cheered and they all galloped out to greet them. Metal hooves sounded a joyful cadence as they danced merrily across the cobbles of the Halstable's terrace. The mares took Ghel away to clean and examine her wounds, while the stallions went off to the Great Room to pepper Nix with questions.

After fifty-something years of assisting Dr. Zinko in patching up wounded warriors, Lauda's own medical knowledge was extensive, so she took over and cleaned the dried blood off Ghel's leg in order to better examine the damage.

While the lead-horned unicorn worked, the others listened, wide-eyed, as Ghel recounted her terrifying night-adventure. Finally, her tale ended, and she said, "I just wish we could've found Blue." Her voice broke in the middle of speaking his name.

"It wasn't wise for you to take off alone like that," Alumna stated in a clipped tone. "You know how dangerous it is out there. You could've been killed!"

"Or worse," Lauda said. "You might have been captured and handed over to Magh. He could have stripped your hooves and horn!" The hide on her back rippled fearfully.

Ghel shuddered too and for a brief moment, that grim possibility felt just like the fear she had felt when the manticore leered at her.

All the other unicorns put on brave faces, but the thought scared them, as well.

"I can't really say why I left like that, but I suppose I was so worried about Blue taking off on his own that I just ran after him," Ghel admitted, feeling foolish in retrospect. "I thought I could easily find him."

After a moment of reflection, she said, "I'm so sorry I didn't tell anyone before I left. That was very foolish, but so is all of us sitting around here." She urged, "We have got to find Blue before he gets hurt!"

"Yes," Alumna agreed. "But first, we must join the stallions in the Great Room. I need to relay the Numen's complete message, because only then can we all decide together how to proceed."

A short time later, ten unicorns sat around the table listening as Alumna spoke.

"As you all know by now, I went to see Blue before he left. I don't always get clear messages from the Moon-Star Spirit. They are usually garbled and difficult to make out. This time, however, the Numen came through bright and clear and without hesitation to convey a message to me."

The aluminum-horned oracle looked significantly from one unicorn to the other. "You all know unicorn lives have been in grave danger for over a century. Leaving the Halstable is perilous as there are few safe places away from our home. We chance being menaced by the manticore and the Lethean warriors who do Magh's bidding. Just before he left, Blue told me that Magh has gotten to the Cusser's, too. That evil sorcerer will not stop until he has collected the horns of every last unicorn, so it is nothing short of a miracle that it's been eight years since the last unicorn death."

All the unicorns tried to look brave, but fear was a palpable entity in the room. Everyone at the table had lost friends and family members to Magh. To him, metal unicorn horns were the most valuable of potion ingredients. He sought them out at all costs. Rumors claimed that a unicorn's metal was the very source of his magic, so if that were true, he needed them to feed his power.

There had been a time when Magh even tried breeding captured unicorns so that he could maintain a constant supply of their metal magic.

To *breed* them...the indignity was unimaginable, but unicorns were not some ordinary animal to be domesticated so without a healthy aura no offspring came into being.

That was when most of the remaining adult unicorns rose as one in a final attempt at defending of the honor of their tribe. The tribe agreed that, if it came to it, death was preferable to becoming Magh's captured slaves. No one had truly believed it would come to that drastic outcome, though.

Before leaving the Halstable for the ultimate conflict, it had been decided that all personal possessions would be left behind to protect against the sorcerer using them to trace a path back to their remaining loved ones.

The unicorns who went into that final battle believed in their hearts and minds that their fighting force was large enough, and their magic strong enough, to defeat Magh.

They all fought valiantly. . .to the last breath.

None survived.

Magh's forces were too strong. . .too evil. Only a few adults and ponies had been left behind at the Halstable. The few elders who lingered were now old, and the young unicorns they had vowed to protect were all adults.

For the last eight years, twelve survivors had hung on.

Now, ten of those twelve looked to Alumna for guidance. Where the twelfth was—no one knew.

Cuprum coughed nervously, and Lauda chewed her hoof to the point that Alumna feared it would soon bleed.

The agitation of the others reinforced the importance of what she had to say, so she chose her next words carefully. "The Numen reasserted that Blue is destined to save our Tribe. He said that the time has come for Blue to join with the Moon-Star."

No one hid their shock. "Join with the Moon-Star!" They shouted in unison.

"Is he gonna sprout wings to accomplish this trick?" Lauda exploded. "The Moon-Star's in the sky and Blue sure as heck can't fly!"

Silubhra shushed everyone, "Please, quiet down. Let Alumna finish."

"Please," Ghel urged before asking, "What do you mean, Alumna? How is Blue supposed to join with the Moon-Star?"

Alumna shifted her hooves, looking down at the ground for a moment before answering, "Apparently, the Moon-Star will descend to meet him and at the moment of their joining, Blue will acquire all of its knowledge and power.

That news was just too much, and was greeted with more protests.

"He's not strong enough!" Style cried.

"It will kill him!" Cornum shouted.

"He's just a plain blue unicorn," Nix insisted.

"We're doomed," Lauda gasped.

Ghel slumped forward until her chin rested on the table, "First, Blue nearly died from his encounter with the Buzzy-Biter. Then, he left to go on this quest alone, and now, we're talking about him joining with the Moon-Star? Oh, Blue. . ." She began to cry little sniffly sobs.

"There, there," Cuprum tried to console her, nuzzling the back of her ear.

Around them, the others continued to protest.

"This all sounds absurd!" Tinam bellowed.

Cuprum's sympathetic ministrations calmed Ghel enough to raise her head and say, "I believe the Numen's words."

Cuprum drew her head back, astonished. "You do? Why, Ghel?"

"Because, I saw proof," Ghel ventured.

The skeptical faces all focused on her now.

"Pshaw," Lauda murmured.

"Impossible," Dr. Zinko said.

"No, it's. . .it's true. When Blue was near death from the Buzzy-Biter venom, I put my horn to his heart and a vision came to me. In a flash, I saw a magnificent blue stallion surrounded by the tribe. He was strong, powerful, and full of magic. It was Blue."

Ghel caught the lead-horned unicorn's eye and held it before saying, "Lauda, you know it, too."

Lauda hemmed and hawed. "I don't know what you mean," she said, breaking away from Ghel's accusing gaze.

"Yes, Lauda. You do." Ghel said gently. "We both saw signs of magic in Blue's horn-tip that day."

The old gray mare shifted her hooves back and forth. She looked everywhere, but at Ghel. Finally, she admitted, "I saw something. But what if it was Zinko's horn magic and not Blue's?"

"It wasn't, and we both know it."

Chapter Nineteen
The Long Way Around

Alumna recovered first and said, "We must trust in the Numen, no matter how strange the events sound. Blue's destiny has been set for years. We must do everything we can to assist him!"

She looked pointedly at each unicorn before continuing. "As is our nature, we've tried to overlook the bad and continue to live our merry lives despite the losses and dangers. But with this news from the Numen, and the revelation of Ghel's vision, we can no longer ignore the role we each must play in our own destiny."

"Yes," Iown agreed. "We have all tried to pretend everything will 'iron' itself out on its own, but in our hearts every one of us knows it just isn't going to happen that way."

Dr. Zinko interjected, "Our magic has become undependable. Even the safety sensors on the Halstable doors don't always work as expected."

"That's right," Tinam exclaimed. "We were all surprised when that big buck, Gaiso, wandered right into this very room! Luckily, he turned out to be a friend, and not a foe."

No one alive knew how the safety locks of the Halstable operated or how to repair them but operating and maintaining the Halstable had not always been an unknown science. After the Metal-Horn Massacre years, apprenticeships ended. With no one left to teach common skills, they were not passed down, as they once had been. Much knowledge was lost.

Alumna had recovered some things, and much of the history via the books in the Sanctuary Room, but not everything had been captured in writing.

Some elements of their existence continued to work through the sheer force of magic. For instance, Lauda had an innate ability to maintain the integrity of the Halstable's outer shell using her lead-horn to seal little cracks. At first, these structural defects appeared only sporadically, but small fissures appeared every few days now, and the repairs took up more time than Lauda wanted to spend. Still, her magic quietly urged her on because that was just the nature of it, but Lauda was not getting any younger.

None of them were.

Alumna resumed, "I wish Blue hadn't left to take on this quest alone." She rolled out the rectangular map she had drawn and placed some heavy objects on each of the four corners to hold it flat. She pointed to the bottom right corner. "This is Muzika Woods, where the Moon-Star will arrive."

"Muzika Woods? Sounds like a nice place," Silubhra crooned. Anything musical quickly captured her attention.

"Possibly," Alumna said. "But I fear what lies between here and there that might not be so pleasant." Next, she pointed at her rendering of the Halstable on the left side of the map. "This is where we are."

Everyone leaned in closer so that they could see. "It might not look like it, but I believe there's a lot of land to cover between here and there."

"How long will it take to get there?" Tinam asked. He was not much for exercise, and he gave away his fears by rubbing his rather rotund belly.

"Oh look, there's the Guarded Forest," Cuprum noted, placing the tip of her hoof on the group of trees labeled the same. "And there's the land bridge leading to it. That's not terribly far."

"Half a day at a slow walk," Dr. Zinko agreed.

"Longer now," Nix confessed. "The bridge is gone."

"Gone?" Several voices shouted at once. That revelation caused quite a commotion, but the group fell silent as Nix told the story.

"It is unfortunate," Alumna said, "Now we have no choice but to travel southeast."

"I wonder which way Blue went," Ghel wondered aloud. "How will he find Muzika Woods? Did he see your map, Alumna?"

"No. I was going to show it to everyone at the same time," she responded. "He does, however know the Muzika Woods are where the Moon-Star is to arrive."

"Hmm … he doesn't know where the Muzika Woods are, or even the best route to get there," Iown mused. "This is not very promising."

"It's worse than that," Alumna admitted. "He doesn't know the danger the entire tribe faces if we're not all together when the Moon-Star arrives. He doesn't know that's just nine days away."

"Nine days? That's not enough time," Nix said.

"It has to be enough," Alumna said. "Also, Blue knows he's the one who will receive the Numen's knowledge and power, but he doesn't know it will take all of our horns to usher in the star."

"How is that, Alumna?" Ghel asked.

"If we're not all together, horn-tip to horn-tip, he will be killed by the impact and any chance we ever had at being saved will be lost!" Alumna revealed.

"Killed!"

"Lost!"

So many voices joined in at once that it was impossible to know who had spoken.

"The power of the Moon-Star will destroy Blue if he tries to meet it without us," she finished, hanging her head in sorrow.

"Then, we must reach Muzika Woods and hope that Blue does, too," Iown said reasonably. "And we must do it before the Moon-Star's appearance.

"You make it all sound so easy," Lauda said sarcastically. "Seems more likely the impact will kill all of us!"

Style stood and announced, "I can't take anymore. All this sober talking is seriously stressing me out."

She then stunned everyone by bursting into a rousing song and dance. She went from one filly to the other, swishing her horn around each head as she sang.

> *"Enough, enough of this morbid chatter;*
> *gloomy faces over serious matters.*
> *Let Style raise you up out of these dumps.*
> *No, No Lauda, don't you harrumph.*
> *We have some time before we leave.*
> *Even if we're sad, we can look good, at least."*

As she sang, she transformed the look of each filly. Her horn of steel created ridiculously ludicrous gewgaws for unicorns preparing for a strenuous journey. Even Alumna's oracle cap received extra pizzazz with shiny carmine tinsel tassels dangling from the top.

Lauda jerked her head back and to the side as shooting star dust gusted around her head. "What's with all this twinkling and dancing? What in tarnation? Style, what have you done?"

Style did not take time to answer. She moved on to Silubhra. A touch of her steel horn conjured up fluttery multicolored butterflies in the baby's breath and posies that were already in her mane.

Style twirled around to face Cuprum. She swirled her horn causing satin ribbons and tiny glass balls in shades of jade and garnet to appear in the copper-horned unicorn's mane.

Tinam was delighted with the decorative effect, "Sweety-cakes, you remind me of the centerpiece for a holiday table," he exclaimed.

Iown watched the unicorn stylist's frenzied movements as long as he could stand it, but it all finally became too much for him and he butted in.

"Style, as you just noted, these are serious matters. We don't have time for all of this frilly-frally."

The steel-horned unicorn threw him a look that warned; *Don't mess with me while I'm working!* She spat the words, "This is serious business! There's always time to look good. When you look good..."

Iown finished her thought, "You feel good. Yes, we know."

They all knew. And deep down they understood this was her way of contributing. "By all means, continue," Iown capitulated, backing slowly away from the wild-eyed mare.

Style did stop long enough to take a deep breath and slow her manic movements. Eyeing the golden-horned unicorn for a few moments, she finally said in a singsong cadence,

"Now, something very special for you, dear Ghel.
A glowing yellow light will be your sorrow's veil.
It will shine like a candle until Blue comes home.
It will burn in his mind wherever he may roam."

Her horn gyrated in huge circles, three times around Ghel's head. The after-effect was astonishing, as a halo of golden light surrounded the golden-horned unicorn. Flowing down from a ring around the base of her horn shone a glorious luminescent veil. It swept bright, shining light across her mane and her shoulders.

The other fillies exclaimed:

"Beautiful!"

"Amazing!"

"Stunning!" "

Magnificent!"

Style soaked up the praise for her handiwork before she drew everyone's attention back to herself. "Now, I mustn't forget me," she said with a wink.

The purple unicorn raised her head so that her horn pointed skyward. She moved it in an S-pattern, causing translucent purple bubbles to float around her head.

Everyone had to admit the fillies certainly did look beautiful, but these were absurdly outrageous decorations for unicorns preparing for a grueling journey. They all seemed ridiculous except the one she'd given Ghel. Despite Style's best magical efforts, no one felt much better.

Cornum sidled over to Style and burst one of those purple

bubbles. That sent a few titters around the room and some outright guffaws.

"Cornum, stop that!" the steel-horned unicorn cried. "I'm attempting to lift spirits and you just want to ruin everything!" She started to sob.

"Sorry," Cornum said, trying to loosen up one of the much-too-tightly attached lemons from his scalp with the point of his hoof, "but sometimes you overdo things."

His words were true enough that everyone mumbled some sort of agreement. They felt badly for her, but they also understood Cornum's little moment of rebellion.

Alumna sobered up quickly. "Alright, everyone. We've had no sleep since yesterday. Since it will be safer for us to travel at night, let's retire to our quarters and try to get a few hours of rest before we strike out at dark."

"Let's meet here in the courtyard when the sun goes down," Iown suggested. "We can make our final plans then."

Everyone lined up behind the iron-horned unicorn to exit the Great Room in single file. Iown bent his head to place his horn into the notch to open the door leading back into the main hall, and the lights in the big chandelier over the table flickered out.

"Ahhhhh!" the iron-horned unicorn screamed, as a big, bright spark arced from the indentation and connected with the tip of his horn. The gripping power of the unexpected electrical charge kept him pinned in place.

Horrified gasps erupted around the room as the realization dawned that the magic intended to guard the Halstable was failing. More than that, it was actually reaching out to attack one of their own.

Lauda bounded to the front of the line, but hesitated once she arrived. The sparks had whipped themselves into a brilliant, yellow flame that traveled fast through Iown's iron horn, moving dangerously close to his head. The impressive glow and hum spoke of powers much bigger and far older than any of the unicorns.

Nix watched, too. "I don't think I'll be able to nix this danger. A lightning bolt would only make that worse."

"Someone make it stop," Cornum cried. "What's happening to the Halstable? Has it stopped protecting us?"

"Go on, Lauda," Tinam urged. "What are you waiting for? Fix the Halstable."

"But I ... I can't!" Lauda said.

"Of course you can," Silubhra countered. "It's what you do."

"Oh no, this is not at all what I do," Lauda exclaimed. "I repair damage to wires and other metal surfaces. I don't put out flames, and I certainly don't stop surging electricity!"

The wild eyes of the unicorns watching Iown were frightened at the angry red rod his horn was becoming. The diamonds embedded there had become glowing white eyes.

Iown remained trapped by the surging electrical link as sparks began to fly from other electrical devices around the room. The magical properties of the Halstable's protective field were failing—along with Iown's own life force.

The old unicorn's knees buckled as sweat beaded on his coat.

Alumna could not stand helplessly watching for another moment. Her stable-mate's life was at stake. "Out of my way," she commanded those between her and Iown.

Everyone scattered as she ran to her mate. With a yelp, the aluminum-horned unicorn dove at Iown with every bit of physical force she could muster in her body. As their bodies collided, Iown's horn disconnected from the electrical charge so abruptly that they both fell into a heap.

"Iown, are you ok?" Alumna asked, searching his face for any sign of recognition.

He stared back blankly.

She caressed his face with the soft pad of her hoof, turning his gaze to meet her own. He remained expressionless for a moment longer, then shook his head and blinked.

"My head feels really hot," he finally managed to pant.

She said, "It's a good thing you're so tough. You're probably the only one of us who could've gone through that ordeal and lived!"

Alumna stood, but Iown remained on the ground, breathless. The flame had gone out, but Iown's horn still crackled with electricity. The intensity of it froze all the other unicorns in their tracks. Everyone moved in slow motion as the heat continued to ravage his horn.

"Quick! We need water!" the copper-horned unicorn finally called, breaking the stillness. "We've got to cool Iown's horn!"

That snapped everyone into action.

Tinam and Cuprum ran through the open door of the kitchen and came back with four buckets of water. The thin metal containers clanged as the unicorns rushed back into the Great Room.

Water hissed as it was splashed onto Iown's red-hot horn. He lay still on the ground as clouds of steam roiled through the air.

Alumna encouraged them to keep drenching his nearly molten horn with water. Finally, the heat, was completely doused and his horn began to return to its normal color and temperature.

A sigh of relief finally rippled through the group of unicorns. Most of them had been afraid something awful had happened to him, so they were relieved to see him rise to his hooves again. Shakily, Dr. Zinko observed Iown's horn to see if permanent damage had occurred. He found none on the surface, but that did not mean there were no internal fissures or other injuries.

Dr. Zinko took Iown away through the kitchen to do a more thorough examination. The rest of tribe left the Great Room the same way since it was currently the only way out of the room, with the main door seized shut.

The horrifying event was over, but they were still frightened, so sleep would not come easily for any of them.

The entry door from the Great Room into the Main Hall still would not open, and it was up to Lauda to fix it. Alumna wanted to be with Iown, but she did not want to leave the lead-horned unicorn alone as she went about the task of performing maintenance on the fried power lines of the door lock.

She stood quietly, watching and thinking. It stood to reason that the Moon-Star was coming closer with every moment. *Could its approach be causing trouble with their magic?*

The frame around the doorway was scarred black from the sustained energized current surging through it, but there were no more sparks and no more fire, and Lauda soon had the locking mechanism of the door repaired. Unfortunately, the tribe had precious few hours to sleep before they must set off on their journey into the unknown.

"We're lucky to have you, Lauda," Alumna told her old friend.

The lead-horned unicorn gave her a tired smile and nodded. "Let's go get some sleep."

*T*he day passed too quickly and the moon was already rising when the group gathered in the Halstable Courtyard. Following the recent scare, the mood remained solemn and serious.

The outdoor space was not really 'outdoors' at all, but it had that appearance because of the translucent dome which covered the entire area. Both sunlight and moonlight shone clearly through that big, round, vaulted window into the rectangular Courtyard.

The tribe usually gathered there in the courtyard at the time of Lunation, the beginning of each moon cycle, when the moon was on the opposite side of the planet from the sun.

Alumna typically led the meetings and it was then that she presented any new messages from the Numen.

Cornum and Silubhra would lead the others in song and dance during each gathering. In these uncertain times, the meetings helped lift everyone's spirits. However, on this night the moon was already half full and there was no song or dance. . .only silent communing.

The unicorns had made their final travel plans and were about to leave the Halstable. No one knew when, or if, they would return.

Ghel gazed into a night sky sprinkled with a multitude of

brightly shining points of light. Golden yellow auras shimmered around her like candle light. "Oh Blue," she said taking some comfort that he was out there somewhere possibly looking up at the same moon and stars as she. "I'll wear this veil and keep it shining for you, my love. I know we will meet again, and when we do, you will be that magnificent stallion from my vision."

She spoke these words to the night sky, hoping her words might carry to Blue on the winds of dreams.

"I'm afraid," Silubhra sang a sad note.

"I'm not afraid," Cornum bragged. Rearing up on his back legs, he blew a loud note from his horn for emphasis.

"We may have a long, rough road ahead of us," Iown remarked. "We need to pull together."

"Yes, and when we get to Muzika Woods, the blue unicorn is going to whisk us all to Unimaise," Lauda said derisively. "Right . . ." Fear and sarcasm colored her tone.

Alumna gently reminded her, "Lauda, this is not the time for negativity. We need all the positive energy we can muster."

"I'm willing to give it a shot," said Style. "I'm in shape to face whatever we encounter." She stretched her long, athletic legs.

"I wish I was," Tinam said quietly.

No one responded.

Chapter Twenty
Flaming Ball of Fire

*T*he first two days were easy, uneventful traveling for the unicorn and stag. They moved through the Guarded Forest, relying on Gaiso's knowledge of the geography. They stopped at watering holes for fresh water and made good time.

Blue had a decent supply of Cuprum's water purification pebbles, but he didn't use them since chances were there might be a critical need for them somewhere else along the way. The copper-horned unicorn usually distilled water on the spot, but there were occasions when she might not be available. For those times, she concentrated her magic into little pebbles for the other unicorns to use.

Blue feared there would be many places along the route where the water proved undrinkable, so he had brought blue pebbles to remove salt from marsh water, green ones to extract water from thick mud, and red ones to purify harsh chemicals from water that otherwise looked safe to drink.

Once they left the Guarded Forest, Blue figured to use the red ones in any water source, even those that looked clean ... just in case they were not. He and Gaiso grazed on what vegetation was available, rather than squander Tinam's magical tins of food, which, like the pebbles, they saved for what might lay ahead.

There was no fear of being attacked by an unknown, unseen enemy, because of the benevolent magic curtaining the woods from the rest of the world, but as the sun set on the second day of their journey, they both knew the rest of the route would not be quite so pleasant.

Blue bedded down, but remained tired and restless. He tried to settle in for the night, but there seemed no way to make a comfortable spot on the hard ground. His traveling companion, however, did not share this problem.

Gaiso's snoring did not help. Blue tossed this way and that before finally jumping up on all fours. He walked in a tight little circle before lying down again. Even after he found a comfortable position, hours slipped by before he drifted off to sleep. His mind remained full of thoughts of the Moon-Star.

Will the impact kill me? Will I be paralyzed? Will I be burned alive? It is a star after all. . .and I'm just a plain blue unicorn."

He finally began to drift off just as the moon reached its zenith, but before he entered the land of dreams, he thought ... *I have to achieve my destiny. The future of the Tribe of the Metal-Horned Unicorns depends on me.*

In his dreams, the entire tribe left the Halstable headed south. He saw the black outline of a large castle on a hilltop. Pure malice emanated from the tallest tower. He saw the tribe cross a drawbridge. The bridge immediately raised behind them.

"No, don't go there," he silently screamed.

In mid-scream, the sun peeked under his eyelids, prying them open against his will. Startled awake by the nightmare, Blue's mouth felt dry. He clamped his jaws shut and gulped twice before he finally had enough moisture to swallow away the dream, which had felt far too real.

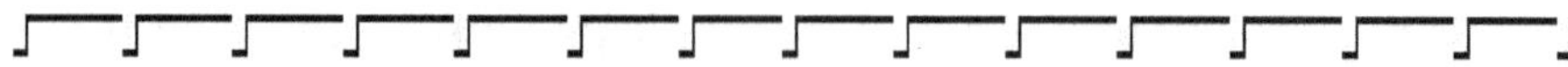

$\mathcal{A}$t high noon, Blue and Gaiso burst through the trees at the northern arc of the Guarded Forest. By then, the dream had nearly faded, but the burst of sun reminded him of the light shining brightly on the tribe as they crossed the drawbridge into the darkness of that castle.

Remembrance of his nightmare caused him to shiver involuntarily. He rolled his head from side to side, trying to displace the feeling of impending doom.

The air had become noticeably colder. Maybe that was where the shiver originated. Way off in the distance, the tip-top of the tallest of the Hedron Mountains stood visible. That was where he and the stag were headed.

An hour out of the woods, the traveling companions stopped short when they saw a strange fiery streak in the sky, not unlike a shooting star. It was the middle of a bright, sunny day, so the sight left them confused.

"What is that?" Gaiso asked, his eyes big, round O's.

The object hurtled toward them, surrounded by brilliant orange and scarlet streaks that cut through the air with such combustible force that fire flamed all around. As the flaming thing rushed straight at them, Gaiso ducked behind a bush, as if that would keep him safe from his impending fiery death.

The stag yelled to Blue, "Protect yourself!"

Blue was about to obey the command when he recognized what—or, rather, who—was hurtling toward them.

The first time he had encountered her, he had been passing under a Pepo tree. She had nearly scared the living daylights out of him when she swooped down in a fiery flame to pluck a nice juicy fruit from the tree. After that initial scare, they quickly became friends who spent much time together whenever Blue traveled beyond the Halstable.

The large, colorful bird came to rest on a big boulder near the unicorn. As she slowed the fanning of her wings, her flames doused, but dark smoke drifted out and surrounded them all.

"I can't believe you've never met her!" Blue laughed and then coughed. All the smoke from the flaming bird tickled his throat a little. "Don't worry, the Firebird is friendly. Come out from behind that bush!"

"Well, if it isn't the blue unicorn!" she cheerfully greeted Blue. Turning a fire-opal eye toward the stag, she asked, "Who's your friend?"

Blue laughed and opened his mouth to answer, but a puff of smoke snuck into his lungs. Gasping, he lapsed into a coughing fit as Gaiso gingerly stepped out from behind the bush.

"I was. . ." the stag stammered, ". . . just moving out of the way! I thought. . . I—"

"No need for explanation." Girasol laughed. "I know the effect I have on others when they first meet me!"

"Gaiso, this is Girasol," Blue finally recovered and introduced his two friends to each other. "Girasol, please give a *warm* greeting to my friend, Gaiso!"

The Firebird 'tsk-tsked' at his poor attempt at humor, then said, "Hello, Gaiso. Nice to meet 'cha! So, Blue, what are you up to? You unicorns never wander this far from the Halstable."

She knew that most of the Tribe of Metal Horn Unicorns stuck to the safety of their magically protected home, rather than brave the hostile outside world. Other than Blue, Nix Nickel-Horn was the only other adventurous member of the tribe. However, even he did not venture this far from the Halstable and his beloved, Silubhra.

"We're on a quest. Our destination is the Muzika Woods," Blue told Girasol simply. He knew she, of all creatures, would be interested in a little adventure.

She cocked her head, inviting him to say more.

"Unfortunately, we're not absolutely certain how to get there. We planned to head east and hopefully get directions along the way," he admitted. "You don't happen to know how to get there, do you?"

"Why, yes, I do," she told them. "I've flown over the place many times."

"Think you might be able to guide us?" Blue asked.

"Of course! You can count on me," the bird declared, just as Blue had hoped she would.

She stretched her wings to the fullest extent of their five-foot span and leapt into the sky. A long trail of orangey fire and white smoke discharged as she rose up into the clouds. "What are you waiting for?" she called over her shoulder to the bemused buck and still coughing unicorn. "Come on! Get a move on!"

"She jumped into this adventure quickly," Gaiso said, trying to stifle a cough.

"That's the nature of her kind," Blue said. "Firebirds have a difficult time sitting still. They have a lot of energy and build up too much heat unless they keep moving."

"Hmmph! I hope she doesn't aim too much of that heat at us," Gaiso said, eyeing the trail of fire.

"She can help us stay warm on cold nights," Blue hacked around the tickling in his throat, "And she can be very handy to have around in the dark."

Gaiso sputtered at the smoke still swirling around them. "Sure, if we can avoid getting singed in the process."

"We'll be ok," Blue assured him. "She'll spend most of her time up in the air. We just have to follow her smoke trails."

"About those smoke trails," Gaiso pointed out. "They look like a big banner saying, 'Here I am!' I hope no one else thinks to follow them."

"Why would anyone bother?" Blue asked naively.

The stag shook his head. "No reason at all. It's perfectly normal to see a blue unicorn, a stag from the Guarded Forest, and a big, flaming bird in the sky all out for a nice, relaxing stroll. Nope," the stag said, "Nothing here to attract attention. Nothing at all."

Chapter Twenty-One
Bugged By Survival

Girasol quickly proved to be an excellent guide for her earthbound companions. She flew slowly enough for Blue and Gaiso to easily follow, but high enough to seek out the best routes for the earth-bound travelers. Tireless, she could literally fly rings around them, it seemed. And she never needed sleep. The only sustenance she required was the seed of the ever- abundant Pepo tree. Every so often, she swooped down to grab one.

Plucking a likely candidate about the size and color of a purple plum, she gave it a little squeeze to make sure it was ripe and then popped the whole thing into her mouth. Instantly reenergized—as if by a jolt of electricity—she bolted back into the sky to continue her survey of the landscape.

"A single Pepo seed gives me energy for two whole days," she told Blue.

For now, those trees seemed to be everywhere, but not knowing if they might thin out or even disappear altogether somewhere along the route, Blue decided to put a store of them in his bag ... just in case.

Girasol flew high above the Phlat Plains. In the midst of the tall, waving grass, there was not much for Blue and Gaiso to see except for an occasional wide-spreading tree. It would have been easy to stray off course and get lost here, but with the Firebird guiding them, that was not a concern. So, they plodded along for hours, weary and bored by the unchanging landscape.

The monotony came to an end when the Firebird swooped lower and then made a few broad circles, which left the duo on the ground confused about her intentions—until she zoomed in low near them. In a cloud of smoke, she yelled, "Blue! Gaiso! Trouble up ahead! Someone is being attacked, and they desperately need our help."

"Who?" Gaiso asked, ready to charge to the rescue. "What sort of creature is in trouble?"

"An Elutron. . .a very big bug," Girasol said.

"A bug?" Blue flinched, as if the word itself could hurt him. He had barely recovered from his encounter with the Buzzy-Biter. Now, he was being asked to *defend* a bug.

"I don't know, Girasol. Me and bugs. . .We don't really get along," he said uncertainly.

Girasol insisted, "This one's nice, Blue. He's a giant beetle, but he's completely defenseless. Right now, he's being tied to a stake by a bunch of two-leggers!"

"Two-leggers?" Gaiso inquired. "From where?"

"Bugansville ... it's a village at the base of the Hedron Mountains. The Bugans are a filthy crew of bug bashers. I've never seen the likes of them anywhere else in MarBryn." Anxiety rose in her voice the more she thought of what they were doing to that Elutron. "There's no time for twenty questions. We've got to stop them," she urged.

"Ummm, I don't know," Blue hedged, as a little frisson of residual pain poked the place where he had so recently been stung. He was more afraid of an encounter with the bug than he was with the Bugans at this point. A bug was a bug, after all. . .wasn't it?

With a catch in her voice, the Firebird made her case, "If we don't rescue him, those Bugans will cut his forewings off to use the stiff elytra for shields and shoes. Those fiends prize the filmy membrane of Elutron hindwings for scarves and veils. And after they've ripped it all away, they'll just leave him to die, defenseless. Once the male has been dispatched, the Bugans will sneak into the Elutron's den to gather the eggs for a feast." A tear escaped her opalescent eye.

"Bugans are a strange lot. They don't eat the bugs but they love Elutron eggs. They rob and steal from all kinds of nests, but Humongas Elutron eggs are their main food source. The females lay up to three hundred eggs at a time that are each the size of the bright green outer husk of the seed of a Juglan Nigra tree. One clutch of eggs is enough for several large meals."

"The Bugans wipe out entire families. Entire species. They work fast because Elutron eggs have a very short incubation time and not even the gnarliest Bugan wants to chomp down on a hatched Elutron.

"Ugh!" Blue almost puked. The very thought of eating bugs was just too gross to contemplate.

"Elutrons are one of the few friendly species left in MarBryn," she pleaded. "But the Bugans answer to Magh."

That was enough for Blue and Gaiso to agree that they had to, at least, try save the helpless Humongas Elutron.

Blue tried to swallow his fear of the bug. He found some comfort in remembering that he had brought along some of Lauda's pest repellant, but he was still worried. "What if I can't fight without magic?"

"You can fight, Blue," Gaiso assured the nervous unicorn. "Use the gifts you were given at birth. Spear with your horn. Punch with your hooves. Look at me. That's exactly what I do. I don't have magic, but I can fight and so can you."

"What if I can't remember what you taught me?" He did not

want to let Gaiso down.

"It will be fine, Blue," Gaiso assured him. "You will know what to do once we are engaged in battle. Rely on your instincts."

The three companions arrived on the scene and were greeted by an eerie wailing as a stocky Bugan began to hack at the humongous left wing of the Elutron. The bug was tethered to the ground by a large net.

Blue snorted a battle charge that he did not even know he had in him. Rearing up on his hind legs to paw the air with his front hooves, he stormed forward with his horn poised for a deadly strike. A strange tingling sensation in the tip grew stronger as he neared the Bugan and his whole body thrummed with the anticipation of plunging it into one of Magh's minions, but the stag beat him there.

Gaiso gouged the Bugan through the spleen with an antler and the two-legger silently crumpled to the ground. Blue considered finishing him off, but before his horn could even touch the Elutron's assaulter, the evil fiend had already expired.

The unicorn galloped around the captive Elutron, ready to engage a stick-thin creature just beginning to climb onto the giant bug's back. That two-legger saw him coming and leaped across the top of the bug, nearly finding himself shish-ka-bobbed on the point of Gaiso's rack.

The stag charged, but the two-legger slid to the ground neatly avoiding being skewered. He lunged toward Gaiso, but the big buck spun around and caught him with the sharp points of his antlers and tossed him away like a rag doll.

Blue thought the battle had been won, but then the Firebird shrieked a war cry and dove. A Bugan had sunk a cleaver at least an inch into the Elutron's flesh, but the would-be bug-slayer fell, screaming in pain, as he found himself shrouded in flame.

The blue unicorn's stomach lurched as the stench of singed flesh filled the air. He surveyed the carnage while breathing in the aura of death that now pervaded the area. Blue wondered if, somehow, this bloodshed could have all been prevented. A killing fever had overtaken him and his companions so easily, but maybe the Bugans were just trying to survive in the only way they knew how?

"Blue, are you hurt?" Girasol asked. "You don't look so good?"

"I'm okay." He looked around for Gaiso and momentarily panicked when he couldn't see the stag. "Where's Gaiso?"

"Over here," the stag called from the other side of the Humongas Elutron.

Blue could not see Gaiso at all with the giant bug lying between them. "Are you okay?" he called out to his friend.

"I'm fine. Just got the wind knocked out of me a bit," Gaiso said, rounding the bug and pulling the net away with his antlers.

Blue heaved a sigh of relief, until he saw that Gaiso had been wounded. Blood flowed freely from a gash in the big buck's side. One of the Bugans had managed to slash right through his thick hide with a razor thin blade.

The cut was not deep, but it was long. Gaiso had not even noticed he was bleeding.

"You got more than wind knocked out of you," Girasol screeched. "Lucky for you, I can fix that." As she spoke, one of her talons glowed to a bright orange. In moments, its tip was white-hot.

Blue watched as she approached the stag with that talon

extended.

Gaiso saw her coming and backed away, yelling, "Stay away from me, you crazy bird!"

"Come back here!" the Firebird shouted back. "We've got to stop that leak! Can't have you wandering all over the countryside, leaving a trail of blood!"

Gaiso paused in his retreat. They all knew that Girasol was right and that Magh had trackers looking out for just that sort of thing. "What's your plan?" the stag asked with trepidation coloring his voice

"I will stop the bleeding with a blast of heat. It's called cauterization. Now, you should bite down on something. This is going to hurt."

Blue did not want to witness his friend's pain, so he worked to pull a stake from the ground to finish freeing the Elutron. He heard his friend yowl as the Firebird sealed his torn hide. The smell of burnt hair and the horrific sound of sizzling flesh were the worst parts.

Blue might never clear them from his mind.

Thankfully, the process did not take long and once Girasol finished, Gaiso's flesh was nearly as good as new. Both of his friends had survived the battle without lasting injury, but the altercation had left him confused. He was the only one of the three who had not ended a life that day, though he had felt the urge to defend that bug just as strongly as they had.

Given the opportunity, he felt he would have killed as well, but the stag had intervened.

"Why did you stop me, Gaiso? I was ready for that fight!"

Blue was indignant.

"Ah, my young friend. Why hurry into the termination of life?" Gaiso said.

Disbelieving, the unicorn said, "But isn't this what you've been training me for?"

"No, I've trained you for survival! I've trained you to defend yourself. This was different. Living with the knowledge that you've ended the life of another is much harsher when the fight is not actually your own. You'll be fighting your own battles soon enough."

"Gaiso's right, Blue. Be happy you didn't have to deliver a lethal blow," Girasol interjected. "Let's see what we can to do help this Elutron. He's been wounded, too."

Blue pondered their words. They seemed wise, and he still had much to learn. Arguing with them about this was not going to get him anywhere, so he dropped the subject and helped to free the Humongas Elutron from his bonds so they could all leave this horrific scene.

"Many thanks," the bug said. "I am Leder."

"Don't mention it," Gaiso replied. "You were outnumbered."

"We're just glad we were passing by and got here in time," Girasol told him.

"Are you ok?" Blue asked. He could not help noticing slimy yellow ooze dripping from a jagged tear in the beetle's flesh.

"Hurts," Leder said, trying to raise his injured wing.

"I can't cauterize that," Girasol observed, looking the bug over. "The wound is too raggedy."

"That looks bad. We need to clean that cut right away," said Blue as he looked around for some water. "That might help to stop any infection."

"Over there," Leder pointed with one chitinous front leg toward a muddy puddle near a low, squatty tree.

"I don't think we'll be able to sanitize your wound with that muck," Blue said. "But don't worry, I can clean that scummy water with one of these." He proudly showed the big bug a green pebble. "It will turn that mess into fresh, clean water."

"Noooo," Leder protested. "Need mud," he insisted. The Elutron waddled over to the mud pit and, to Blue's astonishment, plunged himself up to his eyeballs in the thick, gooey stuff. He rolled his body all the way over so that his little legs stuck straight up in the air and then rocked his body back and forth until he was thoroughly coated with mud.

"Feel better now," he whirred.

Blue shook his head at Leder's self-doctoring.

"Don't worry, Blue," Girasol said. "That's how Humongas Elutrons heal themselves. The minerals in the mud have healing powers."

"I say," Gaiso interrupted, "I'm feeling absolutely parched. Do you happen to have any more water in your canteen?"

"I could use a drink after all of those exertions, myself," Blue said. He took a container from his backpack and shook it. A little bit of water sloshed around, but not much.

"Here, Gaiso. You take it." He passed it to the big buck.

Gaiso took a small sip and then offered it back. "You need

this as much as I do.”

“Honestly, it’s alright. You drink it. I’m going to use this water extraction tablet of Cuprum’s on some of that mud,” he insisted, holding up the green pebble.

“I hope Cuprum’s magic works on pond scum,” Gaiso said, looking as if he did not believe it would.

“Me, too. I’ve witnessed Cuprum using her horn magic on plenty of mud puddles, but I’ve never actually seen one of these little doo-dads in action.”

He took a tin cup from his pack and scooped up a big glob of mud with it. “Here goes nothing,” He said as he dropped the pebble in.

At first, that’s exactly what happened—nothing. The pebble just lay on top of the mud. It did not float; it just sort of sat there.

Gaiso tilted his head and looked quite dubious. Blue could almost see the ‘*I told you so*‘ forming on the deer’s lips. Then, the stone started to sink very slowly and a ring of clear liquid formed around and under it. Within moments, every bit of mud was gone, leaving the cup full of clean water. Blue slowly lifted the cup to his lips, taking a tiny sip.

“This is fantastic,” he grinned. “The copper-horned unicorn has some amazing magic.” After downing the rest of the water, he offered, “Let me just clean up this whole pond.”

“Nooo ...” Leder rasped out. “Bad idea.”

Girasol said, “Blue, that magic would change the entire ecosystem around here. It’s best not to mess with nature. It could have disastrous effects on the Elutron population.”

Blue saw the wisdom in the Firebird’s words. “I hadn’t even

thought about that." He and Gaiso needed crystal clear water, but the Humongas Elutron did not. The bugs needed the microscopic entities residing in the mud to maintain their health.

He scooped his empty cup back into the mud to prepare another drink for Gaiso.

The stag did not even take a little sip first. He downed it in one gulp. "Amazing, indeed," he agreed, feeling much better. "Cuprum's water magic is wondrous! And speaking of wonders, Blue why did your horn glow when we were engaged in battle? It never does that when we spar."

"My horn doesn't glow," he answered, feeling confident that he was right. But both the Firebird and the stag shot looks at each other, which made Blue feel a bit less certain about that fact.

"Maybe it was the sun, or a reflection from Girasol's heat," he offered.

His two companions said nothing but continued to stare. The awkward silence lasted for only a few seconds before Leder crawled out of the mud with his wound looking considerably less dire.

When he rejoined his saviors, he told them, "Someday, repay. . ." He made it sound like a promise. "Home now," he said. "Check on eggs." To everyone's astonishment, he scuttled but a few feet before diving into a large hole in the ground hidden by tall grasses.

When he had disappeared, Blue said, "Wow, that's a really big hole. I didn't even see it there."

Gaiso remarked, "Me, either. I'm glad neither of us broke a leg in it."

"Guess that's the last we'll see of him," the stag said, looking back toward the Bugans on the battlefield.

"You can never be certain," said the Firebird. "I should take care of those bodies. It wouldn't be good to leave them lying about in the open," she said, launching herself back into the air.

She blasted each one with a roaring flame until they were little more than roasted ash. Paper-thin coal-black flakes rose into the air and scattered about the landscape on a mild breeze.

Blue shivered and remarked, "I'm glad the wind is blowing the other way."

"Me, too," the stag replied with a shudder of disgust.

All things considered, Blue was glad they had helped the giant beetle. The bug was not so bad after all, but he could not help wondering about the Bugans.

True, they slaughtered Humongas Elutron for food and clothing, but they were not doing it out of viciousness and spite. They had to survive, and that was their way. Life was so complicated. Thinking about it made his young mind spin. It seemed there was no true black or white in the big picture. . .just millions of shades of gray.

Chapter Twenty-Two
Cheers, Jeers and Fears:
The Unicorn Audience

*T*he tribe of metal-horned unicorns had been trudging along for two days and already, their spirits were starting to flag. They remained focused on finding their way to Muzika Woods in time for the arrival of the Moon-Star, but not all of them were convinced they could make the journey in time, or that Blue would be there to meet them, even if they did.

Forced into taking a riskier southeasterly route due to the unfortunate destruction of the natural bridge leading to the Guarded Forest, not a single one of them felt completely confident they were going the best way. The road they travelled had been surprisingly free of traffic, giving Nix mixed feelings. Fewer encounters with others meant less danger for the tribe, but they had not come across a single soul who could point them in the right direction. This fact had left the group unsure and anxious.

Though there were no obvious threats in sight, Nix's senses constantly tingled this far out from the Halstable. Uncomfortable that he could not pinpoint the source of potential peril out here in the open, he remained perpetually alert, and it was this heightened awareness that made him the first to spot the castle, ahead in the distance.

Something about that tallest tower did not sit right with him, and for a few brief seconds he thought about guiding the tribe away from the place, but instead he pointed the rocky structure out to the tribe as they walked. "That city on the hill," Nix indicated with his horn. "Maybe someone there can tell us the way to Muzika Woods."

Nix was the only tribe member with battle experience. Most

were barely adept at self-defense, so he was unsure how many unicorns he could save if the tribe encountered a large group of hostiles. He hoped the magic of their horns would be enough to help them protect themselves—if it came to that. These thoughts left the nickel-horned unicorn feeling forced into making an uneasy decision.

He asked Alumna to unroll her map so he could get his bearings.

"Style, do you mind?" the oracle asked, indicating the purple unicorn's back would make a good table on which to study the map.

"Of course not," Style said, positioning herself so Alumna could lay it out.

After she smoothed the map flat, the others gathered around and the unicorn oracle said, "I think we are here." She pointed to what looked like a castle on the scroll. "It's labeled Kudos, so that must be the name of that city."

"We don't know anything about the place, or what kind of two-leggers might live there." Cornum sounded worried.

"There are walls all around it," Style hedged, looking up at the castle on the hilltop. "I don't like the look of that. We could be trapped there."

"Trapped." Cuprum gasped. "Maybe we should just skirt around it." The moss-green filly looked around the group for a sign of agreement.

"We have no idea if we are even going in the right direction," Iown prompted. "It's possible we could find someone there willing to guide us to Muzika Woods."

"I've heard that guides can be found in cities and towns," Dr. Zinko said. "It might be worth the risk to see if we can find one."

"We have a decision to make," Nix said. "I don't feel comfortable about being trapped within those walls. . ." He paused and gave Alumna a penetrating stare. "No offense, Alumna, but your map is really hard to follow. There's just not enough detail. Given we are short on time, I fear we have little to waste wandering around. I think we need to find a guide."

The aluminum-horned unicorn nodded. "I wish I'd been able to record better images from the orb, but given my limited artistic talents and the haziness of the messages, this is all we have." She rolled up the map and stashed it in her pack. "So I agree. We need more help than the map provides."

No one felt good about the decision, but they needed to venture into the city. Maybe they would get lucky and discover the two-leggers were friendly.

The tribe marched toward the city. They tried to be quiet, yet there was no way to hide the metallic clatter of their hooves as they crossed the wooden surface of an old weathered bridge. The echoing sounds lent the procession an eerily hollow sound. Spanning a narrow but deep moat, the bridge seemed to be the only way in or out.

As they moved closer, the drawbridge lowered, allowing them to pass through an archway carved from dark granite. As a group, the tribe stepped directly into a large open market square. No soldiers or menacing faces appeared, but loud creaks from the shuddering wood reverberated in their spines as the drawbridge was immediately raised behind them.

Nix took one look back and thought, *I don't like that. I need to look for another way out of this place.* The unicorn defender kept his eyes peeled for a secondary exit as the tribe passed shops and eateries along the way to the town center.

City-dwellers took immediate notice and some followed the little group at a short distance. No one spoke but before long they all noticed they had gathered quite a crowd of lookey-loos.

These unicorns had little experience with two-leggers and were not sure how to interact with those who were obviously suspicious. Some appeared outright afraid as if they had never seen a unicorn before.

Then again, it had been a very long time ago since the Metal Horns had moved freely about MarBryn so in all likelihood no one here had ever seen a unicorn in the flesh.

"Maybe you should sing for them, Silubhra," Alumna suggested. "Hearing you might introduce us in a positive light."

"Good idea. I think Ghel's song would work best," the silver-horned unicorn said, nodding her head almost imperceptibly in agreement.

There was a little round stage right in the center of the town square. She and Cornum stepped up on it and turned to face the crowd of curious onlookers. The lime-green unicorn started with a clear, mellow melody consisting of the uniquely haunting sounds of a French horn.

After a short solo, Silubhra's mesmerizing soprano joined in.

"We're unicorns, unicorns...
known as the tribe of the Metal-horn.
We're magical beasts promoting peace...
that's the way of the unicorn..."

Upon hearing Silubhra's magical silver-tongued voice, the facial expressions of most of the crowd transformed from outright fear and suspicion to sheer delight. Her rhythms of speech, the tones and timbre of her melodious vocal patterns conveyed so much positive emotion that it uplifted the moods of her listeners, and that brought a sense of relief to the tribe.

Silubhra's magical voice made it easier for the other unicorns to approach select citizens in the growing throng.

"Hello," Alumna greeted a young two-legger, who held a basket of fruit. He stood, swaying his head to the song's rhythm and tapping his feet. At the sound of the unicorn oracle's voice, he looked up into her eyes and smiled. "Young sir," she began, "I was wondering if I might have a word with you." He continued to smile, but otherwise said nothing. Then, he slowly reached into his basket. "How about a nice crisp apple?" He asked, lifting the big red globe right up to her mouth.

The stunned scarlet-colored unicorn oracle jerked her head away. She certainly would not eat straight from the hand of a stranger. Sputtering a "No, thank you" she tried again. "We are looking for some help."

He just kept smiling and bobbing his head in time to the unicorn concert. "You unicorns sure make beautiful music." He turned his attention back to Silubhra and Cornum.

"We do a lot more than that," Alumna told the back of his head.

She moved on to another two-legger, but this time when she spoke the woman looked both frightened and confused. "Go away!" She spat. "No singing!" And then, she hissed like an angry snake and gave a menacing leer, leaving Alumna to wonder what kind of being could hate such a beautiful melody.

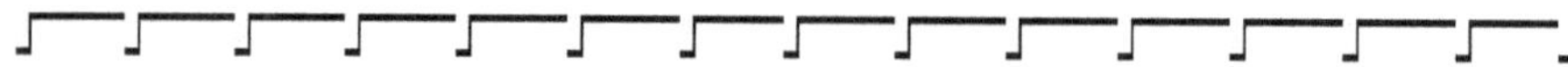

The music floated up through the highest window of the castle tower, straight into Magh's ears. A thin smile twisted his face as he stared at the action in the square below. He did not view the scene from a window; instead, his gaze was fixed upon a small, ornate wall mirror. His features were etched with both joy and disbelief at this impossible good fortune.

Unicorns! Right here in my own city!

The thought filled his body and left him vibrating with excitement as he stood before the mirror. If he could have seen his own reflection instead of the scene of the town square, he would have been appalled. He rarely smiled, and when he did, the expression was not one most would find joyful.

Of course, the same could be said about all of his expressions. A scary mix of a two-legger and unicorn with a smidgeon of manticore thrown in for good measure, the sorcerer had swirling wisps of hot pink hair on the sides of his head. This fringe curled upward a full, gravity-defying foot above the bald strips on his head. Down the middle, a short, grape-purple line of hair sprouted from his splotchy pale forehead and trailed off at the nape of his neck.

Pig-pink mutton chop sideburns hid most of his ears, revealing only the long pointy tips. Smack dab in the middle of his chin sat a mauvish patch of beard scraggle.

Overcome with evil glee, Magh hopped around in time to the brass-horned unicorn's tune. Unable to contain his joy, he tipped one foot out this way and the other out that way. He felt so giddy that he threw his head forward, shaking his arms above it.

The mirror had finally given him what he wanted. He remembered the indium-horned unicorn he had killed to create this mirror. He had thought he would be able to see the other unicorns through the powers of her horn, but the spell had not worked out that way. The mirror allowed him to see anything else, he wanted to see in the Land of MarBryn, but had never shown him any unicorns.

Until now.

As of late, Magh had begun to fear he would never capture another horn, until a manticore recently reported an unfortunate incident involving two unicorns. The creature had been beside himself at the loss of the pointy end of his tail, but that was of no consequence to the sorcerer, so he ignored the pleas to bestow a new one upon the beast.

Manticores were of no use, anyway, except as brutish henchmen. And though, he would never admit such to anyone, Magh lacked the power to reverse unicorn magic once it had been cast. All he could do was fight. . .and overpower their supernatural abilities with his own brand of dark sorcery.

Over the years, he had become quite adept at doing exactly that, and now, with a whole tribe of unicorns at his feet, he could conquer them. . .once and for all.

Chapter Twenty-Three
Something Wicked Is Born

Magh closed his eyes and savored his good fortune. The lilting music wafting up from the town square took him back a couple of centuries, to his first encounter with a unicorn—to another time of good fortune.

Things had been much different before Magh was Magh.
Back then, he went by his given name, Jenin. The apprentice of a middling wizard in the town of Jeribild, he was a good lad who tried hard to follow every instruction from his mentor. He stayed out of trouble and kept a low profile. Some considered him handsome, but no one would have called him brave.

Alone in the forest, his mentor had sent him to collect a Buzzy-Biter hive for the wax. Young Jenin had just about given up on finding one, but he feared the wrath of his mentor. Returning without the needed ingredients for the potion was not a fate he relished so young Jenin wandered about the forest, hoping for a miracle.

He traipsed about with his head tilted toward to the tree-tops looking for a hive, or even any sign of Buzzy-Biter's nearby, when a frightened neighing caught his attention. He followed the noise until he came upon a beautiful creature with a long, flowing mane of violet. From her forehead emerged a long, spiraling horn made of some sort of metal. Her hooves shone with the same metallic light.

A unicorn, he realized having heard stories of the majestic creatures. Many had seen them, and some had even met them. Some wizards had learned their magical craft directly from them, but this was Jenin's first encounter with one.

Only after a few heartbeats did he realize the magical creature was recoiling against the back wall of an open-aired ruin. Fear prominently exposed the whites of her eyes, but still, he marveled at her beauty even in extreme distress.

Then he caught sight of the source of her fear.

A manticore had trapped her within the remaining three walls of the ramshackle building. A temple, or shrine of some sort in the distant past, the place was now nothing more than crumbling remains from a forgotten time.

The brutish creature menaced her with sharp-claws and there appeared to be no escape. The manticore's body blocked the only exit, so it was taking its time. The hungry beast swiped superficial cuts across the unicorn's chest and haunch.

Each slash caused her to shrink away, crying. The cruel creature clearly enjoyed torturing the poor thing, and every swipe drew a thin line of blood that ran in rivulets across her exquisite mauveine coat.

Jenin stood mesmerized by the precision of the malevolent creature. It was almost as if he were designing an abstract work of art across her hide. A shrill cry brought his attention back to the unicorn's terrified eyes. She had seen him standing there, and now begged for his help.

She sank to one knee and said, "Please. Help me."

The manticore was much larger than Jenin, but her words and voice tugged hard at his heart.

He drew his sword just as the manticore turned on him.

"Stay back, if you know what's good for you," it threatened. Raising a giant paw it said, "This is none of your concern."

"I'm making it my concern," Jenin said decisively.

The manticore laughed at his audacity and in the time it took to blink, blood appeared on Jenin's shirt from the swift movement of those sharp claws. He fell heavily as the beast turned back to the business of the unicorn.

The more fearful the prey, the better the flavor.

But Jenin had yet to hear that motto back then. Though bleeding profusely, he was not mortally wounded.

Forcing himself to his feet, he softly approached the monster. *If I die, I'm taking you with me.* With a strength propelled by terror, Jenin slashed his sword down across the manticore's neck with all his might, and the force of the blow sent the head of the beast rolling.

But the manticore's body rose into the air a few feet. Wings fluttering madly, it hovered aloft for several terrifying moments before thudding back to the ground.

The massive, headless body crashed into Jenin as it fell, sending the young apprentice falling toward the spear of the unicorn's horn. Though he tried to avoid being impaled, his momentum and the weight of his body crashing forward, forced the horn clean through his shoulder. He jerked back violently, and the force of his movement snapped the horn from the top of the unicorn's skull.

Horrified, he fell forward and found himself flat on his face, lodged between the manticore's headless corpse, and the wounded unicorn. The horn was deeply imbedded. . .and protruded through the top of Jenin's shoulder blade.

Blood spurted from the unicorn's head, where her horn had been torn away. The other cuts on her body oozed with no sign of stopping, and her lifeblood was quickly draining away.

"I didn't mean for this to happen," Jenin cried, agonized over the result of his actions. "I was trying to help!" Tears poured from his eyes.

"It is not your fault," she whispered hoarsely, trying to absolve him of guilt. "There's nothing you could have done."

And then. . .she was gone.

He caught a lingering image of ancient rust blowing across a desert plain from the spiraled horn of a long dead metal-horned unicorn and wondered what it meant.

A virtual fountain of blood spouted from the manticore's headless body. Jenin struggled to get up. He was desperate to get away from all the viscous liquid, but his leg was trapped beneath the monster.

Try as he might, he could not budge the beast. All he had managed to do was open his own wounds further and weaken himself to the point of exhaustion. With his last bit of strength, he wrenched the spiraled horn from his flesh. His last thought before sinking into oblivion was, "I'm going to die, too."

There are a myriad of ways for a new being to come into existence, and given the delicate balance of nature, it is always a gamble whether that new being will ultimately become a source for good or evil.

That day, there in the dirt, the life forces of three such beings ran together into a pool of blood. Two were destined for death, and the third remained vulnerable. . .and weak. . .and susceptible.

One contained the essence of all that was good. Another embodied pure brute force violence. The third was a sentient being capable of making choices between good and what could only be thought of as evil. Having the ability to make those choices negates any chance of neutrality, but in nature there is always something to tip the balance of free will.

The more dire the situation, the greater the opportunity for the lust for power, moral weakness, or plain old greed to weight the scale toward darkness, and this particular blend, mixed with the magic of the unicorn horn was something which should never have come to be.

The blood coalesced and vibrated on the ground as if it had a life of its own. The three tributaries rushed together into a roiling lake beneath Jenin and saturated his clothing until the primal concoction seeped into the very pores of his skin.

Every shallow breath he took sucked the essence into his nose and mouth. Filling his lungs and entering his blood stream, the mixture marinated his entire body in chaotic echoes of tears and fears, and a seething rage of discontent.

Whoever he might have been was drowned, replaced by this swift exchange. The new magical blood permutation surged through his system right into his brain like a drug—powerful enough to change its very structure.

His eyes flashed open.

Young Jenin was gone.

The entity now staring out of these eyes was momentarily confused. The weight of the manticore now felt no heavier than a blanket, so he cast off the spent corpse as if it were an insignificant nuisance. He rose from the ground, swaying slightly back and forth. He gazed curiously at the hand, which still clutched the mauve unicorn's potassium horn.

Of its own accord, that hand thrust the silvery white horn toward the sky. Lilac lightening crackled and rose from the spire as if it were a lightning rod. Every raindrop was met with loud booms of thunder.

A brilliant light show emitted from the spiraled tusk, up to the angry swirling clouds and back down into his own blackened heart.

One word erupted from his throat: "Magh!"

The new cognizant being became aware, that he now possessed a magical power which only he could wield.

Sheer joy filled him until he was bursting with perverse delight. This was a relishing of something evil, a dizzying giddiness, that pulled maniacal laughter from his throat. A sense of depravity settled over him, and he liked the wicked feeling. He had never stopped liking that sensation, and with each new rush of power he gained, he craved the next all the more.

*N*ow, with the unicorns so close, his need for more had grown insatiable. Magh grinned widely at the mirror, revealing sharp, blackened teeth.

He had been chasing the euphoria of that day for centuries now, and nothing would distract him from completing his mission.

He swung away from the mirror with such deliberate movement that his robes snapped at his legs like rabid rats. Those colorful robes were stitched together from the hides of many unicorns and the remnants of their former occupants were lashing out at him in useless fury. But he barely noticed as he stomped out the door, shouting, "Battalion Commander! Gather your troops!"

Chapter Twenty-Four
Rag-Bag Magic

Silubhra's beautiful voice captured the hearts of her audience. . .most of them, anyway. A few had fled, looking absolutely terrified by the arrival of the unicorns.

After the first song ended, applause erupted. From all corners of the square, expressions of praise and awe could be heard. "Did you hear the melodious sound coming from that unicorn?" said one citizen, referring to Silubhra's beautiful voice.

Unaccustomed to hearing compliments, Silubhra's white hide blushed to a cherry cream.

"Do you see this one's mane? It's magnificent!" another two-legger asked, pointing to Style's mane-do.

Style patted the pouf at the top of her head and flashed an enormous smile. She soaked up the compliments and could not help blurting out, "Well, I'm glad *somebody* can appreciate my art!"

"This one sounds just like a flute!" an excited two-legger exclaimed, edging closer to Cornum.

The lime-green unicorn cheerfully let out a couple of prideful toots, which made those gathered around the square burst into a small round of applause.

"More!" the crowd demanded. They liked being entertained.

As the music started up again, a child-like imp watched the unicorn performance from the shadows.

Enraptured by the beauty of these magical beings, the willowy little two-legger instantly fell in love with the unicorns. Many years had passed since she had last heard music or seen dancing, and this scene was a reminder of the good times from her past.

Like many other things, song and dance were forbidden in Kudos. Magh did not allow his subjects to participate in any events, which might remind them of their previous lives. Music brought back memories, but Imroz was not going to stop the unicorns. Their performance made her happy.

The wide brim of the Ragamoffyn's red leather hat swayed up and down as she nodded her head in time with the melody. The unicorn's voice wrapped itself around her, bringing back memories of her childhood in the Red Band of Weita.

Life for Ragamoffyns had once been easy. They possessed no magic, and by nature, were also immune to it. As such, no one in the Red Band of Weita could be placed in the thrall of the evil sorcerer. Because of that, they had lived freely for a long time. Imroz had once been free.

Before Magh, the little sun-reddened people of her village had had easy access to everything they needed in the Red Fir Forest. There had been no such thing as hunger or sadness. In her mind, she could see the red deer peacefully grazing on red wheatgrass as clearly, as if she were watching the field from the forest edge.

Peace. She longed for it again.

The sound of a single, deep horn blast in the distance tore her attention away from the mesmerizing music. Then, heavy tramping. All over the city, low horn notes called out.

Soldiers are coming!

All too familiar with the cadence of marching feet, Imroz would never forget that same sound when Magh's soldiers had marched through her village, plundering and pillaging. They had stopped only long enough to set huts afire and to place all able-bodied Ragamoffyn's in chains. It had happened in villages, towns, and cities all across MarBryn as populations of two-leggers too numerous to count were either killed, mesmerized, or involuntarily pressed into service for the sorcerer.

Back then, most places throughout MarBryn had wizards and sorcerers of some ability, or another. Most were trained in the ways of magical arts by the unicorns as part of their outreach program. Some two-leggers developed practical magical skills like making delicious feasts of tasty food appear out of thin air or purifying murky water around the land.

Others went through more extensive training to learn battle magic—like shooting powerful streams of energy from their swords.

Some were taught the art of holding the glow of the sun in magical globes, bringing light into the dark of night. These magical lights warded off the evil beings that were new and frightening products of dark magic.

With the rise of Magh, magical defense arts had become more important. The highest level of magical training involved sensing when others were in danger and learning to see into the future. Very few two-leggers ever reached that level.

Some of MarBryn's natives took to magic naturally, while others struggled with the concept. All of them fought valiantly against Magh's magic but, in the end, only one sorcerer remained in MarBryn. Now, Magh was in total control, but still, he was not satisfied. He wanted to control every living creature in the land.

Hearing the sound of marching feet, Imroz felt a moment of

panic. *Magh knows the unicorns are in Kudos.*

When the Ragamoffyn had been captured as a child, she was placed in Magh's servantry corps. After working for a few years, following the instructions of her superiors and quietly going about her business, she gradually gained their trust. By the time she turned fifteen, she had been assigned to work in Magh's personal quarters.

At first, such nearness to the sorcerer had struck absolute fear in her heart, but he had paid little mind to the comings and goings of a wayward Ragamoffyn. Imroz soon came to use her close proximity to learn more about his evil ways. She had vowed to stop him from gaining more power. It was this vow, that first brought her into the magical realm of unicorns, and now, she knew that she would defend this tribe with everything she had.

Imroz had been preparing for such a moment and now her time to help had arrived. She reached into a ragbag of stolen tricks. Some were very powerful, and each possessed a bit of the magic from the unicorn from which it was extracted. She had seen the sorcerer use these on different enemies and over time, she had learned how to activate his magical potions by observing and mimicking his actions.

As the first soldiers came into view, the little red two-legger pulled a powder called Implant from the bag. She tore open the packet and blew the substance into the path of Magh's soldiers.

Their feet instantly stopped moving. In fact, they seemed rooted to the ground.

*N*ix felt danger coming even before he heard the sound of marching feet. His eyes searched for an escape, but found nothing. The soldiers rounded a corner, and Nix's senses flared.

They were trapped!

He spied a little impish two-legger off to one side of the marketplace. He watched as she drew a packet from the ragbag slung across her shoulder. Opening it, she blew a raspberry-colored powder at the feet of the onrushing soldiers.

Nix raised an eyebrow when he saw that the magic halted their forward movement. The potion had literally planted their feet into the road. The first line of soldiers were stuck fast, but those behind them ran around the sides and again, the imp dug into the rag-bag and pulled out a bottle.

She tossed the contents onto several more soldiers, causing them to fall to the ground in a heap. She looked at Nix and yelled, "Hey you! Can't you see I'm trying to help?"

That startled the nickel-horned unicorn. He looked at Alumna, who had also been stunned into inaction, and then back at the little red imp who was valiantly trying to stop yet more soldiers.

"A little assistance would be nice," she challenged.

Nix wanted to assist her, but he did not want to use his horn's blasting power. Hurting Kudos' citizens would not do at all. After such a friendly start, he did not want to leave any with a fearful impression of unicorns.

The little Ragamoffyn seemed to be everywhere at once. In between drawing several more tricks out of the bag, the tiny magician introduced herself. "I'm Imroz," she said, while continuing to toss spells this way and that.

Her goal was to stop as many soldiers as possible and it aggravated her to see the unicorns standing as if frozen in place. She literally screamed, this time. "What are you just standing there for? Get out of here!"

The nickel-horned unicorn hesitated a moment longer while looking around for an escape route.

"Quickly," she urged. "These magical effects won't last forever. Come on. . .I can get you out of the city!"

Nix did not detect anything dangerous about the little two-legger. He believed she could be trusted, so he ordered the rest of the unicorns, "Let's go! Follow her!"

Imroz led them away from the market square while the battalion of soldiers were disabled.

For extra cover, she lit a yellow stick of Impasse and tossed it back behind her. A thick cloud of yellow fog swirled up, blocking sight of the unicorns from the soldiers' view and filling the air with the stench of sulfur.

She guided the unicorns down and through a dimly lit underground tunnel system for a few minutes. No one followed Imroz and her charges. They soon burst out into the bright sunshine in a large open area beside an outer wall of the city.

"This is the best place for you to depart," she said, stopping before a sturdy rock barrier measuring about thirty feet high and several feet thick.

"Here?" Cornum asked, tilting his head back to find the top of the wall.

"There's no door!" Alumna said, worriedly. "I'm too old for rock climbing."

"Me, too!" Lauda cried. "I knew it. We have finally met our doom!"

"Now, now, Lauda," Dr. Zinko comforted his elderly mate. "I'm sure Imroz has something in mind to get us through." He looked to the little imp for confirmation.

They all did.

Imroz was too busy studying the wall to answer. She made a square with the thumbs and pointers of each hand and looked through it. She moved it up and down, and right and left several times. Finally, she reported, "There's no one on the other side of that wall. This will do."

Withdrawing a small clear glass bottle filled with some glittery substance from her bag of tricks, she used her teeth to yank the cork stopper free. She ordered the entire tribe of unicorns to form a closed circle, tips of their horns pointing inward.

Not everyone hopped to her command. There was some grumbling from Lauda and Cornum, but Nix's stern urging convinced them to move into place around the Ragamoffyn.

Once they were all arranged, Imroz emptied the contents of the bottle into her leather hat. She shook it around to spread the sparkly shards of metal evenly and said, "Inverse Ibidem!"

Keeping a firm hold of her hat with both hands, she thrust it up into the air above the unicorns. A big puff of glitter flew upward and as it connected with their horns, everything around them started shimmering.

All they could see was bright white, followed by complete darkness. A moment later, it was bright white again, with more shimmering. When everyone could again see clearly, they found they were safely out of the city—on the other side of the wall.

"How?" Ghel asked.

"Magic," Imroz said without a smile. "Inverse Ibidem means other side, same vicinity. Now, I must be gone."

The Ragamoffyn turned to take her leave.

"Thank you. We would have been trapped without you," Ghel told the little imp.

Imroz blushed a deep apple red. She could not believe she was standing with such marvelous creatures. "My pleasure." She smiled. "I had no choice but to help."

At Ghel's questioning look, Imroz explained, "I've spoken with the blue unicorn's mother."

Lauda was aghast at such a pronouncement. "That's impossible! Miral died at the hands of Magh years ago!"

Imroz was quick to agree. "I communicate with her spirit. She remains trapped in the mirror that Magh fashioned from her horn. She has reached out to me many times, while alone in his quarters."

Lauda expressed the horror that everyone felt. "Oh, poor Miral! How awful it must be for her to be bound to that monster!"

Imroz assured the tribe that Magh did not know Miral was there. In fact, Miral had prevented Magh from seeing the tribe within the mirror until that day. But with the unicorns so close, Miral could not hide their images. "That is why you need to get as far away, as fast as you can," she added.

"What about your safety?" Nix asked.

Imroz shook away his concern. "I am a survivor and I, too, have magic, thanks to Miral. She encouraged me to start collecting magical potions from Magh. I told her I couldn't use them. . .that Ragamoffyns have no magical abilities, but she told me that didn't matter. She said these potions would be different, and she was right. With her help, I watched Magh and paid attention to his spells. She helped me learn to use them. She hoped I would be able to help her tribe someday."

"She also told me that Magh is searching for the most powerful of all ingredients for his potions. With it, he would become unstoppable. She called it Osmium. It is the key to making his reign last forever. If Magh ever finds it, no one in MarBryn will ever be free again." Her voice trembled on the last words.

Though Miral knew exactly what osmium was, Magh had heard of it only in rumors. The idea of it was so appealing that he was determined to find it and use its properties for his own evil purposes.

"Once, a long time ago, there were unicorns with osmium horns," Alumna said, remembering what the Numen had told her, "but no more. They are all gone now, and there will never be another."

Everyone was quiet as she hung her head in what she hoped they would take as silent contemplation. In truth, Alumna knew things she could not reveal, though she hated deceiving her tribe in such a manner.

After a moment, Imroz broke the silence. "I started collecting potions. . .a little bit here, a little bit there, with instructions from Blue's mother regarding the different properties and strengths of various magical powers."

The imp did not mention it as part of her story to the unicorns, but the bag she hid the potions in was magical, too—a remnant of a vanquished unicorn. No matter how many bottles or packets she placed in the ragbag, it never filled to the brim and it remained light as a feather, but its origin made her conflicted about using such an item, even for a good cause.

Finally, she had acquired many different magical concoctions from Magh's enormous supply. There was so much to choose from, and he never missed those she had pilfered. It broke her heart to know each potion came at the cost of the life of a unicorn, but she could not think about such horrors now.

At least the unicorns whose magic had been used to make these particular potions would be contributing to the survival of the tribe. She might be powerless to stop the sorcerer's evil intent, but she would give her very life to help these remaining unicorns evade the fate of their ancestors. Now, time was of the essence.

Nix felt a tingling in his warning sensors and said, "Thank you for helping us, Imroz. We could not have made it out of the city on our own." Then, to the others, he urged, "We must flee now, or we will have wasted her efforts to help us escape."

"Yes. You've lingered too long," the Ragamoffyn said. Her outstretched hand pointed eastward, "That way lies the Barricad Mountains. If you make it there, you may find safety. But beware. . .Magh's soldiers are in his thrall. They will not stop searching for you."

She placed her hat back on her head, then tipped it respectfully as she turned back toward the city of Kudos.

"Come with us. I will carry you," Silubhra encouraged the little Ragamoffyn.

Imroz stopped and turned back toward the silver-horned unicorn. She was tempted. Never in her wildest dreams had she imagined that she would ever receive such an offer, and it took all of her will to decline.

It would be like a dream to travel with these magnificent creatures, but she was compelled to reject the offer, "I cannot go. I must stay and offer what protection I can to Miral and her mirror."

Nix sprang into action, "We must leave. Now!" He led the way up a hill, away from the outer wall of Kudos. They stopped briefly at the top to look back at the city where they had come so close to meeting their doom.

Imroz was still right where they had left her. Not far beyond the small Ragamoffyn's brave silhouette, soldiers crested the wall.

The unicorn's last sight of Imroz was of her planting a stick into the ground. Instantly a wide wooden barricade sprang up between her and the warriors. It was much taller than the city wall and was tipped with sharpened points like spears.

Imroz dashed away through another cloud of smoke disappearing from sight.

Chapter Twenty-Five

Tea Party Tantrum

A bright, sunny morning broke open the fourth day for the three travelers. Despite the sunshine, a brisk chill filled the air here, so close to the rugged mountain range ahead. The combination of the sun's rays and the cool air felt nice on Girasol's feathers. Below her, she could see the unicorn and stag were enjoying it too. The pair broke into a steady trot that soon turned into a full-fledged gallop.

Flying close to sixty miles per hour, the Firebird was happy for them to pick up the pace, but it did not take long to see that Gaiso's legs were not intended for such extended strides. Even at a sprint, his top speed barely broke forty and the unicorn began to pull away. After a few minutes, Blue took pity on his friend and slowed his pace to an easy canter.

Girasol soared above them, circling back so she could keep them in sight. She had enjoyed the race, and flying fast was something she could do all day, so with another check of her companions, she took off fast again to scout the coming terrain.

After about fifteen minutes, she curled back to check on them, but they were nowhere to be seen. The terrain had become pretty rugged as they neared the Hedron Mountains, so she dipped lower and weaved back and forth, searching for her traveling companions.

The mountains were named for the varied shapes of the surfaces comprising them. Strewn out for miles were three-sided crystalline rhombohedrons and six-sided hexahedrons of hard, shiny marble and slate. Mixed in were seven-sided rough granite heptahedrons and ten-sided sand-stone decahedrons in various stages of decay. In between the peaks were concave polyhedrons, making up valleys of different configurations.

"Maybe they got caught up trying to find a way through," she said aloud, though there was no one around to hear.

She backtracked, covering areas she had already flown over, while hoping their absence was nothing to worry about. To her relief and annoyance, she finally spotted them down in the seven-sided Heptagonos Valley, smack dab in the middle of the mountains.

"I hope they've not been forced to dally among the Hoipolloi!" Girasol flared. That chatty group of two-legged commoners loved to brag to strangers about the metal working gods they served. Of course, the metal-workers were not gods at all, but Heptads, a band of seven giants, each two times seven feet tall.

Each Heptad had seven arms. . .three on each side and one right in the middle of his chest. This strong middle arm held bars of iron upon rock slabs while four huge hammers struck in a continuous braided pattern of ringing strikes. Upper right, lower left, upper left, lower right. Like living machines, they never ceased flattening metal into implements of war.

These giants, along with most other two-leggers in MarBryn, were in Magh's thrall. They had no choice. The sorcerer bid them to create weapons for his warriors and minions, and they had to obey.

By nature, the Heptads were gentle beings, preferring to use their skills for peaceful purposes like the construction of farming implements or hunting tools, but Magh had bound them by magic, so now, they forever forged weapons of war for the evil mage.

The Heptads and the Hoipolloi had a symbiotic relationship. The enslaved giants endlessly clanked and banged rock and metal, while the Hoipolloi gathered and catalogued the weapons the Heptads crafted until they could be distributed throughout MarBryn. The Hoipolloi took pride in keeping the Heptads fed and well, and relished their trusted role in Magh's regime.

Blue and Gaiso were not among the Hoipolloi, though. The duo had somehow wandered through a narrow path into a small box-shaped canyon, where they seemed to be in pleasant conversation with something which looked like a cross between a giant penguin and a dragon.

Standing on two webbed feet, the furry creature had two tiny flipper wings and was at least fifteen feet long from the top of its black head to the tip of its feathered dragon tail. It had the face of a happy dragon adorned with a comical penguin's beak.

"What in the heck?" Girasol asked aloud as she spiraled down for a better view. *A Pendragon?* But they were *extinct!* She flew down, landing beside them.

The Pendragon greeted her, "Welcome to the land of eternal spring!"

"Spring? More like eternal winter!" Girasol pantomimed an exaggerated shiver. "It is freezing in this canyon."

Something was out of whack in this place. No plants grew. No flowers bloomed. And it was unnaturally cold, even for this altitude.

"My name is Gwyn," the Pendragon said. Plopping down on her smooth white belly, she slid across the slippery stone surface toward Girasol, propelling herself forward with her webbed feet. "Never thought I'd see another Pendragon again," she babbled happily, eyeing the Firebird with onyx eyes.

Everyone turned to look back the way Girasol had come. No other Pendragons had appeared, so they were all confused.

"She thinks I'm a Pendragon," the Firebird whispered to Blue.

"She's pretty big. Maybe we should just play along," Blue cautioned.

The Pendragon gestured with a flipper, "Aren't these the loveliest flowers you've ever seen?" She bent to sniff a rock. "*Mmm, jasmine, my favorite.*"

Blue and Gaiso exchanged glances. The Firebird made circling motions at the side of her head with a wing-tip.

"I don't really want to stray from our course to Muzika Wood," Blue said, "but maybe we should follow her for a while to see if there's anything we can do to help her."

"There's definitely something bonkers about her. Imagine, sniffing a rock and thinking it smells like a flower."

"Why is it so cold in this canyon?" Gaiso wondered.

"She thinks it's springtime," Girasol reminded them.

"She's going our way, anyway. Let's keep an eye on her to make sure she's okay," Blue urged. "If she seems to be alright after an hour or so, we'll just pass on through."

It was Blue's quest, so Girasol said nothing even though she didn't think an hour of walking would fix whatever was wrong with the daft creature.

The Pendragon noticed they were still with her. "I'm so glad you've decided to stay and visit a while! Will you join me for tea?" she asked politely. Without waiting for their response, she kicked herself off and slid away down the path.

The frozen ground was so slippery, even Blue had a difficult time grasping for traction, and Gaiso had a terrible go of it, even with the help of his big cloven hooves. He slipped and slid hopelessly on the slick surface. Time after time, he fell flat on his belly with his legs splayed out like a newborn fawn trying to walk for the first time.

The stag soon gave up on trying to walk normally and adapted a skating motion that worked so well, he sailed past the blue unicorn and around the corner, out of sight.

"Whoa!" His shout was followed by a loud thud and an anguished cry of "Oomph!" Girasol and Blue hurried to see what had happened and were met with a funny sight. Gaiso had skated side-long into the Pendragon, and while she seemed unfazed, he struggled to regain his grip on the slippery ice. Oblivious to the stag's struggles, the Pendragon ambled on as he fell yet again.

The deer shot the others a look as he finally managed to stand upright. Once again, the trio followed after Gwyn until they came to a small clearing scattered about with large rocks.

"This is my home," the Pendragon declared, beaming proudly. "What do you think? Have I over decorated?"

"Over decorated what?" Blue wondered, staring at the rocks and boulders.

"No, you have exquisite taste," Gaiso said. "This chair looks very inviting." He plopped himself down, rear-end first. "Ahh ... this is quite comfortable."

"Uh, Gaiso, that's a big boulder, not a chair," Blue said, squinting at his friend.

"Don't be silly. I know the difference between a boulder and a chair," the stag chided.

Blue blinked a few times, then smiled broadly. "Oh, now I see. This place must work like the Halstable. Now, I can see that your home is absolutely beautiful."

"Yes, I never expected to see anything so cozy in these mountains," Gaiso agreed. "It's even warm inside this room!"

"What are you two talking about?" the Firebird whispered to Blue. "There's nothing here but a bunch of boulders, and it's certainly not warm!" She flapped her wings a few time to generate a little more body heat.

The Pendragon handed Blue a fist-sized stone. "One lump or two?" she asked.

"Oh, thank you. Just one, please," he replied and then brought the stone up to his lips, blowing on it.

"You are trying to cool off a frozen rock!" the Firebird yelled.

The blue unicorn looked at her and laughed. "Girasol, you are so funny!" He winked at the Pendragon and said, "Don't mind her. She's always making jokes."

Gwyn set a small rock in front of Gaiso. The stag breathed deeply and said, "Umm. . .black tea. . .with cinnamon and cloves, I believe. . ."

"Yes, it certainly is," she replied, looking quite pleased.

Girasol shook her head. Were her friends playing a game, or did they actually believe Gwyn was serving high tea?

"How do you take yours, dear?" the Pendragon asked.

"Umm. . .none for me, thank you," she answered, thinking about the trouble Blue and Gaiso were in if they were truly having delusions of some kind. Looking straight at the stag, the bird cocked her head to one side a few times, trying to get Gaiso's attention. He refused to notice her. "Gaiso, please tell me you don't see anything here but stones."

He ignored her, while intently trying to eat what he called a crumpet. Little pebbles fell from his mouth as he tried crunching the rock between his strong lower molars and the hard palate of his mouth.

Desperately, Girasol turned to Blue. "Come on, we've got to go! Something's happening to you," she cawed, trying to make him understand the seriousness of the situation.

"If you're just going to be rude, you should go and wait outside." Blue turned back to Gwyn and said, "Some folks simply do not have a taste for the finer things."

"Alright, I'll just go then," she threatened, but neither the unicorn nor stag seemed to mind.

Maybe the loss of her heat would shiver them back to reality.

She flew away and stopped at the edge of the canyon to watch and ponder how exactly the Pendragon had bamboozled the two of them.

Chapter Twenty-Six
Speed And A Pepo Seed

*T*he Firebird hovered at the entrance of the canyon watching the three of them. Blue "sipped" on his second rock and giggled something that sounded like "silly bird" to the Pendragon. They all laughed.

Girasol felt completely powerless, and her feelings stung, but she had no idea how to help. "How can I make them listen?" she demanded of the mountains.

"You can't," came a voice from nowhere and everywhere at the same time. "I have induced hebephrenia in their feeble minds."

"Who are you? And what is heb-phren-what-ever you called it?" Girasol flared, melting some of the ice from the nearby rock faces.

"My, aren't you a hot-head?" the voice chuckled at her display of wrath. "I am Yegwa, the Spirit of False Springtime. I have put your companions and the Pendragon under a spell, which makes them think this is a wondrous place. I've altered the way their senses perceive things. They believe their delusions are reality." The unseen entity let out a peal of laughter at that.

"Let them go," the Firebird demanded. Blue-white sparks spouted from her feathered crown. She could not see the spirit, and was getting more frustrated by the moment.

"Let them go? I wouldn't dream of it," Yegwa said in a voice hungry with anticipation. "It's not often I have this much fun! Their antics will provide me with hours of entertainment. It gets so boring sometimes. You seem to be immune to my magic, though.

Must be that hot blood of yours."

"What kind of spirit are you? How can you enjoy watching your victims freeze to death?" Girasol asked. "Are you so wicked? Are you an evil sorcerer, like Magh?"

"Magh? Sorcerer? Do tell," Yegwa inquired. "He sounds like someone after my own soulless heart. Is he single?"

"Single? What?!" Girasol blazed. "Never you mind about Magh. I don't have time for this back and forth with you."

"Oh, you are indeed a peppery dish." Yegwa let loose a shrill cackle. "If I had teeth, I'd eat you right up!"

"What about my friends?" the Firebird pursued. She looked around the top of the canyon walls for the source of the disembodied voice.

"You're welcome to keep company with them, if you wish. I don't keep anyone imprisoned, you know," the spirit said, trying to sound sugary sweet. "My guests are quite free to wander about, as you witnessed when you met the Pendragon."

"You're too kind," Girasol thanked her in a voice drenched with sarcasm. The Firebird wanted to keep a close watch on Blue and Gaiso, and now that she knew Gwyn was in the same predicament, she worried about her, as well. She tapped her head with her right wing, trying to figure out a way to save her friends.

Hot blood ... hmmm ... Warmth ... that's it. They need to be warm!

They would freeze to death, if she did not help soon. She remembered the pepo seeds Blue had stashed for her, so she flew down to where the delusional trio were still playing house. They were not even aware of her presence, as she rummaged in the sack slung across Blue's shoulder.

Thank-goodness, Blue brought these along, she thought. *Nothing grows up here!*

She brought one out of the bag and bit into the nutmeg flavored treat. It all depended on how much she exerted herself but under normal conditions, one Pepo seed equated to at least two days of revitalization. As she launched into the air, she hoped this one would be enough to warm up her friends and get them away from this canyon of certain death. She started slowly, flying continually around the oblivious little group, fanning her wings so that warm gusts circulated through the square-shaped space.

"If nothing else, I'll keep them from turning into ice lollys."

As the warm air encouraged the blood to flow through their veins, they noticed her once more.

"Look at that," Blue exclaimed. He pointed at the Firebird with his horn. "It's a flying unicorn!"

"No, it isn't," Gaiso corrected him. "That, Sir Unicorn is a flying doe!"

"You're both mistaken," Gwyn informed them. "It's the Pendragon who was being so rude. Remember? You told her to wait outside."

"They see me!" Girasol exclaimed, relieved that her efforts were working.

Each of them saw her as a different creature, and as they argued with each other so vehemently, Girasol wondered how they could communicate at all. The fact that they could at least see her gave her some hope, and an idea.

Needing to generate more heat, she continued circling her

friends, picking up speed as she flew. She raced around and around inside the canyon with the speed of a peregrine diving to strike its prey.

Strawberry-colored flames licked the thin, melting ice from the frozen mountainsides until they were drier than the surface of the moon. The very walls stretched themselves toward the unaccustomed sunny glow.

Still, she flew faster.

The Firebird now generated a blue-flamed heat rivaling that of a star. Round and round the canyon she spiraled, as if chased by hounds from a netherworld.

The screaming of the Yegwa broke through the trance that held her captives. "This isn't fair! You're ruining my fun!" she yelled in savage irritation.

Her voice echoed throughout the canyon and her screams frightened them all, but Girasol was joyful that her friends had recovered. They stood in the middle of the canyon, dripping with sweat, but had regained their faculties.

"What's going on?" Blue asked, trying to see the Firebird through the glaring light.

"There's no time to answer questions. Follow me. You too, Gwyn," she ordered them. "I'll lead you to safety."

Blue and Gaiso scrambled after her, but the bigger bird hesitated. "Do I know you?" the Pendragon asked, wavering.

Another of Yegwa's terrible screeches echoed.

With the increasing screeching of the enraged Yegwa, Gwyn decided it did not matter whether she knew these creatures or not. She hastily followed Blue and Gaiso down the trail after Girasol.

The Firebird was frantic to find an escape for her charges. Their lives depended on it. If they got cold again, the Yegwa would regain her power over them.

No matter how far they ran, they could still hear her venomous taunts. "There's no escape from Yegwa! Your friends are doomed, Firebird." Her laughter rang obscenely.

Girasol's energy began to wane, but she refused to give up hope. She flew far ahead, seeking an exit from the canyon for her land-bound friends. She never stayed away from them longer than a minute, so that they would not lose too much body heat.

The Firebird was growing tired from over exertion. Never had she flown so fast before, but Yegwa easily kept up, laughing evilly at her attempt to save her friends.

"You will fail!" the evil spirit screeched. Her voice bounced around the canyon walls, and it was this that finally allowed Girasol to see it. . .well, she saw *something*.

A crystalline vapor chased after the group. It shimmered like a mirage in the desert, but this quivering apparition was born from the cold, rather than the heat.

Girasol did not stop to stare at Yegwa. She had to find an exit. She could not give up. All their lives all depended on it.

The Firebird was expending her energy reserves quicker than usual, and there was no time to stop for another Pepo seed. Besides, she had no idea what the effects might be of eating another one so soon. For all she knew, she might completely flame out. She could not chance losing her strength, or her fire. Her friends needed her.

The Yegwa was always right with her, laughing and taunting her failing strength, "You're growing weak. You'll never beat me at my own game. My essence will turn even you icy cold!"

Hearing those words, Girasol faltered, dropping like a stone toward the ground. "No!" she yelled defiantly. Her fall halted just two feet from the icy surface. A mighty surge of her wings pushed her back into the sky.

There, just a little ahead, the tired bird saw a small opening in the rock face. Through it, she could see a wide band of purple land. Her heart lifted. That was the way to freedom!

She had flown over the rainbow-colored Bands of Weita. The colored bands were laid out exactly like a rainbow shining in the sky after a storm. First purple. . .then, blue, green, yellow, orange and red. The bands flowed seamlessly together, with only gentle hills and dells in the distance. Crossing should be easy. She smiled happily. Her energy could not have lasted much longer.

"Here," she called triumphantly. "This is the way to safety!"

The opening proved smaller than she had thought. Blue exited first. The hole was a little wider than his shoulders, so he made it through with room to spare, but Gwyn got stuck half way through. Blue heard her cries for help and turned back. Grasping her flippers with his cloven hooves, he pulled, but could not budge the large Pendragon.

Gaiso immediately positioned his antlers under her tail so that the sharp tines would not puncture the poor chick-drake. Pushing and pulling until the rocks crashed and crumbled, Gwyn finally squeezed through with a grunt and a groan. The hole was now large enough for the stag's antlers to pass through without even touching the sides. He leapt through in a single bound and the three survivors waited anxiously for the Firebird to join them.

Seeing them flee to safety, Yegwa called caustically, "Go that way, if you dare! You won't be any safer from those who dwell within the Bands of Weita than you are with me!" She laughed with harsh malice, and then vaporized back into nothing.

Girasol had soared back and forth before the opening in the side of the mountain, protecting her companions as they escaped the canyon. Now, they were all safe. "We'll take our chances," she said wearily, exiting behind them.

The instant they were all through, the screeching of the Yegwa mercifully ceased, as if an invisible sound barrier had sprung up between them.

Chapter Twenty-Seven
Running The Rainbow

*T*he group did not stop moving even though Girasol was near the extreme limits of her stamina.

Flapping her wings was such an effort that she was forced to take advantage of air currents to hold her up and push her along. A rising thermal would lift her, then, she would soar a few miles, slowly losing altitude until she caught another thermal to help her rise again.

The land-bound group followed the Firebird as she led them through the rainbow colored Bands of Weita. After Yegwa's warning, the travelers were so certain that danger would jump out at them at every turn that they would have run at a full sprint all the way through the Purple Band. Unfortunately, the Pendragon considerably slowed them down, so, their speed was more of a fast waddle.

Despite that, they passed through the Purple Band so quickly that they almost missed hearing the love songs of empurpled passerina. Those chirpy twitterers glittered in the sun as they sang from the branches of purple heart trees. Lavender fields were the last thing they crossed before reaching the Blue Band and despite the hurried rush, the travelers took a moment to savor the peaceful aroma.

The floating blue bills, wild blue foxes and aromatic blue gum trees were just a blur to the trio as they maintained a rapid pace through that part of the Weita. The group began to relax as Yegwa's threats of impending danger failed to come to fruition. To their great relief, they had not been challenged once, so they slowed their pace through the last mile of the Blue Band.

"Everything seems so peaceful," Gwyn remarked. "After Yegwa's warning, I expected horrible things."

"Obviously, she was just angry that we escaped," Blue said.

Gaiso nodded. "She lost her only entertainment."

"You remember anything about that?" Blue asked. He couldn't recall a thing between the time he started seeing paintings on the walls, and waking up to find himself standing in the little box canyon drenched in sweat, hearing the Firebird screeching at them all to RUN!

"Sure. Don't you?" Gaiso seemed confused. "I distinctly remember having tea and crunching on crum. . .no. . .wait. Those were rocks!" He lowered his head to take a nip of knee-high blue grass. "I can't believe I thought those rocks were food." He chewed a moment and said with a laugh, "I hope this grass is actually grass, because it sure feels moist and savory."

"I'm so glad we got away from that monstrous spirit!" Gwyn said. "What if the Firebird had been affected, too? We would have been doomed!"

"We never would have escaped without Girasol's help," Blue agreed.

Gaiso chewed yet more grass and said, "As you thed in the beginning, Bwue ... Girathol hath turned out to be vewy handy to haf awound."

Gaiso's marbly-mouthed speech caused Blue to explode with laughter. It felt good to feel so free again, but they still had a long dangerous journey ahead. "Things seem safe now, but I fear we may have other perils ahead. Girasol will warn us if anything looks awry."

Some stupid words inserted themselves into Blue's memory. "Silly bird," he remembered himself saying. Girasol had not deserved that kind of derision. He hoped his callousness had not hurt her feelings, but either way, he would apologize to her the next time they stopped.

When the group crested the top of a small blue hill, they could see all the way across a narrow swatch of green land dotted with tall stands of skinny olive-colored trees. Beyond that, the organized stripes of the rainbow land's colors popped surreally against the white of the distant mountains.

As the group started down the robin's egg blue slope Gwyn surprised everyone by jumping into the air. She landed on her stomach and slid down the hill, picking up speed as she went. Just before reaching the bottom, she flew up into the air and landed firmly on green soil near a slow-moving emerald stream.

In the extra time it took for Blue and Gaiso to reach the bottom, the Pendragon jumped into the water and washed the dirt away from her belly with a wiggle.

Blue laughed and said, "Wish I could travel like that."

In the Green Band of Weita, the travelers marveled at trilling green finches, which danced like butterflies around nests brimming with brown-spotted green eggs. Warbling Greenlets produced magnificently bold songs from their surprisingly small bodies. Long-legged green shanks, all perched precariously in towering green heart trees.

The group stopped to slake their thirst at a pond that was covered by a green blanket of algae. But this was no problem for the thirsty travelers, since Blue had a good supply of Cuprum's magic pebbles.

Scooping up a cup full, Blue dropped the pebble inside, but having already seen this magic in action, he did not pay close attention as it went about transforming the thick green slime into clear water.

This proved to be a mistake, as the algae reacted violently. Green shoots boiled up out of the cup and latched onto Blue's right eyelid. He recoiled, but the slime did not let go. Focused as he was, he never saw a long string of algae rear up and slap his other eye with the force of a boxer landing a strong right jab.

The struggle ended just as quickly as it had begun as Cuprum's magic won out, but Blue was left with a swollen eye, which quickly turned green, like a bruise on the mend.

Gaiso smirked, but Blue did not find the short-lived battle nearly as funny, so he snapped back, "Don't say a word."

At that, the stag laughed and laughed, finally saying in a very serious voice, "Pond water is known far and wide to be a very tough combatant."

That finally made Blue laugh as well. "If nothing else, it should remind us that we can't be too careful out here. Danger is everywhere."

Upon reaching the Yellow Band, Gwyn finally declared,
"We've got to stop. My head is spinning and all these colors are blending together."

Blue and Gaiso agreed it was worth the risk to take a break.

They had not seen any civilization to speak of in the other rainbow bands, but as far as the eye could see, this yellow ribbon was dotted with groupings of round saffron-yellow houses. Some looked like single occupancy dwellings, while others were large enough for big crowds to gather.

As they made their way along the sand-colored road, Blue

saw a sign on one building that read *Yodler's Yurt.*

A jonquil-shaded two-legger rode shakily by on a two-wheeled contraption. He gave them a strange look and then dashed into the yurt. The sweet scent of corn fritters wafted its way from the open door right into the unicorn's nostrils. Blue's stomach rumbled. "Ummm, that sure smells good," he said. "I wonder if we can get a meal in that place."

"I don't know, Blue," Gaiso said. "That looks like a lot of two-leggers and Magh has spies everywhere. Who knows who's in there."

"Yes," Gwyn noted warily. "And I've heard some two-leggers eat meat."

"Civilized carnivores don't eat other things that speak. . .well, on second thought. . .manticores do but they are not actually civilized," Gaiso explained in a roundabout fashion. "Anyway, there are no manticores here, so I don't think we have to worry about getting eaten."

Just then, a couple of yellow-skinned fellows burst out of the door, laughing and making raucous warbling sounds. Their hands clutched clear mugs of gold liquid, which they slopped about as they toasted each other in some sort of celebration.

The commotion stopped as soon as they spied Blue and his traveling companions

"Oh look! A stag and a unicorn!" The two gents swayed as they stared at the trio. "And a. . .um, I don't know what that one is." He pointed at Gwyn. "But it's kind of cute." He laughed, launching again into the high-pitched quavering. . .maybe it was a song?

"Of the three, I've only ever seen deer before," his lanky ginger-yellow friend exclaimed. "I always thought unicorns were just a myth. And this black and white bird looks like something out of a folklore tale, too. Let's invite them to the party. It will be a hoot!"

So, they did, and Blue accepted for himself and his friends.

"Come on, you two," he cajoled Gwyn and Gaiso. "We're all hungry. We'll only stay long enough to eat and then we'll get right back on the road." It did not take much more encouragement, because the smell of the cooking fires was overwhelmingly tempting.

Girasol had been lazily circling above them on air currents. When Blue looked up to check with her, she waved them to go on in, saying, "Don't worry about me. I'll be up here keeping watch from the sky."

The Yodler's Yurt turned out to be a surprisingly crowded and rowdy establishment. The yellow-skinned two-leggers were all about having a good time. Food and drink flowed freely. Yummy yams and yellow cake were the specialties and everything was free of charge for the distinguished guests. They ate their fill, but the grainy aroma of the yellow beverage smelled fermented to the travelers so they drank nary a drop of the stuff.

Judging from all the applause and singing-along, it appeared the locals really enjoyed a good old spine curdling yodeling accompaniment with their meals. In fact, the noise never seemed to stop. Before long, the bards were making up lyrics on the spot about their legendary visitors.

It was the first time Blue had ever been honored for being born a unicorn. These two-leggers did not know he was an outcast. They made no mention of his plain hide horn, but still Blue knew he did not deserve to be praised in song. He had done nothing worthy of such praise. Nix Nickel-Horn, on the other hand was a real hero. His bravery was known far and wide, and *he* truly deserved a hero's celebration.

All the noise and excitement dialed down to a low murmur as he thought about Nix and the rest of his tribe. He missed Ghel ever so much. It would have been more fun to hear the two-leggers yodel with her at his side. Loneliness washed over him at how much he missed her. He wondered if she missed him, too.

The tribe was probably angry he had left alone. He remembered how insistent Alumna had been that the entire tribe make plans together. A twinge of guilt settled in his stomach, but this was his mission and he alone needed to see it through. He wondered how much time was left before the Moon-Star arrived, but with his belly so full, his mind couldn't quite focus, and his body was tired from the rigors of the day. Still, dark thoughts took hold.

He looked at his friends and could tell weariness had set upon them, too. "I think it's time we head toward the next colored band of land," he suggested to Gaiso, whose head was just beginning to nod down onto his chest.

"Great idea," Gwyn said, jumping up to leave. "This noise is too much."

As they made their farewells and exited the establishment, their hosts cheered them along, but no one followed or tried to stop them.

Seeing the group exit the yurt, Girasol dropped from the sky, flapping her wings to halt her fall just before touching the ground. "Yikes! I couldn't soar high enough to get away from that noise."

"At least you could fly away," Gwyn complained, as they moved on down the road. "For us, it was positively hideous! I worried my eardrums would burst."

Blue said, "At least they were a friendly bunch."

To that, Gaiso replied thoughtfully, "We got lucky. We took a chance going there. It could have been dangerous."

"If it was so awful I don't understand why you stayed all those hours," Girasol said.

"Hours?" Blue and Gaiso said in unison.

"You were in there half the night! I thought I was going to have to rescue you three all over again," the Firebird said.

"I'm just glad they weren't meat eaters," Gwyn chimed in. "I did not want to end up like a big, headless chicken on a pike!"

Blue ignored her irrational fears, because he was now fixated on one of his own.

Hours? They did not have hours to waste away on corn fritters. The Moon-Star was coming and already he had lingered too much along the way.

Chapter Twenty-Eight
The Pendragon's Quest

*T*hey trudged on through the night and into the next day. By dusk, they finally reached the Orange Band of Weita.

Girasol landed on an organ-pipe cactus that happened to be in full flower. The sweet, musky perfume drifting off the tubular white flowers was intoxicating; especially after the adventure she'd had so far. For the first time, since joining Blue and Gaiso, she allowed herself to become completely motionless.

That was all it took to send her into a deep slumber. The faintest orange glow emanated from her, allowing the others to make out several huge longhaired orangutans and bejeweled Oread forest nymphs, who skirted past them before disappearing into their orangewood tree houses.

A couple of the nymphs peeked out a window to get another look at the strangers in their land. Their long, gem-encrusted wings sparkled and reflected the light of the setting sun as they gazed at the unknown visitors. Their faces were a mixture of fearsome seriousness and gentle somberness. They pointed at Blue and the Pendragon and whispered amongst themselves behind their tiny hands.

"I don't like this," Blue said. "They don't look all that happy to see us."

"Don't be so paranoid," Gaiso replied. "We are a long way from Magh's stronghold."

Before anything else could be said, an orangutan lifted up his head so that his neck was fully stretched. He pursed his lips and issued a long, roaring howl. It seemed to echo through the air for miles.

"Do you think they're dangerous?" Gwyn asked the others. Quivers of fear rippled through her feathers.

"Who? The long-armed simians? No," Gaiso told them, "don't worry about them. Rumor is, they're gentle beings. That roar was just a signal that they want to be left alone." He was already lying down, massive head resting on his forelegs.

"Let's hope that is the case, and they aren't sending some signal to Magh," Blue said, trying to suppress a yawn. "I fear there could be spies anywhere but I'm too tired to keep going tonight."

"I'm tired too," the Pendragon admitted. She looked at Girasol, who was snoozing with long, deep breaths. "Poor bird," she noted with a mix of sympathy and gratefulness. "She wore herself out trying to save us from that horrible Yegwa."

"We'd better let her sleep awhile," Blue decided. "She certainly deserves any down time we can give her."

"Yes, let's all get some rest," Gaiso mumbled ... and immediately started snoring.

Blue, tired as he was, remained on edge. He felt like time was working against him. He would let the others sleep a while, but he would stay awake to keep watch, and to make sure they got an early start in the morning.

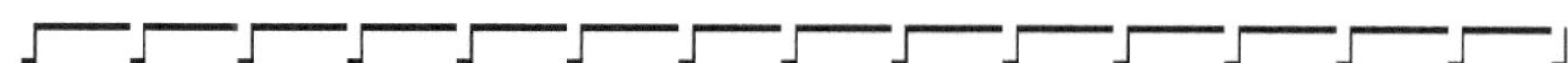

*A*lmost twelve hours later, an unimaginable light lit up the darkness. Blue bolted upright and squinted. "Girasol, could you please dial it down a little bit?"

"Whups!" the Firebird clucked, "Sorry for the abrupt wake

up call." She decreased her power output, stretching one scarlet wing up high over her head and the other down toward her talons. "Was I really asleep?" she yawned. "I haven't done that since I was a young chick."

"Yes, we all slept, even though I didn't mean to. We should get going. I am very anxious to get to the Muzika Woods before the Moon Star arrives and to get out of here before anyone comes looking for us.

"Good idea," Girasol stretched and spread her wings to take flight.

The Pendragon had asked them about their adventure the day before, and they had filled her in on the journey from meeting up in the Guarded Forest to the battle to save the Humongous Elutron. Today, Blue decided they should learn more about her. So, as the land trio set out, he said, "Tell us about your home and your life, Gwyn."

She clucked a few times before saying, "What's to tell? My true home and family are gone. Now I live above the Icy Cold Lake with my adoptive father. Icel, the Ice Blink, is nice, but life there is boring. He spends most of his time communicating with some spirit or other supernatural creature."

"Sounds like Alumna," Blue said.

"Alum who?" Gwyn asked.

"She is the unicorn Oracle. She talks to the Numen through a crystal ball. That is why we are on this journey to meet the Moon Star."

"Ohh, you are that Blue Unicorn," Gwyn said in the most peculiar tone.

Blue and the stag stopped and stared at Gwyn until her

white chest feathers blushed bright red.

"I feel like a complete fool, but my mind hasn't worked quite right since the Yegwa took over. Now that I have gotten some rest, my focus is coming back." She looked to her webbed feet and kicked at a small stone before saying, "Icel sent me to find you, but of course I thought you'd be with a big group of unicorns, not a stag and a Firebird, so between that and the Yegwa's spell, I got mixed up."

Sparkling tears brightened her eyes as she said, "Icel is the only friend I've ever had until you guys. I was dropped from the sky as a baby, abandoned in the courtyard of his home at the top of the Ice Falls in the Smaul Mountains. He is the only parent I've ever known."

"Oh Gwyn, that is awful," Gaiso said.

"When I wasn't much older than a hatchling I asked Icel why there were no other Pendragons in the Smaul Mountains. That's when he told me, there were no more Pendragons left in all of MarBryn."

Icel's gentle voice still filled her memories. *"Your parents didn't abandon you, Gwyn. They left you in my protection to escape Magh. The evil sorcerer snuffed out all the others. You are the only one left."*

"He killed my family too," Blue said. "That is why I must complete this journey. . .to avenge them and to save the remaining unicorns."

"I know." A tear rolled down Gwyn's cheek before she continued. "Icel has protected me always. He feeds me and takes care of things, but he is bound to the mountain. You guys are different. You are taking action to stop Magh and without your help, I would have died under Yegwa's spell, without fulfilling my mission, which was to give you a message, Blue.”

Blue’s ears perked up. “A message? What is it?”

“I don’t know,” the Pendragon said. “Only Icel knows. I was only supposed to find you and bring you to him.”

“Icel?” Girasol flew down and hovered closer to them “You mean, the Ice Blink?”

Blue, the stag, and Gwyn all nodded before the unicorn added, “He is Gwyn’s adoptive father. She says he has a message for me.”

“Why didn’t you say something sooner, Gwyn?” The Firebird asked.

“I’m sorry, Girasol. My memory was totally gone back in Yegwa’s lair. And we’ve moved so quickly since. . .well. . .except for the time in that yurt, and all that yodeling scrambled my brain even more. I think I needed to sleep to let my mind sort itself out.”

“Don’t be mad at her, Girasol,” Blue said. “My brain has been scrambled, too. In fact, now that I’ve remembered a few things, I. . .I want to apologize for being so rude to you back there, when I was under Yegwa’s spell. I feel terrible about calling you a silly bird.”

“It’s okay, Blue,” Girasol assured him. “All is forgiven and forgotten.”

They went a short way in silence before Girasol said, “I met Icel once. I was flying by when a mighty voice called out from the top of Smaul Mountain. An icy gust filled the air as he spoke, but he was a friendly sort, complimenting me on my thermal gliding skills.”

“We need to get back to Icel as quickly as possible,” Gwyn said. “His message must be urgent for him to send me to find you. He’s usually very protective.”

"Yes, of course we should," the Firebird cackled harshly. "There's no reason to stay here gabbling about it. Let's get a move on!"

The four travelers continued across the Weita. The Red Band was the last of the rainbow-colored lands. Passing through, they saw a Ragamoffyn watching them intently from the edge of a red fir forest. The imp's squinting eyes never blinked as they passed, but when Blue looked back over his shoulder only a short distance later, he was surprised to find that the Ragamoffyn was nowhere to be seen.

At mealtime, they stopped long enough to enjoy a restorative snack of red pepper hummus and red lentil soup underneath a rowan tree. After eating, they left the Red Band of Weita, bound for their next destination: Smaul Mountain.

There, they would find the Ice Blink with his mysterious message, and Blue could only hope it did not deliver an icy blast to what was already a thin sheet of hope.

Chapter Twenty-Nine

Between A Rock
And A Hard Place

*T*hanks to Imroz, the unicorn tribe had a small head start, but Magh's experienced and motivated warriors soon dogged their tails. The peaks and valleys of the Barricad Mountains were their normal scouting area, giving them an advantage at every turn.

The soldiers knew every trail and short cut allowing the henchmen to gain on their prey every step of the way.

Time and again, the Metal Horns were forced to change direction, and were only able to maintain distance from their pursuers because running on four legs was naturally faster than the two-leggers could move. However, as the unicorns moved deeper into the mountains, running up the steep trails became nearly impossible.

Magh's troops struggled as well but still they followed using every advantage they could.

By the time the tribe reached a narrow mountain pass, some of the unicorns lagged behind the others. Tinam huffed and puffed to keep up with the rest.

His lungs felt too big for his chest, and he could barely breathe. He quickly fell behind.

I can't go on at this pace. I need to rest ... just for a moment.

He stopped and leaned sideways against a big boulder, trying to catch his breath. He was so winded, he couldn't even call out. All he could do was watch his tribe disappear around the bend.

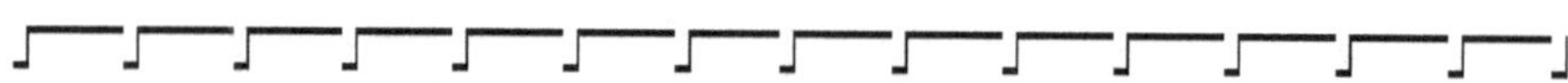

Cuprum realized she could no longer hear the constant trot-a-trot of Tinam's hooves behind her and when she peered back down the narrow mountain trail, her mate was nowhere in sight.

"Everyone, wait!" she called. "Tinam's gone!"

The urgency in her voice stopped the others in their tracks.

Nix ran to her side, stirring the pine-scented air with the tip of his horn. "I don't feel like he's in immediate danger. I'll track back the way we came. The rest of you stay here and catch your breath," Nix said. "I'll find Tinam. He can't have fallen far behind."

There was just enough room on the narrow trail for each unicorn to turn around and face the way they had come. Worried eyes watched Nix as he disappeared around a tall rock face.

Cornum did not do an about-face when the others did. Instead, he said, "I'm not winded. I'm going to scout ahead."

He trotted away before anyone could argue that he should stay.

"Hey, buddy, you ok?" Nix asked as he approached the unicorn chef.

Tinam looked wretched. His normally bright yellow face had taken on a green pallor, and the color had drained from the outer edges of his eyes, making him the same shade of pewter as his packing tins. He looked like he had eaten something spoiled.

"I think so," he answered. "I'm just not used to all this

activity." He grimaced. "I'll be ok in a minute."

Tinam leaned against a huge boulder. As Nix got closer, he noticed that it was not attached to the side of the mountain. A small opening existed between the two rock formations.

"Wonder how I missed this when I passed by," Nix said. Curiosity led him to poke his head into the space. "Well, I'll be…"

"What's that?" Tinam asked.

"Our lucky break," Nix replied. "You stay here while I get the others."

*C*ornum slowed his trot to a soft step. He heard voices up ahead, but they had not heard him. Magh's troops must have taken another short-cut, intending to head off the tribe.

Suddenly, a trio of two-leggers propelled themselves down the mountainside. The first one's feet thudded softly when they hit the dirt, but his sword clunked loudly against his armor.

"Not so loud," his compatriot shushed. "We don't want them turning tail and running back the other way!"

"Don't matter if they do," the first laughed harshly. "We've got them surrounded."

Oh no! Cornum thought. *I've got to warn the others. We must prepare to make a stand.* He spun around, throwing up rocks, pebbles and a cloud of fine dirt as he made a mad dash back to the tribe. Nix returned as Cornum ran up, panting.

"They're coming," the lime-green unicorn blurted between gulps for air. He skidded to a stop, chest heaving. "It's do or die time.

Get ready to fight!"

"Good job, scouting ahead, Cornum," the unicorn defender said. "I knew I could count on you, but we might not need to fight just yet. Everyone, follow me," he ordered.

"But I heard them say they've got us surrounded. We'll run right into them that way, too," Cornum warned.

"Not if we're quick enough!" Nix told him. "Come on. I know a way out. Let's go!"

*A*s Tinam's breathing slowed, the pounding in his ears quieted. He heard a skittering sound and whirled around. Small pebbles skipped and popped their way along little ledges on the mountainside. He looked up to a rope slowly swinging in the breeze. Then, another dropped over the side, followed by even more ropes.

"Two-leggers! They've caught us," he cried, hoping to alert the others. He lunged towards the opening behind the boulder.

Hearing his alarm, the base of Nix's horn began shivering. Real danger surrounded the tribe. He lurched to a stop when he saw Tinam's back-end protruding from between the boulder and the mountainside. The pudgy chef was stuck. The opening was too small for him to squeeze all the way through and with Tinam's body plugging the hole, no one else could make it inside.

"This is it. No escape now," Lauda whispered.

"No, we'll not end this way," Nix said. "Cornum, get up here and help me pull Tinam out."

Working together, they each grasped a back leg of the yellow unicorn and pulled. He was not wedged too tightly so they soon extracted him.

Once Tinam was safely out of the way, Nix ordered everyone to move back. Carefully aiming his nickel-horn at the side of the boulder, he released a blast that had exactly the effect he had hoped. The expanded hole allowed everyone entry and no one needed to be ordered inside.

Nix stood guard, while the others passed through. Something brushed against the side of his neck. It swished past his shoulder and fell to the ground. A rope. With a noose.

One of Magh's henchmen had attempted to lasso himself a unicorn, but his puny attempt had failed.

Nix looked the two-legger over and snorted disdainfully. "Is that all you've got?" he asked.

The two-legger snorted back, drew his sword, and ran at Nix full throttle. So did half a dozen others. Nix took one step backward into the cave opening and grinned. "Not this time fellas," he said, aiming the power of his nickel-horn. An explosive blast shattered the rocks above the entrance to the cave.

The rocky pile-up tumbled down, rendering the entrance to the cave impassable, at least for the time being.

Nix had stopped the Kudos army on the other side. . .but for how long, was anyone's guess. A thunderous rumbling echoed after the unicorn defender as he followed his friends around a corner only to lose his footing and begin sliding along in a dark, dizzying spiral downward. Below him, he heard the others being pulled by gravity into unknown territory.

Nix had chosen not to mention it, but if there was no way out they were now trapped inside the mountain. Inside what could very well be their eternal graves.

Chapter Thirty
Slip Sliding Away

The narrow, winding shaft wound downward for at least a mile. A film of moisture made the tunnel floor slick and left them with no way to gain a foothold, so one by one the unicorns accepted their fate and descended deeper into the mountain.

Slipping and sliding helplessly to an unknown end, they were incapable of stopping anywhere along the course. At least the passage was smooth and not as dark as it might have been thanks to the veil of golden light Style had given Ghel, and the shooting stars decorating Lauda's mane. These magical ornaments allowed the tribe to see ahead, instead of skidding along in total darkness.

After a number of harrowing turns, drops, and seemingly endless sliding, the ground began to level. The descent became a slow glide until they finally tumbled roughly into each other into a rather large cavern. The ceiling was so high it seemed to reach the inner peak of the mountain.

"Does anyone require medical attention?" Dr. Zinko queried, as he scrambled gracelessly to his hooves. His voice echoed around the cavern walls. "Any scrapes or gashes that need tending?"

Everyone took a few moments to examine each other in the dim light. Luckily, all had survived without serious injury, though some were sore and bruised.

Nix called attention to the fact that everyone looked unbloodied. "I can't believe no one's horn gored anyone on the way down."

"Where are we?" Cuprum practically bleated. Fear infiltrated her tone so that she sounded more like a squealing little lamb than a full-grown unicorn. The sage-green filly turned around in place, making a complete circle.

Here in the dark, it was hard to make out details of any kind, but above them long stalactites menaced from the high ceiling. Their sharp, pointy tips shone with soft, star-like glows.

"How are we ever going to find our way to Muzika Woods now?" Cornum moaned.

All the unicorns felt fearful. The soldiers could come careening down that tunnel at any moment and even if they did not, no one knew how to get out of the caverns. . .or which way to proceed.

They would get nowhere if they could not think calmly so Iown took control of the situation. "Everyone, chirk up now. I have just the thing to set you all to rights."

He approached Lauda first. All the unicorns knew what came next and were happy to receive this gift from the iron-horned unicorn.

The old gray mare bowed her head so the elder male could easily reach her forehead. Iown positioned his horn tip right over the base of her horn and gently pressed it into the soft flesh surrounding Lauda's horn.

Holding the pressure for a few seconds, they both felt a slight pulse as his horn drew the energy inside her to the surface of her skin. This location was where her third eye resided, just under the horn growing there.

Opening the flow of energy to the eye reset her ability to perceive realities she had become blind to.

"This will increase the energy of your life-force," he assured her.

It was true. That little burst of positive energy gave Lauda an increased feeling of well-being and a renewed sense of clarity.

Iown repeated the procedure for the rest of the unicorns, and they all felt more capable of handling their current situation.

After the procedure, Nix's senses were sharper, but he still felt the need to shake his head and flutter his ears to rid them of the swish-swashing sound his body had made, brushing against the walls of the slick tunnel. It seemed as if the sound had been imprinted upon his eardrums.

Inexplicably, as he stepped further into the cavern, the sensation became more intense, like water splashing and rushing through a restricted space. He twitched his ears again, hard.

The sound was water. Actual rushing water!

Beyond that, there was also a sound he could not quite identify—something like a child sobbing, but how could that be?

Nix strained to hear it over other sounds echoing around the cavern. No, whatever was out there sounded like an adult—a blubbering, miserable adult. He called to the others, "Someone is in trouble."

Everyone became quiet and still. They could hear an, "uh-hoomp, uh-haump, uh-hump," followed by a strange whomping noise, like a heavy object being dragged around and set back down. Whoever, or whatever, it was, was between them and the water.

"Maybe someone has a problem that needs ironing out,"

Iown said, swiveling his ears toward the sound. "We'd better see if we can help."

"Do you think that's wise?" Silubhra asked, looking into each of their faces. "We don't have any idea what's down here."

"No matter what it is, we don't have a choice. We must go forward," Nix said. He angled his head to point back the way they had come. "There's no going back, now. We can't climb back up that slippery slide, and even if we could, those soldiers are up there, looking for a way in."

"And we can't go this way either, even if we wanted," Cornum told them, looking over a cliff ledge that no one else had noticed just yet. "It only goes further down."

Dr. Zinko leaned over to see what Cornum meant. "He's right. It's a deep, dark crevasse. And it's no slippery slide, either. That route spells nothing but doom."

Alumna advocated for helping, "If someone is in need, we couldn't live with ourselves if we ignored them."

So, that was that. Nothing to do but proceed toward the sound. . .with caution, of course.

The roar of rushing water filled their ears as they rounded the bend and stepped into another monstrously cavernous place. Not one hundred yards ahead ran a wide strip of wild water, which could only have originated from the Smuthe River. Foamy white tipped waves crashed violently against the rocky shore that bordered both sides.

The roar was deafening here, but it was the realization that somehow, they had to ford these raging waters, that hit the hardest. Unicorns were marginal swimmers at best and this angry river was anything but marginal.

Chapter Thirty-One

A Blubbering Mess

*B*etween the unicorns and the river, about fifty yards distant, they discovered the source of the strange blubbering noises. At first sight, they could not be certain whether the dirty white lump was anything more than a mountain of mushy lard. At least twenty-six feet wide at its base, the blob loomed just as tall, but near the top its shape narrowed almost to a point. The bulging entity gave off a faint, dim light like blue coals on the verge of burning out.

Sensing their approach, the gelatinous goop revolved to face them. Near the top of its pulpy mass, two long antennae, tipped with what looked like eyelashes, swung around searchingly.

All the while, it continued blubbering, "uh-hoomp, uh-haump, uh-hump. Booo-hooo-hooo!" It was crying, all right, but it had no eyes from which tears could fall.

Iown whispered, "It's a Blind Blober. I saw a picture of one in the MarBryn Compendium once, a long time ago. They can't see but their antennae serve as their eyes, ears, and nose, too. See how its lashes are fluttering in a frenzy? We must smell pretty tasty, because I can't imagine a lot of food wanders down this way."

The creature suddenly became rigidly still, and something about its stiff posture set off an alarm within Nix's brain.

"Why is it crying?" Ghel asked, starting toward the creature with the intention of offering comfort. Before anyone could stop her, she took a step, slipped, and found herself sliding across the slimy, water-sprayed floor.

The antennae came alive as the creature sensed her approach. Eager to receive her, the Blober yawned, revealing a huge toothless cave of a mouth, ready to catch prey.

With Ghel in danger, Nix rushed forward, intent on placing himself between her and the Blober, but his hooves lost their grip on the slippery floor. In the blink of an eye, Ghel slammed into the nickel-horned unicorn, causing him to disappear all the way up to his flailing back legs into the gaping black hole.

Nix willed his horn to blast an exit through the Blober. A mighty discharge flared forcefully from his horn-tip, but by the time it travelled a few inches into the blubbery goo, it fizzled away into nothing.

He tried again. Same effect.

Fear took hold of Nix and climbed across his hind quarters and up to his shoulders like creepy spidery legs dancing across his hide. His heart beat faster than normal as impending doom made itself known. He had to get out fast or he would perish.

Inside the translucent creature, Nix thrashed violently. He tried to stab his way out, but the viscous nature of the Blober made that impossible. There was no breathable air inside the thing's gut, and gripped tightly, Nix felt his own lungs being squeezed. Weak from exertion, and lack of oxygen, Nix fought hard to stay conscious.

The Blind Blober did not seem to notice any of Nix's efforts. No longer crying, it made happy, cooing *um-mm, um-mm* sounds.

"Aaieee!" Silubhra cried. "My Nix! We've got to save him before he is eaten alive!"

"It thinks Nix is dinner!" Tinam exclaimed. "Why can't he blast his way out?"

Dr. Zinko worried aloud, "He won't be able to hold his breath much longer."

Cuprum studied the gelatinous monstrosity with a hydroistic eye. "If this is some sort of water spirit, I might be able to use my magic to purify it."

"Please try something. Fast!" Silubhra screamed.

"I hope this works," Cuprum said. The Blober looked to be mainly liquid with some kind of membrane bonding it all together.

Acting on the hypothesis that her water magic might work on it, Cuprum aimed her copper-horn. A bright stream of green light flashed out, connecting with the creature, right between where its eyes should have been.

For an agonizing moment, all the unicorns held their collective breaths, hoping her magic would release Nix.

It did not.

In fact, Cuprum's magic bolstered the Blober. It swelled to an even bigger glob than before and vibrated in what seemed like excited glee.

"Let our friend go, you big dirty marshmallow!" Style bellowed. She charged the fat, swollen lump with her horn, prepared to thrust like a rapier. Plunging it in for the kill, she found herself sinking up to her shoulders in the soft, gooey substance.

Her sharp-pointed horn did not hurt the creature. But now, her entire head was immersed in blubber. The Blober opened its mouth wide, surprised by the attack. It burped, ejecting a giant purple bubble from the gaping orifice.

It rose to the ceiling, like a lighter-than-air balloon escaping from the hand of a small child. Now, two unicorns were stuck in the blubbery mess.

"My magic didn't work," Cuprum cried in disbelief. "What now?"

"I'm not going to let Nix and Style be that blob's dinner," Tinam exclaimed. Thinking fast, he started twirling his horn in a big wide circle, chanting, "Feed the beast. Feed the beast. Bring me what this beast will eat!"

Poof! A huge heap of foodstuffs began piling up in the center of the cavern.

Well, not exactly foodstuffs, more like food waste. The larger the garbage pile grew, the greater the stench became. Reeking of fetid meat, soured milk, and oozy farts the mound of stench contained random fish heads and the entrails of who knew what poor creatures.

Whatever it contained, the horrendous aroma caught the Blober's attention. It turned toward that odiferous delicacy in a frenzy of blubbering noises and jiggling movements.

The blue glow inside its gelatinous body excited into a bright cherry red as it wrenched itself away from Style's embedded head.

Her bubbles were all gone, but she was none the worse for the experience.

Alumna, Dr. Zinko and Cornum ran over to the big squishy thing just as the Blober went for its newly conjured malodorous meal.

As soon as the Blober's mouth opened, they grasped Nix's legs and tail with their cloven hooves and in unison jerked backward with all the might they could muster, falling on their rumps in the process. Like a newborn from the womb, the nickel-horned unicorn popped free from his gummy fate.

The tribe scrambled to their hooves and made their getaway from that messy situation, as quickly as they could—half running—half sliding toward the river.

They made it about twenty yards before they came to a wall, which blocked their path. Turning back was not an option. Though the Blober was happy for now, the tribe did not want to chance another encounter with the gluttonous glob.

That left them out of options. They had no choice but to forge across the river, which passed from view through an opening at the bottom of the wall. One by one, they threw themselves into the swiftly flowing river, leaving behind the contented sounds of the Blind Blober's satisfied *Ummm, ummmm, ummm* sounds.

They were in near complete darkness then, as the cold water completely doused the shooting stars around Lauda's head. Only Ghel's shimmering veil kept them from being totally blind.

Bobbing and flailing, they were swept down-river in a raging current of darkness. After a few harrowing minutes, they burst through the other side of the wall into great gold swaths of light.

Bright sunshine flooded the choppy surface of the river with jeweled luminescence, but still the unicorns struggled to keep their heads above water.

There, just ahead, was definitely a way out. They had to take it. If they stayed in the water much longer, the current would sweep them beyond the exit and the water was bone-chilling, so they needed to escape before hypothermia set in.

Everyone flailed about in the surging river. Aching with cold and exhaustion, each unicorn was dependent on their own capacity to fight the currents. Sheer will-power kept their heads above water.

Battling against the force of the raging river, they somehow managed to reach the golden light-splayed north bank. One by one they dragged themselves wearily upon land.

All except Lauda, who disappeared in a swirling whirlpool of water.

Without a second to spare, Ghel dove in just ahead of the spot where Lauda disappeared and for a heartbeat in time neither of the unicorns was visible.

Then, Ghel's head popped back up. She kicked and flailed her way back toward shore and as she found hold of solid ground the others could see Lauda clinging desperately to the shiny gold veil.

Somehow, against the odds, they had all survived, but cold, wet, and shivering as they were, the Metal Horns all feared what they would next encounter, in this terrible place.

Chapter Thirty-Two
Miral's Shiny Little Secret

After helping the unicorn tribe escape, Imroz raced back to the castle to report to Blue's mother through the mirror.

"I'm so sorry, Miral. I wasn't able to save your son. He wasn't with the tribe." She swiped at the corner of her eye to blot away a tear. "I did assist the tribe in their escape from the city, but Magh's soldiers are still pursuing them and I fear the worst!"

"Do not fear, my child. They are all safe for now," a voice answered from within the magical mirror.

"How dare you!"

Imroz spun around at the sound of Magh's voice to find the sorcerer and his Battalion Commander standing in the doorway. Instinctively, the Ragamoffyn hunkered into a defensive posture, but for the moment, the sorcerer's wrath was fixated on the mirror.

"You've been hiding from me all this time!" Magh spat the words at the mirror. "I should smash your essence into a million shards."

Imroz threw herself in front of the mirror, stretching her arms out protectively. She could not win against Magh and his commander, but she would try her best.

They moved toward her with raised weapons. She was cornered like a cat trapped by a rabid dog in a dark alley, but she refused to back down. Facing the full force of his wrath, she challenged, "No, I won't allow it!"

Magh blinked at her audacity.

"You … won't … allow it?" he seethed.

Imroz swallowed hard. "Miral is too precious. You mustn't destroy her mirror."

Magh grinned sadistically. "Hmmm. Too precious… Perhaps you are right. Now that I know she's in there, that mirror may be of more use to me, than ever before." In a flash, he grabbed Imroz, spinning her around to face the mirror. Holding her arms firmly at her sides, he forced her to peer into Miral's eyes.

The Ragamoffyn and unicorn never broke eye contact, not even as the sorcerer placed a sharp dagger at the little imp's throat, tilting it so that its shiny surface caught the candle light.

"So you're the little Ragamoffyn who caused so much havoc," he growled. "The Battalion Commander told me of the tricks you cast to help the unicorns escape."

Kata, the Lethean Battalion Commander, stood silently by, hand on sword, watching the scene unfold.

The Ragamoffyn tried to twist away, but Magh's grip was too tight. Defiantly, she shouted, "I'd do it again…a thousand times! Anything to impede you from killing off the Metal Horn tribe."

Magh let out a peal of genuine delight at her impertinence. "Impede me, you have…but stop me…Never! Now, what should I do with you? With your natural skill, it seems a shame to end your life but I can't be bothered with the interference of mortal peasants so kill you I must." He pricked the point of the dagger into her neck, causing a small bead of blood to trail down her skin.

"Wait," came the voice from the mirror. "The child can still be of service to you."

"I will never do his bidding!" Imroz spat. "There's nothing he can do to make me." She hated Magh. Her eyes threw daggers at him. If only she could kill with a look.

But magic does not work that way. "Kill me and get it over with," she said without blinking. She would not to give him the satisfaction of seeing her tremble in fear.

"As you wish," Magh said, and increased the pressure on the blade against her neck.

Kata turned her head away. She did not want to witness a murder. Besides, she liked Imroz, and she despised Magh for entrapping most of her Lethean clan with his binding spell. Some. . .more so than others.

The measure of his power varied from one victim to another. The weakest among them were in a nearly zombie-like state. "Yes, master. No, master," were the only words spoken as they mindlessly served his will.

Others felt an intensely irrational urge to please the sorcerer. Like a drug surging through their brains, his voice soothed and manipulated their actions.

As for Kata, it struck like an intense itch she could not scratch, every time she tried to resist his bidding.

She knew this very well, as she had tried many times.

Every effort thus far had been futile.

She had decided long ago that her best option was to be his top warrior, and it did not take long for her to rise in the ranks, but she was not proud of her actions, along the way. She was thankful, at least, that she had never killed a unicorn. And she had managed to keep many Letheans from Magh's worst punishments.

Kata would give anything to save them all from their mental imprisonment, but that task seemed impossible.

A pained cry pulled her out of her reverie. She looked back up to see Magh's wide soulless grin as he dragged the sharp blade slowly down Imroz's long neck toward the high collar of her jacket.

The Lethean yearned to do something, but if the sorcerer meant to kill the Ragamoffyn, nothing would stop him. Just the thought of trying to intervene caused that deep, internal itching in the core of Kata's spine. Magh's magic was too strong and pervasive.

Except for some. . .like Imroz. The Ragamoffyn seemed completely immune. She twisted and turned, trying to fight with Magh as he toyed with her. Cat and mouse. Kata could not help marveling at her spunk.

How is she able to resist? If only I could!

"Stop! There's no need for this violence. I will cooperate but only as long as Imroz lives," the unicorn called out from the mirror.

Magh grinned like a sneaky snake, slowly lowering the knife from Imroz's throat. "You are right. Violence shall not be required. Not at this time, anyway." He turned to Kata. "Search the little thief and strip her of the rest of my property. Then, put her in chains. I'll deal with her later."

He turned back to the mirror with a calculating look and said, "Time to reveal your secrets."

Imroz fought against Kata all the way to the dungeon but said nothing until she was shackled. Then, she looked Kata in the eye and said, "I don't care about my safety, but if something happens to the unicorn in that mirror, Magh will gain even more power. Surely, not even you want that to happen."

Kata started to speak, but looked away when that itch in her spine became more than she could bear. She left the Ragamoffyn there in the cold dungeon while feeling the heat of shame burn somewhere deep down in her soul.

Chapter Thirty-Three
All Hail Icel

Smaul Mountain loomed ahead of Blue and his traveling companions. The prattle between them had dropped off after walking so far and so fast, but as they neared the mountain, the Pendragon got chatty.

Pointing at the mountaintop with her little flipper, she said, "You can barely see it from here, but the Ice Falls are over there near the top of the Smaul Mountains." She swung her entire body around to point to the left. "And see that lake? It is full of living cubes of ice. They are the Cubose. They're produced by my adopted father, the Ice Blink. Icel lives at the top of the falls," Gwyn said proudly.

"Well, I'll be horn-swaggled. I've never seen the likes," Gaiso asserted.

"There are no other creatures like those little Cubose in the whole world!" Gwyn told them.

"Icel sounds like a most unusual fellow," Blue said, impressed by the Ice Blink's ability to create living ice cubes.

When they reached the lake, he looked into the water near the shore and was surprised to see several little Cubose waving hellos. They were friendly, miniscule creatures that emitted a warm glow, despite their icy appearance. As they passed, the group proclaimed in funny little chattering voices, "All hail Icel. . .giver of life and purveyor of intel."

"Look at that!" Blue said and eagerly lifted his leg to wave back.

Gaiso raised his eyes skyward at the idea of the Cubose and at the sight of Blue moving his leg in a waving motion. Unicorns were double jointed, but waving was not something Blue routinely did.

"They certainly seem to love Icel," the stag said, smiling.

"Oh, they do," Gwyn assured them.

Girasol flew closer. A wave of heat trailed behind her, which caused several of the Cubose to immediately melt together, making them produce high-pitched little noises, which might have been screams.

Alarmed at the trouble she had caused, the Firebird kept her distance afterward as the group skirted around the lake. They soon came to the base of the Ice Falls. The group peered up toward the top of it, but they could not make it out due to thick, gray clouds that seemed to be snow-laden.

Thunderous crunching sounds accompanied the delighted yelps of tiny Cubose as they rode the falls for their first and only time into the lake.

The mountain face seemed to be sheer ice. Blue and Gaiso were both pretty good at climbing mountains with footholds, but a steep icy surface was another story. A brisk wind kicked up, adding another risk to the climb. The unicorn and the stag both shivered.

"How are we supposed to get to the top of that?" Blue asked Gwyn in wonderment.

Girasol flew high above her friends to keep the heat produced by her body from melting the icy ground.

Blue looked up and said, "We could ask Girasol to fly up and take a message."

Gwyn nodded her head in acknowledgement before asking, "Girasol, will you please fly up to the top of the falls and let Icel know that I've returned with the blue unicorn?"

Turning to the unicorn and the stag she added, "He will send a transport once he knows we're here."

Girasol saluted with a wing and lifted higher leaving a stream of smoke behind.

In the few minutes that the group waited, they stood shivering in the shade of the mountainside. Blue and Gaiso shuffled from side to side, trying to stay warm. Their hot breath rose, visible in the cold air. They both looked over at Gwyn, who seemed unaffected by the bitterness of the winds. In fact, she stared longingly up the mountain.

"How can you not be at least a little cold?" Blue asked through chattering teeth.

"This is my home. The chill doesn't bother me." She tore her eyes away from the mountain. "It's actually refreshing," she added.

The Firebird returned a few minutes later with the news that the Ice Blink had invited them all to dinner. "He is relieved you've returned, Gwyn. He's really missed you."

The Pendragon allowed a huge grin to spread across her face. "I have missed him, as well as my home."

Girasol continued, "He also said he is looking forward to meeting the blue unicorn."

Blue heard that and replied, "I'm really curious to hear what he has to say. What could be so important that he would risk Gwyn to find us?"

The wall of the mountain began to make a loud, grinding noise as a door slid open. "Enter," a booming voice from an invisible source commanded.

Blue held back. "Is it safe?" he asked, feeling a bit light-headed. Skeptical of receiving a smooth ride to the top of the mountain in the brightly lit chamber, he hesitated with one hoof inside the entrance and the rest of his body well outside. *What if the door slammed shut, never to open again?*

The idea of freezing to death while packed into such a tiny room with the others, like a bunch of sardines in a tin can was not appealing.

Gwyn dismissed his fears. "It will be a quick ride, don't worry." She stepped inside and said, "This magical room will transport us to the top."

Neither Blue nor Gaiso moved.

"Are you coming up or not?" an authoritative voice asked from inside the box. "I've got to close that door down there. Too much warm air is drifting up the shaft."

"I'll fly on up and meet you at the top," the Firebird said. "I wouldn't want to melt that room on the way."

The unicorn and stag stepped into the cube-shaped chamber. The door began sliding shut before Blue's tail cleared the entrance. He jerked it in before the door clamped down on it. He and Gaiso both staggered off-balance as the elevator lurched upward.

"I'm not sure this was a good idea," Blue muttered to Gwyn. She looked perfectly calm but the walls of the small space seemed to close in on him.

"It will be ok, really," she assured him. "I've done this many times, sometimes twice a day!"

At the top of the falls, the moving room came to a jerky halt. Blue stumbled trying to balance himself. Without a sound, the door slid open to a blast of frigid air that cut like a knife. Again, Gwyn did not seem bothered by the cold.

Not too far off in the distance, the soft high-pitched sound of many voices sang in a hypnotic way that made Blue feel strange.

Icy-hard snow crunched underfoot as the three companions stepped out into the glaring white atmosphere. The dark snow clouds they had seen from down at the base of the mountain were now hovering below them and the top of the Ice Falls.

Blue squinted so tightly from the glare that his eyes nearly shut. The light seemed to emanate from an iceberg. Any features it might have were indistinguishable, but the bright glow somehow seemed animated. This had to be the Ice Blink.

To the left of the creature, the splishy sounds of ice splashing into water caught Blue's ear.

Girasol flew over to Blue and Gaiso, dropping a pair of dark eye coverings on the ground for each of them. Here," she told them. "Icel had me get these for you. You'll need them to look at him."

When Blue and Gaiso put on the lenses, the glare immediately dimmed so they could see much clearer. Gwyn did not need such a device, as a yellowish film flickered down over each of her eyes.

Blue watched, open-mouthed, as it started at the top of each eyelid, and slowly trickled down until it securely reached the bottom rim.

She laughed at Blue's confusion. "Extra eyelids ... all

Pendragons have them," she giggled before remembering and correcting herself. *"Had them. . ."* In a more subdued tone, she continued, "Comes in handy, especially around this guy. Works just like those glare reducers you're wearing."

Taking in their surroundings, Blue turned toward the splashing sound. He saw a large pool containing many Cubose. They floated slowly toward a cliff-like ledge until those closest dropped out of sight. It was the first of many waterfalls that emptied into the lake. Blue looked closer at the water and saw it was thick and slushy. He wondered why it was not a complete sheet of ice.

"Hey, Gwyn? If there are so many Cubose in the water, why isn't it frozen solid?" he asked.

"It's because of how fast the Cubose are moving through the water. There are so many of them that it creates a slight heat."

Blue slowly nodded his head. It made sense.

He tried to interpret the words of the song coming from them. It sounded kind of like the little floating ice creatures were singing praises for Icel as they disappeared from view, but he could not quite tell for sure.

Gwynn dropped on her belly and pushed forward with her rear legs. Her body skimmed smoothly across the ice like a sled made for this kind of surface. She slid over to a huge face embedded in the ice on the mountainside. Halting just before she was close enough to kiss him, she cooed, "Icel! It's so good to be home. You can't imagine what it's like out there!"

The big guy blinked. When he did, the entire mountaintop darkened. Within seconds, as he opened his eyes, it was brightly lit again. A single frozen tear had appeared on what could only be called his cheek.

At his change of emotion, the singing changed from voices raised in worshipful praise to subdued sounds of sadness. Whatever his feeling, the voices changed to perfectly compliment his mood.

"I worried I'd never see you again," Icel said in a low, composed manner.

Gwyn offered a huge grin, assuring him, "I never want to leave again. If it weren't for these three, I never would have survived."

At that, the Ice Blink blinked again. When he did, it caused the sunlight to blink out for another moment. The singing stopped each time he blinked. "Then, they have my undying gratitude," he affirmed in a low, mellow tone. "I am glad you found them."

When Blue could see again, Icel was literally beaming with pleasure and gratefulness. The singing swelled in voluminous joy as the whole place flooded with his light.

Despite the light, it remained arctic cold.

The unicorn stamped his hooves to keep warm.

"Truth is, they found me," Gwyn said, glancing shyly at Blue. Noticing his apparent discomfort, she slid across the icy floor to a frosty wall and pushed a button.

A panel slid open, revealing a big stack of colorful fringed blankets. She retrieved one for the unicorn and one for the stag.

Gaiso was pleased with the warm sensation on his back. "Oh! This feels amazing. Thank you, Gwyn."

"Me and Girasol will be fine, but the cold will get to you guys pretty quick," she said while settling a nice warm purple cover on Blue's back. It made him feel snug enough to ask Icel how he could put out so much light and still be so cold.

The Ice Blink explained, "I am able to reflect, rather than absorb the light of the sun. My surface is so cold, living here at the Top of the World as I do, that the sun's rays could never penetrate my outer layers."

He was so cold, in fact, Girasol's heat did not harm him. Blue remembered the little frightened squeals emanating from the ice creatures in the lake when Girasol got too close. Heat could certainly harm them.

As if he was a mind reader, the Ice Blink said, "The Cubose aren't immune to the sun's heat." He paused before asking, "Would you care for some ice milk or flavored ices?"

Blue politely declined. "Ice? I don't think I need anything cold. I'm already freezing."

Gwyn laughed chirpily and said, "These will warm your insides. Come on! Try one. You'll be surprised."

"Warm my insides? Yes, please!" Gaiso declared happily. A panel in the ice wall right next to the stag slid open with a swishing sound. Inside were several frozen treats.

"Help yourself to whatever you wish," Icel offered generously.

Gaiso took out something, which looked like a fruit sorbet on a stick. He sniffed it before he tried it. Inhaling deeply, it did not smell like anything in particular and the cold air entering his nose stung so he cautiously bit into the concoction.

His eyes widened and he exclaimed, "Tastes like steamed cauliflower soup with crispy buckwheat croutons. How can something so cold taste so warm?"

The blue unicorn reached for what looked like frozen chocolate milk. He, too smelled his drink first, but did not detect any scent, so he brought it closer to his nose. A little too close. In fact, so close, that he accidentally dipped his snout into it. Taking a taste, he recognized the flavor of roasted sweet potato soup mixed with brown rice. Warmth spread through him, followed by the sensation of standing in the middle of a large field in the summer with the hot sun beaming down.

Despite his enjoyment of the meal, he guiltily glanced Girasol's way. He could not shake the memory of the Cubose who had been melted earlier. The shrieks reverberated in his head.

It was then that the Firebird admitted to Icel, "Yes, we found out about the frailty of the Cubose the hard way. There was an unfortunate accident." She told Icel the story.

The Ice Blink responded with booming laughter. "Cubose don't have very long life spans," he divulged. "Most of them are here today and gone tomorrow."

Blue said, "That is sad. Why manufacture them if they only live one day?" His belly felt warmer, but it still churned with pity for the short-lived Cubose.

"Manufacture?" the Ice Blink asked and blinked, once again blocking out the sun's reflection from his surface for a fleeting second. "I don't manufacture them. They are merely the rejectamenta of my body. I have no control over their arrival. None what-so-ever. They are in essence, refuse," he said, convulsing so with laughter that it shook the ground.

"You mean like … poooo?" The word was so distasteful that Blue practically had to squeeze it out of his mouth.

The Pendragon tittered at that idea, and the big guy's laughter boomed so loudly this time that cracks could be heard splintering the ice all around them. "Well, not exactly. Call it that if you must, but I assure you the water they are formed from is completely pure after the filtering processes."

"Would anyone care for an iced-cake?" he asked through his mirth.

Gaiso accepted, but the blue unicorn shook his head, declining the offer. He was too interested in the moral dilemma of the Cubose.

"But, listen to them. The way they sing. . .it seems the Cubose think of you as their God." He sighed, trying to find a satisfactory answer to the question which plagued him.

How sad that their God had so little regard for their lives that he could laugh at their demise, he thought morosely.

"Yes, I suppose, they do," Icel agreed. There were sounds of ice cracking as what must have been his lips turned down into a solemn arc.

Blue was relieved the Ice Blink did not find this particular remark amusing.

"After all, it is through me, they have their origins," he acknowledged, as the inner corner of one eye produced a thick liquid. It fell, tracing a tiny furrow down his cheek. It froze before going very far. The singing became doleful after that.

Blue could not take it anymore. He had to ask. "What's with all the singing anyway?"

"They just come out that way," the Ice Blink said. "They only sing until they take the long plunge over the falls into the Icy Cold Lake."

"What happens to them after that? Do they die?" Girasol asked.

"Oh, they don't die. They just melt and mingle with the waters of the Icy Cold Lake," Icel told them, regaining a little of his old humor.

This was even more curious to Blue. "Why doesn't the lake overflow, then?" he asked, astonished at the concept. That seemed the logical result of a continuous supply of water.

"Why, the lake can't overflow," the Ice Blink said, pompously, as if this was something they should know. "Once the water reaches a certain level, it begins to flow out through thousands of channels situated around its upper rim. The excess water flows into underground springs which feed rivers and streams all throughout this great land of ours."

Blue pondered this for a moment. The singing did not make sense to him before, and he was even more perplexed that they would sing even up to the time of their plunge, possibly knowing that they would die. He was beginning to think they continued singing because they knew how much good they did and how their existence was part of a larger one; much bigger than themselves.

Somehow, that thought made the blue unicorn feel better about the fate of the Cubose. Their God had a purpose for them after all. They were there to make sure the land of MarBryn never thirsted.

Nightfall was fast approaching. The yellow glare reflecting off of Icel began to dim, so Blue removed his dark lenses and let his eyes readjust for a couple of seconds.

Icel had grown silent, so the unicorn took a moment to closely study the massive face on the mountainside. It had kind crystalline eyes, but a sharp hooked nose dripping with ice gave him a stern look. A massive beard of icicles cascaded down the lower half of his face, all but obscuring his mouth. Blue wondered if Icel's lips even moved when he spoke.

Just then, the low, ponderous voice of the Ice Blink rolled across Blue's drowsy brain. With a lulling effect, he said. "We'll continue this conversation in the morning. It's time to sleep now."

"Wait!" Blue shouted. "What about the message? The one you sent Gwyn to find me for?"

"Tomorrow," Icel said. "It is a very important message, and one you need to hear, but first, you must sleep."

The thought of arguing quickly became futile. Blue was suddenly bone tired. There was no fighting it. In a blink, he fell fast asleep alongside the snoring stag.

Girasol stayed close to them, to provide the warmth she generated from the constant movement of her wings. Like a hummingbird, she could remain stationary while beating her wings at a tremendous rate.

The blankets Gwyn provided were nice, but if it were not for the Firebird, Blue and Gaiso would surely have frozen to death that night, as there was no place colder than the Top of the World.

Just before morning, Blue dreamed that he and Ghel stood together in a field of flowers watching their colt happily chase a sunbow across a bridge of water sprays. The blue unicorn, flushed with pride and love, nuzzled the beautiful golden mare's neck, promising, "Our son will live in an age of peace." Blue did not want to leave that dream. . .it seemed so real.

All too quickly, dawn broke and Blue's dream lost its realness. In its wake, he felt a sadness unlike any he had felt since the untimely death of his parents. For reasons he could not explain he was grieving a reality that had never been, but still the loss felt no less genuine.

Breakfast with Icel was more cold fare. Even so, the food had the same warming effect it had, the previous day. Blue had been too curious about the fate of the Cubose to think about where the food came from, but now the question dominated his thoughts. After he finished chewing and swallowing a delicious bite of an iced donut, he asked Icel about the phenomena.

"Oh, it's not so complicated," the Ice Blink said. "All I have to do is think of meals that Gwyn enjoys, and the ingredients appear by magic. I use a process of flash-freezing to preserve the meals so they may be enjoyed later."

Blue realized Icel's magic worked in a similar manner to Tinam's tinning procedure. "Oh, are you saying that any food which starts out hot, remains that way even though it is contained in an outer wrapper of ice?"

"You are absolutely correct." Icel beamed at Blue's ability to reason out the concept.

Blue had to admit, "You have a most convenient way of preserving food."

The Ice Blink agreed, then said, "Enough about me. Tell me more about your quest. What do you hope to find in Muzika Woods?"

"I am to meet the Moon Star," Blue replied. A memory of his tribe flashed through his mind. He wondered briefly if they were still safe in the Halstable. He wished Alumna were here. For the first time in his life, the thought occurred to him that she was so much wiser than he was. She had always just irritated him, like some old aunt always telling him what to do. A sensation like guilt lodged in his gut and with it came a realization that he should have taken her more seriously.

Blue bowed his head, feeling a rush of remorse. "I'm supposed to join with the Moon-Star. It's supposed to help me save my tribe. I wish I knew more."

"I can help you there," Icel began carefully. "It's why I sent Gwyn to find you. For eons, this land and I have been connected. I have been here for untold centuries, so I remember when the Moon-Star Spirit first sent unicorns to this world.

Centuries have come and gone, and few things are unchanged since the Numen first transported a tribe of metal-horned unicorns here to MarBryn. There are at least a dozen other species of unicorn on Unimaise, so I have long wondered why the Numen chose only to send the Metal Horns."

Blue became all the more confused when Icel mentioned other breeds of unicorns. His thoughts became a tangled mess. *There are other breeds of unicorns besides the Metal Horns? What can it all mean? Will I find out when I join with the Moon-Star?*

"Ahem. . ." the Ice Blink cleared his frosty throat, bringing Blue's focus back to him. "As I was saying, bringing the metal-horned unicorns here was some sort of experiment by the Numen to see how well your kind would interact in a world of two-leggers."

Blue was astonished. "Experiment? What sort of experiment?" *Unicorns were sent to MarBryn as an experiment?* It all seemed so cold and scientific.

"I believe the initial reasons for bringing your tribe here were to learn from the natives and impart Metal Horn knowledge and magic to them. They were to compile and transcribe their findings into a book. . .*The MarBryn Compendium*. Long ago, a wise zinc-horned ancestor of yours scaled my mountain looking for me, but I remained silent because I did not understand these new creatures and I feared what they might do with the knowledge they gained. They were to return to Unimaise, but the rise of Magh changed everything, as you know and between the dangers and the deaths, the communication and link became severed."

Dumbfounded, Blue asked, "How did Numen send the tribe here in the first place? And why couldn't he just bring everyone back?"

"Your ancestors arrived on MarBryn in the Halstable," Icel told the incredulous unicorn. "It is not only your home, but also a craft capable of traveling through space and time. The tribe was only meant to stay for a few years, but once Magh came into power, they felt partially responsible. Evil tends to rise one way or another, so one cannot say there would be no dark powers here on MarBryn if the Numen had never dispatched a magical sector to come here, but there is no doubt that this particular evil partly originated from unicorns.

So, out of both duty and guilt, the Metal Horns stayed longer than planned. They worked hard to train and protect the two-leggers. . .even at great cost to themselves. There were so many deaths during the wars between the unicorns and the sorcerer, that the remaining members of the tribe lost all knowledge of the interspatial mechanisms of the Halstable. Without that knowledge, they could not return to their ancestral home."

This information overwhelmed the blue unicorn. Icel's words were disturbingly familiar. Alumna had told him some of the same things, but like most of the unicorns, he had ignored her words.

He even remembered her rattling on about a book called *The MarBryn Compendium*, but his focus had always been on getting bigger, stronger, faster. "So, the tribe was abandoned here?" he asked sadly.

"No, you shouldn't think of it that way," Icel assured him. "After the last Pilot died, your tribe was unable to continue using the Halstable for travel. Also, over time, the ability to communicate with the Numen was severely lessened, but he never stopped trying to find a way to get you back home."

"How do you communicate with the Numen?" Blue asked.

"Deep beneath me, in the bowels of the planet, are crystal caves. The crystals act as transmitters for radio waves traveling through space. Large copper deposits in the walls of the caves absorb the waves and reflect them back up here to me. I am able to both send and receive messages from many places."

As he spoke, images magically filled the minds of Blue and his three companions. They all saw giant copper coils towering up through the clear ice walls lining the inner shale rock of the mountain. The pink and green spirals encircled needles of white rose quartz crystals. In the rock of the mountain, veins of gold glimmered reflecting back light from the Ice Blink.

After seeing the images planted in their minds, Blue and the others had no reason not to believe that the Ice Blink spoke the truth.

Icel continued, "The Numen has communicated with me many times over the years. He had hoped I would be able to relay what I'd learned to those of the metal-horned tribe. I have managed to route some of the signals through the crystals beneath me to other signal receivers throughout the land.

There are crystals and metals everywhere below us, and some are directly under the Halstable. Through them, I was able to activate one of the communication devices there, but it was many years before anyone paid attention."

The crystal orb! That must be the communication device, Blue realized with a new sense of clarity. The only one who had ever made an attempt to listen or understand the words and images was Alumna. Without her efforts, he wouldn't even be on this quest.

That thought hit his brain like a splash of cold water.

Blue now understood that Alumna was more important to him and the rest of tribe than he ever imagined. He remembered Alumna's many stories. The others had stopped believing they were prophecies when the one about him had not come true. Now, he wondered if it might, after all.

"The communication signal to the Halstable is not very strong, so I'm afraid the Numen has had great difficulty making his messages clear. And alas, I am unable to move about, as you can see. So most of what I learn stays here with me," Icel finished.

"That's why you sent Gwyn to find us," Gaiso commented.

Icel confirmed and said, "You need to know. . .the Spirit of the Moon-Star has never stopped trying to find a way to return your tribe back to Unimaise. For a long time, there was no reason to fear for your safety. MarBryn was a serene land. Then, unexpectedly, Magh came along and everything changed. . .for unicorns and many other creatures."

At those words, Gwyn cried out, turning to hide a sorrowful tear.

"I'm sorry to broach this painful subject, Gwyn. I know how much it distresses you," Icel lamented. Then, he did the most amazing thing. The entire area vibrated as the Ice Blink extended a limb made from icy light and reached out to pat Gwyn on the back.

The lines on Gwyn's face disappeared as she visibly relaxed from his caring touch. Even still, she took a shattered breath before saying, "Oh, just tell them. They need to know."

Chapter Thirty-Four
The Beginning Of A Pilot,
The End For A Dragon

*B*lue looked from Gwyn to Icel and said, "Tell us what?"

No one replied for the longest while, and Blue felt his heart rate quicken. After all the shocking and confusing things they had already learned, he was half-excited and half-afraid of what would come next.

The cold seemed colder all of a sudden as he waited.

Finally, the Ice Blink said, "It is because of Magh that Gwyn became an orphan and the sole survivor of her tribe. The evil sorcerer introduced the Bugans to Pendragon eggs. He taught them to hunt for him and harvest the eggs while doing all manner of his bidding. The eggs quickly became those gluttonous ovivore's most sought-after delicacy. Bugans voraciously hunted all Pendragons to extinction in their lust for that prized food source."

"Oh, Gwyn. . ." Girasol began but her voice trailed off in despair.

"The Pendragons fought back, but sadly, they were all killed … except Gwyn," Icel finished. "She is the last of her kind."

The companions were stunned.

All gone, except for one, Blue mused. *And my tribe is on its way to becoming extinct, too.*

He and Gwyn eyed each other in a long moment of shared grief.

Icel cut into the fog of sadness that surrounded them. "I'm sure the Numen never imagined the atrocities your tribe would come to suffer. And once the reality became known, it became imperative to discover a way to get the survivors back to Unimaise. You are that way, Blue. Being a direct descendant of the Pilot herd, you are the last hope. Only a natural born Pilot can command the Halstable. You are the last Pilot."

"A Pilot? I don't even know what that means," Blue snorted. His confusion was absolute now.

"You will. . .once you join with the Numen," Icel said simply.

"Can't you just let the Numen know I'm here. Connect us up with the radio?" Blue asked.

"No. The communication window closed yesterday. It won't be open again for two more days, and even if you could talk directly to the Numen, you would need ten lifetimes to learn all you need to learn." The Ice Blink said, "There is a better way, but you will need to use the music of the Nebul orchestra in Muzika Woods to communicate with the Numen in the wake of the Moon-Star, before it drops out of orbit."

"Thank goodness you sent Gwyn to find us," Gaiso said.

Getting to Muzika Woods now took on a new urgency in Blue's mind.

He had to join with the Moon-Star Spirit to find out exactly what was expected of him.

He had to save his tribe from Magh.

He had to learn how to get them back to Unimaise.

"But there's a caveat," the Ice Blink interrupted his thoughts.

"Your entire tribe must be with you when you meet the Numen."

This news hit Blue like a big, jagged chunk of ice-cold granite thudding into his gut. The tribe would not be with him. He had left them behind.

"What happens if they're not?" he heard a tiny voice ask. His own voice. . .sounding as if it came from the other end of a very long tunnel.

"You will die!" Icel said with such booming force that the unicorn's ears hurt from the vibration. The words echoed through Blue's skull and that metaphorical boulder in his belly busted into a thousand tiny shards.

You will die. . .entire tribe. . .

His ears rang and his temples throbbed. It was all too much, the burden too big for a unicorn with no metal and no magic. Blue feared his head and his heart would split wide open from the pressure within. A range of emotions played with his mind—sadness, fear, sheer rage at his own stupidity.

What have I done? I only wanted to save the tribe, but it seems I'm ensuring their doom. What made me think I could do this without them?

Gaiso stared first at Blue and then at Icel before saying, "We haven't come all this way just so he can die. There's got to be a way."

"There is a possibility that all will be well," Icel answered the stag. "I can tell you the tribe is on their way to Muzika Woods as we speak."

"On their way?" Blue was ecstatic. "Then, there's hope!"

I don't have to die. I can merge with the Moon-Star. Ghel and I will be together again.

"Yes, there still is hope. The important thing is that you all make it to the Nebul's within the next two days. That is when the Moon-Star will arrive."

"Thank you, Icel. I have dallied here and all along the way for far too long. I must get to Muzika Woods to join with my tribe so that we can face our destiny together. I fear time has become my enemy."

The Ice Blink said, "You can make it in time for the Moon-Star's arrival, but you have to hurry."

Gaiso finally understood the urgency of the situation. "Blue, now that you know how vital it is for all of your tribe to be together, we should go right away."

"Wait," Icel said. "Gaiso, open that storage unit over there and pull out the silver bag."

The bag was springy to the touch. Gaiso could not imagine its contents.

"Go ahead. Open it," the Ice Blink commanded.

The stag grinned and opened it. When he looked inside, his face fell. It only contained ice cream.

"Something for you to snack on later," Icel told him.

Gaiso was more than a little disappointed. He was hoping their frigorific friend was giving them some magical something that could help them along on the journey.

He had to laugh when Icel said, "Don't worry, it won't melt before you're ready to eat it. That's an insulated bag. It keeps food cold for the longest time.”

Blue told the ice-bound giant. “We thank you for everything.” Then he turned to Gwyn. “Are you coming with us?”

She shook her head. “I would like to, but I literally cannot take the heat. I belong here with Icel. I’m really glad to have met the three of you and I sincerely hope you succeed in your mission, but this has to be the end of the adventure for me.”

“What?” Girasol erupted. “What do you mean, ‘the end’, Gwyn?”

“We thought you were with us for the long haul,” Gaiso emphasized his disappointment with a shake of his big head.

“You’d make a great addition to our team, Gwyn.” Blue told her. “Are you sure you don’t want to continue on to Muzika Woods?”

“I’m sorry, I can’t. I was absolutely wilting in that climate away from Icel. All I could think about was finding my way back to the comforting coldness of the Ice Blink as quickly as possible.”

“We understand.” Gaiso nodded his head in comprehension.

“Yes, this is your home,” Girasol agreed. “It’s where you need to be.”

With that, the three companions set off.

They chose a path through the Smaul Mountains to continue their now southerly course. This seemed a shorter distance than going back around the Icy Cold Lake. They wound their way through the passes, which were sometimes narrow and at other times, surprisingly wide, but at least there was no fear of landslides given the rocks were frozen solid against the icy walls.

If only they could freeze the sands of time before the last grain slipped through the hour-glass.

Chapter Thirty-Five
Lulled To Sleep

*T*he group travelled hard and fast after leaving the top of the world. Sleeping little and pushing themselves forward, they covered a lot of ground. Ahead of schedule, the Firebird guided Blue and Gaiso straight toward the Muzika Woods.

They could sort of make out the tall stand of old-growth trees off in the distance, but if they stared directly at it for more than a second or two the image blurred and shifted like a mirage.

So focused were they on closing the last of the distance that they did not notice the pair of scouts watching them for the longest time.

Blue saw them first, off to their right. "Don't look now," he said to Gaiso. "But we are being watched."

Girasol swooped down and said, "We have company. . .two Lethean soldiers from Magh's army."

"I saw them," Blue added. "Are there more?"

"Not that I can see," the Firebird answered. "But there will be once they report back."

The big stag turned his head this way and that, cracking his neck as he did so. "Then I say we make sure they don't have a chance to report back."

The trio formed a quick battle plan, making careful note of Girasol's knowledge that each scout carried Lethean Longswords.

The Firebird took off first. She lifted into the air and pretended to forge ahead as Blue and Gaiso slowly veered apart. With a screech, Girasol peeled back high and fast to cut off the scouts' retreat, while Blue raced to the left and Gaiso to the right.

With Girasol's speed, they were able to trap the scouts within a big triangle before the Lethean's even knew they'd been spotted. Magh's two warriors tried to flee backward, but a stream of fire from above changed their mind. On two legs, they were no match for Blue or Gaiso's pace, but after a quick appraisal of the situation, they headed mostly toward Blue. No doubt, his single plain hide horn did not seem as menacing as the many sharp points of Gaiso's broad antlers.

They did not know that Blue had been training for years for just such an encounter. He cut off their escape and hit the first one hard with his shoulder, sending him face down into the dirt. Blue whirled back around just as the second scout cleared leather with his longsword. Lethean's were fitted with a sword about the same time they learn to walk, so the scout swung the blade with speed and precision and, with no place to run, advanced on the unicorn.

The Lethean on the ground tried to stand just as the stag reached the scene, but Gaiso quickly stood on his back to render him immobile. "Watch that blade," he said to Blue.

The warning was not lost on Blue. Truth be told, he had been watching the shiny steel sword ever since the Lethean yanked it free from his scabbard.

The two combatants faced each other, slowly circling one another.

"Drop your sword and there will be no bloodshed here today," Blue said.

Something like regret flickered within the scout's eyes, before he said, "If I drop my sword," Magh will cut off my head for letting you escape." And then, he lunged.

Blue reared up on his hind legs and lashed out with both of his front hooves. The sword caught him square in the middle of one of them.

He expected to feel pain, but the blade clanged off his hoof unexpectedly and in that brief second while the metal rang out, he dropped down and brought his hide-covered horn down like a club atop the scouts head. The blow split the man's forehead open and laid him out cold.

"Are you hurt?" Girasol pointed a wing toward Blue's hoof.

He lifted it for inspection. The hide was cleaved and damaged, but there was no blood. It looked like perhaps a piece of the sword had imbedded there, but it was hard to tell given the mangled divot. As he stared, the hide seemed to grow over the deep gash. He started to probe at the wound, but Girasol stopped him.

"Don't touch it. It's not bleeding now, but if you mess with your hoof it might start. And we are too close now to let anything stop us. Let's tie these two up and get them out of sight so they can't summon Magh."

They drug the scouts deeper into the forested area and bound them to trees, using their own britches and a tangle of gourd vines they found nearby. No doubt they would eventually escape, but hopefully not anytime soon. To be safe, they took the two long swords with them.

Blue didn't say anything to the others, but when he inspected the blade that was used against him, he was surprised to find it dinged but intact.

Very odd, given that for one brief instant, he would have sworn he saw a sliver of metal imbedded in his hoof.

There was little time to ponder any of this as they raced toward the mirage they had seen earlier. They reached their destination soon enough, and as the travelers entered the mystic place, the trees grew more substantial, though just around the edges the place still seemed mist-like.

Under the canopy, the leaves responded like wind chimes to the little breezes, which stirred as the trio passed. The gentle wind created a reverberating symphony of zen bells. The occasional, low vibrations of a meditation gong rang out, from an indeterminate distance.

Girasol was so focused on the sounds of tinkling chimes and baritone gongs; she nearly collided with a bird that looked much like a stiff-tailed woodpecker.

"Whoa! Pardon me," Girasol exclaimed, screeching to a halt in mid-air. The last thing she had expected was an in-flight collision with another bird.

"Ho, there," called the other bird. Girasol immediately recognized it as a woodthumper.

"Welcome to Muzika Woods. I've just come to lead you to Bab. It was foretold long ago to the Nebuls who reside here that a blue unicorn would be coming to commune with them on this day, at this appointed hour. . .and here you are!"

Blue's ears perked up at that bit of information. "You knew I was coming? Has the rest of my tribe made it already?" he asked hopefully.

The Firebird and stag exchanged a questioning look, then directed their attention back to the other bird.

"No, you are the first unicorn to visit the Muzika Woods in over a century," the woodthumper said. "The Numen told us you would be coming on this very day, so I have been watching out for your arrival."

"You've been in communication with the Numen?" Blue asked.

"Yes. This prophecy came from the Moon-Star Spirit. I'm Pici. I'm so excited you are finally here! We must find Bab, my harmonizer. She's been waiting for this moment for a long time," the woodthumper told them.

Pici led them into the soft green forest to find the Nebul, Bab. Moving deeper into Muzika Wood, the bright, full soprano timbres, melodious tenors and heavy baritone sounds continued.

Approaching a dwelling, they saw a young, almost translucent nymph playing a pear-shaped instrument with only three-strings. Sawing back and forth lightly with a short bow across the long straight neck of the instrument, she had the appearance of being. . .not quite fully materialized.

"Ah, Pici. my harmonizer," Bab said in a singsong voice, perfectly matched to her music. "I see you've found the blue unicorn."

"What's a harmonizer?" Gaiso asked.

Pici and Bab looked at each other and then the latter said, "When a Nebul reaches their seventh year, they are selected by an animal of Muzika Woods to become their harmonizing partner. The Nebul and the animal bond together for the rest of their lives. The harmonizer pair produces a special blend of music that can never be duplicated by any other duo." The two launched into song to demonstrate.

Pici provided rhythmic beats in flawless compliment to Bab's melodic compositions.

When they finished, Bab spoke once more, "Blue, the Nebuls are connected to both the physical and the spirit world, so we're able to receive messages from the ether. We learned of the prophecy long ago and have been waiting many years to assist you."

Turning to Pici, Bab said, "Please enter the Nebulium Circle to summon the rest of the Nebuls and their harmonizers. They will be happy to know the blue unicorn has at long last arrived."

Promptly, the woodthumper did as Bab bade. He alighted near a long, hollow piece of wood, on the outer edge of a circular space filled with dark, luxuriant grass. The circle was outlined by large, irregularly shaped stones, which seemed to be cut or broken in half. Each exposed a wide cavity lined with brilliant points of quartz in yellow sunstone, orange topaz, white diamond, green jasper and sapphire rose tones.

Propping himself back on his stiff tail, Pici began to tap out a summoning rhythm on the wood with his flat-ended beak. Unlike the Nebuls, their companion animals were more corporeal, their bodies more substantial, so Pici could perform tasks like making tapping sounds with his beak with ease.

Bab looked at Blue and gestured toward the grassy area, saying, "Please move into the center of the Nebulium Circle to await the Moon-Star's arrival."

Remembering the Ice Blink's words, he hesitated. "I think the rest of the tribe is supposed to be here."

The Nebul nodded and said, "I know, but you must trust me. Please, step into the circle to wait."

Blue did trust the Nebul, and if he wanted to save his tribe he had little choice but to take a few chances. As the unicorn moved into the space, a male Nebul named Monken and his howling harmonizer, Houlen, appeared through a break in the hedge surrounding the house they shared with Bab.

Monken turned the crank on the side of his hurda-gurda, which had the tinkling sounds of a music box. The organ grinder's harmonizer was a small monkey, who gently howled along in mild accompaniment to the choppy pan-flute and piccolo pipe sounds coming from the box.

The next Nebul to arrive was a tall, slender female named Sallein. She floated in like a beautiful ghost, plucking on the strings of a psaltery with her fingertips as she approached. The triangular harp-like contraption glided along beside her of its own accord.

Her harmonizer, Cita, was a tiny cat with the body of a spotless cheetah. The cat's most outstanding features were her extremely long legs. She picked at the lower strings of the psaltery with the non-retractable claws of her right front paw, creating a lovely counterpoint bass to Sallien's melody.

One by one, as if on parade, many more Nebuls and their harmonizers arrived. Bab introduced them all to the trio. "Baba, meet the Blue Unicorn," she said to a young male Nebul.

He stopped plucking the strings of his balalaika to wave hello. When he started up again Chirope, a light-gray bat chirped and cooed in accompaniment.

"That's Dari," Bab said, as another female Nebul appeared, blowing lightly through a hollow piece of wood. "Her instrument is a fipple. It is carved from the single branch from a recorder tree." Dari's rock dove companion trilled along in fluting notes.

Lura strummed her lyre as her lyrebird sang a warbling song, and Aeol played his wind harp as a longhaired goat emitted harmonic bleating and baa-ing sounds. In all, at least one hundred Nebuls had come to the Nebulium Circle to help usher in the Moon-Star Spirit.

Once assembled, all of the harmonious duos joined in an elaborate orchestration of otherworldly music in concert with the melodious chiming of the trees of Muzika Wood. It had a transient effect of drifting and floating here and there, touching every part of Blue's brain until the essence of the music moved his spirit right out of his body, leaving him in a dreamlike trance. It felt strangely good.

Then, the hollow spaces in some of the trees began to emit a harmonic droning which sounded like, *didjerry, didjerry, didjerry, didjerry…*

This provided a constant undertone to a kaleidoscope of sounds unlike anything the three questers had ever heard.

This synchronization between the Nebuls, their harmonizers, and the trees combined to induce a symphonic euphoria. The three questers had never heard such a sound.

"Blue, you are now experiencing the rapturous harmonization of the Nebuls and Muzika Wood," Bab sang in a soft soothing tone. "This symphony will spark the arrival of the Moon-Star."

With those words, the music began to lull Blue into a trance. Part of him wanted to fight the flood of calm engulfing him, because the rest of the tribe had not yet arrived.

I'm not ready! The tribe's not here! He wanted to scream, but no words emerged from his mouth.

Bab heard his thoughts and told him in a silent soothing voice that only his mind could hear, *"They will arrive in time."*

He wanted to be awake when the tribe arrived. He wanted to be completely aware of his surroundings, but after speaking with the Ice Blink, he knew his part would be vital to ensure the success of this mission. So, he let go and let the music have its way with him.

The music did not lull Gaiso to sleep this time, although the Ice Blink's voice had. And the Yegwa's magic had affected him and Blue, but not Girasol. The stag was confused by all of this. There had to be some sort of explanation.

With the Yegwa, it seemed to be about body heat and the ability to fight off chill. Maybe the same thing had occurred with Icel. Here, the stag felt like the music vibrated his very antler tips, keeping him on edge. Maybe the hide on Blue's horn dampened those reverberations, because the melody obviously left him subdued.

Gaiso watched as his friend easily succumbed to the hypnotic effects of the music, and even Girasol seemed to be nodding off. Relieved that he was not falling into a trance as well, the stag knew someone should stand guard, so he was glad to remain alert, just in case his fighting skills were needed.

While drifting in a dreamlike state, Girasol heard voices calling to her through the musical veil.

The clear notes of Bab's song finally reached her, "Firebird. . .the unicorn must awaken from his slumber before the Moon-Star arrives. Only a kiss from a unicorn with the purest heart can wake him."

The Nebuls planted an image into the Firebird's mind. As if from high above, she saw the rest of the metal-horned unicorns beside the Icy Cold Lake. One of the unicorns appeared to be enveloped in a shimmering golden veil. The filly beneath that veil must be Blue's mate.

The golden-horned unicorn was the only one who could fit their description. She was kind. She was good. Everyone said she had a heart of gold.

The vision was clear, and it filled the Firebird with hope until she spotted a line of soldiers not far behind the unicorns. With a shriek, Girasol bolted into the sky, breaking free of the musical spell. Before disappearing over the treetops, she called back, "I'll bring Ghel to you, Blue! The Nebuls have shown me where to find her!"

She would go there and she would guide Ghel and the rest of the tribe to Blue. But first, she had to reach the tribe before Magh's soldiers did.

Chapter Thirty-Six

A Clean Slate

Leaving the bone-chilling water of the Smuthe River came as a relief, but the dripping tribe still shivered as they exited the Caulis Caverns. Outside, the sun shone brightly, yet the air possessed a chill so cold that tiny droplets of water and ice condensed into a swirling fog with each shake of their manes.

Style had lost her floating purple bubbles, and to Lauda's relief, there were no longer any pesky shooting stars zipping around her head. Somehow, though, the butterflies fluttering around Silubhra's head had survived, and those danged lemons and limes had managed to stubbornly cling to Cornum's dripping wet mane.

The tribe found themselves in a long, narrow natural chasm with nowhere to go but forward. And forward they went whether they wanted or not, because the very ground beneath their hooves moved them that direction. Slowly at first but then increasing in speed the Metal Horns were carried along through the narrow open-aired crevasse. Short of launching into the sky, there was no way to escape. None of these metal-horned unicorns could fly or jump nearly that high, so as a group, they were propelled forward without moving a muscle.

Long, wiggly projections jutted from the side walls. The things looked suspiciously like tongues, and as the unicorns passed, the appendages began to make grotesque licking motions.

Warm, wet, and slimy, they lapped at the cold and soggy unicorns.

Despite the newfound warmth, the unicorns did not like this

new sensation. They tried to squeeze together in the middle of the passageway to get as far away from the tongues as possible, but there was not room enough to avoid the assault. The slimy, wiggly, gooey ribbons got to them, lapping at their sides, like living things, in long, drawn-out licks.

As soon as they were past one tongue, another took up the action.

The copper-horned unicorn sniffed and declared, "Hey, this smells like scented soap!"

The fast-moving projections were licking the sweet smelling slimy stuff into a thick lavender scented lather on each unicorn. Before long, they were completely covered in the stuff.

"Consarnit," Nix yelled. He rubbed furiously with his right pastern, attempting to wipe soap from his eyes without much luck.

"Botheration!" Dr. Zinko wrinkled his nose to dislodge a bubbly glob. When that did not work, he expelled a forceful breath through his nostrils to get rid of it. Along with the soap came a slimy, ropelike dangle of snotty mucus. Frustrated he, shouted, "Could this possibly get any worse?"

Little nozzles continued spritzing water on them as they moved down the line.

By this time, everyone had warmed up from the constant lapping and the thick soapy lather.

What had initially seemed revolting became surprisingly soothing. Further down the line, sprayed streams of warm water, which cascaded over the group.

"Ach! That's a strong blast," Cornum complained as water shot up his nose. He sneezed dramatically and then shuddered violently.

"Tee-hee, that tickles." Silubhra blushed at a watery gust directed at a sensitive spot at the back of her knee. "What could this be?"

"I don't know," Cornum replied. "But it actually feels pretty good, once you get over the shock of it."

The spraying continued until all the soap had been washed away from each and every unicorn, leaving their coats shiny and clean.

Up ahead, a frightening growling reverberated through the place.

"What is that? Another monster?" Lauda asked in a shaky voice. The insides of her body shook, as she cringed away from the sound, but there was no way to stop the moving ground from carrying her and the rest of the unicorns toward this new, unknown danger. Lauda's vision blurred over with fright.

"Oh, I hope not," Cuprum replied. Worry sat squarely in the middle of her pupils, a dull glint in her eyes.

The ground carried them around the bend.

The roaring grew louder.

Gusts of warm air blew with hurricane force from holes on either side of the crevasse.

The wind was so strong it blew their manes and tails dry as they passed through the crevasse. The force blew all of Silubhra's butterflies up into the air and off into the sky.

"Phew," Lauda sighed, feeling her heartbeat return to normal.

At the same time, more projections rubbed at their coats. Not so much tongue–like this time, but soft and fluffy. The unicorns tittered and giggled as the makeshift towels ruffled their manes and scrubbed every hair. The group was completely disheveled by the time they were ejected into an open area at the end of their little journey.

They arrived clean, warm, and dry.

"Oh, my," Lauda exclaimed, looking at Style with wide open eyes. The steel-horned unicorn was a mess, and it appeared she had no idea how tousled and unkempt she looked. The purple unicorn looked especially comical because it was unusual to see her looking less than perfect. In fact, every hair was out of place, a rare occurrence indeed.

Style seemed completely oblivious to her new mane 'do. She rolled her eyes exaggeratedly. "I want one of those for the Groomane Salon," she exclaimed with delight. "I could call it the Lickety Split!"

"Great name," Cuprum agreed. "But I can't imagine where you'd get one. It would take some powerful magic to conjure up one of these. It was like nothing I've ever seen." Her eyes were bright with awe and wonder as she spoke of the place they had just experienced.

"Too bad it's not closer to the Halstable. I'd use it every day," Silubhra laughed.

"I haven't felt this rejuvenated in years." Alumna announced, taking a moment to adjust her oracle hat. It had come askew with all the windy blasts. Once situated, it balanced on her head like a yogi on a mountaintop.

"*Blatt, Bleep, Bloop,*" grumbled Cornum, who shook his mussed up mane-do. He was really tired, and those unwanted citrus fruits seemed extra heavy. "I'm thirsty."

"Stop, Cornum. Let me help you with that," Style offered gently. She used her steel horn to magically remove all of the lemons and limes and smiled at the brass-horned unicorn.

He grinned back, barely containing himself. "Oh! Thank you, Style," the surprised Cornum rejoiced. "The weight of those things has been giving me a terrible headache. I'm so glad to be free of them. My head feels lighter than air, now." He lifted his head skyward and raised up on his back legs as if he were about to float away. With the load removed, he felt like he could take to the sky. Instead, he blew a note so sweet and pure that it filled the air with the spirit of love.

Style smiled again, happy to see a genuine smile spreading all over his face. It was the first one she had seen in quite a while. "I am sorry I made you wear them so long," she said in a small voice, but still smiling. She really did feel bad about it. She should have done something before now, to reduce his burden.

She remembered the other unicorns and took a quick moment to freshen up their manes and tails, but she did not add any extra accessories this time. It just was not realistic. It would be silly to continue on this arduous journey dressed as if they were going to a ball.

She took particular care with Ghel's golden veil, which had surprisingly suffered no harm, making sure it was situated just so across her withers. "Perfect," she whispered, complimenting her own handiwork.

"I'd love a refreshing drink, about now," Lauda said, licking her parched lips with a bone-dry tongue.

"Toot-ta-too!" trilled Silubhra. "There's a lake! We'll get water there."

"Great," Iown replied. "All that warm, dry air has built up quite a thirst in me, too."

They trooped to the water together, each trying to get there before the other, while Style walked slowly behind. Cornum fell back beside her, silently matching his step to hers. He walked alongside her without saying anything until they got close to the lake.

"Aren't you thirsty, Cornum?" the steel-horned unicorn asked her mate.

"Of course," the lime-green unicorn replied.

"Why are you lolly-gagging back here instead of running out front of the others?" she asked.

"I wanted to be close to you," he said, surprising himself and his stable-mate. "You seem different. I like that," he told her before running ahead to catch up to the front of the line.

Style watched him as he moved off, a smile spreading slowly across her face. He seemed different to her, too. *I like that, as well,* she thought as her stress floated away for the first time since the tribe started their quest.

Chapter Thirty-Seven
Of Fire And Ice

The lake gleamed clean and clear as a glass of pure water. A tall, sparkling waterfall splashed noisily into it. What looked like ice cubes floated around everywhere in the lake. Cornum raced over and plunged his muzzle into the cold water to take a giant slurp.

"Hey, watch who you're nosing around, buddy!" a voice shouted.

The lime-green unicorn inhaled sharply sucking water in through his horn. Coughing and spitting he shook his head. When he could breathe again, he faced Silubhra. "Did you say something?" he asked.

"No, I didn't," she replied.

"Not up there, you yahoo," the voice admonished. "Down here!"

The unicorn jerked his head toward the water again. Nothing but a bunch of little ice blocks. He poked his horn in among them and vigorously stirred, causing the ice cubes to spin around in a maelstrom.

"You bumbling hare-brained unicorn!"

Cornum jumped back.

Just then, from high up in the sky, a blazing red fire trail came barreling down toward the group.

The stiff hairs on the back of Nix's neck tingled at their roots. "Danger!" he shouted, sending a swirling shower of magic sparkles aloft.

"It's the Moon-Star! We're too late," cried Lauda dramatically. "We're all going to die." She hid her face from the light.

"I'm not a star!" exclaimed the Firebird, as she landed among them. "It's me, Girasol. You all know me!"

Of course, they did know her. She was a constant sight on the road between the Halstable and the Guarded Forest. Sometimes, she would swoop down for a chat. Other times, she would tip a wing in greeting and fly on.

Jittery from recent dangers, they were not expecting to see her all the way out here at the Icy Cold Lake.

"Oh, Girasol, you gave us quite a fright; flaming down toward us like a comet," Nix exhaled a huge sigh of relief.

"Yes, we've all got Moon-Star on the brain. . .expecting to see it hurtling down upon us at every turn," Iown explained.

Girasol said, "Sorry about that, but this is urgent! I'm here to bring you to Blue!"

"You know where he is?" Ghel asked, frantic to know his whereabouts.

"Yes, he's in the Muzika Woods. The Nebuls have lulled him into a trance so that upon awakening he will be ready to join with the Moon-Star Spirit. You need to get to him right away! Magh's troops are not far behind you. A large force is gathering on the mountain tops behind you."

As she paused for the tribe to absorb the bad news, the beating of her wings blew hot gusts across the water.

"Help! Save us!" several voices melted together. "That bird's going to boil us!"

Sure enough, the heat Girasol generated melted a good number of the little ice cubes. She immediately backed off upon hearing their desperate cries.

"Oh! I'm sorry, Cubose!" Girasol withdrew, startled.

"Cubose?"

Cornum and the rest of the tribe peered closer at the water, confused.

"Talking ice cubes?"

"Better back off some more, hot stuff," cautioned Nix. "Those cubes are melting fast!"

Alumna did a double take as one of the Cubose detached a previously invisible arm from the side of its body and pointed at the other ice cubes. "We, Cubose, are the sole inhabitants of the Icy Cold Lake. We live at the pleasure of the Ice Blink."

"All hail Icel," several voices chattered.

"It's true," Girasol said. "I've recently learned they will all eventually melt and merge with the other waters of MarBryn, so no real damage has been done."

The unicorns did not know anything about the Cubose or Icel, the Ice Blink, but they all felt terrible for the havoc they had wreaked on the little ice creatures.

"We never meant to cause any harm," Iown soothed.

"No harm at all," Silubhra crooned in a calming voice. "Please accept our profound apologies."

"It's alright. We'll forgive you, since you didn't know any better," allowed a bumpy blob of ice having several sets of eyes, noses and mouths all running together. This one blob represented about five ice cubes. "We are just as happy living in groups as we are individually, so all is well."

"If everyone is really okay, then please excuse us, Cubose. We must get to Blue," Ghel urged. "Girasol, please, lead us to him."

The Firebird streaked into the sky.

She looked back to make sure they were following and saw Magh's army crest the nearest of the Barricad mountains. Far ahead of the marching troops, the golden veil waved out behind the golden-horned unicorn as she raced to her mate with no time to spare.

Chapter Thirty-Eight
A Veil Of Love

Ghel and the metal-horned unicorns followed Girasol's smoke trail to Muzika Woods. By the time they arrived, it was nearly dark. The planet's buttery moon looked like an ostrich egg in the night sky. Normally round, tonight a batch of swirling clouds distorted its shape.

Approaching a large crowd, they were greeted by sights and sounds that exceeded their most fantastical imaginings. Even Alumna had never witnessed such wondrous beings in all of her viewings of the crystal orb.

Nebuls and their harmonizers were positioned in musical duos around a large grass circle. Each played a different instrument that seemed like it would never harmoniously compliment the one beside it. But, somehow, it did.

Cornum stared at a stocky Nebul playing a five-foot long alpenhorn. The lower half sat on wheels. As he blew through the mouthpiece, five offspring of a white trumpeter swan continuously stood up, then sat down again rhythmically over what would normally be the finger holes of the instrument. The result filled the air with an amazingly fluid melody, but the brass-horned unicorn whispered to Ghel, "I'm glad I don't have to have swanlings hopping up and down on my horn to make music."

Ghel watched in amazement as two Nebuls worked together with their harmonizing insects. One Nebul pressed the keys on a small keyboard, which were connected to bells suspended inside the wooden framework of a carillon. His harmonizer, produced music with wings joined together by bellows. When the bee-like creature flapped his wings, it produced a series of droning swishing notes. The other played a glocka with two light hammers. Her harmonizer rubbed its front wings together to create a musical accompaniment much like the chirping of a cricket.

There were many more musical duos, too many to count, all adding their unique sounds to the mix. Once all the unicorns finally reached the edge of the circle, all music ceased. Even the tree leaves were still, undisturbed by any breath of wind. The silence became deafening before Bab finally greeted the tribe.

"Welcome to Muzika Woods." She embraced them in her persuasive sing-song voice. "We have been awaiting your arrival," she revealed.

"Thankfully, you're here," Gaiso said, racing over to the tribe. "Blue must be awakened from this spell."

Several Nebuls moved away from the outer ring of the Nebulium Circle so that the unicorns had a clear view. The only occupant of the circle was Blue. The phosphorescent geodes surrounding it were now emitting a soft glow, which fell upon and illuminated his unconscious body.

As everyone watched Blue, the radiant moon began to dim, causing the glowing stones to brighten. The unicorns looked up, afraid.

"He looks too deep into the trance," said Dr. Zinko in alarm. He asked Bab. "Is it alright for me to enter the circle?"

She nodded her permission.

The unicorn doctor infused Blue with restorative power from his zinc-horn and waited for the energy blast to take effect.

Nothing happened.

"It's not working," he declared in hushed tones. He spoke

quietly, but they all heard and began to worry.

Ghel longed to run to Blue's side, but shyness left her hesitant. Instead, she called to him from her place outside the circle, "Blue, please wake up. Blue! Can you hear us? We are all here now."

He did not respond.

Suddenly, as if a dark cloud had settled across its face, the moon changed to a luminous black. From behind it, a black star emerged. The glow surrounding it burned bright as white neon.

Alumna fretted. "If we aren't all in position at the precise time, we will lose everything."

"Try using water to wake him," Cuprum suggested. She removed the canteen from around her neck, reached across the stones, and splashed water onto his face.

He offered no reaction.

"It's no use, he's not waking up!"

Tinam beat on a tin can with his hoof, thinking the noise would break through to Blue. *Clang-ity-clang!*

Blue did not stir

"It's hopeless!" Lauda choked out. "We're doomed. We'll be eaten alive by the manticores. Magh's soldiers will strip us of our horns and hooves! My spirit will forever be trapped in his porridge bowl" The poor old thing had wound herself up with fear and worry and was clearly on the very edge of losing her sanity, altogether.

"The one whose love for Blue is pure of heart," sang Bab. "You must enter the circle. Only you can break the spell ... with a kiss." She motioned to Ghel.

Ghel's face flushed a pearly pink.

She looked to one side, then the other.

All eyes were on her. She asked, "Me?"

When Bab nodded, the golden-horned unicorn stepped hesitantly into the circle. She approached Blue and bent down to softly kiss his cheek. Immediately, her luminous veil moved so that they were both encompassed within its filmy layers.

"Please work. Please, please, please." Cuprum silently mouthed the words repeatedly while pacing back and forth around an arc of the circle.

Nothing changed. Blue remained locked in the trance.

"Oh no, it didn't work." Ghel was dejected. "My kiss wasn't enough." A feeling of complete inadequacy descended upon her. *Maybe my love is not as pure as it should be.*

Her feelings were exacerbated when Lauda exclaimed, "I knew we were doomed."

"Lauda, my dear, please calm down," her mate, Dr. Zinko chided. "It's not good for your heart to stay in such a tizzy."

The worse Ghel felt, the more her shimmering veil shied away from Blue. Its glowing points of light began to dissipate.

Bab addressed the golden unicorn again, "That kiss only indicated friendship, Ghel. Blue must feel your love. Embrace him. Meet his lips with yours."

This time, Ghel understood. She bent over the prone unicorn and caressed his neck with the soft pads of her golden hoof. "I love you, Blue. I need you. We all do," she said earnestly.

She tipped his chin upward so that she could easily reach his muzzle with her own. Then, she placed her lips upon his, breathing vitality back into him with a long, loving kiss.

The kiss was soft and gentle, but not in the way she had imagined it, because it was unrequited. She had wanted her first kiss with him to be romantic and passionate. But maybe saving his life— all their lives—*was* romantic.

This time the veil moved outward, extending to wrap around all of the unicorns, drawing them into the circle with Blue and Ghel. Luminosity returned, glowing with such warmth that everyone in the circle felt hugged by love.

Blue thought he was dreaming again, but something called him to open his eyes. When he did, there was the vision of his love, Ghel, kneeling beside him with a worried look.

He reached out to touch the translucent veil covering her golden mane, saying, "You're here ... but how?"

Ghel reared back slightly when she noticed that a strange glowing light was emanating from inside the plain leathery hide of Blue's horn. All eyes around the Nebulium circle were focused on what was quickly becoming a blindingly bright phenomenon.

Blue saw it, too. More than that, he *felt* it. The light from his horn-tip pulsed in time to that of a falling star careening across the black night sky.

The star was already so close to the ground that he bellowed, "The Moon-Star! It's here!"

Chapter Thirty-Nine

The Joining

A blinding white corona surrounded what loomed like a huge black sun that would soon destroy them all. Falling rapidly from the sky, the object struck fear into those gathered, but before anyone lost their nerve and retreated, the radiant light quickly began to shrink as it neared.

The expansive nimbus masked the true size of the Moon-Star. It also cloaked the nature of the device. The Moon-Star contained the essence of the Numen and it was hurtling through the atmosphere with the speed of a comet.

"Hurry, everyone…it's time!" commanded Alumna. Everything she had hoped, and carefully planned for all these years, was finally coming to pass.

Ghel jumped up to join with the rest of the Tribe of the Metal Horn. The unicorns positioned themselves horn-tip to horn-tip in a perfect, protective ring around Blue. The golden veil rose up of its own accord, swiftly weaving itself in and out between the ribs of the vaguely pyramidal shape formed by the tribe's metal horns. Soon, the cone of horns was completely tented by the magical gold-threaded fabric. Still on the ground in the middle of the circle, Blue's head pointed skyward with his horn tip in the very center of all the others.

The fluorescent black star gathered speed, trailing swirls of silvery star-dust. It plunged toward the center of the Nebulium Circle, straight for the tips of the magical metal-horns.

An energy arc reached out from Ghel's golden horn toward the now marble-sized object in the center of the bright white halo. Gold, a natural connection to the stars, became the catalyst to align the Moon-Star with its destination. The rest of the tribe's horns sent metallic arcs upward.

The closer the entity got to the gold-shrouded horns, the brighter the crystals in the geodes glowed. Crackling sounds emerged from them as electrical charges flew back and forth; connecting the energy of the crystals into a ring of lightning that sparked all around the Nebulium Circle.

Static discharges rose in colorful arcs to meet at the point where the metal-horns were connected. This amplified the power of the horns and focused the energy of the Moon-Star straight toward the blue unicorn's own glowing horn.

Blue felt his body pulled upright, as if a powerful magnet drew his horn forward. His head shot straight up through the shimmering gold cone surrounding the other horns. As his horn joined with the Moon-Star, the cloth flashed like tissue paper treated with nitric acid and disappeared in puffs of white smoke and ash.

The Moon-Star continued to shrink. By the time it touched Blue's horn, it had condensed to the size of a pinpoint.

Instantly, Blue became aware that the Moon-Star was not really a star at all, but a satellite, which held the records of all known unicorn knowledge. The vessel contained the Nomadic Unicorn Magic Extender Network—the N.U.M.E.N.

The data stream of the Numen followed a direct path to the light beneath the leather shielding his plain blue horn. The river of knowledge shredded the old leathery hide with its kinetic energy. Like a heavy rain purging a dusty dry land, the flood of information exposed a gleaming platinum shaft. Rising from its base like a crown, were hundreds of fine hair-like metal and alloy filaments weaving and braiding themselves around the shaft, spiraling up toward the star. The spiral ended at the foundation of the horn's spear tip, which shined a brilliant blue osmium, the strongest of all metals.

The young unicorn had a metal-horn—a shaft comprised of all known metals tipped with shining blue osmium, with a hardness and toughness never before witnessed in any metal or combination of metals

Nix, the nickel-horned unicorn defender exclaimed, "He *did* have a metal-horn! That hide obstructed the signal. No wonder Magh had never detected him."

Ghel gasped as the blue unicorn's mane and tail began to shimmer, taking on every shade of blue imaginable. From celeste to cerulean, and painted like bright skies over dark seas, his hide held all of the awe of nature, and then some. Azure feather streamed down his fetlocks to the tops of his hooves. The colors were sheer artistry.

Before all their eyes, the plain blue unicorn transformed into something new and wonderful.

Muscles began bulging from his shoulders, withers, and haunches. His physique became perfectly gracilian, and his proportions matched those of ancient carved statues. Pure power rolled off him in waves.

The Moon-Star's powers transformed his body with such force that the unicorn reared high on his hind legs.

Developments were also occurring in his mental faculties at the same time the Numen's essence entered his horn. A cavalcade of knowledge marched into his brain, coursing through channels so thirsty that every scrap of information was sucked up instantaneously. All things past and present were revealed to his mind in an explosion of infinite proportions.

His perceptions were amplified. Sight, smell, taste, and

sound each brought forth overwhelming sensations of newness. Concepts and ideas that he had never imagined coalesced into bright spokes leading to circles of sturdy conclusions. Confusion and chaos became insignificant little nits that could not disturb a drop of water. Any erroneous conceptions he had previously harbored were ejected by the sheer force of his new will.

In that instant, the blue unicorn's obligation to guide and protect his tribe fully manifested.

He whinnied and neighed, flinging his head from side to side, as the entire star was drawn into his horn tip, until it had vanished completely. With its disappearance, he proclaimed, "I am Osm, and I now have the tools to save our tribe, once and for all!"

Chapter Forty
The Revelation

*E*very last being gathered around the circle gazed upon the newly transformed unicorn with expressions varying from sheer wonderment, to awed appreciation. Alumna felt those same emotions and then some, because she of course knew more about this moment than any of the others.

A proud smile bloomed over Ghel's face. "I knew it!" she whispered. Joyful tears trickled down her cheeks. "I've always known you were special, even when you thought you were ordinary."

"Oh!" Lauda lead-horn's mouth opened in obvious shock.

Cornum gave Osm a sheepish grin. No doubt, he was thinking about all the teasing and tormenting he had done. No doubt, he now wished he had been kinder.

Alumna's memory flashed back to the night of the blue unicorn's birth. . .to the sorrow in Miral's eyes as she looked at her foal's plain blue hide horn. She remembered the gasps of shock from all the other unicorns of the tribe.

"No metal ... No magic!"

"We're doomed!"

The entire tribe had thought the Numen's prophecy a cruel joke. Or maybe they thought Alumna was a crackpot. Either way they had all been greatly disappointed.

Only Alumna, Blue's parents and a small select group had known the truth.

A truth which had been hidden for two decades now.

The unicorn Oracle lowered her head and the silver tassels on her oracle cap shivered. Tears welled in her eyes as she thought again of Blue's dam. She wished Miral were here to share in this moment of her son's triumph.

Back when the Numen predicted that Blue would save the tribe, he had told her the new foal would be born with an osmium-horn and hooves. And he had told her that the truth must be hidden from everyone—for if Magh discovered a vulnerable newborn unicorn with an osmium-horn, he would have stopped at nothing to gain such powerful magic.

The blue unicorn would not have survived childhood.

She smiled and touched her heart with her right fore-hoof. The emotions dancing inside her were so varied and complex that she was nearly overwhelmed, but she still had one task left.

The time had arrived. She had to tell the tribe the truth— that she had known all along. She nervously cleared her throat to draw attention to herself.

"Now that the truth has been revealed for all to behold," she said, "I can reveal how Osm's metal attributes and magical powers were hidden in the first place."

She turned to look at the heart-shaped charm hanging from the ribbon lying flat against Ghel's chest. Everyone followed the path of her gaze. "It all begins with the ring in the center of that necklace ...

... The Numen had learned via communications with the Ice Blink and the Nebuls that the sorcerer, Magh, was already in search of an osmium-horned unicorn to reach the highest realms of power.

The prophecy made it clear to Miral and her mate, Anion that their foal would be born with such a horn. They were willing to do anything to protect their son, even after the Moon-Star Spirit warned that the cost of hiding osmium from the prying eyes of the world would be very great."

No one said a word so Alumna continued …

"Anion, a platinum-horned unicorn, was of royal blood. On Unimaise, the metal-horned unicorn herds ruled over all of the land. Those from the platinum group were the highest ranked of all. The platinum group consisted of unicorns with Platinum, Ruthenium, Rhodium, Palladium, Iridium and Osmium horns.

Together, these six noble-metal unicorn herds were known as the Platinides. The Platinides shared a bond of loyalty which could not be broken and no Platinide group's bond had ever been stronger than that of Anion, Ruten, Rod, Pally and Iris.

The fight for life on MarBryn had brought them together in ways that no unicorn from Unimaise had ever dreamed. So, when Anion confided his plight to them, they willingly pledged to sacrifice all to save the life of his unborn foal. The five Platinides conspired to craft a special ring to surround Miral's indium horn. It would contain five magical elements—one from each of their horns."

The tribe inched closer to Alumna, hanging on every word of this history lesson.

"The platinum from Anion's horn, was a magical metal of invisibility, used to keep things hidden in plain sight. Anion's metal would keep his osmium-horned foal safe from searching eyes.

The strong metal of Ruten's Ruthenium horn provided defensive strength. Unicorns with Ruthenium horns rarely fought physical battles. They simply activated their horns to build magical protections around themselves. They were the hardest for Magh's forces to conquer. Ruten's metal magic would build a protective force around the new foal's horn and hooves.

Horns of Rhodium enhanced physical capabilities. These tough unicorns stood brave in the face of turmoil. Rod donated this metal from his horn in order to enhance the osmium-horned unicorn's physical strength.

Palladium horns contained incredible blasting power and were feared and respected. A palladium horn could blast through most anything. Pally was such a unicorn. His metal would go into the mixture to protect Miral and Anion's foal."

Alumna stared at the metal-horns gathered around her. She knew that they had all doubted her at one time or another, but now she held their undivided attention. Turns out both she and Blue were being redeemed here today. She continued on ...

"Finally, Iris donated Iridium, a magical metal which provided insights and glimpses into the future. Most times, unicorns with this metal are unable to utilize their magic if not guided through the process. Iridium provided the ability for vision. Iris hoped that, with it, the little osmium-horned unicorn would be able to foresee danger.

Anion had hoped that all of the Platinide-group metals combined with that of his little osmium-horned foal's would create an impenetrable shield. He, Pally, Iris, Rod, and Ruten journeyed to the Heptagonos Valley to appeal to the Heptads to forge a ring from the metals, though of course, they did not reveal the true purpose. The Heptads agreed nonetheless as, in that not too distant past, they were good friends to all unicorns.

Their first task was to retrieve the metals from the Platinide group's horns. Though great care was given to scraping the metals from each horn, the process was not easy. Unfortunately, the deep grooves which were gouged into them weakened the integrity of magic wielded by each unicorn. The loss of so much magic also took a dangerous toll on their bodies' physical strengths. But these Platinides had all sworn their allegiance to Anion. They willingly gave away vital parts of their horn magic in order to protect the first osmium-horned unicorn to be born in over a century.

The magical properties of platinum and the other four metal elements would flow from the ring around Miral's horn into that of her unborn baby's osmium-horn and hooves. The iridescent properties of Miral's horn reflected and intensified the magic of the other metals, making it the perfect conduit. Together, the magical metals would create a protective barrier to keep him safe from Magh and give him strength to protect himself as he grew older. Because of his parents' and his own properties, this combination made Blue the only candidate to lead the Metal Horns back home.

When he was born, the barrier which covered his horn and hooves looked like plain blue hide, but it was so much more. It kept Blue's magic hidden, which also disallowed its use by him. No one, not even Blue was to know that he possessed any metal or had any magical ability."

Alumna paused to let that all sink in and then finished revealing what she knew about Blue's birth.

"There was a strong possibility that Blue, himself would never know. If that were the case, his parents had been willing to risk it in order to protect him from Magh. Everyone else had been sworn to secrecy—a secret which died with all of the participating unicorns, except me. I am the only unicorn who survived to see the clandestine plan come to fruition. Now that Osm is here, Magh will sense his presence." Fear gripped her throat as she spoke these last words.

In the instant that Osm had gained all knowledge of his unicorn ancestors from the Moon-Star Numen, he had also learned the story Alumna had just finished. He also understood the sacrifice not only of his parents, who like most would do whatever was necessary to save their offspring, but also the five Platinides who had weakened their own magic, to protect him.

This selfless act had effectively surrendered their lives to Magh, as without their full magic, the five of them were doomed. Osm did not take any of this lightly. He felt the full weight of all that had led to this point, and he was afraid that, despite all the knowledge handed to him, he would somehow not know what to do with it all.

He had not yet used his power and did not know what he would be capable of when it came time so even he felt some of that fear, but Numen had also shown him many other things that convinced him of a bright future for his tribe.

Because of that, Osm chose to believe he would have what it took to save them from Magh. . .and to pilot the Metal Horns back to their homeland.

All that stood in the way was the army of miscreants marching toward them. . .and Magh.

Chapter Forty-One
A Gathering Of Forces

A stranger in a strange body.

Osm felt a little like that, and a little like the most confident and comfortable being in the universe. His newfound strength, poise, and self-assurance left no room for self-doubt. And yet, he also held memories of the old Blue, and how he'd felt then. Those lifelong memories were impossible to simply forget in one fell moment.

He said nothing about any of this because he didn't feel right burdening the others with his conflicted memories. And even if he did, how would he express such a thing? Who would understand anyway?

Am I supposed to hold every feeling inside now? Am I allowed to have conflicting emotions?

Upon joining with the Moon-Star, he now possessed knowledge of the past, present, and future meant to give him the tools to save the tribe from extinction. That seemed fantastic, but while everyone cheered, Osm somberly wondered, *Am I still me?*

I can still feel the old part of me inside, but it feels stripped away, just like my old blue hide. I feel more powerful and confident than ever, but that's not the Blue I know.

Osm experienced a heaviness in his chest, contrary to the energy he was feeling. He would lead his tribe, but all this new responsibility added to the overwhelming feeling that his life was no longer his own.

The Moon-star had really done something to him.

The prophecy was true.

The unicorns broke into a victorious shout at his transformation, but a lifetime of isolation was hard to forget in the blink of an eye.

Clearly he had been foolish to seclude himself from the tribe, all those years. His newly acquired wisdom, allowed him to see that so many things could have been handled differently. Very differently.

The pains he had felt and all of his loneliness were now crammed into a tiny nook somewhere in the back of his brain, and yet he felt foolish realizing all the mistakes he had made in arriving here. This phenomenon left him feeling detached from his own body. A strange experience, even for one who knew everything, as did Osm.

Osm was now someone, but Blue no longer was anyone. Then again, Osm had been born from Blue, and somehow they were both the same.

Somehow, he understood all of this and even thought that perhaps he should tell one of his fellow unicorns. His wisdom, however, held him back from saying anything. He simply looked around proudly. Proud of what he had become—and of the tribe to which he fully belonged.

"It worked. Our magic has been saved!" Cornum's cheer broke through his thoughts, and his former tormenter blew a celebratory tune to accompany his declaration.

"Not so fast," Osm cautioned. "Listen. Hear that uproar rising from just beyond the forest."

The distant sound of war drums beat in time to the tramping of hundreds, maybe thousands of feet marching in unison.

"This quest is not yet complete," Osm told them. "Magh has found us, and now there will be a reckoning for all of MarBryn."

"I'll scout the area and tell you what I see." Girasol announced as she launched herself into the air.

As the Firebird flew to the edge of Muzika Woods, the others waited impatiently.

They did not have to wait long. Girasol returned quickly which meant Magh's army lurked very near.

Girasol landed with a thud and said, "Magh's entire army is fast approaching. Hordes of two-leggers, and many other creatures as well. I saw Lethean warriors, manticores, the Cussers of Egada, and pretty much all of the other two-legger clans. Magh has a slew of Bugans marching with him, and even *Heptads*!"

The gathering gasped.

"The giants stand separate from the core of the army, but all seven of them are marching in this direction. I could see the land tremble beneath their feet. The Heptad's unsmiling faces are truly terrifying," she added.

Before Magh's enchantment, they had been gentle beings, and friends of the unicorns. They had forged the very ring that had protected Osm, but now they were under the sorcerer's thrall and that made them part of the enemy. No one could predict how the sorcerer might use them, given his magical hold over the giants.

Girasol continued her report. "Magh himself is riding out front of his army on a gigantic manticore. Beside him, is the female Lethean warrior who serves as his battalion commander. She is said to be Magh's fiercest warrior. There was a Ragamoffyn out front as well, but she is bound with rope and looks like she's been beaten."

The tribe of unicorns gasped at this news, and then Silubhra cried, "He must have captured Imroz. We must save her!"

The Metal Horns answered with various affirmations of this statement, but then the heavy sound of war drums arrived on the wind, and everyone went stone silent.

Osm broke the silence by saying, "I shall face Magh's army outside of Muzika Woods. No harm shall come to the Nebuls or this beautiful forest."

"Do not worry about us," Bab assured him. "The moment you step beyond the forest, we will use cloaking spells to keep everyone inside safely hidden from this evil battalion. Go. Do what you must to defend your tribe."

Osm nodded gravely and said, "I will go but not solely to defend us unicorns. I go with the intent of defending all of MarBryn."

"I'm going with you," Nix declared.

Osm began to shake his head, but Nix would not be deterred.

"I have done my best to defend our tribe for years, and I will not stop in this moment of need. You do not need to fight this, or any other battle alone. We need you to lead us, Osm, but trust that I have your back. Now and always."

"Me, too!" called a voice.

"I, as well ..."

"And I ..."

"We are with you!"

The entire tribe would do this together, come what may. This was their battle—their shared destiny.

Osm's heart swelled with pride for the bravery of his tribe. Each member held powerful magic and special abilities and he knew they would use these skills to battle Magh. Despite their fears, no one would stay behind.

Girasol launched herself back into the air, declaring, "You're sure as heck not going to face that army without me."

Gaiso raised his right foreleg, placing his hoof across his chest. "You have my allegiance Sir Unicorn. Horn and antler stand together!"

Their pledges did not surprise Osm. His friends had always had his back. He was delighted to hear all of the support from his tribe and friends, but his focus came to rest on Ghel.

She blinked back a tear, before saying, "If this is the end, we go together, my love."

She looked so fragile and delicate in that moment. The ring, which had tethered that amazing golden veil to her horn had disappeared along with the cloth when his horn connected with the Moon-Star. That veil had bonded the tribe together in such an unexpected way. It unified them—made them strong.

Even still, Osm's first instinct was to try to convince Ghel to stay behind. He did not want her in harm's way. But, he knew she was anything but delicate. No—she possessed a well of strength and like the others, she would demand to do her part to defend the tribe as a matter of honor. So, instead, he said, "Don't worry. I have been training for this day all of my life."

He smiled and gave her an encouraging wink before commanding the others. "All! With me now! To victory!"

The Metal Horns echoed his rallying cry. "To victory!"

Chapter Forty-Two
The Power Of Osmium

*T*hunderous gallops filled the air as the tribe and their valiant companions burst through the western wall of the forest. Once the last of them emerged into the open, the trees faded away behind them, becoming misty and ghostlike, just like the Nebuls themselves. The inhabitants there would be safe.

After all, you can't grasp the mist. It just slips through the fingers, as if it were not even there.

Up ahead, full moonlight silhouetted three figures on a low rise. At the furthest left was the sorcerer, Magh, with the mirror tucked into his belt. Osm could feel the pull of his mother calling to him from the glint of that mirror.

In the center, stood the battalion commander, Kata, formerly of the Lethean Silva. Osm felt this knowledge emanate to him from his mother. The commander held a rope with leather bindings attached to the wrists of Imroz, the Ragamoffyn that Osm understood had saved not only his mother's spirit, but the members of his tribe.

The Ragamoffyn had been forced to her knees. Her head was bowed as if in prayer, but Osm understood she was plotting more than praying. This Ragamoffyn would assist in any way she could, but only if she survived long enough to be freed.

Spread across the wide-open space between where Osm stood and the trio on the hill was a moving mass of various beings, all marching toward Muzika Woods and the Metal Horn Unicorns.

Magh watched the phenomenon of the disappearing woods very closely from his vantage point on the hill. His slanted eyes became slits in their sockets. Even in this vital moment, he thought of it as his next acquisition. Somehow, he would conquer the Muzika Woods.

A good trick, he thought to himself. *Once this battle is won, I will ferret out a way to claim the forest and its inhabitants as my own.*

Kata blinked at the disappearance of the forest. *Where did it go?* She wondered.

She had never seen anything like it. In that moment, with her attention diverted away from Imroz, the little imp took advantage of the distraction. Imroz rushed toward Magh and, with an acrobatic flip, jumped over the manticore, snatching the mirror from the sorcerer's belt as she did so.

Landing with grace, she lifted her bound wrists as high as her small stature would allow. The bright moonlight gleamed off the magical surface, and that touch of moonbeam triggered the most amazing event . . . one that no one could ever have predicted.

All movement stopped.

Even Magh stood stone-still as the visage of Miral filled the air high above the mirror.

Lauda gasped, "It's true! Miral is in that mirror."

The indium-horned unicorn called to her son, "Osm, you know what must be done."

Her voice had taken on an otherworldly quality. She was Miral, but she was also much more. She was a wise spirit. She was a friend. But above all. . .she was a mother. Her eyes shone with pride at the strong unicorn her son had become.

"Mother," Osm replied simply, but it was not simple; none of this was. He bravely fought back the tears struggling to escape from his eyes.

"You cannot fail, son," Miral said. Her eyes, too, held the shimmering glitter, which betrayed unshed tears.

"I will not fail."

The transformed unicorn bowed low beneath his mother's image. His heart ached with both sadness and joy upon seeing her. He would give anything to be with her for one more day. A tear slipped unattended from his eyes. His mother's presence filled him with a certain longing, a longing he fully understood for the first time. . .a longing wrought by the fiend on that low hill, up ahead.

"I will avenge the atrocities Magh inflicted upon you and the other metal-horns," he promised.

He rose, and to everyone's shock, pointed his horn directly at the mirror. A laser-like stream of azure light shot through the air, connecting with the glass and shattering it into a million shards. The pieces of glass cascaded down like well-aimed arrows, finding targets all over the field.

One sliver delicately freed the bonds from Imroz's wrists as smoothly as if it had been guided by a practiced hand.

Scores of the sorcerer's warriors went down from that discharge, but those closest to Imroz were saved from the blast. Miral's image exploded when the mirror did, sending an array of shooting stars from her simulacrum to light up the night. Rather than feeling sadness, a sense of calm descended upon the unicorns and their friends.

Miral's spirit had been released from the accursed mirror. Finally free, her magic could no longer be used for Magh's evil deeds.

When Miral's mirror shattered, she was not the only spirit freed from his domination. Magh's spell over the multitudes also broke. All creatures that had been in his thrall were mercifully unbound.

Chaos erupted as skirmishes broke out between various factions of Magh's army.

The beings who held no quarrel with the unicorns stopped their battle march. With a loud roar, the Heptads stomped away from the evil sorcerer. Hundreds followed the Heptads to the other side of the battlefield, but groups who had spent centuries bickering with each other now resumed their old ways even though they had been spellbound for years or even decades.

Many other creatures simply dropped their weapons and left for home, but the dark and the gruesome lingered still. Bunching up closer to Magh, these foul beasts snarled and sneered, because they thrived on carnage and destruction, and the air here was palpable with the over-whelming anticipation of war.

Chapter Forty-Three

A Promise Kept

The dark beings on Magh's side of the battlefield erupted in a chorus of "Chaaaarge!"

"To victory!" Osm responded.

Cornum blew a battle charge from his brass-horn as the Metal Horns galloped toward the enemy.

Volleys of arrows were unleashed from Magh's archers. The thudding plucks of so many bows letting loose arrows at once caught the lime-green unicorn's attention. He stood frozen as a cluster of sharp arrows gathered in flight. A swarm, climbing upward, the flock of deadly points reached their apex and began a descent aimed straight for the hearts of the unicorns.

The battle would be over before it began. Time seemed to stand still until Cornum heard Osm's sharp command. "Sound the recall signal," he ordered and Cornum did just that.

"Take cover wherever you can!" Osm shouted, and the tribe turned and ran from the approaching onslaught of lethal arrows. A futile stand would not win this battle.

Gaiso shook his antlered head. "I will not run." The ferocity of the stag's spirit held ground even as arrows hurled downward. The projectiles picked up speed as gravity grabbed them and pulled them downward.

Osm looked back to see Gaiso standing under a hail of arrows. He watched, stunned as the deer rapidly shook his antlers back and forth. Twisting his massive rack, he parried the arrows away from his body. Most of the deadly projectiles landed in the tall grass, but a few dozen impaled the dirt. Not a single sharp point touched the mighty stag.

I never thought to do something like that, Osm mused, somewhat embarrassed about his call for retreat. Then, a second hail of sharpened metal rushed skyward from Magh's bowmen. Three times as many rose into the air as the first round.

"Gaiso!" he shouted. "Do not try to fend these off. There are too many! Run!"

Just as the torrent of arrows began to fall, a low droning settled between the bowmen and Osm's battalion. The sound emanated from a troop of Humongas Elutron rising from the tall grass, elytrum wings outspread to deflect the remaining arrows. The sharp projectiles bounced away, harmlessly falling to the ground.

The tough wings of the Humongas Elutron could not be pierced by mere arrows. That required axes and saws.

"Air defense, at your service," Leder stated, his voice softly whirring.

Gaiso addressed the big bug, "Leder, your arrival is most fortuitous."

The other unicorns stopped and turned to hail their saviors.

"We welcome your help." Nix gratefully saluted the beetle. "You've saved our lives from that attack."

"Elutron keep promises," Leder murmured in reply. "Debt repaid?"

Osm bowed his head in thanks, saying, "There was never any debt to be repaid, but thank you for saving us, Leder. Now, lead your swarm away to safety."

The beetles left the battlefield together, flying high over where Muzika Woods should have been.

The blue unicorn pointed his osmium-tipped horn skyward like a wand, painting blue streams of thin contrails above the archers. The streams spread quickly, like a fine mesh net; to snag any newly released arrows. There would be no more assault from that front, but the battle continued to rage.

*O*n the other side of the battlefield, Magh gripped his staff tightly as he contemplated his next move. The staff contained a conglomeration of several entities. The mauve unicorn's potassium horn made up the main shaft and the skull of a youngling manticore capped off the powerful rod.

Forged from the metal hooves of several steel-horned unicorns, the lower half formed a razor sharp sword. The large curved blade was attached with windings made up of woven strands of many colors. Fibers plucked from the tails of many different unicorns had been carefully blended to create the strands. The sword's edge was honed to such razor sharpness, that a single swipe could decapitate any beast, and it had done so many times.

The sorcerer had infused the staff with such powerful magic, that it could literally change the landscape and even the weather when wielded in anger. Now, Magh smiled viciously and aimed this might toward the fleeing Elutron. A sinister tornado coiled down from the dark clouds above.

The twister spun and bounced through the sorcerer's own minions, tossing them about like rag dolls as it churned toward the big, slow-moving bugs.

Seeing what the sorcerer was doing, Cuprum tried to suck the impure energy away from the twister using her water magic. The vortex began to shrink in size, but Magh was more powerful and quickly brought it back to full force.

Exhausted, Cuprum fell to her knees in defeat.

Osm saw her fall and aimed his powerful horn between the big twister and the Elutron. A blue beam streaked up and out, turning the sky from gray to blue-black. The temperature dropped as a fast moving cold front blew high winds back toward the tornado with the full force of a blue norther. In no time, the raging whirlwind was completely unspun to nothing more than a gentle breeze.

Infuriated, Magh stabbed the staff into the ground. A great fissure ripped open across a wide swath of ground. An entire contingent of Bugans tumbled into the recesses of the earth.

Bodies sank deep into the ground as the chasm widened. Fiery sparks erupted from the deep, dark gash in the landscape. The horrific whining of the Bugans filled the air. The painful sound tormented the ears of those on both sides of the battle as the gap lengthened toward the unicorns.

For a moment, Osm froze as he flashed on the memory of a long forgotten dream ... *Dark, scabrous hands pushing ... pushing him down.*

He shook off the memory and turned to see Iown shoot a blast of earth magic from his horn toward the long gorge. The torn land began to close up slowly.

Far too slowly.

Osm threw an ice-blue blast at the ground to help his elder. Working together as a team, they healed the gaping maw before it reached them.

Frustrated that his power had again been disrupted; Magh felt something he had long ago forgotten.

Fear.

Livid at the power this unicorn possessed, he realized he could not be so reckless with his infantry. He was going to need them more than he ever had.

Watching the chaos, the Battalion Commander knew the time to take action had arrived. *Now or never* she thought, steeling herself for the familiar on rush of crawling itch to snake up her spine at each and every treasonous thought. No such itch came this time.

I'm free, she realized with relief and amazement. *The others must surely be, too. Now is the time to win back my clan's freedom.*

She tossed the ragbag of tricks to the imp. "I saved these for you. You are strong. Maybe together, we'll have a chance." She gave Imroz a respectful nod before turning to bring her sword to bear upon the sorcerer himself.

Despite his preoccupations, he saw his own battalion commander swing her blade straight at him.

He blocked Kata's attack despite a moment of confusion. *Her, too? She was my best.* Still much stronger than she was, he suppressed his disappointment and easily forced her back.

Enraged at being double-crossed by the highest level of his command, he struck back with vengeance. She tried to turn and move away, but he sliced the flesh behind her knee with the razor-sharp blade of his staff.

As she fell, he moved in swiftly to slash her neck and remove her head.

But the Ragamoffyn intervened.

Blowing a powdered potion toward the former Battalion Commander, Imroz's breath spun the resulting cloud into a small, dense vortex. Magh watched the Lethean warrior as she was whisked safely away from his descending blade, all in the blink of an eye.

"You will *die* for this!" he screamed, spewing spittle with his vitriolic words. Blinded by rage at the petulant Ragamoffyn, he temporarily forgot about the larger battle at hand. He wanted her to suffer for her many acts of defiance.

He raised the staff, ready to boil the very blood within the Ragamoffyn's veins, but his incantation was cut short when Osm called.

"*Magh!*"

The word thundered across the distance between them.

The sorcerer turned to gaze upon the face of Osm. He would deal with Kata and Imroz at his leisure. They were nothing, and could be easily dismissed, but this unicorn required his full attention.

"Ah, there you are ... the one who has remained hidden all these years ... the one with the osmium horn," Magh exclaimed with sinister delight. "What a fine specimen to add to my collection."

"I am not a specimen. And I am not yours to collect," Osm challenged in a voice that echoed throughout the hills. "The lives of others are not yours to steal. It's time for you to pay for your high crimes against my tribe, and all inhabitants of MarBryn."

I will take that horn!

It's so close.

I can nearly touch it.

It's as good as mine.

Magh was overcome with a perverse glee as all of these thoughts paraded through his mind. A rush of power that he did not yet possess, but wanted so badly. He had to have it for his own.

"It is *you*, who will pay," Magh laughed disdainfully, "...with your life. Your horn *will* be mine," he shrieked.

"Never!" Osm shouted, rearing up to his full height in anticipation of this ultimate battle against this unnatural threat. Behind him, his trusty companions readied themselves for an onslaught of evil from all of MarBryn's darker elements. Two prides of manticore, each containing three powerful males, moved across the field to flank the sorcerer. With his staff, Magh signaled them to advance upon the tasty unicorns.

The lust for blood and power and magic made them all insane for carnage.

Chapter Forty-Four
Unicorn Warriors

*T*he tribe readily dove into battle, but as the conflict escalated Nix worried about the others. He did not question their bravery or willingness to fight against evil, but except for the blunt force damage their horns could inflict, most of them were not really equipped to attack or defend.

Nix used the power of his nickel-horn to phase from one to the next, doing his best to keep everyone safe, but the war quickly fell into pandemonium with attacks coming from all sides.

Using his magic to leap from one place on the battlefield to another, he began to tire as the conflict raged on. Continually assaulted, he found nary a moment of rest. Out of breath and feeling his magic wane, Nix knew the help he could provide was growing more and more limited by the second.

The nickel-horned unicorn watched in horror as a brutish manticore headed straight for Silubhra. He had tried to stay close to his stable-mate, but the battle had carried him well away from her, and now she was in real trouble. He could still detect that much, but he could barely see her through all the battling bodies between them and try as he might, Nix could not make the magical jump to her side.

He summoned all he had and tried to make one last gargantuan leap.

But he could only generate enough magical energy to sparkle and fizzle out in an agonizing sputter.

Desperately, he ran toward the silver-horned unicorn solely

focused upon saving Silubhra.

Imroz also noticed the silver-horned unicorn in peril. Closer than Nix, the Ragamoffyn managed to race across the battlefield and leap right onto Silubhra's back, where she leaned over to whisper in the filly's ear, "I won't let you come to harm."

Withdrawing a potion from her bag, she splashed the contents on a drooling manticore that had reared up to slash his mighty claws at Silubhra's neck. Instantly, the huge monster shrank to the size of a rat. The creature did not realize how small it had become until it looked up to see a massive hoof come smashing down on its head.

That particular manticore would not bother anyone else.

Despite a lack of battle hardened experience, the tribe of unicorns adapted quickly.

Style aimed her horn straight at one macho brute that made the mistake of thinking she would be an easy target. The manticore lurched toward her and got a surprise when his big head thudded to the ground. Roaring in outrage, he tried to rise, but despite his anger and enormous strength, he could not lift his head off the ground.

With a figure-eight twirl of her horn, Style had festooned his ears with two ginormous earrings, the weight and shape of steel kettlebells. Jubilant at her victory, she gave a snort of triumph. "That should keep him pinned awhile."

Cornum had raced over when he thought his mate needed aid. Pleased she had defended herself so ably, the thought of possibly losing Style had instilled bravery in him that he'd never before possessed. He gave a swift kick to the beast's temple just to make certain it stayed down.

Style looked the brass-horned unicorn over with a new

sense of appreciation. "Oh Cornum. I never knew you could be so strong!"

She pranced over to him, horn swirling green sparkles over his head . "This attire will be much more suitable to your new persona."

On his head appeared an elegant green silk top hat. In one cloven hoof, he now held a magnificent cane with a brass manticore for the handle.

"That's much more dignified," she said, approving of her work.

Cornum thwacked the ground with the cane tip. "Much more distinguished," Cornum agreed. He was about to slip his cane into its custom leather case that was slung over his shoulder, when he caught an immediate necessity for it out of the corner of his eye.

It turned out to be a handy weapon against a two-legger preparing to attack him with a spiked spear.

Cornum engaged the little two-legger in a joust of sorts while Style used her magical styling horn to turn the evildoer's two pant legs into one. The stocky ruffian fell flat on his face as he tried to take a step forward, allowing Cornum to give him a good whack on the noggin.

A few yards away, a mean looking Lethean threatened Lauda Lead-Horn with a metal blade. A well-aimed blast from her magical horn turned his sword to molten steel. This was the same process she used when sealing cracks in the Halstable walls.

The warrior screamed as liquid metal splashed him. "You'll pay for that with your blood!" He pulled a dagger from his belt. "I always did want to skin me a unicorn," he sneered.

Most of the Letheans still on the battlefield were now helping unicorns but this one had either been bad from the start or had spent too many years under Magh's influence.

He moved forward, thrusting his blade as he charged, but the Lethean stopped suddenly as the ground trembled. He looked up to see a Heptad looming above.

"Now, you're in trouble!" the Lethean said with an evil smile. The grin disappeared when the Heptad brought a war hammer crashing down on his head.

"I fight for unicorns, now," the giant said, then left to fight another of Magh's minions.

The battle was going well for the unicorns. Even in the midst of intense danger and surrounded on all sides by enemies, the metal-horned tribe thrived against these lesser enemies.

But somewhere, Magh lurked and his power was still a menace to be feared.

Chapter Forty-Five
Of Boundless Sorrow

*E*lsewhere on the field, Kata rallied her most loyal warriors. Newly freed from Magh's binding spell, many of the battle-hardened Letheans were now ready to wage war against their former captor.

Imroz had used a potion to heal the battalion commander's wound, so Kata once again fought at full strength as sword fights between good and evil erupted all over the field. Letheans raged against Lethean in a battle for free will and the right of freedom for the dwellers of the Silvan Forest—and for all of MarBryn.

Fighting her way across the battlefield, Kata saw Nix in trouble. "We've got to get to the northern field," she directed her troops. "The nickel-horned unicorn needs our help."

Nix had worked his way halfway to Silubhra before being surrounded by foes. With his power to nix a disaster gone, he could no longer escape enemies in a magical flash, but he could wield his horn and punch with his hooves. Doing both, he ferociously fought for his life.

Three manticores assailed him, claws slashing through his thick hide as if it were paper. A Bugan leapt on his back, bringing an already bloodied hatchet down upon his neck. The unicorn tried to shake off the two-legger, but the vile creature's legs tightly gripped the barrel of his body. The Bugan hacked as the manticores slashed.

Blood dripped and ran from Nix's tattered body.

"No!" Kata shouted, anguished. *This is all my fault.*

*S*he could not help thinking about the battle plan she had helped form as Magh's commander.

Attack the famed nickel horn early and often.

Do not let him rest.

Do not attack him head on but from every side at once.

She sprinted toward Nix, but the distance proved too great and all Kata could do was unleash a furious battle cry.

Silubhra and Imroz turned to see what had the Lethean so upset. They saw her sprinting across the field toward Nix as he sunk to one knee, head bowed low.

Silubhra broke into a gallop, racing like the wind to his aid.

Across the field, a Heptad lopped off a manticore's head with his axe in the same moment Kata shouted. He looked around to see the nickel-horned unicorn fall. The ground shook as he lumbered toward the unicorn.

Nix looked up to see Silubhra plowing toward him through two-leggers, as if they were mere blades of grass. She stopped short at the look in his eyes. For a long moment, he gazed lovingly at his mate, finally saying, "I am done." Then, he fell on his side, lifeless.

"No, Nix, no," Silubhra whispered.

Imroz slid off her back as the silver-horned unicorn moved closer. Numbed by the vision of her beloved, broken and bleeding, Silubhra became oblivious to all else.

She could not see the menacing manticores or the two-leggers advancing upon her. She could not see Imroz routing them back with potions and spells, or Kata slicing her way through them to defend her. The Heptad finally killed the last manticore threatening her. The giant watched the unicorns silently as a single tear trickled down his massive, dirty cheek.

Silubhra kneeled beside Nix, the unicorn defender and the love of her life lying lifeless on the ground — now just an empty shell. Throwing her head back, she issued a silent scream. The ultrasonic wave shivered through the air, bringing the entire battle to a stop.

And then the silence ended.

The sound of boundless sorrow replaced the silence.

Ranging out across the entire battlefield, it started out as a woeful hum reverberating from deep within her, and by the time it reached her vocal chords, she wailed with the moaning of a thousand lost souls.

That sound reached deep into the bones of those who had attacked her mate and shattered them as if they were glass. The creatures who had dared to take her love from her suffered the most agonizing of deaths.

For everyone else, her keening requiem brought forth sharp painful memories of their most sorrowful moments. Every last eye on the battlefield shed a tear for her sorrow, and their own.

Except one. . .Magh.

To him, her mournful soliloquy registered as the most beautiful sound he had ever heard—an elixir to his addled essence, for he fed off the misery of others.

The Heptad knelt beside Silubhra. Her pain rang through him like the clanging of his iron hammer on an anvil. He dropped the sword that he himself had forged and said, "Never again will I make weapons like these."

He lifted Nix gently. Muzika Woods uncloaked long enough for him to carry the nickel-horned unicorn away from the battlefield and into its lush green canopy.

Imroz touched Silubhra gently on her cheek. "Come, I'll go with you."

The silver-horned unicorn nodded once and let herself be led away from the site of death and destruction.

Dr. Zinko and Lauda followed to prepare Nix's body for the transition ritual.

Alumna slugged her way behind the procession with a heavy heart.

Nix is gone, she thought. His was the first unicorn death in eight years, but he had been the one to keep them all alive during that difficult time. She looked upwards and asked the careless skies, "Without his protection, how many more of us will die today?"

Chapter Forty-Six
To The Reaches of Egada

$\mathcal{A}$s the procession left the battlefield with Nix's body, Osm took the measure of Magh. The hideous two-legger had smiled sadistically and swayed to the sound of Silubhra's mournful keening.

Now, locking eyes with his enemy Osm read the evil sorcerer's lips as he said, "Such a beautiful sound."

Osm drew closer. Those repugnant words infuriated him, and compelled him to speak out. "How can a sound that rips the very heart strings from every decent creature's chest sound beautiful to you?"

Magh turned to Osm, clearly delighted that the unicorn showed so much interest. "I'm glad to explain it to you," he said. A twisted grin spread across the sorcerer's face as he explained, "You see, pain—the concept of it, the sight of it, the very sound—makes me shiver with delicious waves of ecstasy." He gave a cheery chirp of laughter and wiggled his body. "It positively makes me want to dance."

Osm shook his head with appalled understanding of evil at its worst.

The sorcerer took advantage of his opponent's disgust and whipped his staff around to send a blast of force straight at Osm. "I'm going to love the sound of your pain the most!" He shouted over the crackling charge. "This is going to hurt badly, I guarantee it!"

Magh pushed a stream of purple fire right at Osm's face, but the unicorn stopped the lethal blast halfway between them with a searing blue beam from his horn. The two forces pushed against each other filling the air with a sizzling energy.

Ghel stood close behind Osm, nearly tail to tail, with the resolution to guard his flank regardless of the outcome. From this position, she could not see the one-on-one battle raging behind her, but as the two powerful beings clashed for superiority, Ghel shrank back upon seeing two manticores spring toward her. A searing flame came from the sky, this time from Girasol.

The Firebird focused the full force on one of the brutes, igniting both his fur and wings. When he began rolling around on the ground in an attempt to smother the fires, Girasol did not let up. She kept spouting fire at him until his struggling ceased.

Gaiso bravely tried to defend Ghel from the other manticore. The stag jabbed at the beast this way and that with his massive antlers, managing to keep enough distance between himself and the manticore's swiping claws.

Ghel cringed as those sharpened claws nearly connected with his flesh. To save the stag, Ghel was forced to strike the manticore's heart with her golden horn.

She moved fast. A quick in-and-out thrust, and the manticore went down, never to rise again.

Smoke rose slowly from the manticore's immolated partner.

A sick feeling washed over the golden unicorn as she withdrew her horn. It dripped with blood, and she felt nauseated. It felt wrong to take a life, but one had had to die, to save the other. A hard lesson to learn, but drastic choices were sometimes necessary to stop the advance of evil.

Ghel took no pleasure in the act no matter how justified. She told herself it was either them or her companions, but that did not ease her mind. When Gaiso gave her a huge smile for saving his life, she managed to feel a little better.

She turned to see Osm had advanced toward Magh, one trudging step at a time.

"My — tribe — has — suffered — enough — because of *you*." His words pounded Magh's ears as each hoof beat on the ground like a war drum.

The sorcerer's eyes widened as the bruise-colored flame from his staff shortened incrementally with each stride the blue unicorn made.

Osm's blue flame lengthened and strengthened its hold over Magh's power source. The evil one frantically swept his staff to the side in hopes of deflecting the raging blue flame. Instead, the connection between the purple and the blue beams broke.

That did not stop the advance of icy flame rushing up Magh's arm. He found himself enshrouded in the amplified iceberg-blue ray. His entire body was encased in a block of ice. Only the hand holding the staff was not covered in the frosty stuff.

Magh tried to use the staff against Osm, but it crashed to the ground with such a loud clatter that all activity stopped on the battlefield.

All attention was now glued to the unicorn and the sorcerer.

The flame from the sorcerer's staff flickered and sputtered and finally winked out altogether. The staff lay still on the ground, and the sorcerer himself could only blink from within his icy prison. But blink he did, and his fury and frustration were plain to see.

A moment later, the blue beam from Osm's horn blinked off, too.

Osm watched Magh struggle in his ice block, and felt a struggle in his own mind. His intent was not to kill the evil one. He had questions and he wanted answers.

Many thoughts rattled the cage of his mind. Yes, he was in a cage of his own as well, and he was struggling just like Magh.

Why did Magh want to kill all unicorns?

Why did he want to rule the world?

Why did such evil exist?

No one, but Magh knew the answers to those questions. . .and he was unlikely to ever reveal such things willingly. This meant that Osm could only find the answers he sought by venturing inside the sorcerer's mind. But what else would he find in such a dark place?

Inside the cube of ice, the sorcerer's body began to glisten with a thousand points of blue brilliance.

Is he trying to kill himself? Osm wondered, alarmed. He took a step back as enough ice melted around the crazy fiend that he was able to straighten to his full height. It appeared Magh was either about to explode, releasing himself and all the power he had collected into oblivion, or he was literally absorbing the power of osmium into himself and was indeed becoming unstoppable.

Osm could not be certain of that, but he definitely did not want this sorcerer dead.

That would be too good for him. He wanted him locked away in the deep, dark recesses of the earth forever, being reminded of his atrocities. He deserved such punishment, as the source of so much death and destruction.

So many lost mothers and fathers. . .entire families and

species wiped away as if they had never existed.

A blue ray leapt from his horn and the block of ice melted instantly, showering water onto the ground. The blue pinpoints quickly receded into Magh's body.

The sorcerer laughed in the frenzied tones of a madman, his voice rising and falling in scale as he tried to gain enough control over himself to finally crow, "I am invincible! The power of osmium is mine!" He thought his own magic had melted the ice. Wild-eyed, he looked around for his staff. Madness filled the sorcerer's eyes as he reached for it. At that moment, the unicorn realized he would never have the answers he sought.

Magh cannot be allowed to live.

He is too evil.

Too dangerous.

"This ends now!" Osm shouted, stopping Magh mid-reach. The unicorn directed another laser-like beam of magic toward the evil one. Once again, Magh's body started shimmering and shining … this time with brilliant purple points of light.

The tiny singular points shifted color and shape to form glowing orange stars. The stars grew larger and redder with each passing moment.

Magh screamed, as agonizing white-hot fire lit him from within.

This time Osm took no chances.

Ending Magh was the only real option. He could not chance leaving such an evil monster alive to unleash himself upon MarBryn, again.

He maintained the piercing blue discharge from his osmium horn until the evil sorcerer started to shatter. The battlefield filled with the unnatural sound of the hellish Magh's soul disintegrating.

Osm watched the sorcerer's body collapse under the searing heat of his osmium-horned power. Magh was breaking apart like ceramic doll, each piece crumbling into smaller pieces as they hit the ground. In his screams of pain, Osm heard the incomprehensible babble of many spells that would never work.

One last explosion rocked the field as the remnants of Magh's dark soul exploded into a million jagged shards. It was the sound of the evil magician's final obliteration.

When the last sound had faded away and all trace of the sorcerer had vanished, Osm stood quietly gazing into the space evil had left behind.

Nothing remained. No evil. No good. No answers.

The old sorcerer had not even suffered as much as he had wanted, which left a hollow in his heart where all the pain over his parents death was once stored.

A roar erupted from Osm's lungs, "The power of osmium is mine." He reared up on his hind legs, letting loose a victory shout that echoed to the furthest reaches of Egada.

The Cussers in the town, who heard that sound, were glad they had not gone off to battle with the others.

The remaining manticores immediately fled the battlefield with their scorpion tails tucked meekly between their legs. Cussers, Bugans and other ne'er-do-wells were not too far behind, all of them intent to get far away from Osm as quickly as possible.

$\mathcal{A}$s Osm's victory shout reverberated across the land, the pre-historic vines protecting the Guarded Forest unfurled just long enough for its inhabitants to hear.

Pido skidded to a halt in mid-air. "I think he did it, Fleoge."

"Yes," the little butterfly fairy agreed, hovering near her brother. "The blue unicorn has met his destiny. All is well in MarBryn again."

Chapter Forty-Seven
Ascension Of A Hero

"*H*e really did it," said Lauda in amazement. "We're saved!" Doing a curtsy Osm's way, she atoned, "I'm sorry I ever dared call you a nincompoop, Sir!"

Osm bowed his head in deference to his elder. "Nothing I didn't deserve, at the time. And please, no more of this 'Sir' business.

"I can't imagine a better leader for our tribe, but I am going to miss little Blue," the elderly lead-horned unicorn admitted.

Cuprum agreed, "I can't believe we'll never see him again."

Style looked him over with the appreciation of a master stylist. This unicorn was one for the record books. . .one that only comes along once throughout history. "You certainly have a better sense of fashion than you did as Blue."

"I may not look like him, but he's still here inside me," Osm assured them. "I am him and he is me." Osm looked over at Ghel and suddenly felt like a skittish pony in spite of himself. His old thoughts and feelings still swam in his consciousness along with the new.

She was the most beautiful unicorn he had ever laid eyes on which made it all the more difficult to accurately describe his feelings for her. He loved her. Of that much, he was certain.

He had always been certain but he had never before felt worthy of her love, in return. Part of him still felt that way. Looking at her, he intensely felt every last shred of the pain and affection he had ever experienced. The former worried him but the latter showered him in warmth and love. And these sensations won out above all else.

There was so much he wanted to tell her, but where to start?

His heart would soon do the talking, but first the tribe still had dire business at hand.

Back in Muzika Woods, Nix's lifeless body lay in the center of the Nebulium Circle. Cuprum had provided purified water for Dr. Zinko and Lauda to cleanse the blood, so the nickel-horned unicorn was once again clean and no longer shattered and twisted. Now, he seemed at peace, eyes closed in a forever sleep.

Silubhra lay on the ground beside him, her head against his. She had not spoken another word since uttering her ululations of grief on the battlefield.

There would be no funeral pyre for Nix, as was usual when death occurred on MarBryn. When a unicorn fell to Magh's forces, their body was usually spirited immediately away by his minions, so it was rare that a body was retrieved by other unicorns. Those that were found, out in the open, after their bodies had been ravaged, were brought home and burned to ash so that no further desecration could befall the victim.

This ceremony would be different. It would reflect the ways of their ancestors.

"Nix's body is no longer necessary. With the help of the Nebuls, his spirit will ascend to our ancestral home," Osm told those gathered around the circle.

A single note sublimely floated forth almost timidly from amongst the trees of Muzika Woods. Other soothing, woodsy bamboo tones joined in one by one, causing a peaceful mood to fall upon all those gathered.

Lauda whispered, "This reminds me of the feeling I get when Iown opens up my energy channels." She swayed gently with the music.

Silubhra lifted her head ... as each soothing note of music caressed her numbed mind. The soft colored lights of the geodes began to slowly pulse.

"You must leave the circle, Silubhra," Bab urged. "Nix must be alone for the ascension."

The silver-horned unicorn looked around the circle at the loving faces. She nodded, accepting the Nebul's words with heart-wrenching resignation. Achingly, she rose to her hooves and moved beyond the circle. Leaving his side only served to intensify her sense of loss.

The lighted geodes increased their tempo from gentle, slow pulses to flickering flashes of multi-colored electrical charges. The Nebuls and their harmonizers joined their unique music to that of the trees of Muzika Woods sounding like a joyful electronic symphony.

Inside the circle, Nix's body lifted from the ground, rising with the trilling arches of sound and light. A song that Silubhra had never heard burst from her throat. She sang like she had never sung. It lifted her spirit and those around her to relieve the group's sadness with lyrics of joy. Everyone around the circle and throughout Muzika Woods danced until they laughed in release and cried in relief.

Colors moved and merged with one another around the Nebulium Circle to form such a brilliant light that Nix's form became indiscernible. With a final silent flash, the light show stopped to expose the outline of his body as it disappeared in sparkling pinpoints of shining white lights.

This was not an ending, but a beginning. Despite the

horrifying events of the day, MarBryn was now free to rebuild itself.

Nix, would forever be remembered as a hero to both the Unicorns and peace-loving inhabitants of MarBryn. The Metal Horns had a strong new leader in Osm, and it seemed like they were finally going home.

Silubhra turned to Osm in wonder. "Thank you, for showing us this way of honoring those we've lost."

The transformed blue unicorn said, "Now that the Numen has joined with me, I have many things to share with the tribe."

Chapter Forty-Eight
Never To Be Forgotten

Kata approached Osm with a good number of her clan behind her. They all knelt before him in gratitude. "If not for you, we would still be captives of that horrible power-hoarder," she told him.

Her clan murmured agreement.

"We, of the Lethean Silva, pledge our fealty to you and to your unicorn tribe," she offered on behalf of the forest folk.

"Kata, the Letheans are completely free from pledges of any kind. We are all free now," Osm assured her.

"However, we do want to leave you and Imroz with a remembrance of how much your bravery is appreciated by the Tribe of the Metal Horn. Style, please adorn each of them with a medal of valor."

"My pleasure." The steel-horned unicorn bustled forward, stooping to touch the right shoulder of Kata's uniform with the tip of her horn.

Stepping back, she revealed to all, a five-pointed gold star surrounding a flaming red and orange Firebird. The word VALOR was inscribed upon a gold bar from which the star was suspended by two gold chains. The bar was attached to a green ribbon embroidered at the bottom with the words,

For Kata, Lethean Commander
From the Tribe of the Metal Horn

It was big and gaudy, but Kata smiled in obvious honor. No

one expected less from the unicorn stylist.

Next, the Ragamoffyn bowed her head with deep humility as she received a similar medal. No higher honor could she receive from the unicorn tribe.

"You will never be forgotten," Kata promised.

"Nor will you and everyone here who helped defeat Magh," Osm assured all of the two-leggers. "Now," he proclaimed. "Time to celebrate."

This was indeed a time for celebration. The Firebird created an orange and red display in the sky, and the tribe of the Metal-Horn and their new friends danced and pranced until the night turned to day. A magnetic wave pulsed through the air, causing showers of blue sparkles to sprinkle the trees. The Nebuls and their harmonizers came out to join Cornum and Silubhra in song until the brass-horned unicorn finally started to sound too brassy.

"Oh, Osm, I am so proud of you," Ghel glowed. "I knew you were special all along. I love you so."

Osm lightly tapped her gold heart pendant with his shiny new multi-metal-horn and kissed her cheek. "I love you too, Ghel," he whispered. "If it weren't for you and your heart of gold, so full of love and kindness, I never would have received the power to save our tribe."

He then tapped her golden horn with his own. Strips of gold shredded away to reveal sparkling canary-colored diamonds.

"Oh!," Ghel said in surprise. Her horn suddenly felt more substantial. "What's this?"

"The perfect accoutrement for the golden-horned unicorn," Osm said, smiling at his handiwork.

"Oh my," Iown said, impressed. "You're almost as creative with ornamentation as Style."

The iron-horned unicorn dropped the monocle from his eye socket and replaced it with a jeweler's loupe. Examining each new stone, he pronounced, "Excellent quality...flawless clarity..." He shook his head in wonder at this new Blue.

Pointing at the largest stone, Iown said, "I say, this Fancy Vivid yellow stone is the king of diamonds. Or should I say, Queen...your majesty."

"Please don't call me that, Iown. I'm not," Ghel objected.

Alumna quickly chimed in, "The Platinides are a noble family . . . so if not a queen, as Osm's mate, you're surely a princess!"

"See?" Osm said, winking, "you are now royalty."

Ghel lowered her eyes, overwhelmed by all the attention. Everything felt so strange with Blue now being Osm. The transformed unicorn simply smiled lovingly for a long moment at the unicorn filly who held his heart.

Then, he addressed the rest of his tribe. "We must now return to the Halstable. It is our vehicle home."

"Vehicle? Home?" Ghel asked for all the others. "The Halstable—is—our home."

"Yes, it is where we've always lived and always will, but this planet, and the land of MarBryn, is not our home. The Halstable once brought unicorns here to explore this land and to learn from the inhabitants. But now, it is time for the Halstable to return us to Unimaise, the immortal land of the unicorn, where we belong. There, we may live happily and prosper forever."

He looked lovingly down at Ghel. "There, we can finally be free to raise a family of our own."

Ghel smiled shyly at those words.

Osm turned his attention to the others gathered there, "Friends, sadly, it is time for us to say goodbye," he proclaimed for all to hear. "We leave MarBryn in your care. Be good to it and to each other. And when you recount these times to your offspring, fondly remember the tribe of the metal-horned unicorns."

Gaiso stepped forward to make his farewell. He bent one knee, bowing his massive head toward Osm. Rising and looking him squarely in the eye, he affirmed, "It has been an honor to fight for right alongside you, Osm. You have come a long way from the shy young pony who asked me for jousting lessons."

"The honor was all mine, Gaiso," Osm responded. "I can't imagine a better friend and mentor than you. I might not have stood against Magh today, without your aid and companionship.

"I will miss you," Gaiso confessed. "You're the little brother I never had."

"I will miss you, too, my friend," Osm acknowledged. "Speaking of brothers, I bet Springen is anxious to have hers back home in the Guarded Forest."

"I start my return journey right now. I am anxious to see all of my forest friends. Farewell to all," the stag said, giving another sweeping bow to everyone gathered around.

Girasol swooped down from a boulder, where she had been quietly fanning her wings, "Hey, Gaiso, wait up. I'll go with you. But first, I have something to say." As she dashed a tear from her eye with a fiery feather-tipped wing, a spritz of steam sizzled loudly. "I'm gonna miss you, Blue. . .I mean Osm. You, me and Gaiso. . .we made quite a team."

"Never leave a friend behind … that's what I learned from you," Osm told the Firebird. "It's a lesson I'll never forget, just like I'll never forget you."

"Think of us from time to time, when you're flying out there amongst the stars," Girasol told the unicorns. "I know I'll never fly that high."

As she threw herself into the air in a fireball of orange and yellow flames, the stag saluted his final goodbye, following the little smoke trails the bird left in her wake.

"Safe journey, my friends," Osm addressed the receding backs of his friends.

Imroz stood with the silver-horned unicorn, watching all of the goodbyes from the sidelines. Unable to hold back any longer, she reached up and wrapped her arms as far as they would go around the filly's neck. "I will miss you, Silubhra. I wish we'd had a chance to spend more time together," the little Ragamoffyn sobbed.

The silver-horned unicorn nuzzled her neck with her soft nose. "We certainly would have, had this been another time and another place, little one," she responded sadly, as large tear drops threatened to spill over the lower rims of her eyes. She had suffered so much loss, the loss of this two-legger friend being no less painful than any other.

There were many other protestations and sounds of disappointment, but as the sun fully crested the horizon, Osm knew it was time. "With me now," he instructed. All Metal Horns met once again tip-to-tip. With superluminal speed, the unicorns were transferred to the Halstable's courtyard.

Chapter Forty-Nine
Home In A Hurry

"Wow, what a ride!" Cornum said impressed with Osm's new mode of transporting the tribe.

"Yes, that jump was just a short distance. The next one will be much further," Osm hinted. "Okay, everyone. We still have a grand adventure ahead of us. But first, let's take some time to freshen up. We'll meet back here in the courtyard after we've rested and eaten. Then, we'll go home to Unimaise."

Style and the fillies raced to the Groomane Salon so the steel-horned unicorn could work her magic. They wanted to look their best when they arrived on Unimaise.

Though heartbroken, Silubhra went too. The others were all excited about returning to their home world, but she did not feel their joy. What kind of future could she have there, alone without Nix?

Tinam, the tin-horned unicorn, dashed to the kitchen. He planned to conjure up a feast fit for kings. He wanted to make sure there was a wide array of mouth-watering delicacies for everyone to eat for their last meal in MarBryn.

Soon, the Great Room was filled with tantalizing smells and happy sounds of wonder and excitement. Eating did not take long because everyone wanted to get to Unimaise.

Osm asked everyone to accompany him out to the Halstable courtyard. He followed the walkway around the inside wall to a flat stone that looked like all the others. He tipped his head toward Alumna and smiled. "It's been here all along."

"What do you mean, Osm?" the aluminum-horned unicorn oracle asked.

"Our way home." He tapped on the stone with his right hoof. A column with flashing lights rose with a swish from below the floor. On it were several keys and buttons.

"Whatever is that?" Alumna asked.

"This is the Halstable's control console. Centuries ago, when our ancestors arrived on MarBryn, the craft's navigational system descended beneath the flooring of the courtyard. The crew kept it there, out of the way because it wouldn't be needed again until their outreach mission had successfully ended. After Magh killed the pilots and massacred the navigational crew, it lay hidden and forgotten."

Comprehension dawned on Alumna, then. "We could have gone back home a long time ago, if any of the crew had survived."

"That is true," Osm said. "The eldest among us were too young to know what to do when the crew was decimated. There were no apprentices."

He looked at the sad faces of his tribe and continued, "Instead, we had to wait until the Numen could connect with a descendant of the Navigator herd. As he told you, Alumna, that descendant is you. You were the only one who even tried to communicate with the Nomadic Unicorn Magic Extender Network, which we've always referred to as Numen. Without you and a little help from Icel the Ice Blink, the Moon-Star would have never been able to bring the Numen here to merge with me. I would never have received the knowledge required to take us back to Unimaise. "

"Icel," Alumna said the word slowly. She remembered those strange little talking ice cubes mentioning that name.

"A tale for another time," Osm promised.

"All this time. . .we thought the Halstable was just our home, when it was actually a spacecraft," Iown said. "And we thought Alumna was an oracle when in fact, she was so much more."

The iron-horned unicorn's mind could barely 'iron' out this concept. "Alumna, a Navigator?"

There was a short moment of silence. They thought of all they had lost, and how needless that loss was. Most of their tribe had perished in horrific ways because so much knowledge had been forgotten. It all seemed so unnecessary and it made Alumna unbearably sad.

She wished she could have done more. She wished she had known earlier. But she also knew that, without a pilot, she could have done nothing anyway.

She was glad that little Blue had been born and that he had finally met his destiny. The Numen knew what he was doing after all.

Osm broke the spell of sadness by saying, "We all owe a great debt to Alumna. She opened the line of communications and worked diligently to decipher what all the random messages meant. She navigated us to this point in every sense of the word and now she will navigate us home."

A chart of the stars and planets and various moons appeared from thin air. Hovering there the map of sorts had no buttons or function, but somehow Alumna closed her eyes and thought of Unimaise. A path lit up on the map and she knew without a doubt, it would lead them home.

She had, never in all of her years, felt the satisfactory tingle in her horn that she felt now.

Osm smiled at her then pointed to a flashing blue indention on the panel. The portal somewhat resembled the entry lock the unicorns used to access the Halstable, and now Osm inserted his Osmium horn into it.

Without the slightest shudder, the Halstable rose, hovered for the count of two, and then the sky overhead turned black.

In the blink of an eye, the Halstable flawlessly executed its long unused space-time function, and transported the tribe, through a traversable wormhole, to the home of their ancestors.

Chapter Fifty

A Homecoming To Remember

*T*he sky above looked entirely different beyond the big glass dome over the Halstable courtyard. The blue skies of MarBryn were replaced with a lovely buttercup yellow. No more white clouds—these were cotton candy pink. And two blue suns sprinkled a gentle light upon them. The view was breathtaking.

Alumna and Iown stood side by side. She said, "So, this is the sky of Unimaise. It's absolutely beautiful, but are you absolutely sure it's real? I mean, are we truly home once and for all or is just a dream?"

Beside her, Iown looked up, stunned. He said, "It has to be real, unless we are both having the same dream at the same time."

She nodded.

Iown added. "You captured the colors perfectly in your paintings."

Everyone was in complete awe of the scene above.

"Oooh..."

"Ahhh..."

"Amazing!"

"Listen..." Osm said. Outside the Halstable, a muffled hubbub could be heard. All ears swiveled toward the noise, as it gradually grew louder. Ghel said, "Sounds like voices."

"Yes, many voices," Cornum agreed.

"Almost like singing," Silubhra noted.

The sound grew louder, fuller, until the words were clear. "Osm's here. . .Osm's here. . .Osm's here," was the lilting chant that filled the air. More voices joined in and the chanting turned to shouting. It sounded like a rioting mob.

Lauda felt suspicious of the crowd's intentions. She could not tell if her tribe was being welcomed to Unimaise, or if the herds outside were calling for their heads. "Should we be afraid?" she asked with a tilt of her muzzle.

Osm placed his cloven hoof upon the old mare's shoulder, smiling down at her. "No more fear. Everyone come with me to meet our kith and kin."

Their hooves sounded a joyful drumbeat on the stone floor as the tribe marched down the long hall to the outer doors of the Halstable. Osm inserted his horn into the indentation to unlock the latches, which had always protected those inside. Normally, the gears and chains moved quickly, but this day, they seemed to grind and groan for a long time, before the doors finally swung open to reveal a multitude of horse folk.

The eyes of the tribe were met with a sight that made even the most talkative among them fall silent.

Iown was the first to break that silence. *"It's all just like Alumna's drawings,"* he said in awe.

Fanning out around the slope, unicorns stood together in groups according to their tribal breed.

Beyond them, a gently flowing river was full of Watercorns with gills on the sides of their necks. Each had a long bone horn sprouting from the center of their forehead. They were a type of unicorn no member of this metal-horned tribe had seen before.

"Fish unicorns?" Dr Zinko, wondered aloud. "Astonishing!"

There were many more unicorn species, all unknown to the new arrivals. To the left were hundreds of Alicorn with tiny wings on each ankle. Each sported a single long, spiraled horn—each a unicorn, to be sure. Some Alicorn rested on the ground. Others hovered in the air, wings flittering like those of hummingbirds.

"How in the world do they fly with those teeny-tiny wings?" Style wondered.

To the right were feathered unicorns with no wings. Their heads and necks were covered in shining blue feathers. Their colorfully plumaged tails swept up in displays bursting with vibrant peacock hues. The tail feathers of these Peacorns quivered as they swept back and forth through the air like hand-fans. This movement caused subtle rumbling vibrations in the eardrums. The whispery feelings made the Metal Horns look forward to other joyful noises the Peacorns might create.

Further out to the right were unicorns with giant wings just like the ones Alumna had seen in the crystal orb. "Such magnificent fellows —my renderings certainly didn't do them justice," she said.

The majestic white-winged creatures were called Unicus, and they were gifted with both flight and magic, making them the envy of all their land-bound brothers.

Closer to the center, on the right flank were brown and white unicorns standing nine feet tall at the tiptops of their ears. On the left flank were miniature white unicorns—no more than two feet tall.

Unimaise was a land so diverse, yet so unified. Dozens of unicorn breeds lived together in simple harmony with neither

malice nor anger. Joy trickled in the waters and floated in the air—
happiness a tune carried by the wind. Satisfaction found its way
into each body, through every pore. The unicorns were home.
Nothing had ever felt as right.

In the very center, were hundreds of metal-horned unicorns,
all shouting, "Osm! Osm! Osm!"

Chapter Fifty-One
The Old Is New Again

The recently-arrived tribe were struck silent for the briefest of moments, and then Alumna spoke what they were all no doubt thinking. "Metal-horned unicorns. Just like us." In a whisper full of awe and joy she added, "This truly is our home."

Standing before the tribe were Osm's mother and father, both looking strong and very much alive. Together, they trotted up the hill to welcome the new arrivals.

"Sire, it is so good to finally see you again." Osm bowed his head toward Anion with deep respect.

"And you," his father said proudly. "You achieved what most thought impossible, my son. You saved the tribe, as you know it, as well as those who were lost through the years. All of our spirits were released from the purgatorial stasis Magh had trapped us in."

"Yes," Miral said. "Your father and I received our new bodies the moment that vile sorcerer was obliterated. Many of the Metal Horns here owe you a debt of gratitude."

Ghel beamed at Osm. "I've always said, you can't judge a book by its cover. Never has that saying been truer than with you."

Osm smiled back at Ghel. "I always knew you believed in me, my love, but I had to learn to believe in myself."

"Ah ... my pendant." Miral smiled at the heart-shaped necklace. "You must be sweet Ghel," Miral said to the golden filly. "I'm so glad you were always there for my little Blue. Your love and encouragement helped spur him to find his better self."

"Yes," Anion agreed. "Without you, our son might never have achieved his destiny."

Osm's parents smiled their approval.

Osm's parents were not the only surprises in the homecoming crowd. The group of Platinides who had helped conceal Blue's metal and magic from Magh, as well as several other unicorns that had been thought forever lost on MarBryn were present, including Ghel's parents.

Silubhra moved about the crowd. Raising her head, she peered around the bodies obscuring her vision. She was near frantic. She could not find Nix anywhere.

Then, her eye was caught by a shower of sparkles at the bottom of the hill. Emerging from the glare was a storm-cloud gray unicorn with a shining nickel horn. "Nix!" she shouted.

The new arrivals all turned to look, stunned at her words.

"Nix?"

"We watched him die!"

"Is it really him?"

"It's my Nix. How can this be?" she asked the gathering.

"Transmigration?" Iown pondered aloud, scratching behind his ear with a cloven hoof.

Silubhra galloped away down the hillside to reconnect with her love.

"Not exactly," Osm answered Iown. "This does not involve the movement of a spirit into another body. These are new bodies, each conjured by magic, out of the essence of all they were.

Unicorns never die, but they do get lost from time to time. The magic works much the same way Tinam conjures nutritious meals from far-flung places. But this is much more powerful than Tinam's magic. This magic comfortably houses the spirit of each individual forever."

The results were not ghostly figures or apparitions. They were real, live, flesh and blood reincarnations of their former selves. At the moment of death, as each spirit was released from the world in which it had resided, it had been conveyed to Unimaise. There, a new healthy body, free from scars and imperfections materialized around the unicorn spirit.

Only those from the tribe of metal-horned unicorns who had been murdered by Magh had been forced to wait for their soul's release from perdition before receiving their new bodies. As soon as Magh was gone, they too, had been set free.

"I am grateful that the Numen found the way to release your spirits back to Unimaise," Osm told his parents. "I am honored to be. . ."

"Blaaaat!" he was interrupted by a trumpeting horn from amongst the crowd of metal-horns at the bottom of the slope.

Cornum whirled toward it saying, "I'd know that sound anywhere." It was his brass-horned brother. Next to him, waving frantically, trying to get his attention was his copper-horned dam and his zinc-horned sire. Cornum rushed headlong down the hill toward them, blaring and blasting his own joyous greeting.

A beautiful reunion.

Lauda was mystified. Old as she was, she thought she had seen or at least heard of most everything, but she had not come across any of this information. "How do you know these things?"

Osm said, "Because now the Numen is in me. The spirit of the Moon-Star now inhabits my flesh as it once resided in the Moon-Star satellite. Joining with me was the only way for the Numen to save all of us—those who were trapped in limbo and those of us stranded on MarBryn."

Miral said, "Here in Unimaise, all is made new and lives on forever."

"What about the rest of us?" Lauda worried. "This old body of mine sure isn't new. What's going to happen to me and Zinko and the others who just arrived here?"

"These bodies will remain with you until they reach their natural end. Once your spirit is freed from them, you'll receive a new one that looks just like you did when you were a young filly," Osm said, to Lauda's complete delight.

"Oh, Zinko...remember those days?" she raised her eyebrows up, flirtatious.

"Indeed, I do, Lauda, my dear. You've always been that young filly in my eyes."

No one except Dr. Zinko could remember ever seeing Lauda blush, but they all saw it now, as her cheeks burned as bright and warm as a Firebird in the sky.

Epilogue

Tomorrow Burns Bright

Life on Unimaise filled the unicorns from MarBryn with so much hope and promise that the sadness and conflict faded into dim recollections of their past. The memories never totally disappeared, because the challenges they had faced were a part of their story, and they never wanted to forget what they had experienced.

After all, those experiences on MarBryn were what fashioned their great appreciation for their new life on Unimaise.

Iown, the iron-horned unicorn, was happier than he had ever been. The peaceful life on Unimaise meant the problems here were so small he did not have to spend much time 'ironing' them out. This allowed him to concentrate on his favorite hobby. He smiled fondly at his mate, Alumna, where she sat, reading a book. She looked up and blew him a kiss, which he caught in his cloven hoof in an exaggerated gesture. He looked back at his colorful garden and grinned at the many budding flowers.

Alumna finished her book and took a moment as she often did to think about her new home. Upon arrival on Unimaise, she had donated her most cherished book, *The MarBryn Compendium*, to the university. Scholars there would be studying that massive tome for generations to come. There were many differences between Unimaise and MarBryn and she loved learning and sharing the histories of both. A radiant smile danced on her face, as she walked to the Unimaise library to pick out another book.

Tinam was having the time of his life. The Chef Herd held weekly competitions, and the tin-horned unicorn from MarBryn realized he had a very competitive streak when it came to baking cakes. He and all the other tin-horned unicorns could not help trying to outdo each other with towering creations of confectionary delights, but Tinam's sculpted cake designs were the most unique because he had witnessed things the others never had. His manticore cake was ten feet tall and twenty feet across and looked almost too scary to eat. But of course, nothing could stop anyone from eating this amazing edible art. After all, every unicorn has a sweet tooth that simply cannot be resisted.

Cuprum found that Unimaise had the most pure water of any place in the entire universe. Of course, it would, since it was the original home of the Water Purification Herd. With no need to fashion water-purifying pebbles, Cuprum spent long hours, drawing inspiration and calmness from the lakes and rivers. The copper-horned unicorn soon learned that many members of her herd had artistic bents with their water magic. Her favorite new skill was that of making the river waters dance to the music of the Musical Herd's daily concerts.

Style now had a lot of customers, or fans, as she liked to think of them. Golden veils were all the rage amongst the unicorn fillies who had heard tales of how the steel-horned stylist's magical creation had saved the unicorns of MarBryn. Style also loved to see their smiles as she retold stories about the Lickety-Split. The unicorns from Unimaise were not quite sure whether to believe it was real or something she made up as a fun story. The unicorn stylist knew it was real and one of the things she missed most about her adventures on MarBryn. Still, there was no place like Unimaise. It was a dream, come true.

Cornum, the brass-horned unicorn performed daily with his Musical Herd family. The sounds his horn produced were more sweet than sour because he was now in a good mood more often than not. Sometimes, he visited with Silubhra and together, they attempted to recreate the harmonies of Muzika Woods.

Lauda Lead-Horn joined the group of scientists in the Unimaise laboratory. This was the life she had always dreamed of. Though Unimaise was a rare utopia, there was still room for improvements and innovation. Together with the others, she created wondrous inventions. When each day was over, she and her mate, Dr. Zinko would take long walks, discussing their latest discoveries.

For the zinc-horned unicorn doctor, Unimaise was the perfect place to practice his craft. There were no serious diseases on the planet, but he treated scrapes and bruises of over-active unicorns. He still had a lot to learn for one who had lived so many years, and he was especially fascinated with the watercorns. "Fish unicorns," he laughed. "I could have never imagined such creatures if I hadn't seen them with my own eyes!"

For Silubhra and Nix, the gift of life made them cherish each other more than ever. Now, with the new foal growing within her, happiness radiated from her mane to the soles of her silver hooves. Nix was always by her side. After years of being the tribe's defender, it was his natural instinct to watch for danger, and be her protector.

Miral remembered the night of her little blue foal's birth. She smiled at how worried she had been about the prophecy. Not so much the accuracy, as the viability. Keeping such a secret for years upon years would be tough. And if Magh discovered him the fate of them all would have been vastly different.

She gave silent thanks to Anion and the Platinide family for their sacrifice of horn magic that shielded the metal of little Blue's osmium horn and hooves. She was grateful he and the surviving members of the tribe had been protected until the proper time came for everything to fall into place.

Osm had grown to be everything a mother could hope for and more. The indium-horned unicorn was happy to be together with all of her family and friends again. She never thought about Magh and his evil mirror. The suffering she had gone through as his prisoner was left to burn in the ashes of the past.

Soon, everyone settled into their new routines. The new arrivals quickly made friends with the other breeds. They reunited with long-lost friends and ancestors. The Halstable of the metal-horned unicorns bustled with life again. They had gone from a few unicorns to hundreds, once more.

One day, as Ghel and Osm rested together on soft clover-scented grass, Ghel remembered what Osm had said when they first arrived on Unimaise. She now comprehended his meaning.

"So. . .unicorns never die," Ghel slowly spoke in almost a whisper.

"Nope," the transformed unicorn replied. "They just move on to Unimaise."

She smiled and said,"I can think of no finer place to be."

As the sovereigns of the Platinides, life was certainly fine for Ghel and Osm on Unimaise. Their home world was too beautiful to be left to lie just in the pages of a book, unexplored. Every day was a new adventure for the noble blue unicorn and his golden-horned consort. The more they became acquainted with the majesty of the land of immortal unicorns, the more thankful they were to be home. Most of all, they were grateful that they had each other. The bond between them was a flame burning brightly.

Just beyond Osm, Ghel's attention was captured by a sunbow slicing through a colorful bridge of sparkling water droplets. The colors ruptured into a splendid multi-faceted array as a little blue foal burst right through the prism.

The young metal-horned unicorn played a game of chase on wobbly legs with a pink unicus yearling just learning to use its wings. Osm turned to see what the gold-horned unicorn's gaze had fixed upon and smiled.

"Is he real?" Ghel asked, her voice pregnant with hope.

Osm nuzzled her cheek, replying, "He's real and also a promise of a million tomorrows."

Ghel was so happy she started to sing about her new home:
So far away. . .I never knew such a place
was here for me.
My eyes have opened, now I see.
In Unimaise, we are safe,
We are home.
We are free.
We are home. . .home.
Home after so long.
We are home, home, home.
It's been too long that we've been gone.
Now we've made it here, we'll stay.
Our home is Unimaise. . .
Where we are safe.
We are home.
We are free.

HOME!

The End

Map of MarBryn

THE MAP OF THE LAND shows two paths.

One is the path the Blue Unicorn and his companions travel in their journey to Muzika Woods. Blue meets up with Gaiso, the stag in the Guarded Forest. Then, in the Phlat Plains, Girasol the Firebird joins the unicorn and the stag. Blue and Gaiso meet Gwyn, the Pendragon in the 7-sided Heptagonos Valley. There, they meet Yegwa, the Spirit of Eternal Spring, who casts an enchantment on everyone except Girasol. The Firebird saves them and they flee through the Rainbow Colored Bands of Weita on their way to the Smaul Mountains. First, they pass the Icy Cold Lake and meet the Cubose. Then, they visit with Icel, the Ice Blink at the top of the world. Finally, the traveling companions make it to their destination: Muzika Woods.

The dashed line shows the route that the Tribe of the Metal-Horned Unicorns take to reach the Muzika Woods. They leave the Halstable in search of someone who can tell them how to get to their destination. They stop in the first city they come to: the City of Kudos. The evil sorcerer, Magh, rules over Kudos. A little Ragamoffyn named Imroz comes to their aid, but Magh's soldiers are in hot pursuit. The tribe finally loses them at the entrance of the Caulis Caverns. They have an encounter with the Blind Blober deep inside the caverns. They escape through the Lickety Split and find their way to the Icy Cold Lake where the Firebird finds them. Girasol guides the tribe to Muzika Woods in time for the arrival of the Moon-Star.

Other places of note on the map are Egada, where the Cussers live; Bugansville, where the Bugans dwell: Lethean Silva, where Magh's best Warriors originated; Manticore Domain in the Kinubalu Desert, where Nix and Ghel encounter a Manticore; the Village of Jeribild, where Magh and many of his servants are from; and finally, Muzika Woods, home of the Nebuls and their Harmonizers.

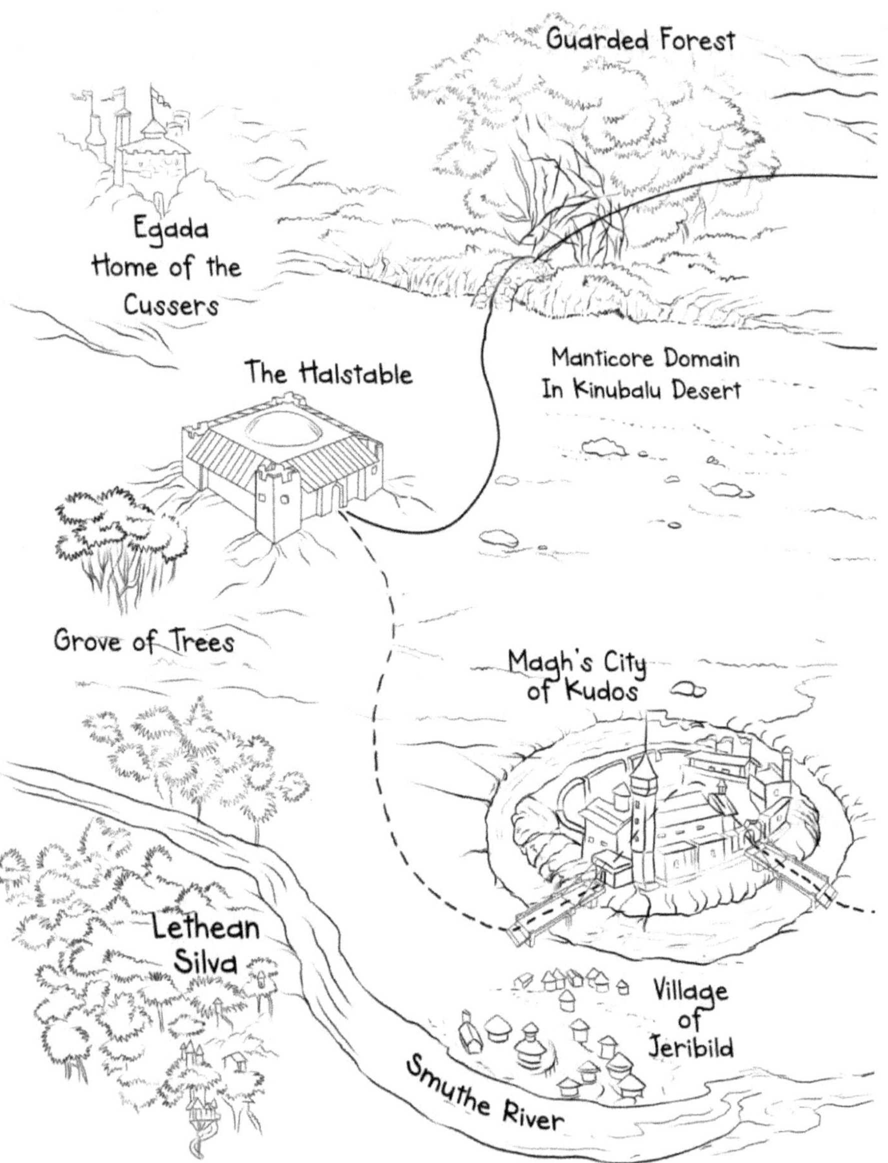

Guarded Forest
Egada
Home of the
Cussers
The Halstable
Manticore Domain
In Kinubalu Desert
Grove of Trees
Magh's City
of Kudos
Lethean
Silva
Village
of
Jeribild
Smuthe River

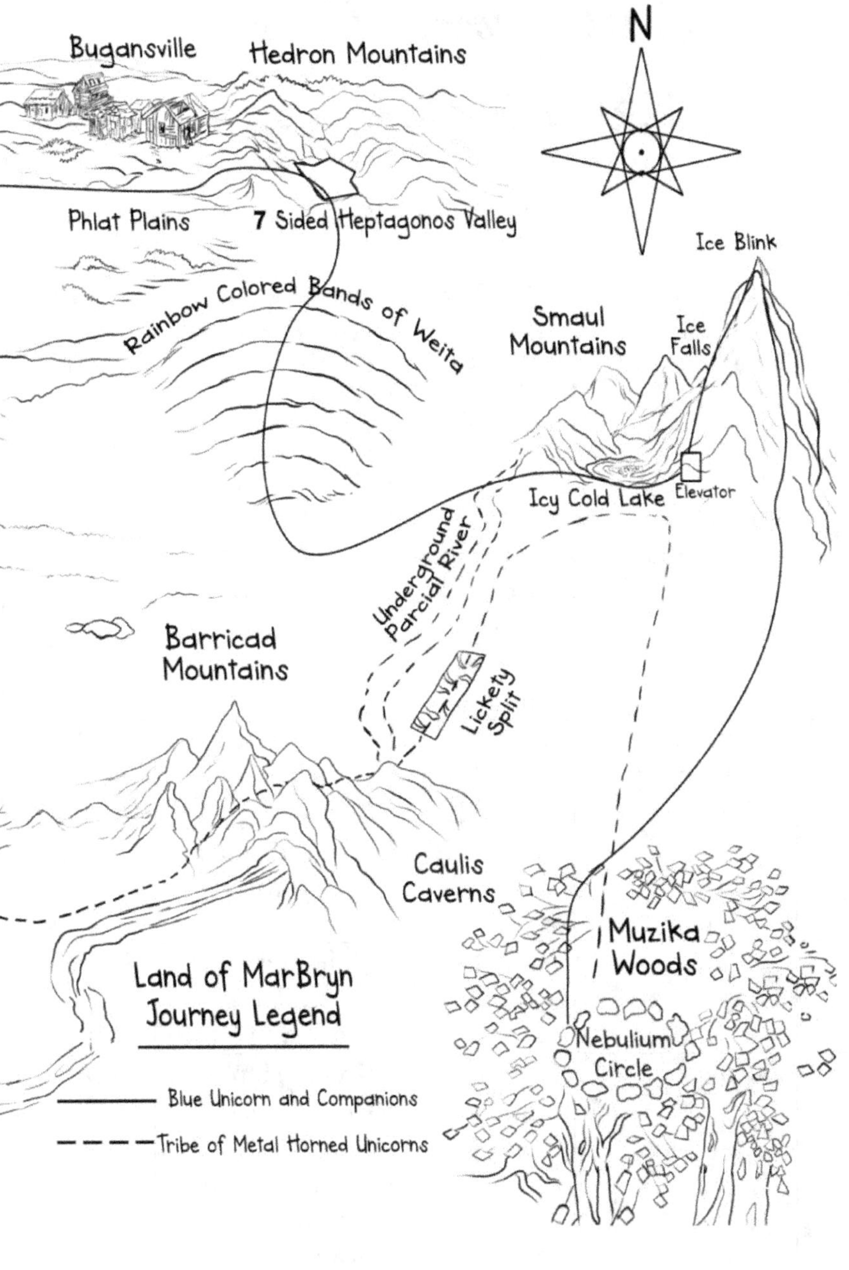

Bugansville
Hedron Mountains
N
Phlat Plains
7 Sided Heptagonos Valley
Ice Blink
Rainbow Colored Bands of Weita
Smaul Mountains
Ice Falls
Icy Cold Lake
Elevator
Underground Parcial River
Barricad Mountains
Lickety Split
Caulis Caverns
Muzika Woods
Land of MarBryn Journey Legend
Nebulium Circle
Blue Unicorn and Companions
Tribe of Metal Horned Unicorns

Metal-Horn Tribe Character Details

This is an introduction to the Metal-Horn Unicorn Tribe.

NAME	COAT & MANE COLORING	HORN & HOOF METAL	MAGICAL HERD & CREST	MATE
Blue	Plain Blue	No Metal	No Magic	Ghel
Ghel	Honey colored beige coat with blonde mane	Just gold at first but later embedded with canary yellow diamonds	Empath Herd - Herd Crest—Open heart surrounding the Celtic symbol for love.	Blue
Silubhra	White coat with silvery mane	Silver with embedded diamonds	Communicator Herd - Herd Crest—A Musical staff and smiling lips	Nix
Nix	Thunder Gray	Nickel	Defender Herd - Herd Crest—Lightning Bolt	Silubhra
Style	Purple	Steel with embedded amethysts	Stylist Herd - Herd Crest—a steel comb engraved with a pretty flower.	Cornum

NAME	COAT & MANE COLORING	HORN & HOOF METAL	MAGICAL HERD & CREST	MATE
Cornum	Lime Green	Brass – his is the only horn flared like a bell	Musical Herd - Herd Crest—Brass bugle to match his flared horn – tip.	Style
Cuprum	Moss Green with a red and green mane	Copper	Water Works Herd - Herd Crest—Cup with Alchemy Symbol for Water	Tinam
Tinam	Lemon Yellow with Mane like uncooked Spaghetti	Tin	Chef Herd - Herd Crest—Chef's Hat or "Toque"	Cuprum
Lauda	Gray	Lead	Scientific Herd - Herd Crest—Potion Bottle	Dr. Zinko
Dr. Zinko	White with Indigo mane	Zinc	Medical Herd - Herd Crest—Stethoscope In The Shape of A Unicorn	Lauda
Alumna	Red	Aluminum with embedded rubies	Navigator Herd - Herd Crest—Crystal Orb as she is the Unicorn Oracle	Iown

NAME	COAT & MANE COLORING	HORN & HOOF METAL	MAGICAL HERD & CREST	MATE
Iown	Black with gray mane and beard	Iron with embedded diamonds	Earthworks Herd - Herd Crest—A vibrant flower growing from the alchemic earth symbol	Alumna
Osm – was the Blue Unicorn	Many shades of blue – from Celeste to Cerulean	All metals tipped with Osmium	Pilot Herd - Herd Crest— A Platinum Wand	Ghel

Pronunciations

Many names of characters and places in this story are somewhat complicated to pronounce. This list is not complete by any means, but it lends insight into the author's thoughts.

Alumna—ah-luhm-nah
Anion—an-Yuhn
Cornum—corn-umm
Cubose—cube-oze
Cuprum—cup-rum
Fleoge—flue-zh
Gaiso—guy-so
Ghel—hard g like gift and rhymes with bell
Girasol—jeer-rah-sawl
Halstable—hall-stah-bull
Icel—I-cell
Imroz – em-rahz
Iown—I-own
Kata—kah-tah
Lauda—loud-ah
Olina—o-lee-nah
Osm—oz-um

Oura—oor-rah
Magh—mm-ah-gh (hard g at end)
MarBryn—mar-brihn
Miral – meer-uhl
Muzika—mew-zee-kah
Nebul—neh-bule
Numen—new-men
Phlat Plains—flat planes
Pici—pee-cee
Pido—pee-doe
Silubhra—sil-loo-bruh
Smaul Mountain – Small Mountain
Tinam—tin-um
Unimaise—you-nih-maze
Weita—wee-tah

Unicorn Anatomy

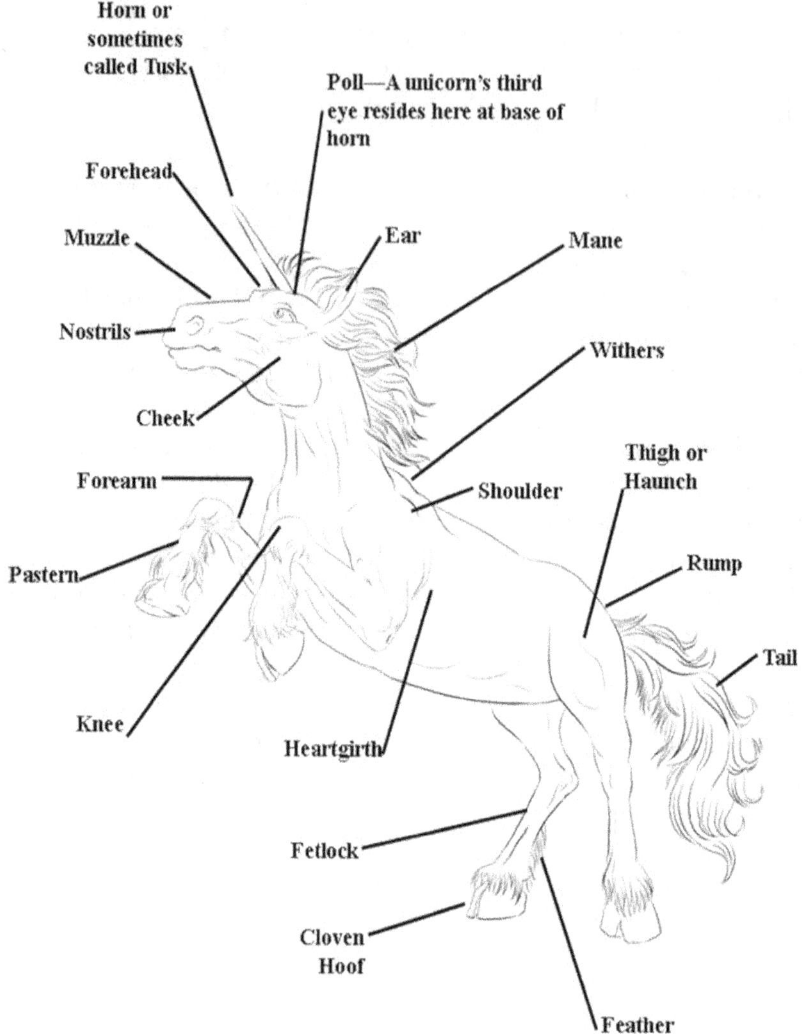

Get the *MarBryn Compendium* to learn much more about its denizens and the Tribe of Metal-Horned Unicorns from Unimaise.

~ ~

Dear Reader:

I hope you enjoyed this book. If you did, please give it a nice review at the online site where you made the purchase or simply at your favorite online review site. You can't begin to imagine how important a review is in helping others learn about a book these days. With over 4,000 new books offered to the public for sale each and every day, it's easy for books by independent authors to get completely lost. Suffice it to say, "The Blue Unicorn needs your help in order for others to know it exists."

This novel has been over 35 years in the making. At the time that I came up with the idea for metal-horned unicorns with magical powers based on the properties of their metal-horns, the only research tools available to me was a hardback dictionary and an incomplete set of encyclopedias.

The world has changed so much since then and I'm so happy to have arrived in a future where the answer for nearly every question I might ever ask is available to me now at the touch of a button. Researching with the internet is the most amazing thing and I truly hope we get to keep it.

I want to take this opportunity to express my immense gratitude to all of the people who contributed to the ideas and concepts in this story. There have been countless readings and feedback by rough draft readers, proofreaders, content editors, line editors, friends, family and many others who have shared insight and given input.

I'd like to give a special thank you to those who have

corrected my spelling and grammar and other writing
frailties. I honestly could not have finished this story
without all of your valuable assistance.

I would be remiss if I did not give my heartfelt thanks to
the most amazing content editor, Travis Erwin, who
understood my vision for the characters and the scenes in
my story and breathed life into them in a way in which no
one else could have.

Finally, I want to thank the man who has made it possible
for me to pursue my writing efforts. Without his loving
encouragement and support, I would have never been able
to realize my dream of finishing and publishing this book.
Thank you, EMR. Thank you for encouraging me to see
how far I can go with my dreams and for always being my
biggest fan. It means the world to me.

The Blue Unicorn stories are available in several different
versions. This novel was written to be enjoyed by any
fantasy lover. . . and it is not aimed at any specific age
range. It is my hope that anyone introduced to the story
through the novel will want to also collect the illustrated
books. They will make great keepsake books for anyone's
fantasy library collection.

The illustrated book contains 42 magnificent full color
fantasy illustrations by Sudipta Dasgupta (Steve to his
friends) and his fellow artists at Dasguptarts. The text for
that book is much shorter than in this novel but the
artwork alone, practically tells the story.

The illustrated book was edited by Kimberly Avery. She
was a great asset in helping me simplify the language and
tame certain situations to ensure they are suitable for

~ ~

teens and younger readers.

Dasguptarts also provided the artwork for a toddler's or very young children's version of the story called "Unicorns From Unimaise – The Magical Metal-Horned Tribe". It was edited by Marissa Elliott.

The illustrated book is also available as a black and white 'Read and Color' book. How cool is that? You read a chapter and then color the following illustration.

Speaking of coloring – there is also a coloring and character description book available. Final editing of that book was by Calyie Martin.

Finally, the text of the illustrated version of the book is available as a whisper-synced audio book, narrated by the multi-talented Troy Hudson. Whisper-sync allows you to enjoy the illustrations as you listen to the story.

Most of these books are available in soft and hard cover print.

Lots of readers become so enamored with the world-building efforts of certain authors that they enjoy reading about the processes that the author went through in detailing characters and places in their book. Some notable examples of this type of encyclopedic tome are "The Star Trek Star Fleet Technical Manual", "The Vampire Companion: The Official Guide To Anne Rice's Vampire Chronicles", or "The Sorcerer's Companion: A Guide to the Magical World of Harry Potter". There are many other books of this type that were written with intention of giving inquisitive readers insight into their favorite author's thoughts. Those books inspired me to compile "The MarBryn Compendium", a rather large pictorial glossary, which delves deeper into the land of MarBryn and its characters.

Over the years, many people have taken an interest in the story of the Blue Unicorn. Britt Brundige, her mother, Sandi Johnson and I co-wrote a sweet little tale titled "The Legend of the Blue Unicorn" that is based on my original story. Britt and her dad, Jim Johnson provided the artwork for that book.

I have future plans to publish a uniquely, interesting version of the Blue Unicorn and the Metal-Horned Tribe's story by the amazingly talented horror writer—Josh Darling. I also plan to publish an epic 4 book series about the Unicorns in MarBryn that I'm co-writing with the incredible word wizard—Luna Davis.

Last but not least - if you're a lover of all things unicorn, you can scoop up lots of book related merchandise from my 'Journey To Osm' Collection at Zazzle dot com. There, you'll find Metal Horn trading cards, mugs, stickers, tee shirts, and much, much more.

Visit sybrinablueunicornbook dot com for more blue unicorn offerings. *If you would like to listen to the song "Home", you can hear it at https://youtu.be/CordwltbeTY*

Happy reading to you all. . .

Sybrina Durant

~ ~

I'd love to hear from you. Email me at
sybrina@sybrina.com

***All books are now (or will soon be) available at all
online bookstores. Look them up today!***